P9-DHF-252

BLOOD JUNCTION

BLOOD JUNCTION

CAROLINE CARVER

Published by Warner Books

An AOL Time Warner Company

This book is a work of fiction. Names, characters, places, and incidents are the product of the author's imagination or are used fictitiously. Any resemblance to actual events, locales, or persons, living or dead, is coincidental.

Warner Books Edition
Copyright © 2001 by Caroline Carver
All rights reserved.

This Warner Books edition is published by arrangement with Orion, an imprint of the Orion Publishing Group Ltd., Orion House, 5 Upper Saint Martin's Lane, London WC2H 9EA

 Mysterious Press books are published by Warner Books, Inc.,
1271 Avenue of the Americas, New York, NY 10020.

Visit our Web site at www.twbookmark.com.

 An AOL Time Warner Company

The Mysterious Press name and logo are registered trademarks of Warner Books, Inc.

Printed in the United States of America

First Warner Books Printing: September 2002

10 9 8 7 6 5 4 3 2 1

Library of Congress Cataloging-in-Publication Data

Carver, Caroline.
    Blood junction / Caroline Carver.
      p. cm.
    ISBN 0-89296-770-6
      1. Women journalists—Fiction. 2. Australian aborigines—Crimes against—Fiction. 3. Massacres—Fiction. I. Title.

PR6103.A78 B58 2002
823'.914—dc21   2002020099

BRUNSWICK

For my mother

BLOOD JUNCTION

Prologue

1952

BERTIE WAS IN THE CENTER OF TOWN WHEN THEY CAME for him.

He knew they would eventually, but he hadn't expected it to be so soon. Or that he'd be with his father and his younger brother, Willy, his two cousins, Jake and Jimmy, and Jake's son, Rick—all six of them collecting their paychecks from the Bamfords for burning off and fencing their property. Backbreaking work for a bloody pittance, he was thinking. We've all aged ten years from that bloody job and I'm not doing another like it again, ever.

The first he knew something was up was when Willy slowed, hissing between his teeth. He'd only heard Willy make that particular sound a couple of times; once when he'd nearly trodden on a death adder out near Benbullen and the other after a bush fire had swept through camp, leaving nothing but a sea of fine gray ash and a clump of eucalyptus trees blackened and split open like shattered sticks of charcoal.

He followed Willy's gaze. There were four horses tethered outside the Royal Hotel and another two standing docilely next to Sam Davis's bakery. He saw a group of men lounging on the hotel's verandah, schooners of beer in their hands, hats shading their faces.

Beyond them a truck turned right at the crossroads, stirring up clouds of red-brown dust. Tin and weatherboard buildings lined the street, and shop awnings painted white offered shade against the raw heat. The rows of iron roofs bounced the sunlight into his eyes, making him squint.

"What's up?" he asked his brother, who was staring at the Royal.

"Those blokes," said Willy.

He saw the men had put down their beers and were watching them. He had the sensation of a pack of dingoes watching a flock of sheep.

"They're all drunk," his father said wearily, and came to a halt.

"Yeah," he muttered, and kicked at the ground. He'd hoped to go out and buy a lathe that afternoon, but with that mob full of grog and looking at them the way they were, they'd be better off coming back another day. He swivelled to head back out of town and felt his stomach swoop. Hank Dundas and five men he didn't know were walking steadily towards them, expressions intent. Three of them carried machetes, and the broad blades flashed like mercury in the sunlight.

"Jesus," Willy said at the same time as Bertie said, "Christ."

"Don't swear," snapped their father.

"I'm buggered if I'm going to hang around—" he started to say but then Hank Dundas was yelling at them, his big round face swelling with the effort. His voice thundered down the dusty street like a truck horn.

"Mullet! Which of you's Bertie Mullett?"

He felt more than saw his father pale. "You didn't do nothing, did you?" he said, his voice shaking. " 'Cos I told you not to. I told you they'd get you for it."

Bertie was staring at the machetes. He felt the blood start to drain from his head.

"Son?"

He found himself unable to speak when he met his father's eye.

"Oh, Christ . . ." His father's black-polished skin had turned gray.

Bertie turned a desperate gaze on the men. They were approaching fast. He swung his head to see the mob from the pub had fanned out, blocking the other end of the street.

"Bertie Mullett!" Dundas yelled. "I want to talk to you!"

"He's not here, mate," Rick said, palms spread. His forehead was beaded with sweat. "He's back at camp."

"Like hell." Dundas stood before them, his face puce. "I know he's one of you lot. The Bamfords told me."

"He's back at camp," Rick insisted.

"You tell us which is Bertie Mullett or you'll all get it in the neck."

Bertie saw his father step forward, shoulders back, head held high. "I'm Bertie," he announced. His voice didn't waver.

Dundas barely glanced at him. "Bertie's a young bloke. Rose told me that much." He studied Rick, then Jake. "A churchgoing lass ruined by a bloody Abo. Perverted son of a bitch! I'm going to make him pay."

Bertie felt a whimper flutter in his throat as the narrow eyes slid to him.

"You Bertie?"

He jerked a negative.

"You?" Dundas asked Jimmy, who shook his head.

Dundas then asked Jake and Rick and Willy, who also shook their heads.

Dundas grinned. "You're all Mulletts, right?"

None of them moved.

"Tarred with the same bloody brush the lot of you." In a single lazy movement he raised his machete above his shoulder. His eyes went quite flat. "You've ruined my daughter."

Everything slowed to half speed.

He saw Dundas swing his machete at his father's neck. From behind came a shout and then Willy screamed. There was a dull chunk, like an axe hitting wood. Bertie watched his father topple to the ground, hands fumbling, desperately trying to stem the river of blood pouring from his neck. He saw Willy dart between two men in an attempt to flee. He saw another machete strike Jake's right arm, almost severing it, and as Dundas came for him, Bertie spun. A man in overalls jabbed Bertie's right kidney with his elbow and he lurched, fell to the ground. Pain blurred his vision. Then a great weight was on top of him, sticky and wet, and Bertie was pushing it away, only half aware it was Willy, that he was bleeding badly, his groans bubbling from a great gash in his throat.

Then Bertie scrambled free and rolled sideways, gasping. The street echoed with shouts and screams. Bertie wavered upright. Dundas lunged for him. Bertie swung sideways and, ducking low, hurdled his father's inert form. Dundas dived to intercept him. Bertie feinted right, then dove left, and sprinted past.

A gunshot cracked behind him.

Bertie increased speed.

Voices were shouting and screaming.

He kept running. Concentrated on nothing but the act of running. Eventually the screams diminished, but he still kept running.

Bent double, lungs heaving, he paused on the town's limits. He put both hands out to steady himself against a metal signpost and found himself almost hugging it to remain upright. After a little while his breathing eased and he straightened and looked back at the town. At the tea-colored weatherboard buildings hunched along a strip of gravel road, paint blistering beneath a remorseless Australian sun.

He lurched into an unsteady jog, heading for the low mound of hills in the distance, where he knew there would be nothing but dry grasses and rocks and lizards and brown-bellied snakes.

Bertie Mullett was unaware he had left three bloody handprints on the signpost. They remained there for seven weeks and two days before a sudden deluge washed them clear. Only then could the local residents look at the sign without flinching: COOINDA.

ONE

1999

INDIA KANE LOOKED UP AND DOWN THE ROAD. THE WIND was blowing hard from the north, hot as a blowtorch and whipping fine grains of sand in her face. The air scorched her nostrils as she breathed. There was no shade, no respite from the sun and sand. She was already thirsty, but caution prevented her from drinking any water. She'd save the small amount she had for when night fell, when it would do her most good.

Hypnotized by the raw heat, she stared southwards, where the road curved around a large clay pan. Then she gazed northwards, at the broad sandy arrow streaking relentlessly into the distance. No cars, no trucks, no rescue in sight. The horizon seemed to waver as she stared, but it was only the heat haze and her dried scratchy eyes playing tricks.

India turned to her stricken Toyota Corolla and cursed it under her breath. Then she cursed the wind and heat and the interminable flies, Toyota generally, the rental-car company and then her work, for putting her here. She'd been stranded in this flat baking tray of scalding wilderness for three hours now and the worm of worry that another vehicle might never come along had grown into a snake that writhed and squirmed in her belly.

The only car she'd seen since she had turned off for Cooinda had been a 4 x 4 ute, a pickup, travelling in the opposite direction. That had been around twelve-thirty, four and a half hours ago.

In silent desperation, she tried the ignition again. Nothing. No electrics, no power, nothing. The inside of the car was like a furnace and smelled of hot plastic. She clambered back outside and stared at the engine block for what must have been the twentieth time. What she knew about engines she could write on a pinhead. What she knew about survival was fractionally more and she had no intention of putting herself at risk by leaving her car yet. She was pretty sure Cooinda was only thirty or forty kilometers away, but she'd last two seconds in this heat. She would wait until it was dark, then follow the road into town. There was no point going the other way. The last homestead she'd seen was about the same distance away as Cooinda.

India sat huddled beside the flank of the car, trying to shelter from the dry, insistent wind. She cupped both hands over her nose in an attempt to prevent herself from breathing more dust, but it didn't seem to help. Her nose and lungs and mouth were being layered with the stuff. She wanted to light a cigarette but it was too windy.

She thought about her friend Lauren, waiting for her at the Royal Hotel in Cooinda. Thought about an ice cold beer, ice cold water, any water. Pulled her mind back to practicalities. Found enormous comfort in knowing Lauren would raise the alarm at the end of the day, come looking for her. Maybe she wouldn't have to walk into town after all.

She rested her head against the car's bodywork and closed her eyes. Breathed in dry air like fire.

She was dozing when she thought she heard a faint hum in the distance. From the south. She scrambled to her feet, praying it wasn't a plane, or a tractor or a four-wheel-drive car taking a short-cut off the road.

Then she saw it, a glimmering black saloon going like a rocket. All four wheels were locked as it drifted around the clay pan, settled briefly, then surged forward with no apparent lessening of power.

India decided against standing in the middle of the road and simply stood by her car with her arm out, knowing the raised bonnet would have the desired effect; the outback code was always to help another in need.

The car hummed towards her, gravel and dust pluming behind it like a meteor tail.

India gave a little wave.

The car shot straight past her without stopping, a BMW with smoked-glass windows.

India stood in great choking clouds of grit and sand with her eyes shut. When she opened them, the flat-six engine note was at least a kilometer away.

"You little shit," she said, astonished. Unless she'd witnessed it with her own eyes, she'd never have believed a fellow Australian would abandon a stranded motorist in the outback.

Perhaps he's from the City, she thought, and doesn't realize that in the bush things are different. That the wind sucks all the moisture out of you until your lips crack and start bleeding, and your throat is so dry you can't swallow. That if you're stranded for several days twenty liters of water per person will only just suffice, and I've only two. That if you don't die of thirst or sunstroke, you might die of snakebite. Brown snakes live out here. Their venom is one of the most potent known. And should you disturb one, the brown snake won't think twice, it will attack with a ferocity and viciousness you won't believe.

India stood and watched the dust settle behind the BMW.

I don't care where the little sod is from, she suddenly thought with a spurt of anger, *because if I ever come across that shitty BMW again, I will lob it with Molotov cocktails. Not that I know how to make one, but I'll learn.*

Then she looked upwards into the dazzling blue-white skies. *Please, God, don't let every driver do that to me. I don't want to die out here.*

TWO

I T WAS NEARLY SEVEN O'CLOCK WHEN A BATTERED BEIGE Holden Commodore pulled up behind India's car. The wind had died to a gentle breeze and the sky had lost its harsh glare. The wilderness was softening into evening.

The man who approached looked to be in his midtwenties. He was dressed in faded jeans and a rough work shirt. He had a thatch of fair hair and eyes the color of burnt toffee, and unlike her was fresh and clean while she was caked in dust, her eyes red and sore, and her hair matted in a thick clump.

"G'day," he said.

"Hi."

His eyes ran from her scuffed boots, up five feet eleven inches of jeans and loose cotton shirt to the wide-hooped earrings, then he gave her one of those grins, impulsive and cheerful, as though he'd just won a prize.

"Name's Terry," he said, and stuck out his hand. "But my friends call me Tiger."

"Mine's India Kane." Her voice was hoarse with dust. "My friends call me Indi."

They shook.

"Cool name," he said, "like Indiana Jones." He stood there, still grinning.

"Know much about cars?" she asked.

He looked momentarily nonplussed, then said, "Oh, yeah. Sure." He shoved his head under her car's hood. She fetched the liter of Evian she'd put beneath the car and unscrewed the cap. She raised it to her mouth, took a large mouthful, closed her eyes. She rolled the heated water around her mouth, swallowed, gave a small groan of intense pleasure.

Heaven, she thought, is a mouthful of hot water.

She carefully sipped the rest of the bottle while she watched Tiger fiddle with the hoses she had fiddled with, wiggle the same electrical wires, check all the levels. "Could you see if she'll start now?" he said.

She tried.

Nothing.

Tiger scratched his head, looked at his watch, then at her. "I'll give you a lift into BJ. We can sort it out from there."

"Not Cooinda?"

"BJ, Cooinda, same place."

She gave him a confused look.

"There was a massacre years back," he said, "at the crossroads in town. Five Abos got wiped out by a bunch of whites armed with machetes. You'll find most of us call it BJ, short for Blood Junction."

Blimey, thought India as she transferred her backpack to his car. *I hope things have changed since then.*

They chatted amicably as he drove. She learned it was his day off and he'd been to Tibooburra to see his parents. She told him she was going on a riding safari from the Goodmans' with her best friend. He liked a cooked breakfast to start his day. She liked coffee and nicotine.

"How come you wanted to holiday out here?" he asked. He was shaking his head slightly, and she could understand his bafflement.

Cooinda wasn't exactly on the tourist map being in what was known as the Corner Country, so-called because it centered around the meeting of three borders: New South Wales, Queensland and South Australia. With Sydney about fifteen hundred kilometers to the east, and Adelaide another eight hundred Ks southwest, Cooinda was pretty much slap bang in the middle of nowhere.

"We were meant to be trekking in Kosciusko," she replied, "but everything turned pear-shaped at the last minute."

He turned his head, brows raised.

"My friend was working in Cooinda, and since I was in Broken Hill . . ." She shrank from disclosing the real reason, then firmed her resolve. If Lauren was right, she'd better get used to the idea, and start talking about it. She picked up her second liter of Evian, where it sat between her thighs, and took another long slug of warm water before saying, "My friend . . . um . . . said she'd found a relative of mine up here."

Tiger didn't seem to make much of this, so she added, "I don't have any, you see. They've all died or emigrated. My mother's family originally came from Cooinda, so when Lauren said she'd found my grandfather . . . well . . ."

"Your grandfather? What's his name?"

"Tremain. Edward Tremain."

Ahead, a flock of crows blackened the corpse of a kangaroo in the middle of the road. As they approached, three birds lumbered heavily into the air but the remainder hopped away a short distance to return the instant they had passed.

"Don't know any Tremains, sorry."

It didn't surprise her. She wasn't certain she believed Lauren anyway, considering both her maternal grandparents had been dead for thirty years.

The Commodore rattled and jarred as they crossed a bridge. Beneath were reaches of red and yellow sand but no water, not even a damp puddle. India asked Tiger how often it rained and wasn't surprised when he told her cheerfully virtually never, and went on to inform her that Cooinda was the second hottest town in New South Wales, after his home town, Tibooburra.

They were discussing the pros and cons of air-conditioning versus ceiling fans when Cooinda came into view. She could see rows of iron roofs, television aerials, a handful of satellite dishes, a white tower with a big black clock. Soon they were driving down streets lined with fibro houses with picket fences. The houses looked fairly new, but the paint had already blistered from the doors and window-sills. Every other building had a ute parked outside.

They reached the main street, called appropriately Main Street. Although the street was flat and very wide—you could have turned a road-train in one sweep—its bitumen was unkempt and dotted with potholes that were full of grit and gravel. They passed a super-market, a post office, a cafe and milk bar, a hardware and sporting store, a hairdressing salon and a dress shop. The dress shop had two headless dummies in its window, both sporting identical floral sleeveless cotton dresses, one in red and blue, the other yellow and green.

Bond Street, eat your heart out, she thought. *At least my credit card will be safe here. I shall look forward to my New Year's statement when I'll owe Visa zero.*

Tiger slowed as he approached the crossroads, then he pulled up outside the Royal Hotel, switched off the ignition. "See if your friend's still there. I'll call Reg Douglas. Get your car towed in tonight."

She tried to open the door, but it was stuck. Tiger leaped out and strode around to release it for her. "Sorry," he said. "Look, if your friend's not there, I'll drive you on to the Goodmans'. I've got to go pretty much past their doorway anyway."

India thanked him and raced for the hotel. Excitement fizzed through her at the thought of Lauren being there. God, it was twelve months since they'd last seen each other. Twelve months too long. As she burst through the swing doors, the noise level instantly dropped ten decibels. She paused, gazed around. The Royal was a typical Australian pub with its horseshoe bar, pool table, poker machines, wide-screen TV bracketed to the wall and unashamedly curious stares reserved for strangers.

India ignored the stares as she scanned the room, felt her smile slip. She told herself to stop being stupid. Would she have waited half the day here for Lauren? Yes, she would. So India checked the restrooms and asked the bar staff if they'd seen a five foot four, slim strawberry blonde.

The barmaid straightened up from emptying the dishwasher and turned around. India surveyed a massive spread of wobbling flesh. The woman resembled a giant roll of uncooked sausage meat, and great dark patches of sweat stained her clothes.

"You India Kane?" she said.

"Yes."

"I'm Debs."

The woman put her pudgy hand out. They shook. Debs's hand was slippery with sweat and India restrained herself from wiping her palm on her jeans afterwards.

"Your friend had to meet some bloke out of town. Said she'd see you at the ranch."

India thanked her. She stood there for a minute, wondering who the bloke could be. She rested her boot on the footrail and lit a cigarette, thought about buying a drink, a gin and tonic perhaps. She wondered if by some miracle they had Bombay Sapphire and checked the optic dispensers. No, just plain old Gordon's. But they did have a telephone directory, which she asked to borrow.

India flipped straight to the *Ts*, ran a finger down the middle column. Tredennick. Tregelles. Treloar. Tremain, R.G., 22 Stonelea Close, Cooinda.

She stared at the telephone number. Her skin suddenly felt clammy. Maybe Lauren had been right. Maybe she did have a grandfather after all. She pulled her notebook and pencil out of her back pocket and wrote down the number.

She jumped when she felt a hand on her shoulder.

"Only me," said Tiger. His grin was in place.

She pushed aside the directory and grinned back. He really was very cute. About five years younger than her, but yes, cute as hell.

"Your friend not here, huh?"

She shook her head.

He touched her shoulder again. "Let's hit the road."

In the mirror opposite, grimed with dust and nicotine, she could see the drinkers at the bar staring after them as they left.

———

Stars danced on the horizon. India saw a huge sandy depression to the southwest with black shadows spreading across it like spilled ink. A brand-new red Nissan ute roared past them. The driver honked twice. Tiger honked back. Two men were standing on the back behind a rack of halogen spotlights. They turned and when they saw India, started whistling and making catcalls. She took a slow drag on her cigarette in a gesture of indifference. Tiger made exasperated shooing motions with his right hand. The men laughed. One wore dungarees, the other a red baseball cap. Red-cap put a hand over his crotch and pumped his hips in a rude gesture.

"Sorry," muttered Tiger.

India shrugged and flicked her stub out of the window. She noted three rifles snicked into leather straps behind the Nissan's cab. 'Roo lampers, out for a bit of sport. They quickly vanished into the distance.

A few minutes later, a small white 4 x 4, headlights blazing, turned right across the road ahead of them.

"Shit," said Tiger, under his breath.

"What is it?"

"Who I'm meeting." He raised his wrist to shine some light onto his watch. "Shit."

India looked across at him. The grin had gone. His eyes were narrowed, his mouth tense.

"You want to drop me back in town?"

He glanced in his rearview mirror, swung left and onto the track where the white 4 x 4 had gone. She saw a sign pockmarked with bullet holes. NINDATHANA BILLABONG. PICNIC SITE.

"Nah. The Goodmans are just around the corner."

He didn't say any more. India decided to keep quiet; she could tell his mind was on his meeting. She wondered who he was seeing, whether it was a woman or a man. Romance or business. She was inclined to think business from the way he'd tensed.

A neatly painted sign next to a rusting mailbox announced Bed and Breakfast for forty dollars, and Tiger pulled off the track and down a smooth sandy road to a traditional low-slung homestead with a tin roof. He kept the engine running as he jumped out and opened her door.

"Sorry about this," he said. "You must think . . ."

"You're wonderful," she said, sincerely.

He popped open the trunk and hefted her backpack to the front steps. He gave her shoulder a quick squeeze, then with a wave and a spurt of gravel, he was gone.

"Your friend'll be back soon," Frank Goodman reassured India. "Her car's here, so she can't have gone far."

While Frank fetched some beers, India slipped onto the verandah, leaned her hands on the railings. The air was full of the sound of insects. It was a moonless night but the sky was scattered with brilliant stars right to the horizon.

"Here you go," he said. "Sorry Mum and Dad aren't here with the red carpet treatment, but they've gone to Milparinka. Some barbie going on they didn't want to miss. They'll be back tomorrow, about lunchtime or so."

India gave a nod, and tipped the cold lager down her throat. Wiped her mouth on the back of her hand, exhaled audibly. "That's better," she said.

Frank smiled. One front tooth was slightly crossed over the other and with his freckled face he appeared ten years younger than he probably was. He opened his mouth to say something, what she never knew, because it was then they heard a gunshot.

"Bloody hell! That sounded close," she said.

"Yeah. Too close." Frank was frowning. "Bet it's Billy's lot. They're out most nights. For a bit of sport."

" 'Roo lamping?"

Frank nodded. They listened some more, but all was silent aside from the hum and chirrup of insects.

"Look, I know you just got here, but would it be okay if I slipped into town? We've a bit of a celebration on. My best mate's gonna tie the knot."

"Sure," she said. "Just show me where the shower is and I'll be fine."

———

India slept badly that night, trying to ignore her travel clock by the bed. Each time she looked across, its vivid green digits read only fifteen minutes had passed since she'd last checked. Where the hell was Lauren? It was ten past three, for God's sake! Lauren couldn't have gone to town to report her missing because her car was still outside. Perhaps she had met a bloke, had an extramarital tryst . . . No. No way. She and Scotto were the happiest couple India knew. There would be a simple explanation. She'd just have to wait.

India lay on her back, staring at the ceiling. Not that she could see the ceiling since it was so dark. Country dark. Bush dark. No lights from neighbors. No streetlights. Just the faintest hint of light from a crack in the curtains.

Eventually she rolled over and firmly shut her eyes. She could hear the occasional creak from the wooden house as it shifted in the cooler air, and smell the dry-hay scent of the bush at night filtering through her window.

You just missed me. By a whisker if I may say so.

Hi, Lauren.

How come you were so damned late? The Australian *didn't pay you enough? Jesus, Indi, why didn't you use Hertz instead of Rent-A-Ruffy? Then at least we'd have caught up this arvo . . .*

India's body suddenly jerked and she snapped her eyes open, unsure whether she had been dreaming or not. Warm yellow light seeped into her room, and she could hear a horse's distant whinny. She pushed back the bedclothes and padded into the hall. Checked Lauren's room. Bed made, unslept in.

Worried now, India dressed and headed for the kitchen, where Frank Goodman was blinking sleep from his eyes and making sandwiches and tea.

"Kip okay?" he asked on a yawn.

"Fine, thanks," she lied.

He asked if she'd like some breakfast. She looked at the four doorsteps of sandwiches on the breadboard. "That's breakfast?"

He laughed. "Nah. That's my lunch. I'm off to Flinders Ranges with my mates in a mo'. Bushwalking. I can rustle up eggs and bacon if you'd like."

"Just coffee would be fine."

He shoved the sandwiches into a cooler and picked up the thermos. "Mum and Dad'll be back at lunchtime," he reminded her. "Don't worry about your friend. If Debs was right and she was meeting someone, they probably gave her a lift into town and she stayed over."

India nodded, unconvinced. She followed him outside, watched him pack his car with backpacks, camping equipment, water, freeze-dried packs of food, rolls of mosquito netting. He paused in his bustle, looked across at her. "I'm going through BJ a bit later. After I pick up my mate Craig. D'ya want a lift? See what's happening with your car? Reg is usually in his workshop around ten, and if we're early you can always get a coffee at Albert's."

She thought about waiting at the homestead for Lauren, the bush silence all around. No distractions from her worried thoughts. "That would be great," she said.

Albert's cafe, where India found herself at ten past eleven that morning, was halfway along the main street of Cooinda. Frank had been wrong about Reg Douglas. He hadn't been open at ten at all. He'd been nursing a ferocious hangover and had been very apologetic that he hadn't collected her car yet, but he would, love, he swore, pick it up early arvo and have it fixed in a shake so she could get on back to Benbullen and her horse-trek, honest.

Albert was pinning up tinsel behind the counter while she sipped her coffee. He was brown and fat and had a thick black moustache. The tinsel was red and gold and still had last year's Sellotape clinging to it.

India was sitting on her stool at the counter, trying not to worry about Lauren, when the door burst open and two men strode inside. She glanced around, recognized the 'roo lampers. Red-cap and Dungarees. They could have been twins. Two walking beer bellies with tattoos.

"Have much luck?" she asked them. To pass the day. To be polite. Above all, to distract herself.

Both stopped talking and stared at her.

"What the . . ." Red-cap said, and took a step backwards. The color was draining from his face as he took her in, and Dungarees' eyes were big as soup plates. Their mouths hung open as though in shock.

"Kangaroos," she added warily. "You were after 'roos, right?"

She heard Dungarees hiss, *"Shit."* Then they turned and were racing each other to be first through the door.

"What the hell was that all about?"

"You scared them," said Albert.

"Sure I did," she said.

"No, honest." He peered at her earnestly. A strand of gold tinsel clung determinedly to the dark stubble beneath his left cheekbone. "You're too good-looking for them. Intimidates them, right? A woman smarter than them." He gave her a quick smile. "You remind me of my missus. Tough as old boots but soft as a peach inside. And just as pretty."

India laughed, went back to her coffee, gazed outside. A Kenworth road-train rumbled past, stirring up clouds of red-brown dust.

"Please, Albert." The voice behind her was a whine, with the faintest of wobbles, as though the speaker might burst into tears.

India glanced around. An incredibly skinny, filthy Aboriginal girl stood at the end of the counter, holding a dirt-encrusted foot behind her with one hand. Her face was pleading.

Albert didn't even look at her. "No."

"But, *please.*"

"If I gave you a feed every time you asked, I'd be broke. Bugger off, Polly."

The girl's lips trembled visibly, India recognizing her struggle not to cry. "Sorry." It came out as a pathetic whimper.

India sighed. "Make it my shout," she said, and pushed a ten-dollar note onto the counter. Albert gave her a startled look. "You sure?"

India nodded and turned to the girl. "What would you like?"

The girl's eyes were huge, dwarfing her narrow face. "Eggs?" she said doubtfully.

"How many?"

Her face lit up. "Two," she said. "With fried bread and sausage and bacon and beans." Then she smiled, a broad smile that showed two rows of small white teeth, a gap where the top left molar should have been. Unwillingly, India found herself smiling back.

"You sound funny," Polly said, then she looked anxious. "Nice funny though."

"I'm from London," India told her, wondering if she knew where it was. Polly nodded sagely.

Albert dropped the tinsel. "Gotta go get your eggs, Poll. Believe it or not I haven't had time to scratch myself. They're still out back under the chooks."

While he went to fetch Polly's eggs, India swung her legs around on her stool to face the window. Expecting to see trucks, perhaps a couple of shoppers loading their utes with groceries, for a second she couldn't believe her eyes. Dungarees and Red-cap were standing at the window. Crowding alongside them was a mob of spectators, staring at her. She could see the hostility burning in their eyes.

To her disbelief, she heard Red-cap yell, "She's still here!" Within seconds the mob was in the room.

India slid off her stool, took two paces back. Her heart was hammering like a road drill. "Look, I don't know what this is about, but I don't want any trouble."

"Well, bitch, you've got it, whether you like it or not." Red-cap stood slightly ahead of the mob, obviously the leader. Pale brown eyes the color of stale mustard ran from her feet to her head, then back down to settle on her breasts. He smiled without showing his teeth. "We're going to carve you up and love every minute."

Dungarees came forward and gripped Red-cap's arm. "Ken, we said we'd wait for Stan."

Red-cap shrugged him off. "Yeah, well, Stan's not going to cry over a bit of spilt milk, is he?" He bunched his fists at his sides.

Albert appeared, carrying an egg in each hand. "Holy moly," he said, and stopped in his tracks. "What're you lot doing here?"

"We came to take this bitch away."

"What for?"

"She killed Tiger."

India's knees suddenly felt very unsteady and she put a hand out and gripped the counter.

"What the hell are you talking about?" asked Albert.

"We saw her last night. She was with him." Red-cap's tone turned vicious. "Murdering bitch!"

"Tiger?" India repeated faintly. "Tiger's dead?"

Red-cap didn't appear to have heard her. He spat on the floor and said, "You killed him. You killed our mate."

The mob started to rumble, like a gathering storm, and India could feel its menace.

"Where's Stan then?" Albert said. He looked at each of the men in turn. "He wouldn't like you taking the law into your own hands."

Red-cap sneered at the cafe owner. "Get back to your stove, fat Albert, this ain't none of your business."

"The hell it isn't," Albert said, his face flushed. "This is my place, and I'll have no lynching in here." Without moving his gaze from Red-cap's he opened his hands and let the eggs drop to splatter softly on the floor. Slowly, he tracked for the counter and picked up a stool. Holding it high over his head, he took three paces towards the mob. "Someone go and get Stan then. Before one of you gets hurt."

Red-cap retreated, as did the mob behind him. "You can't be serious, Albert. I mean, we know you're effing Greek and all, bloody soft in the head for Abos and such . . . But you're protecting a murderer. It'll land you in jail."

India slithered past Polly, who was staring openmouthed at the mob, and took up position behind Albert. Her mouth was dry, and she felt ice cold although she was sweating. "Back door's open," hissed Albert.

India turned and fled.

THREE

INDIA TORE THROUGH A STOREROOM FILLED WITH CARtons and crates, stacks of loo rolls, bleach and cooking oil, then down a corridor for the fly screen at the far end. She opened the screen and slammed it shut, hard as she could in front of her. Then she crept back up the corridor and through the storeroom. She stood by the door behind the counter and listened. Silence. Opening the door a crack, she saw Albert leaning weakly against the counter. Polly was holding his hand, looking anxious.

"Is it safe to go out the front?" India hissed through the crack.

Both Polly and Albert jumped visibly. "Jesus," said Albert as Polly smiled, delighted.

"Albert, could you check for me?"

He gave her a nod and turned to Polly, a finger against his lips. "Keep quiet, will ya?" he whispered. "We'll pretend she's gone out back."

Polly nodded earnestly.

Albert beckoned India behind the counter, whispered, "Duck down here for a bit 'til the coast is clear. I'll check the street, see what's happening."

Polly followed him while India hunched behind the counter, adrenaline pumping. She heard Albert's footsteps, the sound of the fly screen being opened. She heard Albert say brightly, "Hey, Stan, how's it going?"

"Where'd she go, Albert?" The voice was deep and weighted with menace.

There were some shuffling sounds, then Albert said, "Dunno."

"Why are you fucking lying, Albert?"

Another silence. Then Polly's voice, defensive. "She's nice. She's going to buy me my brekkie."

There was a thud, the sound of a struggle, then a high-pitched squeal. India flinched. Her heart was pounding so hard she wondered it didn't explode.

"Polly," the man said in a warning tone, "tell me where she went."

"Stan, c'mon, let Polly—"

"Shut the fuck up! This is police business."

Polly started to yelp, little gasping sounds of panic and distress. India forced herself to move. On her hands and knees she crept to the corner of the counter and peered slowly around. Her wrist caught by the policeman, Polly was trying to free herself. The policeman had raised his arm so her toes barely scraped the ground. She flapped and kicked like a small fish on a line. Her panic-stricken eyes latched on to India. *Help me.*

India ducked back. Her hands were shaking. Her whole body was shaking. Jesus. What the hell was going on? Had Tiger really been murdered? If so, why were they after *her?* Would Albert and Polly keep quiet? The policeman wouldn't really hurt Polly, would he? Then she could sneak out, grab a lift and get the hell out of here, head for her little apartment in Melbourne and safety.

"Tell me, Polly, or I'll give you a belting. A real one with my belt, like I did last year. Remember?"

Polly gave out a single piercing shriek, like a train whistle. That did it. India jumped to her feet, came to the front of the counter and stood there on legs that felt like cotton wool. "No need for that, officer. I'm here." She was amazed how calm her voice sounded. The policeman appeared amazed too, because his jaw dropped. India made a tiny movement, a precursor to stepping forward. In a split second the policeman had shoved Polly aside and was in a crouch, pointing his gun two-handed. Right between India's eyes.

"FREEZE!" he yelled. "DON'T FUCKING MOVE!"

India's hands shot into the air. "Okay, okay, it's okay." Her breathing was uneven, her voice jerky. "It's okay, I'm not armed, I'm—"

"TURN AROUND!" he screamed. "HANDS ON THE COUNTER!"

She turned, put her hands on the counter. Felt a barrel of cold steel pressed hard against her neck.

"One move and I blow your head off, okay?"

"Okay," she managed.

He started to pat her down. Shoulders, arms, armpits, flanks. He exhaled noisily several times. Perhaps as a way of collecting himself, regaining some calm. She felt his boot kick her legs wide. More pats. "I do like a pair of pretty legs spread just so," he murmured when he had finished. "Now, hands behind your back."

She flinched when she felt the cold metal against her skin. He imprisoned her right wrist first, but as he grabbed her left she jerked it free, a bubble of panic forming in her breast. "It's too tight," she gasped.

"They're new." He gave a rasping chuckle. "They'll stretch some after a little wear."

He grabbed her left wrist and still she struggled. India tried to breathe deeply, to halt the panic, but she couldn't allow herself to be handcuffed, she couldn't . . .

Click.

She went quite still. Fear sat in her stomach like a big black bat.

"You're just like a mare I've got," he remarked. "All fidgety at taking the bit. She settles down after a couple of minutes though."

He gave her a little tug. She turned around, looked at him straight. He had eyes the color of dirty ice and a face like boiled beetroot. His nose looked as though it had been broken a few times and his hands were ridged with scars. She found herself staring at his shirt, and a piece of what looked like egg yolk smeared there.

"Name?" he demanded.

"India." Her voice was almost a whisper. "India Kane." She took a breath, firmed her voice. "And yours?"

He seemed to hesitate, gave a mental shrug, then said, "Senior Sergeant Bacon."

"Stan," Polly interjected. "He's called Stan."

"Sergeant Bacon to you," he growled and swung around to glare at Polly. The girl flushed and hung her head.

"Nice to meet you, Stan," said India, and was rewarded with a nervous giggle from Polly.

Sergeant Bacon reached into his breast pocket for a battered white card. He read: "Miz Kane, you are under arrest. You do not have to do or say anything unless you wish to do so. Anything you say or do may be used in evidence in court at a later date." He put the card away. "Do you understand?"

She swallowed drily. She knew the blood had left her face and that she was deathly pale. "No," she said.

He looked at her as though she was being obtuse. "What don't you understand?"

"Why I'm under arrest."

"For Terence Dunn's murder. And we're . . ." He paused and checked his battered card again. "Miz Kane, you are going to be conveyed to Cooinda Police Station, where further enquiries will be made in relation to this matter. Do you understand this?"

India didn't respond.

"Do you understand?"

She looked at him as steadily as she could, hoping he couldn't see that her teeth were clenched. She would wait until she had a so-

licitor before she opened her mouth to Stan. Whatever she said now
he would try to use against her.

He gave an explosive snort, said, "Shit, not again. I try my damn
best to drum up some kind of cooperation but everyone's so into
this silence-is-your-right crap I may as well forget it. Let's go." One
of his hands was in the small of her back, propelling her forwards.
He had her left elbow in the other, gripping it hard as if she might
bolt at any second.

Albert and Polly were standing at the front door. Polly was crying silently. Tears tracked through the dirt on her face and were collecting at the corners of her mouth.

"Can't I do something?" Albert's brown eyes were round and
worried.

India unstuck her tongue from the roof of her mouth. "You
could call my friend Lauren Kennedy at the Goodmans' for me. Tell
her what's happened."

Albert nodded. "I'll do that."

"Thanks."

The policeman gave her a shove that sent her stumbling through
the door. A crowd was waiting in the street, hushed and expectant.

"This woman," Stan said with satisfaction, "is under arrest for
Tiger's murder."

The crowd, which had swelled and now contained a number of
women, gave a muted cheer.

India drew herself up to her full height and stared at them
slowly, one by one. Many of them looked away, but some returned
her look with hostility, others curiosity. When she spoke, her voice
was clear and firm. "I haven't murdered anyone. I'm innocent."

Nobody moved. Nobody spoke.

She glanced over the lawman's shoulder to see a handful of
women watching her from the door of the Royal Hotel. All of them
seemed to be smoking. Their sunglasses flashed blindly at her.

India felt sick and shivery and knew it was the result of shock. The police car smelled of greasy food and disinfectant. She felt strangely grateful that Stan hadn't thrown her in the back of the paddy wagon like a dog, but had allowed her to sit on the rear seat.

They were speeding down the main street, past the supermarket, the clock tower and rows of fibro houses. They flashed past a road on the left signed to Biloella, then what looked like a small court-house. Three doors farther on Stan braked sharply and pulled up outside a long low brick building, painted white.

A large black-and-white sign was stuck in the lawn in front of the entrance: COOINDA POLICE STATION. Someone had planted pur-ple and pink pansies around it and they were drooping in the heat.

Stan got out and opened India's door. "Let's go," he said.

In a single movement she pivoted, twisted out of the car and stood up.

Stan blinked. "You're nothing if not supple. Most folk flap about like beached whales before they get upright."

India didn't respond. She was concentrating on silence. She walked up the concrete path. She could hear a magpie's screech and dogs barking at the end of chains. The sun hammered on her head, and the wind had risen and was blowing hot and hard from the north.

Inside everything was beige and brown, with scuffed linoleum on the floor. A female desk sergeant, framed by two plastic Christ-mas trees, stood behind a long wooden reception counter. A white plastic clock set on the wall stated it was two minutes past twelve. The desk sergeant stared at India as she was marched down a corri-dor and into a room labelled CUSTODY ROOM. It had two filing cab-inets, a table with a phone and computer and one plastic chair.

Stan uncuffed her, then stuck his head outside and yelled, "Donna!" The female desk sergeant entered the room at a trot. She put a book on the desk and switched on the computer, then proceeded to empty each of India's pockets into a large black bag. A handful of coins, receipts, passport, a notebook and pencil. Stan took the notebook and passport.

"Shit," he said, surprised. "You're an Aussie."

India remained silent.

"I thought you were a bloody Pom." He sounded indignant. "And here you are, a bloody Aussie. Bugger me."

"No handbag?" Donna asked India. When she didn't reply, the policewoman glanced at India's watch then across at Stan, who nodded.

"Looks like it's expensive," he said.

She wanted to say: *Looks like you dropped half your egg on your shirt, Stan,* but she held her tongue.

India gave her watch to Donna. The desk sergeant took her photograph. Next, she inked India's fingers, pressed them onto a stiff white card labelled with the number eight, and smiled apologetically as she passed her a tissue. Donna pulled out the chair and sat down. She opened the book and made some notes. She turned to the computer and tapped quickly, looking up at India. "I need your name, address, and date of birth."

"India Rose Kane. Thirty-two Keppel Close, Saint Kilda, Melbourne." She added her date of birth.

"So, that makes you—"

"Twenty-nine."

It didn't take long to complete the custody details and Donna finally pressed Save and printed off a form. Stan gripped India's arm and marched her two doors down and into a room labelled INTERVIEW ROOM. It was also decorated in beige, and had one table, three plastic chairs and no windows except for the small one in the door. A camera was positioned in one corner of the ceiling. On the table was a cassette recorder and a cheap tin ashtray with ash smeared in its center.

Stan told her to sit her ass down, then left the room. The sound of the lock clicking into place made her flinch. She stared blankly at the wall. She guessed they'd leave her isolated for a couple of hours, to make sure she had an urge to talk when someone eventually returned. She'd learned that from her time at *The Courier* in London, when she'd started covering murder stories. She'd been thrilled at her promotion. No more interviewing pet owners or slimmers and self-help junkies, instead she was faced with hard-eyed policemen, solicitors, courts and felons. She had celebrated her first murder story with a bottle of Krug.

And now here she was, sitting in a remote outback jail accused of murder. What an irony that was! She wondered whether Cooinda harbored any half-decent lawyers. She couldn't see any wanting to work out here, in the middle of nowhere.

For the first time since India had left London, she wished she hadn't. She wished she'd never resigned from her post at *The Courier.* Wished she'd overcome her impulse to return to her home country. Wished she'd never taken up Lauren's challenge to find her roots. Above all, she couldn't believe the incongruous fact that Cooinda, translated, means "happy place."

India closed her eyes and told herself she wasn't really in trouble, that there had been a hideous mistake that would soon be rectified and then she would be released. She had to believe that or she wouldn't stand a chance. Especially since the whole town was against her. She crossed her legs, then re-crossed them, feeling vulnerable and inadequate and oddly guilty, even though she hadn't committed a crime. A feeling of powerlessness had seeped into her since her arrival and drowned her self-confidence.

She knew Stan was hoping to make her sweat by leaving her here. Well, she wouldn't crack easily, she'd stay cool, act innocent— hell, she *was* innocent—and stick to her story no matter what. Even if they found a gun with her fingerprints on it she'd stick to the same story.

India jumped when she heard the lock rattle and the door open. A tall black guy was peering inside. Late thirties, maybe forty, he was dressed in immaculately pressed dark gray trousers and jacket. India stared. She hadn't seen an Aborigine in a suit before.

"Good afternoon." His voice was deep, his accent crisp, not quite Australian. "I'm Detective Jeremy Whitelaw."

"Hi." She was surprised. He looked more like a lawyer.

"How long have you been here?"

She made a parody of looking at a watch that wasn't there and shrugged.

"Do you need the Ladies'?"

She shook her head.

"Would you like a coffee?"

"White with two sugars would be nice," she said.

He withdrew his head and a few seconds later, in the distance, she heard his deep voice saying something she couldn't distinguish, and then another man and Donna joined in, their voices raised in protest. A door slammed. Then silence. Footsteps hammered along the linoleum and the door was flung open.

"We've got two lawyers in town," Whitelaw said as he placed a foam cup on the table in front of her. "The one who drinks is Coscarelli and the one who doesn't is Jerome Trumler. Coscarelli comes free thanks to the State of New South Wales but Jerome is usually on time when needed. Who do you want?"

She was pleased that her tone sounded amused, not distressed. "I think I can take the hint."

"Jerome it is. Wise choice."

He went out once more, leaving India sipping her coffee and feeling bemused, but a lot more cheerful now that someone seemed to see her as human.

About half an hour later Whitelaw returned. "Look, I'm sorry, but Jerome's in court and can't get here until later. We'll have to wait. Can I get you some lunch?"

"A sandwich or something would be great. Maybe a soft drink."

The sandwich was corned beef with pickles, the drink a cold Fanta. She didn't have an appetite but made herself eat every crumb. She mightn't be fed again.

A little later Donna came and took the debris away, allowed India to use the Ladies', then locked her back in the interview room. She came back after a while with another Fanta that India thought might indicate it was teatime, put some magazines on the table and left. India flicked through an old copy of *Gourmet* but didn't take in any of it. She could feel the afternoon slowly ticking away. Found herself longing for a cigarette. She pushed the magazine back onto the table. *Please let Jerome get here soon,* she thought. *Get me out of here.*

Finally, Whitelaw ushered the lawyer inside. His appearance did not inspire confidence. He was six inches shorter than she was and seemed flustered.

Within ten minutes India became horribly aware of the financial trouble she was in. The lawyer's retainer was $3,000, his ongoing fee $175 an hour. India felt as though her stomach was full of eels as she tried to work out how to raise that amount of cash.

"How much will my bail be?"

"Anything up to two hundred thousand dollars."

Her palms became slippery with sweat.

"It depends who we see," Jerome added. "If it's Judge Deacon we're in deep trouble. He might not even allow bail."

The black detective was standing outside and she could feel his eyes on her face.

"Perhaps I should have Coscarelli," she said.

Jerome gave her a piercing look. "You still can. But I wouldn't recommend it."

"It's not your money," she snapped.

"True. But it's not my freedom that's at stake either."

She covered her eyes by spreading her fingers against her forehead and tried to stem the desire to scream.

"Shall we proceed?" asked Jerome briskly. "Detective Whitelaw's got a lot of questions for you." When she nodded, he waved in the detective. Whitelaw was followed by Donna carrying a chair, which she put in one corner then sat down on.

Whitelaw took his seat and flipped open a pad. He uncapped his Biro and placed it on top. "Miss Kane, we want to interview you electronically. Do you agree?"

She glanced at Jerome, who gave her a nod.

"Yes."

Whitelaw popped three tapes in the recorder. He pressed Record and checked the red light was on, the tapes running, and leaned back in his chair, hands resting on his lap, relaxed, at ease.

"Detective Whitelaw, Jerome Trumler, Sergeant Hemmel and India Kane are present on Monday, twelfth December, nineteen-ninety-nine," Whitelaw began. "Miss Kane, do you agree the time is six-thirty-three P.M.?"

Jerome held his watch so she could see. Whitelaw did the same. She flicked a glance at Donna but the desk sergeant was absorbed in turning her wedding ring around her finger.

"Yes."

"There will be three audio and one videotape made of all interviews. You will be given one audio tape, one will be sealed in your presence, one will be kept with the interviewing officer. The video remains at the station. We can use these recordings in court." He read her her rights again. "Do you understand?"

"Yes."

"Right. Let's start with your name, address and date of birth."

She repeated what she'd told Donna earlier.

"You sound English."

"I've lived in London since I was twelve."

He made a note. "Miss Kane"—he paused—"tell me exactly what happened."

"You tell me. One minute I'm having breakfast, the next I'm a murderer. Would you mind filling me in?"

Silence. Whitelaw looked at her steadily.

"Would you mind filling me in?" she asked him again.

He stroked his chin slowly, as if contemplating whether to answer her or not.

"Look, I don't know what in hell's going on here, but I'd really appreciate a bit of slack being cut." India was glad she sounded calm, collected. "Fill me in, will you?"

The seconds ticked past. He was going to wait her out, make her speak first. Well, fine by her.

"Can I smoke?" she said. "It might help me pass the time while we play this game."

Whitelaw didn't respond.

"I really, *really* need a cigarette," she said. Hearing the slightly plaintive note in her voice, she was instantly reminded of Polly. "Please."

He flared his nostrils a little, pushed back his chair with a tortuous squeal and went outside. Jerome wouldn't meet her eye. He was puckering his mouth in a peculiar way, as if sucking something sour, and it made his lips elongate like a baboon's.

Whitelaw came back with a pack of Benson & Hedges, cellophane already unwrapped, matches in hand.

India dragged the smoke deep into her lungs. Her head spiralled and for a brief fantastic moment she was displaced, disconnected, as though she were dreaming, but then she was slammed back into the neutral cream-and-brown colors of the interview room, Jerome at her side, the unknown quantity that was Whitelaw opposite.

She exhaled a stream of blue smoke and said, "I won't be saying anything else until you make it a two-way street."

More silence while India smoked and Jerome sucked on his peculiar long lips.

The ashtray had two cigarette stubs in it before Whitelaw finally spoke up.

"All right," he said, nodding a little. "For the record, it's a double homicide—"

"*Double!* You're not telling me I'm up for *two murders?*"

She thought she saw a flash of recognition at the back of his eyes, but it was gone so fast she wasn't sure if she'd imagined it.

"Yes. A policeman, off duty, was shot near Nindathana Billabong last night at close range."

Her mouth went dry as sand. "Tiger."

"Also known as Terence Dunn."

"Tiger," she whispered, "He's a cop."

"A woman's body was found too. Same treatment."

For a second, India's mind seemed to jam solid. A chill started at the top of her head, her scalp, and spread through her as she stared at the detective. Lauren had gone to meet a man last night. Lauren, who was up here working. Lauren, who met with detectives and cops and lawyers all the time.

Lauren.

The chill had spread downwards, towards her heart.

Please, God, not Lauren.

"Both victims were shot twice in the head. Time of death is currently estimated between eight and ten P.M. Pete Davies, Ken Willis and Billy Bryant have signed a statement saying they saw you with Terence Dunn in his car, in the area of the murders, at eight-forty P.M."

Lauren's my family. My mother, my sister, my only true friend. The only person who knows me in the whole world. Please don't let her be dead. Please, please, please.

"Why were you in Terence Dunn's car last night, Miss Kane?"

She took a shaky breath. And another. Tried not to show she was trembling. Concentrated on breathing steadily, in and out. In and out.

"Miss Kane?"

She covered her eyes with her right hand and sat there, her mind still unable to function. She heard Whitelaw cross his legs, the creak of his chair. Then silence. Another shuffle of soft cloth. More silence. Eventually she raised her head.

"Who was the woman?"

Whitelaw fixed her with his steady gaze. "Her purse identifies her as Lauren Kennedy, but we'll need an official ID from her family. Her face isn't recognizable."

India had never fainted before, and didn't now, but somehow her body folded in on itself, her bones and muscles liquified, and the next second she was sprawled on the floor.

Whitelaw was barking commands and she could hear Jerome's flustered response. Then Whitelaw was holding her hands, talking to her gently. After a while, it was only a minute or so but felt much longer, India scrambled to her feet and stood there, clutching the edge of the table.

"Lauren's just turned thirty," she said.

Whitelaw wouldn't look at her. Donna was staring at the floor.

India thought of Lauren's vitality, her mischievousness, her immense love of life, and closed her eyes.

Nobody said anything.

"Can I see her? I have to know it's her for sure. Can you understand that? I have to know."

FOUR

THE MORTUARY WAS ON THE SAME SIDE OF THE STREET AS the courthouse and police station, but five doors down. No pansies here. Just tough-stubbled buffalo grass edging the concrete path. Inside it smelled of oranges, but beneath the cloying sweet smell India could detect the faint aroma of chemicals. A tall, unsmiling man told Whitelaw to give him five minutes to prepare the anteroom, and clattered off down a corridor lit with overhead fluorescent strips.

India stood by the window, vacantly watching a magpie hop across the stubbly lawn and back. A hand landed gently on her shoulder, and she allowed Whitelaw to usher her into a harshly lit room with no windows. The tiles were white and cracked with age and the pale blue linoleum floor had worn to gray in the center. Slowly, India approached the chrome trolley, looked down at her friend's body.

They'd covered Lauren with a stiff gray sheet but her arms lay bare at her sides. Lauren's skin was a peculiar color. It wasn't caramel-colored any longer, more of a dull duckweed green. It was this change in Lauren that upset India more than the fact her friend's face had apparently been blown away; Lauren had always been so proud of her ability to tan.

I always start with factor 20 at the beginning of summer and keep dropping it down until I'm on coconut oil. I do love having a tan; I always look so damned healthy.

On the tender underside of Lauren's wrist were some hastily scribbled initials: CTW/GN1, in purple ink. India gave a twisted smile; Lauren always used her arm and never a piece of paper.

You can lose a piece of paper, darl, but not your arm.

"Is this your friend Lauren Kennedy?" asked Whitelaw gently.

India traced the three small moon-shaped scars on Lauren's upper arm where a dog had bitten her when they were children. It was enough.

"Yes."

"I'm sorry."

India remembered kicking that dog so hard in the mouth it had howled and fled with its tail right between its legs. She loved animals, but Lauren came first, always had.

"Shall I leave you?"

"Thank you."

"Just come out when you're ready."

She heard the rubber seal on the door snick shut behind him.

Her best friend Lauren. India could see over the sheet that she'd had her hair cut short. It suited her personality, this new spikily cropped hair like a boy's.

Thanks, hon. I quite like it too. You should try it. Keeps your nape cool and it's really easy to care for.

India reached out and touched Lauren's hand. It felt greasy and cold, but she cupped her palm in Lauren's and held it tight.

Sorry I can't come to bail you out of trouble again, Indi.

India closed her eyes.

I mean, I always used to look out for you, right? Even in the face of the enemy. God, weren't your mum and dad a mess? We could have opened a recycling unit from the bottles they got through.

I'd rather not remember, said India.

What, you're not going back to Dee Why for a trip down good old memory lane?

No way.

Come on, girl. We had some good times too. What about the beach and all those gorgeous surfies?

What about Dad getting fired for taking bribes?

He was a cop, for heaven's sakes. What do you expect?

Some restraint, India snapped. Especially towards his own family.

Just because little Toby—

Dad had no right to do what he did. It wasn't Mum's fault Toby died. My little brother.

Sure, that was a bad day, darl. A very bad one, I'm the first to admit, but every cloud has a silver—

You call my being shunted to England a silver lining?

Well, you got a good education. A better one than I did, that's for sure. And Aunt Sarah was okay in her own weird way. She paid for my first trip to the UK, remember? I've always had a bit of a soft spot for the old bat, and besides, she always had a good supply of cigarettes. Given up yet?

No.

Me neither.

India bowed her head over Lauren's chilled hand.

Lauren?

I know. I'm sorry too.

I should have come to Sydney—

You said you never wanted to set foot in the place again. I never should have insisted. Can't believe I acted like some psychologist or something, saying it would do you good. I'm sorry as hell for being such a pain in the ass. I should have come to sodding Melbourne.

I wish you had.

"When did you last see Lauren Kennedy?" Whitelaw asked.

They'd been in the interview room for ten minutes, cassette recorder running, Jerome to one side, Donna in the corner.

"Miss Kane?" Whitelaw prompted.

India thought of Lauren's green skin, the way the blood had dried black and flaky on her neck and shoulders.

Whitelaw coughed, scratched the underside of his throat with his fingers. "Before you saw her in the mortuary, that is."

"Twelve months ago."

He flipped through some papers. "You said previously you were close to your friend and spoke every week, if not more. That you used to be neighbors as children. That Lauren Kennedy came to visit you in London just about every year. You sound pretty inseparable."

India wanted to rid herself of her memory of Lauren's dead body, but it remained stubbornly in her mind. She could see every detail: the mole near her elbow, the pale strap where her watch had been, a fresh cut on her right knuckle.

"How come you didn't see each other for so long? You've been living in Australia for six months."

"I wouldn't go to Sydney," she whispered.

"Why not?"

"I hate Sydney."

Silence. A shuffle of paper, the soft brush of cloth as legs were uncrossed and crossed again.

"Why is that?" said Whitelaw.

India reached for a cigarette, lit it, and watched the blue smoke spiral. "It has nothing to do with what's happened."

"Still, I'd like to know."

She put a finger on her tongue, removed an imaginary piece of tobacco and flicked it aside. "Okay. I had a bad experience when I was young. It has tainted my view of Sydney ever since."

"What happened?"

"I ran away from home."

"For how long?"

"Just a night."

Whitelaw frowned. "Why the big deal?"

"No big deal," she lied smoothly, and rolled the tip of her cigarette against the ashtray. "But because I refused to go to Sydney, Lauren then refused to come to Melbourne. Hence arranging a holiday in the middle, so to speak."

He made a note, moved right on. "What job did she do?"

"She's a journalist, like me. But more high-powered. She did investigative stuff, exposés."

"How come she chose Cooinda. You too?"

"I've no idea really," she lied. It was just too complicated to start trying to explain her own bleak family history as well as the fact that she knew Lauren too had another reason for coming to Cooinda. Something about a story she'd been working on—medical ethics or another save-the-world subject. Lauren had always veered towards the crusading side of journalism. Unlike India, who had chosen the easier and more crowd-pleasing route.

"We were all set to go horse-trekking in the Snowy Mountains until five days ago. Then she suggested we trek here instead," was all India volunteered.

"You were happy with the sudden change of plan?"

India tapped a length of ash into the tray and thought about explaining the Grandfather Tremain business, but decided not to bother. She said, "I was in Broken Hill. It's not that far from Cooinda."

"What were you doing in Broken Hill?"

"Hunting down Floyd Harrison."

She felt more than saw Jerome's start of surprise.

"You're the reporter who . . ." Whitelaw trailed off.

"Yes."

She could see he was struggling with his curiosity. "I had a source who knew a man called McCarthy," she added. "McCarthy used to be into currency fraud during the eighties. These guys always seem to know each other. McCarthy gave me the tip-off."

Her thrill at nailing the British fraudster felt unreal now. It had taken her three months to track down Harrison, and when she'd found him hiding out in Broken Hill last week, she'd finally bagged him. Put him in jail. Exposed the slime for defrauding more than a dozen Australian companies out of eight million dollars, and managed to initiate extradition procedures. It had been her first big break since she'd arrived in Melbourne.

Whitelaw gave his head a little shake, studied her in silence for a while.

"What do the initials CTW and GN1 mean to you?"

"Nothing. Apart from the fact they were on Lauren's wrist."

"Are they people's initials?"

"I don't know."

India crushed her cigarette out.

"Perhaps they're a code?" he suggested.

"Perhaps they are. But you're asking the wrong person. Why don't you track down the driver of the white 4 x 4 I told you about and ask them?"

She gazed at the ashtray, thinking about her vow to give up smoking for New Year, wondering if she now cared enough to do so.

Whitelaw sat back, leaned his chin in his hand.

"Tell me about Frank Goodman again."

She gave a long sigh. They'd been over her alibi what felt like a hundred times. "Frank was there when Tiger dropped me off, around nine P.M. His parents were away for the night, at some barbecue in Milparinka. Frank and I had a beer, then we heard the single gunshot, then he went into town to meet some friends, at about nine-thirty. I went to bed at eleven. Got up at eight A.M. He gave me a lift into town around nine."

"Frank Goodman's friends say he was with them at nine. That he couldn't have seen Tiger drop you off."

"They're lying."

"Why would they do that?"

"Because of Red-cap and . . ." She couldn't remember their proper names. "A man wearing dungarees."

"Ken Willis and Pete Davies?"

She gave a shrug. "Whoever."

"And where did you say Frank Goodman went?"

"He said he was going bush walking in the Flinders Ranges with some friends." India paused. "And until he returns, I'm in the shit, right?" she added.

Whitelaw started to nod, stopped himself. "We're doing everything we can to locate him."

"I'm glad to hear that." Her tone was tight. "How come I heard just one shot that night, if Tiger and Lauren took two bullets each?"

"The assailant used a silencer. The single shot you heard was the one Tiger loosed off."

She nodded. "Thanks."

He raised one shoulder, dropped it. "Okay. Let's start from when your car—" He broke off at the sound of a commotion outside. As footsteps clattered up the corridor, all three of them looked towards the door. It burst open and banged against the wall.

Senior Sergeant Bacon strode inside, face puce with fury. He switched off the recorder.

"I can't believe this shit," he said. "Turn my back for a second and you're at it again. Get out, Detective Whitelaw, and let me do my job."

Whitelaw stiffened but his expression remained perfectly cool, as though nothing untoward had occurred.

"She was on Time Out, Detective. Extended Time Out, meaning she was meant to sit here undisturbed. Make her think about her predicament. And all the while I've been working on finding her weapon, you've been cuddling up to her, taking her on field trips outside . . ." Bacon stood rigid as a fighting dog facing an opponent. "As the Senior Sergeant of this police department, I'm ordering you out of here."

A long silence. Whitelaw pushed back his chair, got to his feet. He gave a curt nod to Jerome, then loped outside without a backward glance.

"Sergeant," Stan said to Donna, "call the magistrate and get a detention warrant for an additional eight hours."

Donna said, "Certainly, sir," and left the room.

"Out," Stan growled to Jerome. Jerked a thumb over his shoulder at the door.

The lawyer lingered.

Stan swung around fast, like a snake disturbed. "The interview with your client is over, get it? So get the fuck outta here." And to India's horror, Jerome did just that.

Oh my God, she thought. She found herself shrinking on the chair to appear smaller. Her legs wanted to cross themselves, her arms to wrap themselves around her. She wanted to turn into a protective ball and roll out of there. She willed her legs not to move, and slid her hands over her thighs, fingers outspread, relaxed and confident.

Stan came over and put his mouth near her ear. His lips were so close she could feel the hairs on her cheek stiffen as he spoke. "Now, Miz Kane, let's talk. I'm the boss here, and you're a murdering bitch. You've come into my town and killed one of my officers. So now you're going to make a full confession."

She registered that his breath smelled of onions and stale beer.

"As a journalist, you know what us cops say about homicide. That ninety-nine percent of murders are committed by people the victim knew. And here we are, with one attractive young man dead between two attractive young women. Sounds like an open and shut case of jealousy to me."

He reared back to stare down at her, waiting for a response.

India kept her gaze on a scar in the linoleum, shaped like a lion's head. It had been planned, she realized. Stan the bully. Whitelaw the nice guy. Between them, they would work their hardest to crack her into making a confession for something she hadn't done.

Stan pushed his beetroot face next to hers once more. "You're going to jail," he said. "For life. A life of fear and degradation you don't even know exists. Wardens will hire you out, touting your pretty tanned ass to anyone who can pay. You'll have broom brushes jammed up your fanny, your ass, until your eyes pop clear outta your head."

Because she didn't know what else to do, India continued staring at the floor.

"So," said Stan, "tell me how it happened."

India kept her gaze fixed downwards. She didn't want to antagonize him further. He was already in full flow.

"Tell me how it happened," he said again.

She didn't move a centimeter.

Stan's fist seemed to come from nowhere. One second she was sitting on the chair, the next she was sprawled on the floor, her jaw pounding with pain.

"Look at me when I'm talking to you, bitch," Stan said. He came and stood over her.

India felt a hot flame of rage ignite inside her. She hadn't thought she'd feel anything after seeing Lauren dead, but she'd been wrong. She was alive. And she was angry. She welcomed that, at least.

"Stubborn cow," he hissed.

She ran her tongue around her teeth. All intact, but her tongue was bleeding and the left side of her face already felt hot and swollen. *You've got to take this, and don't even think of fighting back.* If she hit a policeman, she'd be in even bigger trouble. So she lay there, the taste of blood in her mouth, while Stan loomed over her, fists clenching and unclenching at his sides.

"But you won't be so stubborn in a couple of hours. Because you're going to the cells tonight, and you're going to have company. We've only got six cells here, and funnily enough five are currently being redecorated, so you've got to share. His name's Mike Johnson, otherwise known as Mikey the Knife. I'll let you think about why he's called that. He's chilling out after a bit of a bloodbath in town so I wouldn't make too much of a noise. He's got a temper."

India traced the heat along her jawbone. She scrambled to her feet, put her shoulders back, tried not to allow a tremor to show in her voice. "I will not be intimidated into confessing to something I didn't do."

Stan grinned. "Mikey's gonna love you, sweet cakes."

India's tongue seemed to have glued itself to the roof of her mouth. She couldn't confess, she might end up in jail for life. But a night with Mikey might be even worse. She stared at Stan, trans-fixed with indecision.

He shook his head as though helpless against the turn of events. "We may as well go down then. But when you've had enough of old Mikey—I've heard he's hung like a horse—just give us a yell and we'll get you outta there."

Stan took India down the corridor to the cell block, which was divided into six separate holding pens with vertical bars. Every square inch of each cell was visible from outside, and was carpeted with caramel-colored linoleum. Metal bunks were fixed to each wall, along with a stainless steel basin and a toilet with no lid. There was a pervasive smell of urine, cigarette smoke and stale sweat. Stan stopped outside the first cell on the right and unlocked the gate sec-tion.

"Your executive suite, madam," he mocked.

Mikey the Knife was sprawled on the bunk. He lay face up, mouth agape, with one foot and hand resting on the floor as if to anchor himself. A thick brown ponytail with sun-bleached split ends nestled like a pet snake in the nape of his muscular neck. Dwarfing the bunk with his beefiness, he looked like a bouncer who had been in an all-night brawl: his T-shirt was torn in several places, and his jeans were dark with dirt and bloodstains.

Stan pushed her inside, clanged the gate shut.

Mikey gave a muffled groan.

India shrank back and immediately her shoulders connected with the chill of steel bars.

The big black bat of fear returned to flutter through her entrails.

"Truly, you don't have to do this," Stan said, sorrowfully shaking his head at her.

You've been scared half to hell and back before, India told herself. *Don't give in now.*

"Come on," said Stan persuasively. "You don't want to be shut up with the likes of Mikey, all for the sake of signing a little bit of paper." He was holding up the bunch of keys as if to tempt her outside, his expression sympathetic.

India glanced at Mikey, the way he was snuffling in his sleep. She shook her head. She'd never forgive herself for being tricked into confessing to something she hadn't done just to avoid spending the night with a man who—she reminded herself in panicky optimism—she hadn't even met yet.

Stan locked the gate. "Just give us a shout," he said coaxingly, "and I'll get you outta there pronto, no harm done."

Dry-mouthed, India slid along the bars to the corner farthest from Mikey and slowly sank to the floor, listening to Stan's footsteps recede. She barely took in the walls, scratched with names and drawings of male and female genitalia. She was watching Mikey the Knife sprawled on his bunk, sleeping sweetly as a baby.

FIVE

INDIA WAS FIGHTING TO REMAIN AWAKE.

Mikey the Knife had slept continuously for about two hours now, and she had watched him, petrified of what would happen when he regained consciousness. Would he beat her up first? Or would he rape her? Should she bluff it out and face him head on? Or should she curl up in the corner and not move, and let Mikey kick the shit out of her until he tired of it?

But I know what broken ribs feel like, she thought. I know what it is to have a man's fist bury itself into your midriff so hard and fast you can't help but vomit. And when he punches you in your kidneys, just so, with a hard twist right up in the corner, I can recall exactly the thought that goes through your mind: I want to die.

Don't go talking like that, hon. It doesn't do you no good.

Lauren?

Who else? And at the risk of sounding stupid, what the heck are you doing in there?

It's a mistake, that's all.

Well, just you watch out, girl. He looks mean enough to scare a scorpion into hiding.

I'll act tough.

You do that.

India's eyes suddenly flicked open. Mikey was still sprawled on his bunk in the same position. The fluorescent lights continued to glare uncompromisingly.

It was just my imagination talking to Lauren, she thought dazedly. *My subconscious can't cope with the fact she's dead. That she'll never be coming to the rescue again. That I'm alone.*

But what if I do have a grandfather here? Then I won't be alone. Lauren said he was fabulous. Which means he'll look like Father Christmas with a shock of white hair, a thick curly beard and twinkling blue eyes . . . Huh! Knowing my family, he may look sweet, but he's probably into chain-saw massacres in his spare time.

India closed her eyes. Almost immediately she fell into a deep, dreamless sleep.

———————

She had no idea what time it was when Stanley Bacon returned. She was shocked awake by the loud jangle of the gate behind her and immediately sprang to her feet, heart pounding.

"You look just about ready to do business," said Stan with a sly grin.

She glanced at Mikey, who didn't seem to have moved a millimeter since she'd first laid eyes on him. If a brass band had been playing right by him, she reckoned he wouldn't wake up.

"No, I'll never 'do business.'" She turned from him and sat down again.

Stan glared at her. "You'd better confess or I'll wake Mikey. Then you'll be in trouble."

India scrambled to her feet, managed to remain calm. "That's an empty threat if ever I heard one." She checked Mikey's recumbent form. "He's comatose."

"He won't be forever."

She shrugged her shoulders.

"Have it your way. I'll come back in an hour, see if you've changed your stubborn little mind."

"Don't bother." She sat back down again. She was surprised at her own recklessness. "I can wait until morning, when Jerome gets here."

She was so absorbed in watching the policeman stride away that she failed to pick up a movement from the bunk.

". . . the hell's going on?" The voice was deep and gravelly and weighted with confusion.

India jumped. She strove to wipe her face free from all expression and to steady her ragged breathing.

Keep your cool, girl. Don't let him see your fear.

She took three slow, deep breaths through her nose, and assumed a meditative position. She placed her hands on her knees and set her shoulders straight.

With apparent indifference, she let her eyes travel slowly across the floor to Mikey's well-worn leather boots and up his grimy, bloodstained clothes until they came to rest on his face. It was a strong face, with a big beaky nose and a jaw like a shovel. A scar ran up through one eyebrow.

"Are you talking to me?" she said, her tone unfriendly.

"Don't tell me there's more of you in here?" He swivelled his head to check the cell's perimeter, and paled. A sheen of sweat appeared on his skin and he fixed his bloodshot eyes on her, his expression oddly stricken.

"If you're going to be sick," India said, "could you make sure you aim in the middle of the bowl? I really can't stand the smell of drying vomit."

Mikey stumbled to his feet and obediently stuck his head right inside the stainless steel toilet before throwing up noisily.

India sat there trying to look serene while he repeatedly flushed the toilet and then stood over the sink, splashing water over his face and neck and hair and rinsing his mouth. He weaved back to his bunk and sat there, wiping his face on the shoulder of his T-shirt.

He looked marginally better, but she could see his hands were shaking and his skin was still gray.

India concentrated her gaze on a space on the wall ahead, as if meditating.

After a while he said, "What the hell are you doing in here?" sounding genuinely puzzled.

Slowly she counted to ten before turning her head and looking straight at Mikey. He had laughter lines at the corners of his eyes and a generous mouth. His body was broad and lean and fit, his belly flat. If he hadn't been so filthy and reeking of alcohol and vomit he could almost be termed attractive.

"Come on." He sent her what he obviously thought was an engaging smile. "Your secret's safe with me, promise."

"Put it this way, I'm not here to wash your socks or do your ironing."

"Bloody hell," he said. He was gazing at her as though fascinated. "Are you having a bad day or are you just a ball buster? One of those women who think men are a subspecies?"

She pictured her father, then Red-cap, and the mob, and Stan. When she spoke she told him the truth. "I hate men."

He stared at her for some time, seeming to pale further as he watched her. Eventually, he lay back and closed his eyes. When India finally stole a look at him, he was fast asleep. She felt her shoulders slump as she exhaled with relief. More confident now, she rested back against the bars and closed her eyes.

———

"Psst!" a shadow hissed at India, and nudged her.

This time India didn't spring to her feet in a jet of fear. Instead, she groaned her protest at being disturbed. At a second nudge, her consciousness crawled reluctantly out of the deep blanket of sleep and she opened her eyes. They felt as if they had been rolled in grit, and her mouth was sour. She felt hungry, dirty and exhausted.

"I've brung you a coffee," said the shadow, and pushed a steaming foam cup through the railings.

"Oh, Polly." She was touched. "You're a lifesaver, you really are."

"You're glad to see me?" The girl's face was alight with so much eagerness that India recoiled a little.

"I'm glad of the coffee." She saw the hurt in Polly's eyes, but was too tired to care. Curled on her side, she started to sip with her eyes closed. Thin and watery, it was probably the worst cup of coffee she'd had, but the heat and sweetness cut the staleness of her mouth and after a while she opened her eyes and murmured, "Delicious."

Polly's face brightened as though a torchlight had been switched on from inside.

"So where's mine then?"

They both looked at Mikey.

"Didn't know you was here."

"You know this man?" said India.

"Everyone knows Mikey."

"Polly," he said, "what time is it?"

"'Bout seven."

"Bugger off and get Whitelaw, will you? I've had enough of sharing my cell with this woman."

India half turned. Mikey was sitting on his bunk, his face swollen by alcohol, ponytail hanging limply down the back of his torn T-shirt.

"You don't like India?"

Mikey fixed her with a speculative gaze. "Not as yet, no."

Polly squirmed like a puppy in distress.

"I'm sure she's nice deep down, Poll," he said wearily. "Go on, do us a favor and get Whitelaw. I just want to go home is all."

India kept an eye on Mikey as the girl scampered, soft-footed on her dirty bare feet, down the corridor.

Whitelaw appeared five minutes later, freshly shaven and crisply shirted. The clean smell of soap washed through the odor of vomit and sweat like a rainstorm after drought. For a few seconds he stood there staring around him.

"Did this jail go dual-sex overnight?" he remarked. "Or am I seeing things?"

Mikey rolled off his bunk and came to stand by the cell gate. He was taller than Whitelaw, well over six feet. "Just get me out," he said.

"What's your hurry?" Whitelaw inquired. "Your cell mate not pretty enough?"

Mikey flicked her a look. "As it happens I've never found her sort attractive. Too thin, too uptight and altogether too aggressive." He made a gesture of impatience. "Come on, Jed, get on with it, will you?"

The gate swung wide with a metallic groan. Mikey walked into the corridor. Cautiously, India followed him, stood at a wary distance. There was a silence before Whitelaw said, "Miss Kane. Could you fill me in on what's happened here?"

"Ask Sergeant Bacon."

Whitelaw narrowed his eyes at Mikey. "What's the score?"

"The usual." He looked India in the eyes. "Can't believe Stan was so stupid. He ought to have known she'd never crack. That type never does."

Whitelaw gave a sigh. "Let's get you both processed," he said. "Mike, Donna will deal with you. Miss Kane, if you'd follow me, I'll see if we can't get you a shower."

India followed the two men down the beige corridor. Whitelaw pushed the swing door back with a little rubber snap. *Too much sunshine.* It made her eyes ache and her head throb. Donna was talking on the radio, dark hair bobbed and shiny, shirt bright white. The look she sent India made her acutely aware of the grime she'd picked up in the past twenty-four hours. India watched as Donna turned her attention to Mikey, gave him a flirtatious little wave. Mikey ignored her and peered over the counter. He pocketed a wallet, a bunch of keys, and hooked a mobile phone to his belt. He then peered at a pile of forms beside a computer, ruffled them with a finger.

"I collected your backpack this morning," Whitelaw said to India. "Thought you might like a change of clothes. Won't be a minute." He went through a door behind the counter and disappeared.

Donna switched off the radio. "Mikey, you know you're not supposed to read those."

He didn't seem to hear. He'd picked up a white form and was staring at it. He swayed slightly and put a hand against the wall and continued to stare.

"Come on, Mikey, give it back," Donna said.

Mikey ignored her. He looked across at India, his face white and strained. "You're India Kane?"

"Yes."

"You're the woman who killed Tiger."

"No! I didn't have anything to do—"

"Shut your mouth." He didn't shout. His voice was calm yet filled with revulsion. "Or I'll shut it for you."

He pushed the form onto the countertop and stood there, both hands clenched into meaty fists.

She took two steps back, swallowed drily. "I didn't kill Tiger. It's a mistake, I shouldn't be—"

"SHUT UP!"

A clatter of footsteps.

"What the . . ." Whitelaw took in the discarded white form, Mikey's expression. "Hell." He crossed the room to stand by Mikey, gripped his arm. "Mikey, I'm sorry," he said. "I'd planned on telling you later."

His furious expression didn't change. He pulled his arm free and continued glaring at India. "I hope you hang her."

"I think you'd better go. We'll sort your fine out later."

"And hang her high." His voice cracked. "He was only twenty-three, for Christ's sake . . ."

Helpless against his rage, India watched Mikey stumble for the door.

SIX

WHEN HIS MOBILE RANG, MIKEY IGNORED IT. IT RANG again, for longer, and still he ignored it. Two minutes later it rang again, and he gave a groan. He slumped onto the step outside the grocery store and pressed the Answer button.

"Yes." His mouth felt stiff, his tongue too large for his mouth. His mind was foggy with shock.

"Is that Detective Michael Johnson?"

"Not any longer."

"What do you mean?"

"If you want to speak to the police," he said wearily, "I suggest you dial direct. This mobile number belongs to a civilian."

"I have your card here. You've written your home and mobile numbers on the back."

The fog cleared a little. "Who are you?"

The voice lowered. "My name isn't important."

"Okay. So talk to me."

"You're investigating the Patterson case."

"Yes."

A slight pause.

"I might know who killed him. And the other guy."

Mikey leaned forward. "Keep talking."

"I'm scared, okay? I found some files. Notes and stuff. Highly classified . . . It's really serious stuff."

"What's it about?"

"I can't say. But if they knew I'd seen it . . . I'd be dead."

"Who are 'they'?"

Silence.

"Can you send them to me? Or a copy?"

"I don't know if I can do that. They weren't supposed to be found . . ." The voice trailed off.

"Take it easy," Mikey said. "Why don't you give me your name and we'll go from there."

A hesitation.

"Call me Sam."

"Okay, Sam. Where are you calling from?"

"A phone box. In Sydney. I'm worried they've bugged my office and home."

"Where do you work?"

Another silence.

"Sam? Are you still there?"

"I've got to go."

"Will you call me later?"

"I'm scared they might kill me."

"I'd like to promise you protection—"

"You can't protect me. Nobody can."

The man hung up. Mikey stared at his phone. A breakthrough. At long last a fish had tugged at one of the lines he'd cast during November. Not that he'd learned much from Sam, but once a witness started to squeal, they usually found it very hard to stop. He hoped this one would be no different. *Tiger would have been thrilled.*

He wondered if his friend had looked the Kane woman in the eye when she'd shot him. He wondered if Tiger had died in agony, or if he'd known nothing about it. A spasm of emotion, like a physical pain, sliced through him. Unsteadily, Mikey got to his feet and headed for the bottle shop.

It was gloomy inside. Mikey mopped his face with the end of his shirt and glanced around when the fly screen banged to see Skippy standing there, his big black head hanging. The corners of his eyes and mouth were webbed with wrinkles, his skin dark as a log scorched by fire. Gray spotted his mop of black hair, and his bare chest and shoulders were scored with cuts and long red scabs like worms. In one hand he had a smooth wooden carving of a snake and in the other a painted emu's egg.

"Which you like?" he asked Mikey.

"I spent twenty-four hours in the nick because of you," Mikey snapped. "Next time, call the cops."

"They wouldn't come."

"I wish I'd been as sensible. Getting mixed up in a bar brawl between a bunch of pissed Abos and white blokes was not a good move. Cops even think I bloody started it!"

"You saved my life. Jacko's too."

"And what do I get for it? Jail. With a two-hundred-buck fine. My body feels like it's been run over by a steamroller. I've a loose tooth and thanks to you I need a new shirt."

Skippy shuffled his feet and stared at the floor. "Didn't mean to get you into trouble, but . . ."

Mikey paid for his bourbon in silence.

"You're a good man, Mikey," ventured Skippy, and came and laid the carved snake on the counter. "Thanks, mate."

Mikey looked at Skippy's dropping shoulders, the way his raggedy shorts hung on too-thin hips. As he picked up the snake, he wished to God he wasn't so bloody softhearted sometimes.

———

India expected Donna to treat her much as Mikey had, with enmity and contempt, but the young policewoman seemed friendly enough when she asked if she could make a phone call.

"If it's interstate," Donna said. "Make it short, would you?"

"Sure," said India, and dialled Scotto's direct number at the *Sydney Morning Herald.* It was answered briskly. "Sorry," said a man's apologetic voice, "but Scott Kennedy's on holiday. Won't be back for ten days. Can anyone else help?"

India announced herself. "It's extremely urgent," she said. "Pretty much life and death. It's about his wife, Lauren. Can't you get a message to him?"

"What's up with Lauren?"

"I can't say right now, but I need to contact Scotto immediately. It's an emergency. I'm at Cooinda Police Station. Could you take this number? Get him to ring me?"

"Is Lauren okay?"

"I can't . . ." Her voice wavered.

"Right." His voice turned brisk. "I'll get hold of him as soon as I can. It's not going to be easy—the last we heard he was heading into the jungle to spot orangutans. Borneo somewhere. He took his mobile but I doubt if it'll work out there. I'll try and track him down another way, starting with his parents. Okay?"

"Okay."

"My name's Tom Worthington. I'll give you my home and mobile number. You have a mobile?"

"No. But, wait a sec . . ." She asked Donna for a pen and paper and if it was okay for Tom to ring her at the station.

"Sure," Donna said. She tore a scrap from her notebook and passed it and her pen to India.

"Tom, you can leave a message for me here. Give me your numbers." She scribbled them down.

"Don't worry, India. We'll find him fast for you."

Taking a breath India dialled a number she knew by heart from childhood, her fingers trembling. A woman answered, "Hello?"

"Sylvia? It's India Kane."

"Indi!" Lauren's mother said. "What a lovely surprise!"

She felt sick. *They didn't know.*

"How's the trek going? Lauren was so excited about the whole thing she packed a week early . . ."

India concentrated on the clock on the wall to try and stop herself from bursting into tears as Lauren's mother talked. Sylvia Walker, who made the best fruitcake this side of heaven. Lauren had always brought a cake from Sylvia whenever she'd visited.

"How's Lauren?" her mother said. "Bet she's got a sore behind! She hasn't been riding for years."

"Um . . . I don't suppose you've heard from Scotto lately?"

Sylvia laughed. "She's missing him that badly already?"

"I guess."

"I haven't spoken to him since he left for Borneo. Borneo of all places! As if Australia isn't hot enough."

"He didn't leave you a number?"

"Why, no, he didn't." Small silence. "Is everything all right out there, Indi?"

No. No, it's not but I can't tell you, not until I've heard from Scotto.

"Fine," she said. Her throat swelled with the effort of not crying. "Sylvia, I've got to go. Good to talk to you."

"You too, and just you make sure you come over here *soon.* It's been too long. Promise?"

India wanted to repeat "promise" but couldn't. She hung up just before a sob escaped.

Donna passed her a box of man-sized tissues. "Try someone else, why don't you?"

India managed a muffled thank-you and blew her nose. She took several deep breaths, then she made some more calls. People she'd met over the six months she'd been in Melbourne. The first was away until Thursday and India left a message. The next was already on their Christmas break in the UK and not due back until January. The remainder were out. India left more messages. Considered contacting the Broken Hill police but there seemed no point; cops stick together.

She started to shake. *Don't lose it,* she told herself. *Just because the cavalry's on holiday doesn't mean it's not going to get here. You can survive this until Scotto gets here. You* will *survive this.*

"Not having much luck, are you?" said Donna.

India didn't reply. She followed the sergeant to the shower room, where she found her backpack, which had a big red tag on it with the number eight. Donna opened the door. "There's no lock, so I'll wait outside." India wasn't sure whether the policewoman intended to keep intruders out, or to stop her from making a run for it.

Her backpack was a mess. Everything had obviously been pulled out and inspected and then stuffed back in. India emptied it, making separate piles of clothes, books and toiletries. She opened her washbag and pulled out her shampoo and conditioner, soap and a sponge, and set them inside the shower. She put a thin orange towel within reach and turned the water on full blast.

India kicked off her deck shoes and peeled off her shirt and jeans. She dumped her underwear on top. Clouds of hot steam drifted towards her. She checked the shower's temperature and turned it down a fraction.

Finally, she stepped beneath the spray. Involuntarily she made a small sound of intense pleasure. She rotated slowly, luxuriously, letting the water beat on the base of her neck and shoulders, her face and over her head. She closed her eyes and as she breathed in the familiar scent of her soap, she pretended she was in her little Melbourne apartment.

This is the only pleasure you're going to get for a while, so enjoy it.

She shampooed and conditioned her hair, then stood with the jet pounding against her shoulder blades, her eyes still shut.

She pictured the last time she'd seen Sylvia and Lauren together. She'd turned seven the day before they'd taken her to Kingsford Smith airport. Sylvia was trying to be brave for Lauren, Lauren was trying to be brave for India, and India was trying to be brave for them all. All three of them burst into tears when her flight to London was called.

There was a loud knock on the bathroom door. "Time's up," called Donna.

India didn't answer. Her eyes were still closed and she knew she should be preparing herself for the forthcoming interrogation but her mind was stuck on the image of Sylvia, her warmth and kindness.

The door banged open. "Miz Kane, get the hell out of there before I come in and interview you naked."

India turned off the shower and dried herself. She rubbed her hair with the towel and wrapped it around her while she smothered her body with moisturizer. She combed out her hair before she got dressed. Tan jeans, yellow shirt, big brown belt. Refusing to rush, she carefully repacked her backpack.

Eventually, she wiped the small mirror above the washbasin clear. Her face was sallow and gaunt, and her normally olive skin had a gray tinge. There was a bluish bruise on her jaw, not particularly noticeable, but it was sore when she touched it. She stood there for a moment, fingers against the bruise, staring numbly at her reflection. *Jesus. How did I get here? How do I get out?* She closed her eyes. *I must remain strong,* she told herself, strong as iron as steel as rock.

Straightening her shoulders, she turned from the mirror, picked up her backpack and returned to the corridor. Donna took her backpack and made to walk her to the interview room.

"Could I make one more phone call?" India said.

Donna glanced up and down the empty corridor. "If you make it short. Stan's going ballistic." She hustled India into reception.

It took her two attempts before she got the number right. Asked for Mr. Tremain.

"Ron Tremain speaking," a curt male voice said.

"Um," said India, "sorry, this might come as a bit of a surprise. I'm trying to track down a relative of mine, on my mother's side. Her family came from Cooinda, you see. Their name was Tremain."

"Well," said Ron Tremain. "I can tell you straight up that you've got the wrong mob. We're not from Cooinda, we're from New Zealand. Moved here five years ago. My parents emigrated to New Zealand from Germany in the thirties. My grandparents are still in Germany. None of them have ever been to Cooinda."

"What about any other Tremains? Do you know any in or around Cooinda?"

"Nope." He paused, as though thinking. "You tried the phone book?"

"Yes. You're the only Tremain listed."

"The electoral role?"

"I'll do that."

"Good luck."

India rubbed at the frown between her eyes. Had Lauren really found her grandfather? Or had she also seen Ron Tremain in the phone book and simply used it as an excuse to get her friend to Cooinda? Right then it didn't seem to matter because Donna started leading her to the interview room.

SEVEN

JEROME WAS SITTING ON ONE SIDE OF THE TABLE, Whitelaw and Stan the other. All three men appeared to be contemplating a single buff-colored folder, four cups of coffee and a plate of granular sugared doughnuts.

India greeted her lawyer and sat down. Whitelaw immediately pressed the Play button of the tape recorder and leaned forward.

"We need to know where the weapon is. The weapon that killed the two victims. Can you help us?"

She took a gulp of her coffee, then picked up a doughnut, unsure if she could eat it or not. She'd never felt less like eating in her life but knew she had to keep up her strength. She bit into the doughnut and started chewing. The sound of crunching sugar seemed to fill the small interview room.

"For fuck's sake—" Stan started to say but Whitelaw held up a hand and the senior sergeant fell silent, looked away. The muscles in his jaw bulged with the effort to restrain himself.

India didn't allow her surprise to show. She'd thought Stan would be leading the interview, but something had obviously occurred and it was Whitelaw who was in charge today.

"Anything you might remember about the evening of the eleventh, when you heard the shot, would be helpful."

India chewed slowly, concentrating on the yeasty warmth and

teeth-edging sweetness of cheaply manufactured jam. She glanced at Jerome's watch—eight-thirty-five—and continued to eat.

"If you're not careful, Miss Kane," said Whitelaw, "we might start to believe you have something to hide."

The shower and doughnut had revived her, and the caffeine was perking her up surprisingly well.

"Why is Mike called Mikey the Knife?" she asked Whitelaw.

He gave her a measured look. "Why do you think?"

"Because he knifed someone?"

"Correct."

"Who did he knife?"

Stan made a small choking sound but Whitelaw cut in. "You'd do best to ask him yourself." He cast a sidelong glance at Stan, who sat back, looking furious.

India found herself staring at the remaining four doughnuts, the polystyrene cups, in a state of weariness. She looked at the lawyer. "Jerome, surely the police can't hold me here indefinitely without a court order or something?"

"We don't need anything," Stan said.

Whitelaw's expression turned inward as he got to his feet, walked to the door. "Sergeant Bacon's right," he said. "We can hold you for twelve hours without any sort of order."

"Twelve! But I've been here since midday yesterday!"

Jerome hurriedly explained the meaning of Time Out, and that the time she'd spent waiting for her solicitor didn't count. The police were, he went on to say, actually only allowed to hold a suspect for four hours but Cooinda PD had gotten an eight-hour extension. The total of twelve hours in jail started when the questioning did.

India glanced at Jerome's watch again. "It still means they've run out of time. Question time started six-thirty yesterday. They're breaking the law. They've got to let me go."

Stan rose so violently his chair fell to the floor with a crash. "Who says the magistrate hasn't given us special dispensation so we can go to court in an hour and get permission to hang on to you as long as we goddam like?" he ground out. He then gave her a humorless smile and joined Whitelaw at the door. They both stepped outside, letting it bang behind them.

"Is that true?" India asked Jerome weakly.

"Unfortunately, yes."

"This town's completely mad! How can they possibly think I killed Tiger and Lauren out of jealousy when I only arrived yesterday? For God's sake, I only met Tiger because my car broke down, and I never even *saw* Lauren let alone knew what she was up to with Tiger. I've got to get out and find out what the hell's going on or I may never see daylight again. You've got to get me bail!"

"How much bail can you afford, in cash?"

"Ten thousand, tops."

"That's not going to help us much. Don't you have a surety, perhaps a house, you can put up?"

"No."

"What about a car?"

"I've a Honda Civic in Melbourne. I bought it for five hundred bucks."

"Can any friends help?"

"Not yet." She filled him in on Scotto. "I'll get bail, right?"

He sucked on his lips.

"What's wrong?"

"We're in front of Judge Deacon," Jerome said on a sigh. "Judge Dread to you and me."

———

India found out where she stood at her arraignment at ten-thirty: $250,000. She felt suddenly light-headed and knew she was white as chalk. Jerome asked for bail reduction, arguing that she would have a solid alibi within the next few days, that she was a well-known journalist who had never been arrested before and was a tourist from out of town and no danger to anyone. The judge watched him impassively, then said, "Thank you, Mr. Trumler, but may I point out that your client is also a long way from home, and seems to have no family to help her in her current difficulties. In my opinion she is a serious flight risk. The bail stands as is."

They all rose, the judge left and India sank back on the bench between Jerome and a constable with downy-blond stubble like rabbit fur. The constable gave her a sympathetic grimace. He crimped a cuff around her wrist for the trip back to jail.

Tears trembled in her eyes, then spilled down her cheeks. She didn't want to cry, hadn't cried for as long as she could remember, but the strain and fatigue of the last two days had left her with an overwhelming sensation of grief and defeat. Jerome passed her a cream cotton handkerchief. He stood up, patted her distractedly on the shoulder and walked out of the courtroom. At the far end of the room she saw a young man watching her. He was the only spectator. She looked away. She felt like a small child as she clutched Jerome's hanky in her sweaty fist. The constable tugged on her arm and led her outside.

———

The following morning India was sitting on her bunk, staring helplessly at the newspapers on her lap. Whitelaw had brought them, and seemed to be waiting for her reaction. She was the main story. She was HEADLINE NEWS. Her face, blown up grainy and gray from her passport photograph, took up most of the front pages. Like most passport photographs it was unflattering, and her pointed chin seemed sharper, her dark curly hair wilder, her nose longer and eyes black as pits and as emotionless.

Beautiful India Kane in Cooinda custody . . . Melbourne journalist held on suspicion of murder . . . Jealous woman accused of killing best friend and her lover . . .

The Goodmans were reported as being "shocked" and "appalled" at the fate of their house guests. What Lauren's parents were thinking, God alone knew. India thought of Sylvia's cheery voice on the phone.

"They've already found me guilty," India said, her tone subdued.

"Not everyone believes what they read in the papers."

"Don't you?"

When he didn't reply, she looked up at him. "Oh my God," she whispered.

Whitelaw looked away and took a step back. He folded his arms across his chest.

"You know I'm innocent, don't you?" She felt a rush of energy and jumped to her feet. She barely noticed the newspapers sliding to the floor. "Let me go! You can do that, can't you?"

"No, I can't. It's not only Stan who refuses to accept that Frank Goodman's your alibi but Judge—"

"But you're a *detective*! If you think I'm innocent, I shouldn't be here!"

"Keep your voice down," he hissed. With a shock she saw sweat beaded on his brow.

"Jesus Christ, Whitelaw, what the hell's going on? What's put the wind up you? Is there a police conspiracy going down or what?"

He walked to the cell gate and shouted for Donna.

"Whitelaw," she said warningly. "This is my third day in this jail."

He didn't respond but waited until Donna had unlocked the gate, let him through and locked it behind him. He turned his head slightly towards India. "Anything I can get you?"

"A cake with a file in it."

Whitelaw walked away without looking back.

Face pressed against the bars, India watched him follow Donna down the corridor. Think positive, she told herself. Whitelaw thinks you're innocent. Don't think about why he won't or can't help you right now. You've a friend on the inside. That's got to be good.

She turned her mind to her friend on the outside, Tom Worthington, and wondered whether he'd found Scotto. Without his help she stood little chance of regaining her freedom. She had discovered that banks didn't care to loan money to someone charged with murder and whose address was Cooinda jail.

Dispirited, she went and slumped back on her bunk. She couldn't face the newspapers, so she lay down and tried to sleep.

———————

Whitelaw returned two hours later. He gave her a handful of books and put a poinsettia beside her bunk. India was astonished.

"Is this an apology?"

He turned the poinsettia a fraction so the petals faced into the cell.

"Whitelaw?"

"We can't talk here." His voice was low.

"Shall I get Donna to take me to the Ladies'? Then you can—"

"We can't. Not in the station."

She digested this along with his anxiety. "Okay, I get the message." She inhaled deeply and exhaled several times. She rotated her shoulders to ease the tension in her neck. A bone popped audibly. "I need a massage," she said. "Or maybe shiatsu. Any massage parlors in Cooinda, Detective?"

He gave her a small smile and said, "Not in particular, but there is Susie."

"Ah. Susie. Fill me in, will you? It's not like I've anywhere to go, after all."

As they talked, India began to wonder what the hell was going on. And why the plant? It was positively bizarre that one of the investigative officers was chatting away to her, a felon, let alone buying her gifts. After a while she watched Whitelaw's unease gradually dissipate. He showed her the books he'd brought, including one called *The Lost Generation*. "Might help you understand how Australia ticks," he said.

"How come the plant? Do you have a predilection for poinsettias?"

"I didn't want you to forget Christmas is around the corner."

"I'm not a fan of Christmas," India replied, "but it was a nice thought."

He pulled a mock-shocked face. "What, are you telling me you're not a Christian?"

"No less than anyone else." She gave a shrug.

"I'm not a fan either," he admitted. "It's the family thing, I guess."

"Don't you get on with your family?" she asked, curious, ever the journalist.

He looked around as though debating how to redecorate the cell. "I don't have a family. Christmas simply reminds me . . ." His expression darkened.

"Surely you must have *some* family?"

"Nope. Not a single one."

"Are they dead?"

"I wouldn't be able to say. I was stolen when I was four years old."

India looked at him, shocked. "Who on earth stole you?"

He stared at the ceiling. "The Australian government."

She shook her head. "I don't get it. Why did they steal you?"

"Not just me. About a hundred thousand Aboriginal children were taken from their parents and either put in care or adopted by white families. Which looks okay on the surface considering a lot of kids were being abused or their parents were incapable of caring for them. But some folks had a very real plan to wipe out the entire Aboriginal race, to 'breed us white.'"

Appalled, India said, "I'd heard something . . . There were articles about it in the papers back home, but I had no idea of the scale."

He indicated the book he'd brought. "That'll tell you all about it, if you're interested. It's harrowing though. A lot of the kids were used as the sexual toys of the outback . . . by missionaries, clergymen, nuns . . ." He took in her expression, gave a sad smile. "I was one of the lucky ones. Sure, I got shunted around for a while—I was an awkward bastard—but then a solicitor and his wife in Sydney adopted me and kept me for good. It was fashionable to have a mixed-race baby and they were one of the few who really cared about their adopted child."

"I hope you don't mind my saying that you're very dark. You look full-blooded, not mixed race."

"Aborigines can also have very light skin." Whitelaw looked across at her with a glint of amusement. "You could easily be an Abo with your coloring. Sure you weren't a lost child?"

"Is that what you're called? Lost children?"

"Officially, we're known as the stolen generation."

"How sad."

"Genocide usually is."

Eight

IT WAS SEVEN P.M. AND INDIA HAD JUST REACHED THE END of her chapter when a shadow moved outside her cell. She immediately dropped the book on the bed as she recognized the large figure clutching a greasy paper bag in his right hand.

"Steak sandwich all right?"

Her mouth watered as the smell of fresh onion and warm bread and steak hit her nostrils. "Albert, you are an absolute peach, feeding me like this."

"And Polly's brung dessert."

The young girl crept into view, her dress hanging limply, her skin mottled with dust. In her hand was a chipped china plate of Lamingtons: floury yellow cakes topped with sickly chocolate icing and a sprinkling of dessicated coconut.

India looked at Polly, who shrank behind Albert. Given half the chance she would be living outside the cell. India found the puppy-like devotion hard to take and last night she'd almost snapped, told her to find someone else to cling on to. Polly had sensed her irritability and fled.

"I love Lamingtons," India lied, and felt ashamed when Polly flashed Albert a proud smile. "Come on, guys," she said, "don't just stand there, pass them through!"

With Albert and Polly watching her, India devoured her steak sandwich. She was working her way bravely through one of Polly's revolting Lamingtons when Whitelaw appeared. He stared at her as if she were eating boiled sheep's eyes—she had informed him only yesterday she'd rather starve than eat a Lamington.

"I thought you said you loathed them," said the detective.

Instantly Polly looked crestfallen.

"I love them," India said earnestly. The girl's face split into a broad smile.

Whitelaw turned to Albert and Polly and shooed them away. When they were out of earshot, he said bluntly, "Your bail came through."

India nearly choked. "What?"

"It came through, the full two hundred and fifty thousand, in cash. About half an hour ago."

She sat there dumbly, plate on her lap, unable to take it in.

"Jerome asked me to tell you your trial's set for January fifth. In the meantime, you can't leave the town." He gave her a wry smile. "You can't leave the country either. We're going to hold on to your passport."

She put the plate on her bunk, got slowly to her feet. "Who paid my bail? Was it Scotto? Is he here?"

"No, it wasn't him."

Whitelaw appeared discomfited.

"Was it you?"

He gave a bark of startled laughter. "What, on my pay?"

"Who then?"

"A Mr. Arthur Knight paid it."

"Who the hell's Arthur Knight?"

"Well, he's the man who's stumped up the cash, which means you're free to go."

"I don't get it."

Whitelaw unlocked the cell door. "How about you ask Jerome? He arranged it. He'll know who the guy is."

"Yes. Good idea. Yes, I'll do that."

She was still off balance as they walked into reception. Perhaps Tom had gotten a message to Scotto and Arthur Knight was his solicitor? That had to be it, surely. She had no other friends who could raise that sort of cash in under twenty-four hours, even if they wanted.

Whitelaw paused at the reception desk. Constable Crawshaw, rabbit-fur stubble now smoothly shaven, passed him a form and a cassette tape with a white sticker on it: KANE. "You sign for this," Whitelaw said to India. "You also get to report to the station every day until your trial."

India signed where he indicated and pocketed the tape.

The constable gave her a self-conscious smile.

"Backpack?" said Whitelaw.

The constable wiped the smile off his face and bent over and came around the counter to pass India her backpack.

"Thanks," she said. She shrugged the straps over each shoulder and settled the backpack on her back. She had an urge to run for the door but suppressed it and followed Whitelaw outside and into the softened evening heat.

It must have been in the midseventies and the air felt like velvet on her face. She raised her head and looked at a handful of stars set against the darkening sky. She could smell meat barbecuing and hear the faint sound of music. A rush of joy soared from her belly and into her heart. *Freedom.*

She gulped the air over her tongue and into her lungs. Her senses became more refined. Beef sausages and Macy Gray singing about trying to walk away from her love.

I've been inside just three days, she thought, and I'm ready to burst into an insane song and dance routine. Imagine what I'd do if I'd been inside three years. She turned to Whitelaw, a grin on her face.

He was grinning back.

"Thank you," she said.

"No need to thank me. Thank your bail partner."

Despite the heat, she gave a shiver.

"I'm sorry your car's impounded. Will you be okay to walk?" he asked her.

She readjusted the backpack more comfortably on her lower back. "I'll be fine."

"You shouldn't be alone."

India squinted through the darkness and saw the shadow that was Polly slip towards her. "It doesn't look like I'll get the chance," she said. At his frown she added cheerfully, "I'll find some champagne somewhere. Polly will know where to take me."

The girl took India's hand. It was sticky, but India found herself squeezing the small fingers gently, finding the contact a comfort.

"I'll look after her," Polly said shyly to Whitelaw.

"Okay," he said, and made a vague gesture with his hand before letting it drop to his side. "I'll be seeing you."

Polly tugged India along the street, past its fibro houses and utes parked in driveways. Nearly every window sported a plastic Christmas tree, blazing with colored bulbs, and most doors were hung with garlands imported from China and Korea. One house had lights strung around its windows and front door as if declaring itself proud to be a happy family home. India glanced inside as they passed but the rooms were empty.

She found her joyful mood evaporating as she walked with Polly through the muffled streets. A humorless little voice inside her kept saying, "Happy Christmas." Other horrendous Christmases began parading past her eyes: her little brother, Toby, dying the week before Christmas, her mother's fatal heart attack on Christmas Eve, her pet dog having to be put down the week after Christmas.

And now Lauren, two weeks from Christmas, was dead.

———

"I don't think it's a good idea," said Polly, stubbornly tugging India's hand and trying to drag her past the Royal Hotel's front entrance.

"They seemed nice. They've vacancies. Look, it says 'newly renovated charming single and double rooms available.'"

"Not the Royal. Please."

"Polly, I'm knackered. All I want to do is crawl into bed and sleep for a week."

"Come home with me."

"You told me it's over three hours' walk away. I don't have the energy."

"This ain't a good place to stop."

Polly tugged once more and India, in one abrupt movement, yanked her hand free. "I'm staying here tonight."

There was a smell of polish in the foyer. Through the open doorway that gave on to the bar, she saw a man with spiky red hair drink his Scotch straight down and then push the glass to be refilled. "Give me a pack of crisps, will ya?"

Then he glanced up and saw her. She didn't think she recognized him, but he obviously knew her.

"Holy shit," he said. "Look what the cat dragged in."

The barmaid's fleshy face peered around the door and looked at her carefully. "I'd beat it if I was you," Debs advised.

"All I want is a room. Just for tonight."

"Hey, guys," Spiky Hair said over his shoulder. "Lookey who's here."

He was quickly joined by three men with alcohol-reddened faces.

"It's Tiger's killer," one of them said incredulously.

"She's got a fucking nerve."

"Go fetch Ken, he'll have something to say to her, I'll bet."

India picked up her backpack.

"Sorry," said Debs, not unkindly.

Polly didn't say a word when India joined her outside.

After an hour of searching for accommodation and being rejected at every turn—one man even fetched his shotgun and waved it at them through his fly-screen door—they finally bought some fried chicken and chips from Albert's cafe, and sat on the pavement to eat. It had cooled a little and the stars had gone. A breeze was stirring the dust in the gutters. India opened her carton and withdrew a crispy drumstick. Up until now Albert's food had been spot on, but tonight her tastebuds weren't functioning properly and it was like eating battered cardboard.

"India . . ." Polly paused uncertainly.

"What?"

"Stan says he found a teddy bear in your backpack." She sounded dubious, as though she shouldn't believe what she'd heard.

"That's right."

"Why do you have him?"

"Because sometimes he's a comfort."

"But you're grown up!"

"That may be so, but we adults still need comforting from time to time."

"Can't I have him? I don't have any toys."

The miniature teddy bear was the only reminder of Lauren she had with her.

"No. I'm sorry, you can't."

Polly's eyes filled with disappointment but India didn't have the capacity to feel any shame or remorse. She was drained of all emotion. When they'd finished their chicken, a man came out of Albert's and crossed the street towards them.

"I heard you can't find nowhere to stay," he said. He carried a pie and a bag of chips and his face was shadowed under his Akubra hat.

"You heard right," India said.

"It must be tough, having the whole town close their doors against you. Kind of rude in my opinion."

India shrugged.

"How about you come and stay with me?"

"I'm fine, but thank you anyway."

"I saw you in the Royal. Read the papers. Know how you feel, being shunned and all."

She looked up at him, wary.

"I don't live nowhere smart. But I've a sofa. So long as you don't mind Elvis sharing with you."

"Elvis?"

"My cat. Sofa's his space. He's likely to climb aboard any time." He glanced at Polly. "You got somewhere, right?"

Polly was biting her lip but she nodded. India thought about sleeping on the pavement, maybe in a doorway. But what if Red-cap and Dungarees saw her?

"You've no worries from me," the man said, and as she continued to hesitate, gave a shrug. "Just thought I'd ask." He made to walk away.

India hurriedly clambered to her feet. "That would be kind of you," she said. "Do you live far?"

He smiled and pointed south. "Ten minutes."

India walked beside him, Polly tagging their heels.

"Have you lived in Cooinda long?" she asked him.

"Born and bred."

They turned right at the Royal, down Kent Street. The man was eating his chips as they walked and India eyed him cautiously, not entirely sure she was doing the right thing.

"You'll be right with Elvis," the man said. "So long as he don't bring in a mouse. Plays with them for hours. Sick sod."

As he said "sod" she saw him drop his pie and chips. He reached behind him, for something at the small of his back, and came at her with a wrench. She made to dive away but he caught her wrist and she felt the wrench crack against her skull, just above her right ear. Then lights exploded behind her eyes, and went suddenly black.

Nine

INDIA AWAKENED AND THOUGHT SHE WAS DROWNING. Water cascaded over her face and strips of cloth were clamped over her eyes and mouth. She gagged and choked, fighting to get air into her lungs, and felt something like baler twine cut into her wrists and gravel crunch against her ankles. Then someone grabbed her elbows and hauled her upright.

She stood with hands tied behind her, feet braced apart, swaying a little, and waited for the blindfold to let in some light. Nothing. She could taste oil and grease on the gag and smell the sharp rankness of excitement and fear. She turned her head and heard the roar of a truck's engine and knew she couldn't be far from the main road. Only when it faded did she catch the soft shuffle of footsteps, the fainter sound of breathing.

"You're a bit dense, aren't you?" a man said. "Else you've got a kangaroo loose in the top paddock."

Some laughter, a raw gloating sound that made her shudder.

"You should have got the hint and left town while you could."

She was breathing hard. Pumping air in and out through her flared nostrils. Trembling. She opened her eyes as wide as she could but there was still no light. She tentatively slid her foot forward. Someone kicked it sideways and she lurched violently, almost losing her balance.

"Keep still," another man growled.

A finger touched the hollow at the base of her throat. India jerked wildly, was brought up hard by someone gripping her elbows from behind.

Again the finger touched the hollow. Again she jerked. This time lashing out with her feet, her protest strangling in her throat.

"Keep her still," the same voice said, annoyed.

She thought it was Dungarees. Or any one of the ugly mob who'd come for her at the Royal. She felt the bottom of her shirt yanked from her jeans and gripped hard. Cold metal brushed her breastbone. She bucked and squirmed, tried to twist away. There was a tearing sound. Her shirt was slit open to her waist.

Everything went silent. Her throat froze solid. She could almost feel the feasting men's eyes suckered onto her breasts.

Someone chuckled. Then another voice spoke—deep and threatening. "Let her go."

Fear had taken a grip on her, made her imagine things; it sounded like Mikey the Knife.

"Bugger off, will you?" That sounded like Red-cap.

"Sorry, no can do. I've an obligation to fulfil."

She hadn't imagined it: it *was* Mikey.

She heard a muttered babble of outrage: "She's ours." "What's it got to do with you?" "Sod off."

"Let her go," said Mikey again, grimly determined.

"Why the hell should we?"

She heard a dull slapping thud, like a wet leg of lamb hitting a tabletop. A softer sound followed; cloth and leather and flesh collapsing onto the ground.

"Because I'm bigger than you," Mikey said grimly.

Someone said indignantly, "You interfering, self-righteous . . ."

The leg of lamb thudded again, and again. Grit scrabbled and scrunched. Someone grunted, as though the air had been punched out of them. Someone else cursed. Another shouted.

India was hauled sideways, lost her footing. She crashed to the ground. She curled into a tight ball, tried to make herself small. Her breathing was jerky. She shook uncontrollably.

The leg of lamb kept thudding. Wet smacks. Dry thumps. Some groans. A thin cry of pain.

Her eyes were squeezed shut behind the blindfold.

Heavy footsteps running. Running away. Someone breathing hard. Hoarsely panting.

A soft scamper. Fingers tugging at her blindfold. India raised her head. Uncurled a little.

"I can't undo it," Polly said plaintively.

The snick of a knife. Baler twine first, then the gag. Blindfold last.

For a moment India simply lay there.

"Get a move on, woman!" Mikey snapped. He was leaning over her. His face was flushed and sweat ran out of his hair. He rubbed his forehead against the arm of his shirt. The checkered-blue sleeve was dotted with blood.

He straightened up and looked down at her as he would a stubborn dog. The skin of his face was tight and the scar through his eyebrow pulsed red. His big chest heaved up and down. *Saved by Conan the Barbarian,* she thought, feeling slightly hysterical.

She sat up and rubbed her mouth. It was stiff and numb. She could feel a swelling forming behind her ear. Huge clouds rolled slowly across the sky. Two streetlights faintly lit the flat wasteland of sand dotted with leafless bushes and plastic bags, rusting cans and broken glass. She could make out the shadows of half a dozen houses, and there was the cheerful green and gold band of a BP garage at the end of the street. Belatedly, she realized she was on the periphery of a rubbish dump.

A squeal of tires reached them, then the angry roar of a V8 being pushed hard. Mikey immediately reached down and plucked her skywards as though she were made of goose down. She was shuddering and her legs felt rubbery, but under Mikey's scornful eye she stood and clutched the torn rag of her blouse over her breasts and straightened her spine. Mikey unbuttoned his shirt and pulled it off with an angry grunt. Thrusting it at her, he made an irritated gesture at her tattered clothes.

"Thanks," she murmured weakly.

Abruptly he turned his back. India scrambled into the shirt, did the buttons up.

With a chirp of rubber a police Land Cruiser pulled up beneath one of the streetlights. A uniformed cop climbed out and headed their way, followed by a man in plain clothes. The downy-stubbled constable and Whitelaw.

"Jed," Mikey said cautiously, "Justin."

Whitelaw and Justin nodded, came and stood next to them.

India caught herself staring at the muscles shifting under Mikey's skin as he answered their questions, the way the sweat glistened at the hollow of his spine, and hurriedly looked away.

Yes, Mikey said, there had been a fight.

No, it had nothing to do with Miss Kane, it was a misunderstanding over a bet.

Yes, the bet had been with Ken Willis. Yes, everything was settled. Sorry to have troubled you both.

Whitelaw glanced from Mikey's bare torso to India's blood-spattered shirt. "How come I'm finding this hard to swallow?"

"Polly's a witness," Mikey continued stolidly. "And Billy Bryant and Tony Roberts."

"You flattened Fat Tony, too?" the constable said incredulously. "Ken and Billy *and* Fat Tony?"

Mikey rubbed his knuckles and remained silent.

Whitelaw turned to India. "Miss Kane? You have anything to add to this fairy tale?"

Slowly she shook her head.

"Okay," he said, turning brisk. "Let's stop wasting time and go home."

Mikey looked uncomfortable. "I'm not sure if that's such a good idea. My housemate's a bit pissed off with me at present and I don't fancy an all-night lecture."

"Then find a friend. You do have friends, don't you?"

"I guess Debs could help me out."

"Well, so long as I don't find you cluttering up some park bench . . ."

Mikey glowered at the policeman. Whitelaw looked amused, said, "I'll give Miss Kane a lift, sort some accommodation out."

Grateful to rely on someone to make decisions for her, India thanked him.

Whitelaw made to usher her to the Land Cruiser.

"Wait . . ." Fingering the thick cotton of his shirt, she walked to Mikey. "Thank you."

"Don't thank me," said Mikey. He was looking at Polly, who was grinning back happily.

"Mikey didn't want to come," Polly said to India.

"Damn right I didn't."

"I told him if he didn't help you, I'd get a job at Susie's massage parlor. He went mad. I had to promise that if he helped you I'd never, ever work in any sort of massage place ever in my whole life."

If it hadn't been for Polly, India realized, she could well be dead. She thanked the heavens for the little girl's devotion.

Mikey seemed to read her mind.

"Got it in one, India Kane. Next time don't count on me to come to the rescue."

———

India slept fitfully, troubled by dreams. She tried to will her subconscious into driving along a road that stretched like a giant paintbrush stroke to the horizon—but she kept sinking onto a hard bunk and Polly was standing outside the cell asking if she needed help, and India was shouting no, she didn't, why wouldn't she go away and leave her alone.

Don't push her away so, she heard Lauren say.

She's nothing but trouble.

It's not her fault. She's only looking for a friend.

I don't want a friend like that.

Whyever not? She's a sweet kid.

A sweet kid who'll suck me dry.

You've gotta lighten up, hon, and let people in every once in a while. They're not all bad, and some of them are even terrific guys. Why don't you just open your heart before it gets rusted shut?

Lauren.

What is it, hon?

I miss you.

I know you do. Look, I've gotta go. Take care, darl.

India lay in a stranger's bed staring at the ceiling. It was six in the morning and a square of sun the color of butter lay across the bare floorboards on the other side of the room. She swung her legs over the side of the bed and sat there in knickers and T-shirt, rubbing her neck and her face, a burning ache of unshed tears in her throat. Unsteadily she got to her feet and went and used the bathroom before slipping back into bed again.

Whitelaw had told her the room was rented by a cop friend of his, and the mess confirmed it. There were clothes on the floor, boxes in corners, magazines and weekend papers piled by the side of the bed. It was the kind of bedroom India felt at home in: cluttered, keys and change on the bedside table, coffee mugs and gold-rimmed glasses on an open hardcover.

Being an incurable snoop, she slid out of bed and went and peeked inside the chest of drawers. Whitelaw's cop friend wore blue jeans and checkered work shirts. On the floor beside the chest were several pairs of hard-wearing boots. She cracked open one of the larger cardboard boxes to find it full of beautiful Aboriginal carvings; snakes, crocodiles, birds and insects were jumbled together—an array of smooth colored wood and bright paint. The next box was full of cheap secondhand paperbacks by Louis L'Amour. No wonder he likes rugged clothing, she thought, distantly amused, he thinks he's a cowboy.

Knowing she wouldn't sleep again, India went across to her backpack and delved inside. It was a peculiar comfort to realize everything was as she'd packed it in the police station. She went through the same routine, unpacking each item carefully and laying everything in neat piles. It was a form of security, she supposed, arranging her personal things as she liked them. She folded a red and gold towel she'd travelled with since she was nineteen and put it beside her toiletries. Placed an expensive body exfoliator on top of it that smelled of mangoes and had cost far too much, even in duty free. She sent thanks to Whitelaw as she removed each item. He'd produced her backpack like magic from the rear of his Land Cruiser last night, and it meant far more than she'd ever admit.

After a quick shower, she put on a pair of shorts and baggy shirt and headed cautiously for the kitchen, sneaking a look at the broad living room with its cane furniture, scattered rugs and polished floorboards. She pulled open the fridge, expecting to see several shrink-wrapped dishes growing a variety of mold beneath them, and stared.

Fresh green vegetables, fruit, two legs of lamb, a ten-inch stack of steaks and what looked like three dozen eggs stared back at her. There were two liters of milk, all fresh, and butter and bread and what looked like homemade strawberry jam.

Not your typical bachelor residence, she thought. She took a packet of coffee, marked "Fresh ground Continental Roast," from the fridge. She filled the filter machine and turned it on. When she reached for the sugar, she saw a fish tank set to one side. Empty of water, it contained a handful of dry twigs, some dried-up grass, and

in the bottom right-hand corner was what could have been a rudi-
mentary web. India licked her lips, peered a little closer—but not
too close. There were no signs of any insects, but she could see numerous specks of what seemed to be excrement. *Please, God,* she
prayed, *let Whitelaw keep mice, and not what I think it might be.*

She extended her hand, flicked her fingers against the glass just
once, very sharply.

Instantly, the twigs withdrew into the grass.

India stared at the twigs, the multitude of tactile hairs that could
deteced the slightest vibration. The tiny claws at the end of each
leg . . . No, they weren't claws, she remembered, but a dense brush
of hairs to give adhesion on vertical surfaces.

"Good morning," said Whitelaw from just behind her and she
leaped into the air.

"You . . ." India found herself ridiculously short of breath.

"Oh, dear," he said, and glanced at the fish tank, then back at
her. "I suppose I should have warned you, but last night I didn't
think you'd want to hear—"

"That you keep tarantulas as pets."

"Tarantula," he corrected stiffly. "I've just the one."

"A Mexican red-knee."

Whitelaw instantly looked enchanted. "How did you—"

"I wrote a profile of a soldier who had three," she said quickly.
"Sorry, but I can't stand them. All those creepy hairy legs." She
shuddered, managed a smile. "Hope you're not insulted that I don't
like your pet?"

Whitelaw shook his head. "Your reaction's not unusual. Most
people are terrified of spiders."

She sent him a nervous look. "You don't let it out, do you? Take
it for walks on a string or anything?"

"The South Americans do exactly that, I've seen it on the TV.
But they hate it. The spiders, I mean. I made a mistake getting this
one." His expression was sad. "I had no idea how much they loathe

being handled. They're much better off in the wild and are truly miserable having anything to do with us."

India glanced at the hairy twigs poised for action and tried vainly to rustle up some sympathy for a miserably trapped wild creature.

"Want some of this coffee you made?" Whitelaw offered gloomily, obviously depressed by his pet's fate.

"Thanks." She crossed the kitchen to sit on the squishy divan beneath the farthest window from the Mexican red-knee, and lit a cigarette. She proceeded to scan an old copy of *The Australian* while surreptitiously watching Whitelaw pour coffee. He was in gray trousers and a white shirt and looked taller than she remembered, and very black. In the soft morning sun, with a snowy-white shirt against his throat, he was so dark he almost seemed to absorb the light and diffuse it.

India turned a page, and was convinced she saw the hairy legs in the fish tank stiffen at her movement.

"Did you manage to get some sleep?" Whitelaw asked, bringing over her coffee.

"Yes, thanks."

He switched on the portable stereo, flipped in a CD. The kitchen was filled with light jazz. "Would you like breakfast?"

"Coffee's fine. I never have much of an appetite before ten."

The detective liked his orange freshly squeezed. He had a bowl of Special K, followed by three slices of Vogel toast with a scrape of butter and Vegemite. Every so often, he looked across at her and half-smiled. India supposed it was meant to put her at ease but she shifted uneasily on the divan and tried to concentrate on her paper without looking at Whitelaw or the hairy monster in the fish tank. Here she was in the detective's house, drinking his coffee, listening to his music, and it felt as weird as if she'd stayed with Count Dracula. She ground out her cigarette on her saucer.

"What am I doing here, Detective?"

"Keeping out of trouble."

Carefully, India said, "Would I be compromising your position?"

"That's my problem, not yours," said Whitelaw simply.

After he'd eaten, he put his dishes in the dishwasher, replaced the butter in the fridge and wiped down each surface with a damp cloth. The kitchen was as neat and orderly as the other cop's bedroom was messy. It was painfully obvious who did the housecleaning.

The divan made a small twanging sound when he came and sat next to her. He slowly sipped his second mug of coffee, and she could tell he had something on his mind by the way he would glance outside, then back at her.

"Something wrong, Detective?"

"Call me Jeremy. And no, nothing's wrong, yet."

"What do you mean 'yet'?"

He looked at her. "Listen, India—and I'm going to call you India whether you like it or not, whether you call me by my given name or not—I don't want you staying anywhere but here until we can clear this mess up."

She arched an eyebrow at him. "Am I under some sort of unofficial house arrest?"

"You've somewhere else to stay?"

India got up and poured some more coffee and stood opposite the Mexican red-knee's tank, sipping slowly. She had a problem with kindness, she knew, and she tried to work out why she felt so suspicious. Was it because he was a cop, like her father? Or something more simple: *could she trust him?* She hadn't trusted anyone since she was a kid, so there seemed no point in changing her spots just because someone was being nice.

"I'll find a place," she said. He opened his mouth to protest and she added, "Any luck with finding Frank Goodman?"

Whitelaw ducked his head. "The only report we've had was

from a ranger who thought he might have seen Frank's party at the Yourambulla Caves. They've moved on. Could be anywhere."

India rolled her eyes. "Jesus. Give the police an award for efficiency."

"The Flinders Ranges aren't Centennial Park," he snapped. "They run north from the top of Gulf Saint Vincent for eight hundred Ks. It's wild, rugged country, and we've about the same chance of finding a needle in there as Frank and his buddies."

India cursed several times, lit another cigarette.

"He's bound to turn up at a sanctuary or park site shortly," Whitelaw reassured her. "We've sent posters to the national parks office, and they've assured us he won't miss them."

"Great," said India. "And what happens if he falls down a gorge and breaks his neck? I guess I'll have to find my own defense then, huh?"

Whitelaw cleared his throat, which she took for assent.

"Anyway. As I was saying," he said. "I want you to stay away from town, and well away from the Royal Hotel, and Ken and the rest of the mob."

"I can't stay away from town," she said reasonably. "I've got to ask questions, find out what's going on. You of all people should know the procedure: one, establish movements of victim until their death; two, pin down the last positive sighting of the victim; three"—she smiled bitterly at this—"look for someone who knew the victim."

He took a breath and let it out. "Done a lot of police work before?"

"I've snooped a fair bit. Us journos get to know how things work. I'd like to know why Tiger and Lauren were at Nindathana."

Whitelaw reached out to the windowsill, neatened the row of cookery books with a finger. "You're going to write about it, aren't you?"

She looked away. She wanted the story, that was true. But it was much more than a story; it was about her and her past. Her and Lauren.

"I'm not sure if I want myself in the papers," he said.

"You won't be," she assured him.

"Like hell I won't. When a reporter's got a story, everyone gets hauled into the light: cops, witnesses, children. Don't tell me you can keep me out of it."

There were some postcards leaning against the cookery books. The top one had a row of naked women lying on their fronts on the sand. "Bottoms up," it read.

"Writing about it will help me," she said, "help me understand. What happened, why it happened."

He looked into space, and smiled. "I'll copy some relevant stuff for you, but on one condition."

India frowned, knowing from his smile she wouldn't like what was coming next.

"That you base yourself here."

Her lips formed a protest but his palm was raised, like a traffic cop's. "We've already established the only place you're welcome is at Polly's. All that bunch of yobbos have to do is drive out there and pick you up. The Abos over there don't have guns—or a lot of guts," he added quietly.

She felt his eyes study her face.

"Look," he said, "I managed to get a message to Lauren's husband late last night. He's back in Sydney." Whitelaw inclined his head towards the phone on the wall, and took his coffee outside. "Why don't you call him? He might help you come to a decision."

Ten

"SCOTTO, HOW ARE YOU BEARING UP?"

"India?"

"Yes."

Just hearing his voice filled her mind with him. Scott Lewis Kennedy, tall and lean and narrow-waisted, his curly brown hair bleached by years of sailing. Blue eyes, kind eyes.

"I can't go to work." He sounded as if he might start to cry. "I think I might break into pieces if I do."

"Then you're doing the right thing," she assured him. "Stay at home and take it easy for a while. Don't be hard on yourself."

The *Sydney Morning Herald* would be able to cover for him, she thought. Loads of editors there to shoulder the extra workload for a while.

"It's not *fair*."

"No."

"We were going to move. We'd found a house in Balgowlah, overlooking the harbor . . ." She could hear him rummaging around, presumably for tissues, and she wondered why she wasn't crying too. Perhaps Lauren was right, perhaps her heart was rusted shut.

Scotto blew his nose. "Are you okay?" His voice was muffled.

"Much better now that I'm out of jail. And, Scotto, thanks for stumping up my bail. I'll pay you back as soon as I can, I promise."

"What are you talking about?"

"My bail."

"I never paid any bail."

"You must have."

"Your solicitor told me it had already been paid," he said. "I didn't get back into town 'til late yesterday. I assumed you'd sorted it."

"Do you know anyone called Arthur Knight?"

"No, sorry."

She pinched the bridge of her nose. "I don't suppose it could have been Lauren's mum?"

There was a small pause. "I'm sorry, Indi."

"What do you mean?"

"Sylvia's in shock . . ." He trailed off.

India felt her stomach lurch. "She thinks I killed Lauren?"

"Give her some time. She'll come around soon."

"Shall I ring her? Explain the situation?"

"I wouldn't, no."

She tried to swallow the ball of tears rising in her throat. *Don't lose it,* she told herself. *Hold yourself tight like you used to and don't let it get to you.*

"Indi? Are you okay?"

"I'm fine. Honestly. Look, could you do me a favor, when you feel up to it?"

"Sure, anything."

"Could you find out what exactly Lauren was working on? It sounded like it was something pretty heavy. Maybe she got too close, and someone . . ." she hesitated ". . . wanted her out of the way."

A long silence, during which she hoped Scotto wasn't sitting there stricken but was thinking about her question.

"Scotto?"

"She went up there to talk to a man called Mullett. Bertie Mullett."

"What about, do you know?"

"It's to do with someone called Geraldine Child. Hang on a sec." She heard the phone clunking down, some classical music in the background, then he came back and relayed a Sydney phone number. "Geraldine's a doctor. Retired, I think."

"A GP, or another sort of doctor?"

"No idea."

"What was the theme of Lauren's story, can you remember?"

Scotto remained silent.

India took a sudden wild guess. Could the name Mullett be Aboriginal? "Was it to do with the stolen generation?"

"Yeah, that could have been it." He suddenly sounded very tired. "You ought to meet Geraldine too, I guess. Talk to her one to one."

India rubbed her forehead with her hand. "I can't leave town. Not while I'm on the wanted list."

"Yeah. The detective mentioned that. Shall I come to Cooinda? Can I help?"

"No, you stay there." She found herself staring at the receiver on the wall, at the telephone number there. She thought briefly, then gave it to Scotto.

"When you feel up to it, maybe you can call in at Lauren's office? No pressure. Just have a look, okay?"

"Sure. I'll do it tomorrow. Okay?"

"Okay."

"I don't know how I'm going to get through this, but I will, she'd want me to." His voice cracked. "I've gotta go, Indi. Take care."

He hung up. India gazed out into the bright sunlight with a mixture of sadness and relief. Sadness over Sylvia, and relief that

Scotto accepted her simply as she was: innocent. And without a single question. She had a friend. Thank God. She closed her eyes and sent him a blessing, a mental kiss on the cheek, then walked back to the breakfast bar. Whitelaw came and joined her. "You okay to take the sofa tonight? My friend will probably want his bed back."

"The sofa's fine."

He picked up his car keys. "I'm going to work now. I'd like you to leave with me and come back at six o'clock, which is when I get home. I don't usually lock up, but you'll find a key in the gutter above the back door."

A question stood in her eyes at the mixed message: I don't trust you alone in the house but you know where the key is.

But Whitelaw didn't seem to realize what he'd said. "You don't get many people who want to rob a policeman's house out here," was all he added.

It was already hot outside, the sky blue, the yard a dusty green. A couple of cars rumbled past—Cooinda's rush hour—but otherwise all was quiet and still. Whitelaw's was the second to last house on the Biloella road northeast of Cooinda and peaceful, aside from the view next door. India could see bed springs, a butane stove, two prams, a sink and a stack of engine parts including a twisted exhaust pipe.

"Can I get a cab back from town?" she asked. To her astonishment, he gave her a set of keys to a beat-up Volkswagen Beetle parked at the side of the house.

"I'd rather you use it than have to deliver your body to the morgue," he said perfunctorily. "This way it saves me some trouble."

She said thank you faintly, and watched him climb into his Land Cruiser.

"See you at six," he said, and with a spurt of gravel, drove off.

The Beetle looked as if it had been used for log-chopping practice. The body was dented in a dozen places and both bumpers hung precariously. Even the license plates were battered, as if someone had put them on the ground and repeatedly stamped on them.

The seats were split with the stuffing poking out and the steering wheel was cracked, but the engine started first time with a burbling roar. "You little beauty," she said out loud, and glanced at the space where the rear-vision mirror should have been. Shrugging, she reversed into the road and headed for town, to top up the fuel tank—which read zero—and pick up the road to Benbullen and the Goodmans' house.

——————

It was half-past eleven when Mikey saw a dark green Bentley pull up at the gatehouse of the Karamyde Cosmetics Research Institute. The binoculars he'd brought were powerful and he could see the number plate clearly but not the driver; the windows were tinted.

Mikey brushed a fly from his face and studied the Institute again. It was a big semicircular building, dense and ugly, built of concrete and painted pink, which made it look like a cooked crab. It had two floors with close ranks of windows set deeply in the concrete. A high wire-meshed fence topped with razor wire circled the complex, and the only entrance appeared to be the electronic iron gates. They swung shut behind the Bentley and Mikey tracked the vehicle until it was lost from view behind the semicircular curve of the building.

He scanned the area around the Institute. Although the complex was quite large, it was still only a dot on the broad expanse of bush surrounding it. It sat at the end of a three-kilometer private gravel road, which was immaculately maintained all the year round. Well tucked away, Mikey thought, but not too far for the commuters of Cooinda at just twenty minutes door to door. As usual, he had parked along the Jangala road, outside the kangaroo sanctuary where his car wouldn't be conspicuous. He'd then walked two kilometers or so across the bush to the low ridge of hills overlooking the Institute.

He swung his binoculars to the sandy airstrip, empty of any aircraft, then to the loading bay. Two men were rolling a large white tub into the back of an unmarked white transit van. The tub was marked: CAUTION—TOXIC WASTE. He hadn't discovered where they dumped the stuff. They flew it out by plane, and since he couldn't fly . . .

He scrutinized the van and noticed it had a crumpled fender on the driver's side. They'd probably hit some wildlife, a kangaroo or perhaps a wombat.

Mikey switched his focus to study the gate. There were two security guards smoking in the gatehouse. He watched them for a while, and eventually shifted to check the road. All was quiet aside from the tapping calls of birds and the odd rustle of a lizard in dead leaves. The Institute appeared totally innocent.

He threw his binoculars on top of his pack. He didn't care how long it took, he was going to sit and watch the bastards until they made a mistake. Flipping open the front of his pack, he withdrew a battered photograph. Carefully, he smoothed it between his fingers. Four policemen in uniform stood in the sun, grinning at the camera. Whitelaw was on the right, Mikey the left. Between them were Tiger and Sergeant Brian Patterson, both now dead.

Everything stemmed from Alex Thread's murder six months ago. Thread was from the Australian Medical Association, and had been asking questions about the Karamyde Cosmetic Research Institute when he was shot.

Sergeant Patterson, six foot three of balding bean-pole from Wollongong, had been investigating the murder of Alex Thread, when he was found drowned in the public swimming pool.

Mikey took up Patterson's investigation and the day after he'd met the Institute's owner, Roland Knox, a five-year-old girl went missing after school.

Mikey had pulled out all the stops to find her, and fast. He'd quickly ascertained she wasn't staying with friends, that there hadn't been a mix-up within the family about collecting her from school, then he put every cop available on the street to continue the search.

Come midnight they had nothing, but Mikey wouldn't stop searching.

He'd been in his patrol car, scouring the streets in the faint hope of spotting the little girl, when he received an anonymous call on his mobile. It had been six A.M. He'd spun the car around and raced to the local rubbish dump, another squad car close behind. He leaped out of the car to see a bloke bent over a cut-off piece of sewage pipe in the center of the dump. Saw the bloke trying to force something into the pipe . . .

When Mikey had pulled the little girl free from the pipe he thought she was still alive. Her body was soft and pliant in his arms. He heard a groaning sound and realized it was himself. *She'd still been warm.*

Mikey hadn't hidden his feelings for the suspect, Norman Harris. He had told everyone he'd be glad to see him dead. Harris violently protested his innocence, saying someone had called him about where the find the little girl, but he couldn't give a name and nobody listened. He was the child's uncle and they were all sure he'd been abusing the little girl and then killed her for any number of reasons.

The morning after the arrest Norman Harris was found strangled in his cell.

Even now, Mikey found it hard to swallow the fact that his own team had believed he'd popped the perp. Christ, he may have *said* he wanted to, but actually *killing* him . . .

Mikey was suspended that same day, but not before he found out that Harris was an ex-employee of Karamyde Cosmetics and was in the process of suing Karamyde for wrongful dismissal. Harris, Mikey belatedly realized, hadn't been trying to hide the child, he'd been trying to pull her body free.

Karamyde Cosmetics had murdered a five-year-old girl in order to kill two birds with one stone—Mikey and Harris—but nobody had believed either of them, or wanted to believe them.

So Mikey went to Tiger, his friend. And two weeks after Tiger had reopened the investigation, he'd been killed. In the cold light of day Mikey knew now that India Kane hadn't killed Tiger out of jealousy. She, and her dead friend Lauren, were something to do with Karamyde Cosmetics, he was sure of it.

His vision blurred as he stared at the photograph.

A little girl, an innocent man, and two good friends had died because of Karamyde Cosmetics.

He would nail the bastards if it was the last thing he did.

———————

It took India forty-five minutes to get to Benbullen from the BP garage. A shiny bay horse with two white socks stood hitched to the front verandah. It swung its head around sharply as she approached, and reared a little, jerking against its head collar.

A wiry man in jeans and checked shirt came out.

"Nice horse," she said.

"You want the missus, she's over there."

"Over there" was the stables, where Mrs. Goodman was in a loose box, grooming a large dusty brown horse. Like her husband, she was thin and well muscled, and although her face was worn and deeply creased from the merciless Australian sun, her eyes were bright.

"Don't mind if I carry on," she said, brushing the curry comb in quick, circular movements behind the animal's left ear. Dust and horse hair floated in a shaft of sunlight. "Got Freddo coming around with the thought of buying this feller. If he's valeted properly Freddo might go an extra couple of hundred."

India gave a nod and watched the woman work her way briskly down the horse's neck.

"I wanted to ask about your son, Frank," said India. "And my friend Lauren Kennedy."

"Yes. I recognize your face from the papers." She flicked a hank of mane aside, looked at India. "Your friend talked about you. Can't say as I know what happened, I'm no judge, but I believe she'd want me to talk to you. She was here almost a week."

India wasn't sure what to say next, she was flooded with so much relief at the woman's kindness. "Thank you," she managed.

Mrs. Goodman was nodding as she spoke. "Jeremy says your alibi hangs on our Frank," she said. "All the stops are out trying to track him down." She looked proud.

"Without Frank's testimony," India told her, "I'm completely scuppered."

The woman chuckled. "He'll be back in the New Year, no worries."

"Will he be straight, do you think?" she asked.

Mrs. Goodman sent her a sharp look. "What do you mean?"

"Well, his friends in town say he was with them at nine o'clock. But he was with me then. Here. He didn't leave for town until nine-thirty."

The woman's eyes renarrowed. "You're calling them liars?"

India looked at her straight, and nodded.

Mrs. Goodman made a *tsk*ing sound, said, "Well, I don't know nothing about it, but whatever happened, Frank'll tell the truth. I'm sure as eggs are eggs he'll do that."

"I certainly hope so," India murmured. "Could you tell me what you remember about my friend Lauren? Any order. It doesn't matter."

The dust-covered woman seemed to think for a moment, then she made a face. "She arrived bloody late. We'd been in bed for half the night before she rocked up. Made us all a hot chocolate though.

Charlie took quite a shine to her but for her smoking. Smoked like a Trojan, your friend did, and barely ate a bloody thing." As she talked, Mrs. Goodman moved expertly around the horse, deftly shifting his great bulk with a soft touch of the hand, a gentle click of the tongue. India learned what Lauren didn't eat, what time she'd woken, when she went to bed and, finally, that Lauren had only planned on stopping over for two nights but had extended her stay. "She wanted to find Bertie Mullett, but he'd gone walkabout."

"Ah," said India, and Mrs. Goodman rolled her eyes to the ceiling.

"Bloody Abos. Love 'em, hate 'em too. Wish they had blood in their veins, not bloody wanderlust. Upping sticks like they do drives us mad, and we try not to depend on them, but what can you do? Not many white folks want to work way out here, and we can't afford to pay much."

"Why did Lauren want to meet this Bertie Mullett?"

With a flourish, Mrs. Goodman put down the curry comb. She picked up a wide-toothed metal comb and started untangling the horse's forelock. "She never said, but she threw a complete wobbly when she learned he'd gone, just the day before she visited the camp. She went off to find his family instead. That was the last we saw of her. We had to go to Malparinka."

Mrs. Goodman seemed to have supplied an answer for every question that India could have asked, but she tried one more. "Has anyone been up here asking questions about Lauren?"

"Oh, two blokes turned up the day before yesterday to collect her things. Covered the expenses on her room. She hadn't paid up, you see."

India felt as if a cockroach had scurried down her spine. "What were their names?"

Mrs. Goodman paused in her grooming. "Well, bugger me, I'm not sure they ever said," she commented, looking surprised.

India asked her what the men looked like: neat trousers, shirts and jackets, sunglasses, she was told.

"What make of car did they drive?"

"One of those Beemer things. Haven't seen one before. Don't get them out here, that sort of city car."

"A BMW?"

"That's right. Black it was, with tinted windows."

India was back on the hot dusty road, watching a black BMW dwindle into the distance.

"It looked bloody expensive," Mrs. Goodman added.

And very suspicious, thought India. She asked to see Lauren's room.

"I've cleaned it, changed the sheets and the rest. They said it was all right."

"Who did?"

"The two blokes."

"Not the police? Didn't they come out?"

"They *were* the police. Well, sort of. A special branch, they said. They showed me their badges, they looked official enough."

"Not from Cooinda, then?"

"Oh, no. I know everyone at Cooinda PD. Stan was here all last week. Jeremy popped in too. To collect your things." She gave the horse a brisk pat before leading the way to the rear of the house.

India stood at the window of Lauren's room and stared blindly outside. Twenty-three years earlier her little brother, Toby, had died. Now Lauren had died too. She suddenly felt exhausted, and had a longing to crawl into bed and sleep for a month.

Instead she searched the room. She checked the inner pillow cases, peered beneath the bed, the mattress, inside the Bible and the chest of drawers. As India searched, she remembered hiding pocket money Sylvia gave her, so that her father wouldn't take it and spend it on booze. She remembered giving anything precious—comics, books, birthday cards—to Lauren, to prevent them getting thrown out. India searched the room as memories crowded her mind, and her soul felt heavy and inert, knowing she had no one to share them with any longer.

The bottom of the wardrobe had an old bus ticket in it, and she unearthed a receipt that had slipped behind the skirting board, both of which she pocketed. Then she walked downstairs and asked if Mrs. Goodman knew anybody in the area called Tremain.

"You mean Ron?"

"Do you know any others aside from him?"

The woman thought a bit, said, "Sorry, no."

India thanked her, returned to the car.

The shiny bay horse pranced at the end of its rope as she drove away.

—————

Before India headed for Cooinda, she drove to Nindathana Billabong and walked the area where the murders had taken place. She didn't expect to find anything, not after Stan had been crawling all over it looking furiously for her gun, but she'd wanted to see the place for herself.

The billabong was a large and shallow circular depression the size of a tennis court, surrounded by spinifex and saltbush. Two square brick barbecues were set beneath a tall sparse-leafed ghost gum, along with three wooden tables and benches. There was a metal trash bin, empty aside from a jumble of broken brown and green glass in the bottom—the remnants of beer bottles smashed in alcoholic carelessness.

The baking plains around appeared lifeless, but during the hour India was there she saw a variety of desert birds and lizards, and two hopping mice. Tracks abounded in the sand: dingoes, kangaroos, the feathery brush strokes of snakes.

It was a good meeting place; well off the road and easy to find, and difficult for an interloper to intrude upon. You'd see their vehicle for miles. However, the atmosphere was deceptive and she found it hard to believe that pretty much where she stood, beside the police tape strung between some bushes, two people had been violently murdered.

In the heat of midday, India paused at the BP garage to buy a cheese and tomato sandwich and a bottle of mineral water. She toured the streets in the faint hope of finding a public phone in a quiet street where people wouldn't see her. After ten minutes of driving around she gave an exasperated groan, dithered briefly, then headed for the Royal Hotel.

When she entered the bar, she saw to her relief that Red-cap and his cronies weren't there. Aside from a weather-beaten old man at the far end, glued to the wide-screen TV bracketed to the wall, there were just two women drinking at the horseshoe bar. Three men were standing outside clutching schooners of beer and smoking.

The barmaid's upper lip was beaded with moisture. She regarded India with a combination of amusement and surprise. "Well, if it isn't India Kane herself."

India gave a curt nod. "Debs."

Debs extracted a cigarette from a soft pack of Marlboros and lit it. "I think you're maybe a little touched," she said. "Or have you forgotten what this town thinks of you?"

India shrugged. "I wondered if I could use your phone."

Debs jerked her chin towards a door signed RESTROOM and said, "Busy at the moment. Sheryl's ringing around for some part-time work." She appraised India. "Have a beer while you wait. She may be some time."

India raised her eyebrows.

"Not all of us follow the herd," said Debs, and signalled India over. She pulled a midi of Fosters, pushed it across the bar. "This here's India Kane," she said to the other two women. Neither responded. Debs waved her cigarette at the woman farthest from India. "That's Roxy." Another wave at the woman nearest. "And that's Kerry." They didn't take any notice. Simply continued staring glumly into their beers.

"Cheers." India raised her glass before taking a long draft. She could feel the ice-cold lager slide all the way to her stomach.

"You can stuff your bloody cheers," snapped one of the women.

India put down her beer and made to move away, but Debs motioned her to stay. "It's nothing to do with you," she said candidly. "We're usually more friendly, but we've had a bit of a blow."

"No worries," said India. For some reason this innocuous response had a galvanizing effect on Roxy.

"You stupid *cow,*" she said loudly to Debs. "If you had *half* a bloody brain . . ."

"Jesus, Rox, why can't you put a sock in it?" said Debs wearily. She'd obviously heard it all before.

"But it's your *fault,*" Roxy insisted. "If it wasn't for you we'd all still have our jobs."

"You call working for that mob a *job?*" responded Debs. "C'mon, we weren't even on their payroll. Just odd bits here and there. It's not the end of the bloody world."

"It may not be for you but what about *us?* You didn't give us a choice, did you? Christ, Debs, you *knew* the rules. They're practically embossed in our bloody contracts and you went and bloody broke them."

Debs heaved her bulky arms off the counter, raised her head high. The atmosphere was suddenly strung tight as piano wire.

"All you had to do was say sorry," Roxy went on, "it won't happen again. That's *all.* But you couldn't bring yourself to do it, could you? Admit you were wrong. I could *kill* you."

Debs's lips thinned. She said, "You weren't the one being grilled by Gordon bloody Willis. He's unrelenting. You heard him. Had I met with a reporter before? Why me? Why that particular week? Why did I break my contract? Was the reporter going to pay me?

What questions did they ask? Christ, he never stopped. How did they contact me? Had they approached anyone else?"

"I wish you'd kept your mouth shut instead of gloating," Kerry snapped from India's left. "Fame and fortune my bum! Dave's going to throttle me. He won't get his cordless drill for Christmas. Won't get nothing, with me penniless."

"You let him *fire* us!" Roxy's voice was high-pitched and trembling with rage. "Just because we were at school together you thought we'd back you up, carry the blame equally . . ." She ran on and on.

India had stopped listening. Her brain had latched on to the word "reporter" and she stood motionless, staring outside. A small tan dog trotted past the hotel door. One of the men lashed out a foot and caught it in its muzzle. The dog yelped, ran off. One of the men came in to use the Gents'. By the time he went back outside, Roxy had finally ground to a halt.

"What work did you do?" India asked Debs after a while.

"Tested products for Karamyde Cosmetics." She gave a bitter smile. "I liked being on the cutting edge of scientific innovation."

"I liked the extra cash," said Kerry, sounding more resigned than angry. "Easiest money I've ever made was lying facedown for ten minutes. I got two hundred for that. Bet even the hottest lawyers in Melbourne don't charge as much."

India asked the question with raised eyebrows.

"Punch biopsy," Kerry supplied. "We call it the cookie-cutter test. They rotate a circular razor blade through your skin and pull a plug of flesh out."

"You're human guinea pigs?" India said, startled. The mention of a reporter had tipped her off immediately and the more she heard about it, the more Karamyde Cosmetics sounded just Lauren's type of story. If she could only work out how a man called Bertie Mullett and Geraldine Child, a Sydney doctor, came into it, she could be on her way to solving the mystery of her friend's death.

"Got it in one. What with the animal libs and all, they daren't test anything on animals."

"And this reporter?" India looked at Debs. "What did they want?"

She tapped her cigarette against a blue Foster's ashtray. "A story for some women's magazine. How housewives can make some extra money. You know, outline what we get paid, what we're prepared to do."

"Did you meet them?"

"No. Just talked on the phone. She sounded nice—"

"Jesus, Debs! How could you do it!" Roxy was off again and India tuned out. The three men came in to buy another round of beer. One of them stared at India, whispered something to his mates. They stood there looking indecisive, and whispered some more. She pushed her beer aside and hastily walked outside.

The sun pounded down, and a dust devil swirled down the road, picking up crisp packets and cigarette ends from the gutter and discarding them on the pavement. She turned right and headed for the post office. She passed a fair-haired man with a carton of Victoria Bitter on his shoulder and a woman in a tight singlet that outlined her jelly-tot-shaped nipples. The post office was shut for lunch, so India ducked into the newsagent next door, which was a cavern of wooden shelves lined with glass bottles filled with a variety of fluorescent-colored boiled sweets.

"Do you have a phone I could use?" she asked the wizened man behind the counter. He was stacking packets of Silk Cut on the shelf and didn't turn around.

"Post office next door does," he replied.

There was a postcard stand next to the till. India rotated it slowly. Pictures of desert, trees and desert, dilapidated if picturesque farmhouse ruins in desert, sky and desert.

"Do you get many tourists here?" she asked.

"Well, people who venture this far are usually heading for Sturt

National Park," the man replied. "But most often they go via Ti-booburra and if they do come this way, they don't stop for long."

"How come the postcards?"

He half turned his head towards her, then back to the Silk Cut. "There's lots of people who've moved here to work for a factory just out of town. They like sending a picture of what it's like back home."

"Karamyde Cosmetics?"

"Oh, you've heard of it. Mighty big company all up, I'm told."

"Seems a weird place to set up a cosmetics industry."

"We're glad of it," the man said, looking at her fully for the first time. He frowned, but continued. "Tripled my business the second it opened and now we're the capital of the Corner Country. Even have our own courthouse and such." He looked proud.

Some capital, India thought as she let the fly screen bang behind her, where you can't even find a phone. She walked along the uneven concrete pavement towards the police station. It was incredibly hot but her skin was dry; any moisture evaporated the instant it slid from her pores, giving her the illusion that she wasn't sweating. India wondered that everything was so parched and barren but still people managed to make a living. When the rain came here, it was in quick bursts, flooding the countryside overnight and then leaving it drought-ridden until the next deluge, sometimes not for years. It was a land of harshness, a land of extremes; drought or flood, life or death.

She made the first of her daily visits to the Cooinda Police Station, checking in with Donna, then headed back for the VW. She started the car and drove to Whitelaw's. After all, he was at work and would never know she'd snuck back to make a few calls from the comfort of his own home.

When she pulled up the car, Whitelaw's neighbor came over to take a look. He was thick-bodied and wore a string vest, and his upper arms were covered with tattooed dragons. She felt his eyes slide over her as she climbed out, probing at her clothes, under her shirt and over her breasts.

"You staying here?" he said.

India grabbed her bag and headed for the side of the house without looking at him.

"Mind your own business," she said.

"That's not very neighborly."

India spoke to him over her shoulder. "I don't mean to be rude, but I'm not the neighborly type."

He grinned and stretched, scratching a hairy armpit with a hand the size of a hubcap. There was a greedy look on his face.

ELEVEN

WHITELAW'S BACK DOOR WAS OPEN, NO KEY NEEDED. SHE walked into the kitchen, picked up the phone. Dialled directory enquiries. Asked for a list of Tremains in the area.

"We've an R. Tremain in Cooinda," the woman said.

"Is that it?"

"Looks like it."

"Could you try Milparinka or Tibooburra for me?" She heard the woman tapping on a keyboard.

"No Tremains in either place, sorry."

"Broken Hill?"

More taps. "I've a Treeman."

"Could you try Bourke for me?"

The woman sighed. "I really can't do this all day, love."

India hung up. How was she going to find this elusive grandfather of hers? Lauren had said she'd found him by accident. Would India do the same? Right this instant, she didn't honestly care. She felt utterly drained of all energy, mental and physical. She recalled experiencing the same dazed feeling when her mother died, but it was an echo by comparison. Today she could barely stand. She decided to call Jerome later about the man who'd paid her bail and stumbled into the bedroom. She'd move to the sofa later but not now when the house was empty, the bed so soft and comfortable.

India stripped off her boots and jeans and crawled into bed. She tried to weep, but she was beyond tears. She lay curled beneath a strange man's sheets in a strange room, thinking only of Lauren and replaying her strident and infectious laughter.

"Lauren," she said out loud.

Nothing.

"Lauren?" she said again.

India buried her face in the pillow. After two or three minutes, no more, she felt herself drifting asleep.

When she awoke it was late afternoon. Beyond the window the bush was still lit by the hard unforgiving midsummer light. She lay without moving, her mind and limbs filled with a langorous lethargy. The house was very quiet. All she could hear was a raven's long-drawn cawing outside. She closed her eyes, succumbing to the seduction of sleep, drifting, warm and boneless, her whole body relaxed. Suddenly a board creaked.

Her eyes snapped open.

She sensed someone in the room.

She sat up.

Her heart kicked in her chest. A broad figure was standing in the doorway. It was Mikey the Knife. His hair was untied and flowed thickly around his neck, making him look as if he had a mane.

She pulled the sheet tight to her chest.

"What the hell are you doing here?" Mikey demanded. He was taller and broader and more hostile than she remembered.

"I would have thought it was obvious," she said, struggling to keep the fear out of her voice. His big hands flexed menacingly, so she quickly added, "Whitelaw said I could stay."

If she had grown horns and a tail, he couldn't have looked more astonished.

"You're kidding me, right? I thought he said he was going to find you accommodation?"

"This is it," she said stiffly.

He strode forward towards the bed. "I want you out of this house in two minutes."

"Oh," said India, as it suddenly occurred to her. "*You're* Jeremy's tenant."

Mikey's eyes narrowed. "So it's Jeremy now, is it? You certainly suck up to the right people, don't you? Well, I'm sorry I'm not impressed, but as a resident of this house I stand by my right to get rid of undesirables. So I suggest you get your bitch ass out of here." Without another word he turned and left the bedroom, crashing the door shut behind him.

Trembling a little, India clambered out of Mikey's bed and hastily pulled on her jeans and boots. She packed her backpack and took it outside, onto the rear balcony. She could hear Mikey bellowing in the kitchen, and assumed he was giving Whitelaw an earful. For a moment all she could do was stare over the backyard and watch the dry grass blowing in the hot breeze. *I want to sleep,* she thought, *I feel so tired and drained, why couldn't he have come home later?*

But he was home now. So India left her backpack where it was and went for a walk, thinking to find a bed of soft sand beneath the shade of a tree and sleep some more. She climbed the fence at the end of the garden and headed for the sloping hills in the distance; there was a tree line at their base. She didn't care that she was trespassing. She couldn't imagine an irate farmer being upset at her footsteps crunching on nothing but burnt brown grasses and their soft seeds. Raising her face to the sun, she felt something inside her shift, and a little peace trickled through her veins. Ever since she could remember she'd loved heading off like this, preferably on her own. Lauren had found it amusing, but no man she'd met had understood it. They had, in fact, resented it.

Her legs started to stretch out into their ground-eating stride.

Soon she was in the low mound of hills, smelling dust and heat in the company of no one but lizards and brown-bellied snakes.

————

"He's not happy, your friend Mikey," India said to Whitelaw later, over a bottle of wine, a jug of lemonade and a plate of dips and crisps. The wine was for India, the lemonade for Whitelaw. A buff-colored file sat on one side of the table.

"It's all sorted. Don't worry about him."

They were sitting on the front verandah. Whitelaw's Land Cruiser glowed orange, as though lit by a bonfire. The jacaranda flamed red. The sun was a huge bloodred orb lowering into the horizon, and bats flicked past them, snicking midge and mosquitos on the wing.

"Help yourself." He gestured at the dips.

India contemplated the pink and brown goos and lit a cigarette. Whitelaw looked at her closely. "I think you're exhausted," he remarked.

"I am a little tired," she admitted. She exhaled some smoke sideways. "I don't suppose you've any news on who paid my bail? I haven't gotten around to ringing Jerome yet."

Whitelaw smothered a crisp with pink goo and ate it. "Jerome confirms it was paid by Arthur Knight. Knight is based in Geelong, ACT, apparently." He brushed his hands together and fished in his front pocket. He pulled out a piece of paper and passed it to her.

India scanned the address.

"I still don't know him!" She leaned forward, her cigarette dangerously close to her shirt. "The only people I know in Australia are Scotto and Lauren's family—who certainly wouldn't help me at the moment—and some so-called friends in Melbourne who haven't returned my calls."

Whitelaw pointed out her shirt was nearly on fire. She leaned back.

"All that matters is you're out."

"Come on, Whitelaw. Isn't there anything else you know about this guy?"

"Just that for a person to pay anyone's bail they have to be pretty upstanding. Provide supporting documentation as to where the cash has come from, no laundering dodgy money via the police."

"Okay, so Arthur's an upstanding citizen. Albeit a rich one."

"He's also a fed."

She took a drag on her cigarette. Her fingers were trembling. "I don't understand."

"Look, why don't you contact the guy and get him to fill you in? I'm sure there's a simple explanation."

"But I want—"

"We've more important things, okay?" Whitelaw glanced up and down the street, back at her and away.

"What is it?"

He took a few seconds before speaking, and when he did his voice was low and troubled. "Tiger's the second policeman to be murdered around here."

India barely registered that shock when he delivered the next. "Along with an official from the Australian Medical Association called Alex Thread."

"Jesus." She closed her eyes momentarily. "I don't believe this. *Four murders?* Who was the first?"

"Sergeant Brian Patterson."

"Are the murders connected in any way?"

"There's no evidence we can find, but Mikey's sure it's to do with the Karamyde Cosmetics Research—"

"*Karamyde?*"

Whitelaw raised his eyebrows.

India recounted the story of her beer at the Royal Hotel, her meeting Debs, Roxy and Kerry and hearing how they were fired because Debs had spoken to a reporter.

"Your friend was obviously following the same trail as we are," said Whitelaw. "Although how she came to know about it is anyone's guess."

"Perhaps one of the testers rang her. She's . . . *was* pretty well known."

They both looked up as a door slammed. Mikey appeared with a bottle of beer and stood cradling it in front of his chest, hips against the balustrade, watching them.

They both ignored him.

"According to the record book," Whitelaw said, "Tiger got a call from a reporter, which we take to be your friend, asking him to meet her; apparently she had something vital to share with the police regarding the two murders."

"Why didn't she meet him at the police station?"

Whitelaw took a gulp of lemonade. "Apparently she didn't trust everyone there."

"Good heavens," Mikey mocked. "You're not suggesting she didn't trust our homegrown incorruptible Abo?"

Whitelaw's fingers tapped on his knee but he didn't look at Mikey.

"Someone else obviously knew about this meeting," said India. "But who, and how?"

"The last entry in the book was made the day before Tiger died," said Whitelaw. "Tenth December."

"Could be a cop then," she said, and took in Whitelaw's sick expression. "So *that's* why you wouldn't talk to me in the police station."

He gave a brief nod.

"Jesus Christ." She ran a hand over her face. "Didn't it cross Tiger's mind that Lauren was right? There might be a bent copper watching his every move? Was he a total idiot?"

Mikey appeared at the corner of her vision. "He was a bloody good officer," he said tightly.

"So bloody good he got himself and my friend killed," she snapped.

Hurriedly Whitelaw said, "Anyone recognize this?" He showed them a scrap of paper with a telephone number on it. "Found hidden beneath the insole of your friend's shoe just this afternoon by yours truly."

It must be important, India thought, *if Lauren hadn't trusted her wrist with it: she couldn't have wanted anyone to see it.*

"Don't tell me," Mikey drawled, "that it's also unbagged and untagged?"

"Dead right," said Whitelaw with a grin.

Mikey refused to relent and continued to keep his expression stony.

"Whose number is it?" India asked.

"No idea as yet, I haven't even contacted directory inquiries." Whitelaw turned a querying look on India. "Perhaps you might like to give it a try." He gestured at Mikey, who reluctantly passed her his mobile.

India dialled.

"Hello?" A woman, broad Australian, answered on the sixth ring.

"Hi," India said, sounding brisk. "I'm from the AMPS, the Australian Mail Preference Service. Our concern is about the privacy of all Australians. Would you mind answering a couple of questions for me—"

"Sorry, but—"

"I'm doing a survey. It won't take a minute and it would help us enormously . . . Do you receive much junk mail?"

"God, yes. Swamped with the stuff."

"Are you happy with the situation as it stands, or would you prefer not to receive any junk mail?"

"I'd kill to find my mailbox empty of all that bloody rubbish," was the robust response.

"Well, AMPS is working for limits to be put on the scope and extent of junk mail for all Australians. What we do is insert a computer code on your behalf that then prevents any company accessing your address for the purpose of junk mail. Would you be interested in this facility?"

"You'd better believe it."

"If it could be guaranteed that from tomorrow you would never receive any junk mail again, would you be happy for me to arrange it for you? Or would you prefer to wait—"

"Sign me up, Scottie!" said the woman cheerfully.

India laughed, then dropped her voice. "I'm not supposed to do this, but perhaps just this once I could do you a favor since you've been so straight with me. All I need is your address, and I'll punch it in tonight."

"Jesus, that'd be bloody great. I'm at Waratah, Jangala Vale . . . hang on a tic. Does it matter that I'm not on my own phone? It's just that I'm helping Elizabeth out for a bit. Her husband died a few days back. Got bitten by a bloody snake in one of the sheds. They've got antivenom in the house but he never made it. Weak heart, they reckon."

"I'm sorry to hear that."

"Yeah, it's a right bugger." The woman gave a sigh.

"I'll flag your address for you anyway. Jangala Vale . . ."

The woman rattled off the postal code.

"Shall I do your friend Elizabeth's too?"

Short pause. "Why not? Save the poor cow from wading through all that shit every day. She's two properties up, Janga Yong-gar—"

"Could you spell that for me?"

"Everyone says that. Drives me insane." She spelled it out.

"Her surname?"

"Ross. Elizabeth Ross."

"And yours?"

"Gask. John and Joan."

India thanked her, pressed the clear button and passed the phone back to Mikey.

"Sly as a snake," he remarked.

"Thank you," she said, and smiled prettily at him, which made him glower.

"How about I go and see this Elizabeth Ross," she said to Whitelaw, "and do some snooping?"

"Okay. I'll leave these for you to read." He tapped the file.

Mikey looked appalled. "You're going to let her read your stuff?"

"If she's not up to speed, how can she help us?"

"Hell, Jed, we don't really know if she's clean—"

"She's clean as a whistle," snapped Whitelaw.

"You call a man lost in the Flinders Ranges an alibi?"

"Who'd have thought it?" Whitelaw's tone was biting. "Mike Johnson, acting like a wet-behind-the-ears rookie and choosing to believe what suits him rather than the evidence. You've lost your touch, Mikey, admit it. That famous cop's instinct of yours has failed you after all these years. Did it get pickled in bourbon?"

Mikey stared at him.

"Ah," said India into the taut silence. "He's an *ex*-cop?" She looked at Mikey. "What happened? They boot you out for boozing? Taking bribes? Or was it simply a bit of gratuitous violence?"

He took a step towards her. Instinctively India shrank back in her chair.

"I wouldn't have thought a reporter could afford to prejudge," he ground out, "but you took one look at me in jail and stuck me in a convenient pigeonhole—"

"Which fits you perfectly, if I might say, and you're one to talk considering you branded me a killer the instant—"

"Be quiet!" said Whitelaw. "I'll not tolerate any bickering here. We're a team, okay?"

Mikey looked shocked. "A team?" he said.

"Unless we act like one we're going to get nailed, one by one, just like Patterson and Tiger."

India played with the stem of her wineglass. "Okay. No bickering."

There was a long silence as Whitelaw looked at Mikey.

Eventually, he muttered. "Okay."

"Good," said Whitelaw, then to Mikey, "Anything happening out at the Institute?"

He flicked a glance at India and away. "I guess since we're a team"—he accented the word sarcastically—"you should know they received a visitor earlier today. One Bentley owner, Gordon Willis, who used to work at Porton Down in the UK. Porton Down is a government defense establishment. Apparently Willis is a genius, and the British government poached him from us. Five years ago he got a better offer from Karamyde Cosmetics and came back."

"What was he working on in the UK?" asked India.

"Classified stuff. Anything concerned with the defense of the realm, I guess. Guns, germs, missiles . . . You name it, he's probably invented a deterrent for it."

"I find it hard to believe a man like that would be happy working on lipstick and mascara," said India.

"The cosmetic company's a cover," Mikey said. "It has to be."

There was another silence during which he stared long and hard at India.

"How much rent will you be paying?"

"That's our business," said Whitelaw.

Mikey looked expectantly at India. "I hope you can cook."

"Sorry. I've never even learned how to boil an egg. I can burn toast to perfection though."

Mikey opened his mouth and then, seeing Whitelaw's expression, headed inside. The screen door slammed behind him. Whitelaw followed. India finished her glass of wine and poured another. She stared gloomily at the darkened horizon. The prospect of enduring an undefined period of close contact with a bad-tempered ex-cop suddenly made her extremely depressed.

TWELVE

NDIA COULDN'T FIND THE ENERGY TO GO AND SEE ELIZA-
beth Ross for two days, and on the third morning it was
by sheer force of will that she propelled herself to the VW and
turned the ignition key.

Whitelaw had told her to take the road to Jangala from
Cooinda, that Jangala Vale was just out of town, but after ten minutes she wasn't sure if she was on the right road. It was supposed to
be a minor road, but it ran as wide as a runway. She had passed a
disused railway junction, a sheep station, a windmill and two ele-
vated water-storage tanks. After another five minutes, she came to a
smattering of houses interspersed with barren bush, and as she drove
saw a flock of pink galahs beneath a ghost gum and a crow perched
on a telegraph pole.

She hit a pothole and the VW shuddered. She slowed the car
and glanced in her wing mirror. She pulled a face. Mikey was behind her. Whenever they were both at Whitelaw's, he stayed in the
sitting room. Since her first night, when she'd slept in Mikey's bed,
India had taken to living in the kitchen, sleeping on the divan in the
corner, and there were whole hours when she'd forget he was there.
Then he'd stalk in and make some biting remark to which she
would retaliate and they would bicker until he'd made his tea or
toast or poured his bourbon and left. When he wasn't annoying her,

he was racing off in his white Toyota pickup, or hunched over his computer, tapping busily. Yesterday, curious, she'd sneaked a look to see what he was working on. Over his shoulder, she could see the screen. It was filled with a color display of a dogfight between what appeared to be two F18s.

"You're playing *games?*" she'd said, inordinately outraged.

"Hang on . . ." He was tapping furiously, the aircraft spinning wildly, swooping and buzzing at incredible speed over a vista reminiscent of Dartmoor. The screen suddenly exploded into a fireball. "Yo!" he exclaimed. "Imagine what that would have looked like on TV!"

India glanced at Whitelaw's twenty-inch screen. "Well, believe me when I say I'm truly sorry you don't have that facility."

"I will though," he said cheerfully. "Everything's on order. Delivery any day. The sound's going to be amazing. Boy, is this living room going to rock and roll with those little beauties."

"I'm so thrilled for you."

He spun around. "What's your problem, India?"

"I thought we were supposed to be catching killers, not playing computer games."

"You read books to relax. I do this."

"All day?"

He didn't answer. Simply turned around and restarted the game. They hadn't spoken since.

She passed a rusty green mailbox with the name Waratah painted in white and flicked her indicator and slowed, letting Mikey cruise past. She waved her fingers jauntily at him and braked harder, preparing to swing left into the driveway of Janga Yonggar, which had a large green and gold sign that announced: ROSS KANGAROO SANCTUARY. At the moment she downshifted to second gear, she took in the BMW parked in the full sun opposite. Gleamingly clean. No dents, no rust, no dirt. *Black with tinted windows. Bloody expensive.*

India felt the skin at the nape of her neck tighten. She stared at the numberplate and committed the number to memory. OED 128. She noticed a white van parked in front of the BMW, and its logo: A.J. LUFFTON BUILDING CONTRACTORS. The van had a dent in its front fender.

She pulled off the street and parked the VW. She climbed out, dropped her cigarette and stepped on it. The atmosphere was still and hot, even the insects were silent. All she could hear was the tick of the VW's engine as it cooled.

The house was partly concealed by a stand of low trees but as she approached she could see it was neat and well cared for. She reached a gate set in a high wire-mesh fence surrounding a dusty corral and the rear of the house. She saw several tin sheds, a water trough and a kangaroo. She pressed her head against the fence. The kangaroo obligingly hopped over and pushed its nose through the mesh. Unable to resist, India stroked the soft gray muzzle. It felt like velvet.

"That's Billy," a woman's voice said behind her. "His mum was killed in a motor accident so we got him as a very young pinky. Now he's grown he'll be off soon."

India turned. The instant their eyes met, the woman's friendly grin dissolved. "Sweet, Jesus," she said. The color drained from her face. "You . . . You're . . ."

"Yes, I'm India Kane. My friend Lauren Kennedy was murdered and I want to find out what happened, and why. I'm hoping Mrs. Elizabeth Ross can help me."

"Sweet Jesus," she said again.

"Are you Mrs. Ross?"

The woman gave a jerky nod.

India turned back to the kangaroo, who had thrust one furry ear forward, the other back, and was surveying her steadily through liquid brown eyes. "Lauren Kennedy had your phone number," she said, keeping her tone calm. "I wanted to know why."

The woman made a small choking sound and unlatched the gate. Immediately five kangaroos appeared from behind the various sheds and looked across expectantly, standing on their hind legs. The woman stepped inside the corral and headed for the rear of the house. India followed.

"The biggest problem in areas like this," the woman said, her voice unsteady, "where it's heavily bushed, is there's no lights, no nothing, and the animals graze to the edges of the road, from one side to the other, and get hit by cars or trucks or whatever." She pointed at the smallest kangaroo, who was hopping slowly after them. "That's Annie. She lost a fight with a station wagon. And that's Randy, had him since he was a pinky too . . ."

While the woman talked, India studied her. She was slightly built, in her late thirties India guessed, and wore ill-fitting jeans and a T-shirt smeared with what could have been porridge. Her skin was tightly drawn and her eyes looked tired, despite the incongruously bright blue eyeliner on her lower lids.

"Do they all have names?"

India received a strained smile.

"Sure they do. We can have them for up to two years and you can't keep just saying, 'Oi, you.'"

India asked how many 'roos they rescued a year, and they were still discussing it when they entered the house. Three kangaroos followed them. In the living room another kangaroo with a bandaged hind leg and tail lay on a pink quilt and nibbled at a pile of grass left within its reach. Another larger 'roo, at least four feet, was sprawled on the overstuffed couch, tail draping from the armrest and resting on the floor. Neither acknowledged their presence aside from a brief flick of the ears.

India stepped over a pile of pellets, her face puckering as she inhaled. The smell of kangaroos reminded her of a roomful of unhouse-trained cats.

"They're family oriented," Elizabeth Ross said, a little defensively. "You can't just put them in a shed and feed them every four hours. Without the support of their mates they'd never return to the wild, so we have to make them part of our family so they can survive in the bush."

India found herself transfixed by a tiny face peering from an artificial pouch made of an old tartan blanket hanging on the far wall. Its long, delicate silhouette was dwarfed by paper-thin floppy ears and a pair of huge glistening eyes.

Elizabeth Ross smiled. "She arrived yesterday. I'll have to feed her day and night every two hours for the next few months. I've called her Jilly."

"You're a dedicated woman, Mrs. Ross," murmured India.

Pause.

"Call me Elizabeth."

Their eyes met. "Thank you."

Elizabeth gave that strained smile again.

"Would you mind talking about my friend?" India asked gently.

Elizabeth stared at the floor. "I'm not sure."

"You know she was shot," India told her bluntly, to get a reaction. "Twice. At point-blank range in the face."

Elizabeth's body seemed to shrivel. When she spoke, it was in a whisper. "Yes. I know that."

"Please," said India, gentle again. "I need your help. When did you last see her?"

The other woman closed her eyes.

"Please."

"It was . . ." Elizabeth swallowed audibly, took a breath. "Night. There was no moon. Lots of stars though. Brilliant stars. Peter wished he'd brought his telescope. He loved star gazing." She swallowed again.

In her mind India suddenly saw the white four-wheel-drive cross the road ahead of her and Tiger. She put her hands in her pockets to hide their trembling. There was a white 4 x 4 Suzuki out-side.

"Peter didn't want me there. But he'd dislocated his shoulder that morning out bush with the Dunsfords, rounding up sheep. He'd stiffened up and could barely walk, let alone drive. Couldn't even reach the gear lever. He didn't want me there," she said again.

"When was this?"

Elizabeth walked unsteadily out of the room. "For some reason or other, I don't know why, they simply love garlic."

India could feel an obstruction in her throat, like a golf ball. She followed Elizabeth into the kitchen. Found her setting the mi-crowave.

"Maybe there's something in the natural bush that's similar, I don't know," she said, not meeting India's eye, "but as soon as we do garlic bread up, they go nuts."

The two women stood there, staring at the microwave. When it pinged, they both flinched.

Elizabeth opened the microwave door and immediately the air was filled with the rich smell of buttery garlic. She had barely put the first bread stick on the board to slice when three kangaroos bounced in, ears pricked forward, eyes bright and beady. "Now just you wait, you scoundrels." Elizabeth tossed slices into a large wicker basket. "You'll get your share in a minute."

She glanced up at India, smiling. India found herself staring at the woman's eyeliner. It was no longer blue, *it was green.*

Elizabeth ran a finger beneath her right eye, then checked it. "I was testing it for Peter the week he died. I've worn it ever since. For sentimental reasons, I suppose. Not wanting to let go. He was a cos-metic chemist." Elizabeth placed the basket within reach of a dozen ravenous kangaroos. "He loved these guys as much as I did and they loved him back. I'm not the only one who misses him."

"I'm sorry."

Elizabeth gave her a sad smile. "The risks of living in the Australian bush. If the skin cancer doesn't get you, the spiders and snakes will."

India made a noise of sympathy. "The eyeliner's an amazing concept. Is it available to the public yet?"

"Not for ages; it still needs a lot of work. It's supposed to change color depending on temperature. They use special heat-sensitive inks, you see, and it's supposed to go blue when I'm outside, green when I'm inside, but it doesn't always work."

They talked nail polish and permanent lipsticks for a while, but Elizabeth sounded more and more awkward.

"Who did your husband work for?"

Elizabeth gave her a quick, searching look. "You don't know, do you?"

"Know what?"

"Nothing. Nothing at all." She glanced at the kangaroos clustered around the bread basket. Two of them were half-boxing each other with their front paws. "Where on earth is Billy? He loves garlic bread, he really does—"

"I'm sorry," said India, not sounding it at all, "but who did your husband work for?"

"Karamyde Cosmetics."

India kept her face bland.

"They've a research institute just down the road. Well, in Australian terms that is. Ten Ks away. Not a single give way sign or traffic light between them and us. A hop, skip and a jump in kangaroo terms."

Elizabeth suddenly gave her head a sharp shake and looked outside. She was close to tears.

"I'm sorry," she said. "Sorry that your friend died. The way she died."

India immediately went to her, gripped her shoulder. "Tell me. *Please,* tell me what happened when you met Lauren that night. *I have to know.*"

Elizabeth jerked away, picked up the empty bread basket. "Where's Billy?" she said again, anxiously. "First time he's missed his garlic bread." She strode outside. "What's wrong with him? Must be something . . . Never known him to miss a treat."

After the dimness inside, the shimmering brightness made India squint. She followed Elizabeth, who was striding urgently between the tin sheds, calling, "Billy! Come on, Billy, there's a good boy." She checked that the gate was latched. They skirted the perimeter of the fence, its posts irregularly spaced, cracked and twisted from years of torturing heat.

India found a deeply scuffed area on one patch of dirt near the fence, spotted with dots of blood. She followed the bloody track to the back of the feed shed where she saw something dangling from a scrawny tree.

It looked like someone hanging.

Slowly, she approached.

A kangaroo, noose around its neck, looked at her helplessly through liquid brown eyes. Blood, still red and moist, seeped from its nostrils.

Behind her she heard Elizabeth's horrified exclamation.

"Billy!"

THIRTEEN

IT WAS INDIA WHO FETCHED A LADDER AND RELEASED THE dead animal. She didn't bother trying to unknot the rope but simply hacked through it with a saw she'd found in the garage. She had to twist the animal's head around until it was jammed beneath her left armpit to expose enough rope to saw successfully. Tiny black flies swarmed through the kangaroo's coat, and each time the corpse moved they buzzed briefly into the air before settling once more. India had to keep blowing sharply upwards through her mouth to dislodge those on her lips and nostrils, but they returned seconds later.

Finally the rope gave way and the kangaroo crumpled with a soft thump to the ground. The two women dragged it outside the corral, Elizabeth hauling on the tail and India a hind leg. Their progress was slow because the body was surprisingly heavy. India felt sticky with sweat and disgusted at the flies swarming all over her and the blood on her shirt. Elizabeth was in tears. "How could they?" she kept saying. "Oh my God, how could they do such a thing?"

They laid the dead kangaroo to rest beside one of the outbuildings. Elizabeth knelt down and took Billy's head in her lap, stroking his ears and nose, shaking her head back and forth. "Poor little mite." She started to sob in earnest.

India stared down at her, too appalled to say anything.

After a while she fetched the saw and rope, and laid them in front of the garage. She returned to Elizabeth and suggested they go inside.

Elizabeth stood but her legs were so unsteady that India had to help her. She searched the kitchen for brandy and eventually found a bottle in the medicine cupboard. She slopped the liquid into two glasses.

"Drink this."

They both drank.

"I can't believe it," said Elizabeth. Her voice had regained some strength. "How could they!"

"Who's 'they'?"

Elizabeth wouldn't meet her gaze. "I can't say."

"Killing Billy was a warning."

Elizabeth got up and poured herself some more brandy. "I wouldn't know."

India took a deep breath. "I think you know who killed my friend. I think it was your husband that Tiger and Lauren went to meet at Nindathana. He had some information on Karamyde Cosmetics he wanted to share."

"I'd like you to leave."

"No. Not until you tell me what happened."

Elizabeth was moving all the time, unable to keep still. She stood beside the tiled fireplace and toyed with a photograph frame on the mantelpiece.

"I stayed in the Suzuki," she finally said. "I didn't see anything. Not really. Just your friend. And Tiger. Waiting at the Nindathana turnoff. Peter told me to stay where I was. They all went together, in Tiger's car. It wasn't much later when I thought I heard a shot. I didn't think much of it, I assumed it was Ken's mob. They're always after the 'roos. We've had three wounded ones come in here, all messed up because of those blokes."

India remained still, silent.

"Peter was only gone fifteen minutes or so, but he was running when he returned. Really scared. Shaking. He shouted at me. Wanted me to get out of there as fast as I could. He didn't tell me what had happened. It was only when I read the papers that I realized he'd been in terrible danger."

"Did he tell you why he was seeing Tiger and Lauren?"

"No. At the time I was upset he wouldn't talk about it, but now I see he wanted to protect me."

"Do you believe he was bitten by a snake?"

Elizabeth's skin turned ashen. She shook her head.

"Me neither."

The two women stared at each other in silence.

Elizabeth turned and crossed the room to a chest of drawers, pulled out the bottom drawer. She took out a folder and opened it. India saw newspaper clippings and letters and Christmas cards. Elizabeth pulled out a photograph. She stared at it for a long time, then held it out to India.

"Take it." She didn't say anything else, so India took the photograph. It was black and white, of four men standing around an enormous dead shark. Three of them looked to be in their late teens. One of the boys was a full head shorter than the others and his legs were spread aggressively wide, as if to compensate. An older man, about fifty or so, was holding a rod out towards the camera. They had the look of a father and sons.

"Who are they?"

Elizabeth shook her head several times. "Peter took . . . Peter took a similar photograph with him. He also had a disc. A computer disc. It was in his pocket. He kept patting it as we drove. I don't know what's happened to it."

"Did he make a copy?"

"I've no idea."

"Did he return with it?"

Elizabeth shook her head again. "I don't know."

"Are you sure? Perhaps he left it with someone? Hid it some-where?"

Silently, Elizabeth started to cry again. What was left of her eye-liner seeped green-blue with her tears down her cheeks. "I want you to go," she choked. "Please."

India let her walk her to the front door. She stepped outside. The BMW was still there. "Do you know who owns the Beemer?"

Elizabeth glanced at it. "No. Never seen it before."

"Will you be okay?" India was reluctant to leave Elizabeth in such a state. "I'm happy to stay—"

"I'd rather you went."

India said goodbye. She looked down at the photograph and then back at Elizabeth. "Thank you," she said. But in Elizabeth's eyes she saw an expression that chilled her. It was fear. Pure fear.

———

India walked down the driveway. A woman was coming towards her, with what looked like a small milk churn in her right hand. She gave a friendly wave, India waved back.

The woman looked at India as she passed. Her eyes widened. She gave a muffled gasp.

India tried a reassuring smile. The woman backed away.

India glanced down at her bloodstained shirt and jeans, then back at the woman. "It's okay. It's from one of the kangaroos. He got hurt . . ." But the woman was blundering back down the driveway and India wasn't certain if she'd heard. Pushing back her hair, she wiped her face free from sweat and climbed into the VW.

She drove to Whitelaw's, where she showered and changed. She put her clothes in the washing machine with half a bottle of wash-ing liquid and programmed it for cold super wash to loosen the bloodstains. After a coffee and a cigarette, she called inquiries and then rang Arthur Knight, Geelong. A monotone announced the number was no longer in operation.

India replaced the phone and stood there, thinking. The number had to have been operational when Arthur stumped up her bail. From what Whitelaw said, the police would have checked pretty closely to ensure the money was clean. She resolved to write a letter to Arthur that evening. She grabbed her keys and got into the VW, drove into town and checked in at the police station. Then she climbed back into the VW and took the right branch off Main Street onto the country road signed to Jangala. She passed Elizabeth Ross's kangaroo sanctuary and, about three kilometers on, shot past a discreet sign carved out of wood: KARAMYDE COSMETIC RESEARCH INSTITUTE. She had to reverse in order to pick up the gravel road east.

Three minutes later the air was thick with a sickly smell, slightly perfumed, like baby powder. Gravel and dust plumed like a cockscomb behind the VW. Five minutes on she came to the Institute. The first thought that crossed her mind was that the windows were shaped like coffins. The blushing pink paintwork did nothing to detract from the air of morbidity. It reminded her of a piece she had done on the ancient Chinese art of feng shui, and how buildings designed a certain way could enhance or diminish a home or business. She might not be in China, she thought, but this building gave her the creeps.

She eased the VW towards the electronic gate and glanced at the low ridge behind the building, sparsely dotted with trees. She wondered whether Mikey was hiding beneath one today, but her thoughts were interrupted when the security guard came out. India gave him a warm smile. "Hi," she said, and turned off the ignition.

"Why, hello," said the guard, raising his sunglasses to get a better look at her.

"I'm from a national English newspaper," said India, and showed him one of her old business cards from *The Courier.* "I was just doing a recon to see if what I was told about the place was true."

He took the card and studied it carefully. Usually people barely glanced at it. Good security.

Then he checked her against the photograph on the card. India prayed he wouldn't recognize her.

"And what did they tell you?"

"That it looks like a big lump of candy, being so pink."

"Well," he said, glancing over his shoulder, "I guess you could be right."

"Smells like it too. Is it always like this?"

"I guess. I don't notice anymore."

"Look, can you tell me if you have a PR manager here? I'm doing a series of articles on the cosmetics industry and would love to talk to someone here about it."

"I'll ask." He took her card with him into his booth and returned a few minutes later. "Yeah, she's interested all right. Her name's Glynnis Coggins, and she's asked you to ring her." He passed her a card with the company's details. "That okay?"

"Great. I'll call her this afternoon and make an appointment."

————————

India watched Mikey sink down beside her on the verandah steps and stretch out his legs. He held a bottle of bourbon in one hand and a half-full chunky glass in the other. She checked his expression for any signs of overt hostility. Seeing no more than usual, she lit a cigarette and let her hands hang between her knees.

He put the bottle between his feet. "Why show yourself to the dragon?"

She didn't answer.

"Don't you think it was a rather stupid thing to do?"

"I wanted to gauge the enemy." India told him about Elizabeth Ross and the dead kangaroo, Peter Ross's computer disc and the BMW. "I didn't dare go look at it any closer in case someone was inside."

"I'll ask Jed to get a run on the plate," he said.

His eyes met hers. For the first time she saw they were a bright, iridescent green. They were such an unusual color she wondered why she hadn't noticed them before. She put it down to their being bloodshot most of the time.

She looked away. "I'm seeing their PR woman in a couple of days; maybe a direct approach might reveal something. In the meantime I'm going to see if I can't track down Bertie Mullett."

"You'll be lucky. Bertie's like a will-o'-the-wisp. You'll only be able to track him down if he wishes you to."

India reached into her rear pocket, pulled out Elizabeth's photograph and passed it to him.

Mikey frowned. "Know these guys?"

"No. Do you?"

"No," he said, far too quickly.

She was tempted to let it pass, perhaps turn it to her advantage later, but the photograph was obviously important. She ground out her cigarette under her boot.

"Please don't lie."

Mikey looked startled, but said nothing.

"I know you can barely stand the sight of me," she continued, "but we've got to work together on this if we're going to catch Lauren and Tiger's killer."

"Hmm," he said. If she hadn't known better, she would have said he was abashed.

"Shall I leave the photo with you to follow up? Since you know them—"

"Only one. The older guy." He pointed at the ascetic-looking man holding the rod. "He wrote *East Asian Approaches.*"

At her blank look, he added, "John Buchanan-Atkins. He's a well-known historian and has his own school in Sydney: Erskin. His book is a classic work on Central Asia, set in the Caucasus and Turkestan during Stalinist rule."

"You read history books?" she asked, thinking of the box of cheap cowboy paperbacks in his room.

"Mostly I listen to them. In the car. They're useful on a stake-out, and I use them when I'm driving long distances." He gave a thin smile in response to her surprised expression. "I like Peter Hopkirk best. He wrote about Central Asia too, *The Great Game*. In fact, I like most history books. Some are just easier to digest than others."

India adjusted her picture of Mike Johnson as semiliterate. She'd never imagined him reading anything but pulp fiction, with maybe an occasional tabloid newspaper or police journal.

Mikey took a long slug of bourbon and turned a bland face to her. "You seem surprised that I—"

"Not at all! I think history's very interesting too." Hastily she lit another cigarette to cover her confusion. "Enough of hobbies. What have you been up to?"

He passed the photograph back to her then peered into his glass as though it held the answer.

"I've discovered that the owner of Karamyde Cosmetics, one Roland Knox, is away in China for some big meeting with the government there. Nobody will say what it's about. I've also ascertained the Australian Medical Association is as tight as a duck's"—he paused—"gizzard. Everyone who worked with Alex Thread has either left or been transferred overseas since he died, including his boss, Dr. Nathaniel Jameson, who was head of ethics."

India looked down at her shoes, noticed they needed resoling. "Sounds like a cover-up."

"An eiderdown special," he agreed, and took another slug of bourbon.

"Can't we get in touch with Jameson? Ask him what was going on?"

"I reckon they don't want him found. All I managed to glean was that he might be in the United Kingdom. Could be Northern Ireland, Scotland or Wales for all we know."

India considered her contacts in the UK. "I'll call a friend, a medical journalist, see if he can help."

"I hope you'll pay Jed back for the phone call." His usual biting tone was back. "Or will it be at a peppercorn rate, like you pay for his divan?"

She gave him a cool look. "Is that all you've discovered? That Jameson's in the UK? Nothing else? I suppose you spend most of your time gazing into the bottom of a bourbon glass."

His expression hardened. "Actually, I have discovered something fairly vital," he said.

"Oh, yes?"

"That your alibi is shit."

She flung up her hands in exasperation. "What were you, a parking attendant in your previous life? We all know Frank's gone bush, but surely even you can do better than that."

"And that you have a preference for fried egg sandwiches for breakfast—when you have breakfast that is—and cheese and onion toasted sandwiches for lunch, and that you live on a diet of fast food whenever someone doesn't feed you."

India's eyes widened fractionally.

"That kind of diet will kill you eventually. Along with your smoking. Keep up the good work."

She didn't say anything.

"I've also discovered that you and your friend were amazingly stubborn about meeting in the other's home city. That you made a handful of friends in Melbourne, but none of them wants to help you out in your current predicament. That some people loathe you, which I can relate to, whereas others seem to kiss the ground you walk on, like Bill Maynard, your ex-*Courier* colleague."

India struggled to keep her expression neutral. "You have been busy," she said.

"I try to pull my weight."

She refused to be intimidated. "So . . . um . . . what are you going to do next?"

He rose to his feet, drained his glass. "I'm taking the rest of the day off."

"But what about—"

Mikey's face was like stone. "Tiger's sister is coming over. She wants to see him."

FOURTEEN

INDIA DROVE WEST OUT OF COOINDA, THROUGH INCREAS-
ingly tatty streets lined with fibro houses. So she'd forgotten about Tiger, had she? She'd lost her best friend too, for God's
sake! What did Mikey expect? Unbridled sympathy on the dot of
every hour? At least he had the opportunity to remain in touch with
his friend's relatives, whereas she couldn't. Lauren's family would
probably lynch her the second they laid eyes on her.

Telling herself that she didn't care what Mikey thought of her,
she almost missed the turning on the right towards the Aboriginal
settlement and, hopefully, Bertie Mullett. Hastily she jammed on
the brakes and slid, with an ugly screech of rubber, across the road
and onto a dirt track.

Within minutes the car was filled with dust, fine as flour, red as
brick. It coated the dashboard, seats and windscreen. It lined her
nostrils and throat, her lungs, the inside of her mouth, and coated
her hair and skin. The temperature seemed to increase by ten degrees. Wedging the steering wheel with her knees, India grabbed the
bottle of water from the passenger seat and rinsed her mouth. Mikey
had put the water in the car. She'd barely thought about what supplies to take in case of, God forbid, another breakdown, when he
turned up with four bottles of water and a ten-liter jerry can, which
he strapped beneath the hood.

"This shit-heap's air-cooled, so the extra water's for you."

She'd asked him why he didn't cheerfully wave her away to a dry and dusty demise. He'd chuckled humorlessly. "You have your uses. Not that they're apparent quite yet, but I'm sure they'll come in handy one day."

About ten minutes into the hot, red interior, she saw the first signs of habitation. A thick carpet of empty beer cans disfigured both verges. Plastic wrappers and cartons intermingled with blinding, flashing tin made an ugly highway to the Aboriginal encampment. She passed a battered-looking bicycle and a car in the middle of the road. Later she learned it had been abandoned by a drunken driver because he had run out of petrol.

India drove slowly through the dilapidated shantytown and parked the VW beneath a sparse-leaved gum tree in the vague hope it might offer some shelter. Taking a pack of cigarettes from the glove box, she made her way up what appeared to be the main street. The houses were an odd assortment of rickety shacks, built from corrugated iron, old doors and piles of breeze-blocks. Each dwelling had an assortment of plastic tubs and drums outside, presumably to catch water.

Dogs lay everywhere. Brindle, gray, brown, tan and mottled blue. India counted twenty dogs in twenty yards. She saw three young pigs in the shade of a rusting Ford truck and a large pink-brown sow panting on her side, eyes tight shut. A small group of Aboriginal men, apparently impervious to the intense midday heat, squatted beneath a tree playing cards. They regarded her with barely concealed suspicion as she approached. The only sound was the heavy vibration of cicadas.

"Hi," she said, taking out her pack of cigarettes and offering it around. "I'm India Kane. I'm a reporter." Each man took a cigarette, nodded and returned to their cards.

"I'm trying to find Bertie Mullett."

One of the men, of indeterminate age, with grizzled hair and a red bandanna around his head, spat on the ground. None of them met her eye. She already knew she wasn't going to get anywhere, but she didn't want to give up yet. "Do you know where he might be? I can make it worth his while." India withdrew a sheaf of folded notes from her back pocket and flicked through some twenty-dollar bills. "Or yours, if you can help."

Silence.

"You might have seen my friend around. She's much smaller than me, with short blond hair."

The men studied their cards as she watched their faces.

"Did you see my friend Lauren Kennedy?"

Shrugs of indifference.

India raised her hand to shield her eyes from the vicious glare of the sun and searched for someone else to ask, but the shantytown appeared deserted aside from a few crows hopping about. She noticed a curious-looking shelter set just beyond the town's boundary, built of a rusting metal car hood, tires and bits of cardboard. As India studied it, wondering who lived there, she thought she saw a shadow shiver inside. It was a small shadow appropriate to such a small shack, so minute that she doubted whether you could sleep with your legs stretched out.

"I'll give the first man who can tell me where Bertie Mullett is twenty bucks."

The shadow trickled to the shelter's entrance, then it became a figure. Polly was flying towards them as though running at the Olympics, chest thrust out, bare feet pounding. Panting hard, pink tongue showing, she flung herself onto India and wrapped her skinny arms around her neck.

"You came to see me!" The girl's hair was matted, her body smudged with dirt and grit. She smelled of burnt wood and apples and felt light and fragile as a sparrow.

India's breath caught in her throat, which she put down to her windpipe being crushed by Polly's grip.

"Hello, sprat," she said. She sensed the men's curiosity as she put her arm around the little girl. Polly's ribs jutted out like sticks. "When did you last eat?"

"Had some cornflakes this morning," Polly said shyly. "Some last night too."

"What about a proper meal?"

"At Albert's. With you."

"But that's four days ago!"

Polly grinned at her. "Shan't we go to Albert's today, then?"

"Shall we," India corrected.

"Shall we go to Albert's?"

"I think we'd better, before you start shrinking. We don't want you to become so tiny you get gobbled up by a cockroach."

Giggling, Polly turned in India's embrace and stood with her arm possessively around her neck. "Who's winning?" she demanded.

"Never you mind," said the man with the red bandanna.

"That means you are," Polly said, and giggled again when he picked up a stone and mock-threw it at her.

"You're Polly's friend?" the man asked India. "The one who stopped Stan having a go at her, right?"

"Right."

Nods of approval all around. A couple of spits and a crack from someone's knee as he shifted slightly.

"Why do you want to know about Bertie?" said one of the others. "He ain't done nothing of interest to no reporter."

"I'm not sure yet. My friend was looking for him. She was murdered last Sunday. I thought Bertie might help me find out why she died."

A long pause while the flies buzzed.

An old man with a face like a worn polished boot blew smoke from his mouth and said, "I'm not real sure where Bertie is, that's fair dinkum."

"Do you know where he was headed?"

They shook their heads.

"Do you know when he'll be back?"

More shakes of heads.

"Why did he take off, do you know?"

"He's an Abo," said Red Bandanna, and they all chuckled.

At her gesture of frustration, the man said, "We've got something in us that makes us want to keep moving. You white fellers can build yourselves a house and live in it and be happy not moving for years, but we can't."

"Did Bertie work at all? Did he have a job?"

"Used to do odd jobs for the Goodmans over at Benbullen. Burning off, fencing and stuff. Backbreaking stuff for a bloody pittance, he's always said. Hasn't done anything for them for a few years."

India nodded. "What about his family? Is there anyone here I can talk to?"

The faces around her suddenly looked ill-at-ease.

"Is he married? Does he have any children?"

They looked at the ground, towards the sky, anywhere but at her.

"He's married to Rose, but she'd dead and long gone now," ventured the leathery old man who'd spoken before. "Three kids he had, all with their own kids now, but we ain't seen 'em for months."

"Where did they go?"

"There was talk of Sydney," declared Bandanna Man. "Bloody idjits, going to the city. Old Bertie wasn't having none of it, but his kids insisted. Something to do with work up there they couldn't get here. Sounded like a load of old crock to me."

Polly dropped her arm from India's shoulder. "You mean that paper they had?" she said. "Getting money for sleeping?"

Bandanna Man nodded, and Polly scampered off, heading for her shelter. A fly touched India's nostril and she brushed it away, wishing she'd brought a bottle of water from the car; she was sweating liters just sitting here. She offered her cigarettes around a second time, then shifted her position so she was sitting cross-legged.

"Do you think they might all be in Sydney now, working?"

"Not Bertie," the old man said. "The others, maybe, but not him."

Polly returned in a cloud of fine dust, a grin on her face. "Here," she said, and thrust a tattered, filthy copy of *TV Week* at India. "See?" She pointed at a full-page, full-color advertisement. "That's where they went."

How to get paid for sleeping and taking drugs.

The advertisement showed a young girl, hooked up to various monitors, lying on a luxurious bed of white embroidered cotton, and two women in white coats, looking down on her sleeping form with warm professional smiles.

Our research unit is a laboratory funded by the government and the Crane Institute to investigate diverse matters such as the kinds of road that contribute to driver fatigue, Chronic Fatigue Syndrome and the three o'clock sag, when employees across the country lose their concentration. Help us develop cures for these common conditions. Fee: $10 per hour.

The next picture was of a good-looking young Aboriginal man sitting on a chair, half smiling. His chest and upper arms were covered with small round pads connected to multicolored electric wires. He was having his pulse checked by a bespectacled man in a white coat.

We also test drugs, and we need people to help us help the children of tomorrow in this vital research. Applicants must be between 18 and 50 years of age, reasonably healthy, and not be on any medication. Fees vary. $150–200 per day depending on duration of stay, frequency of testing, samples provided, etc. A one-month study fully loaded with tests can command in excess of $2,500; increased payment if urine or feces samples are required.

The address and phone number had been clumsily torn out.

"Are you telling me Bertie's entire family upped sticks to go to Sydney because of this advertisement?"

"Idjits," said Bandanna Man, nodding.

"Can I keep this?" asked India. At their nods she rolled it up and tapped it against her thigh. "When did they leave?"

"Six months back."

"And you haven't heard from them since?"

"Nah."

India brushed flies from her face. "Did they ever do this type of work for the Karamyde Cosmetic Research Institute?"

"Nah. Wouldn't have 'em. Not interested in blacks."

The steady sawlike screech of cicadas rose a notch. She hadn't believed the insects could produce any more noise, but they had just proved her wrong.

"Could I see where they lived before I go?"

"Whatcha want to do that for?"

She made a vague gesture with her hand. "To get the feel of it, perhaps find another clue."

"Skippy's lot's moved in there. You won't find nothing."

India had a look anyway. The shack was larger than most and built mainly out of lengths of wood and sheets of galvanized iron. A group of children were playing noisily inside, and when she called out they smiled at her, white teeth flashing. An enormous woman, barefoot and wearing a filthy floral dress, emerged from another room and demanded to know what she wanted. India explained, but the woman couldn't help.

"They took the Greyhound out of town, and we ain't laid eyes on 'em since." She looked around the room with satisfaction.

"*All* of them?"

"Yeah. The kids were real excited, whistling like pigs they were."

"How many children did the Mulletts have with them?"

"All up . . ." the woman stopped to think ". . . seven kids, five grown-ups. Off to make their bloody fortune. Bet they haven't or they'd be back to crow about it."

"Do you have any idea where they might have gone when they got to Sydney?"

"God knows. But you could try Jinny Pollard. Last heard, Jinny was sponging off some mates in Redfern. She's Louis's sweetheart. Louis is Bertie's eldest grandson."

For no apparent reason, the cicadas stopped their screeching. India was struck by the density of the silence.

"Is it usually this quiet?" she asked.

"Oh, no. Everyone's gone into town to get drunk. They're putting up the millennium lights on the clock tower. Any bloody excuse."

India thanked the woman and returned to her car, where Polly sat in the passenger seat, beaming. India clambered inside, started the engine. "What would you like at Albert's?" she said.

Polly's brown eyes gleamed. "Pie floater."

"Remind me."

"It's a meat pie floating in pea soup."

India shuddered. It sounded so revolting her stomach was already informing her it was full despite the fact she hadn't eaten anything all day.

"And it's really good with lots of tomato sauce."

―――――――――

Mikey left Tiger's sister with Donna and returned to Whitelaw's. He wandered to the back of the house thinking about putting a wash on, and opened the washing-machine door. He was frowning at India's laundry when his mobile rang.

"Yeah?"

"It's Sam."

Mikey's whole body stilled. The mystery caller who'd rung his mobile the day he learned Tiger had died. Sam. Not his real name, but he was the only fish who'd taken one of Mikey's baits and was still wriggling at the end of the line.

"So what's happening, Sam?"

"I can't sleep. I can't eat. I don't know whether they're following me . . ."

"Who might be following you?"

"I can't say."

"What *can* you say, Sam? Come on, talk to me. You said you knew something about Patterson's murder. Some files you found. Classified stuff."

He could see a silky bra the color of raspberries and some matching panties. Would she throw a fit if he hung her laundry on the line? Probably.

"It's still there. They don't know about it. I'm thinking of dumping them—"

"How come?"

"It's too dangerous. They'd kill me if they knew I'd seen it."

"Okay. So how about we meet and talk this over? Share the burden. I can be in Sydney in twelve hours."

"No."

"Why are you calling me, Sam? I thought you wanted to help, but I'm not getting any information from you."

"I'll ring again."

"When? I'm not always able to answer the phone."

"Don't push me."

Sam hung up.

Mikey rammed the phone into his back pocket. Jesus, the guy

wasn't half pussyfooting around. But he'd call again. Mikey hoped it was sooner rather than later, and before another body turned up.

"Hey, I can do that." It was India, with a laundry basket under one arm. "Thanks for the thought though."

He followed her outside, and watched her peg her clothes on the Hills Hoist. He told her about Sam's second call, and she pulled out the magazine advertisement from her jeans pocket and gave it to him. He scanned it. "What do you reckon?"

"I think Karamyde Cosmetics are into some sort of Aboriginal exploitation."

"This says nothing about Karamyde."

"Well, either it has nothing to do with them, or they're being incredibly clever. From what I've gathered, interviewees have to go to Sydney, which keeps any attention well away from Karamyde Cosmetics in northwest New South Wales."

"Hmm." His attention had been diverted by the raspberry panties, which weren't panties at all but a G-string. He'd never known a woman who wore G-strings daily. Most of them said they were uncomfortable and only brought them out for special occasions. Which was a shame because he'd always found them amazingly sexy.

"I rang my medical journalist friend," India said.

"And?"

"Nathaniel Jameson's dead. He was mugged a week after he arrived in London."

"Christ." Mikey ran a hand down his face. "It's turning into a regular massacre." A crow cawed and he could hear the steady creak and rustle from the trees.

"How was Tiger's sister?" she asked.

"Distraught."

"I'm sorry."

She had finished hanging her laundry and was standing still beside the hoist. She looked miserable.

"I'm sorry about your friend," he finally said.

She gave him a sad smile. "Me too."

He noticed she had a tiny mole at the corner of her right eyebrow, and another on her cheek, just where her jaw angled to her neck. They'd have to be watched, he thought, to ensure they didn't turn into melanomas in the sun.

"Mikey?"

"India."

"Why do they call you Mikey the Knife?"

"Hasn't anyone told you?"

"Not yet, no."

"Why do you think?"

"Because you knifed someone?"

"Correct."

"Who did you knife?"

He gave a sigh. "My left foot."

She looked down at his foot. "I haven't seen you limping."

"It was a long time ago. I was fifteen. I was going to show my knife-throwing skills to my mates. I could nail a hair on a board ten feet away. Anyway, I was holding the knife by its blade, to get the right spin, and I was so nervous I was sweating and the bloody thing slid out of my hands and went straight through my shoe and into my foot."

She gave a muffled snort and turned away. He watched the way she walked into the house, hip bones fluid, shoulder blades prominent through her shirt, and felt a wave of confusion wash over him. He didn't want to be attracted to her. She was too complicated for his tastes. She was also smart and hard and very bright, and he liked her taste in underwear. Scowling, he headed into the kitchen, got a beer and took it to the verandah. Sitting on the top step he sipped his beer, trying to wash away his confusion, but still it lingered. He was glad when a police Land Cruiser came into view at the top of the street and cruised into the front yard.

A pair of dusty-booted feet appeared beneath the driver's open door. Not Whitelaw, but Stan.

When the engine died, he called out, "G'day," and waved his bottle at the senior sergeant. "Can I get you a beer?"

Stan slammed the door shut and rearranged his holster before stumping to the bottom step. "Sorry, Mikey. I'm here on police business."

Another police four-wheel-drive appeared and cruised in to park by Stan's. Constable Crawshaw and a sinewy dark-haired man he hadn't seen before, dressed neatly in black jeans and a dark shirt, climbed out. Crawshaw looked at Stan, who shook his head. A confirming nod from Crenshaw, who took up position behind the cars, feet apart, hands free, his whole stance wary.

Slowly, Mikey got to his feet and crossed his arms. "Where's Whitelaw?"

"Bringing in a body."

Stan walked up three steps, trying to peer past Mikey's bulk, but Mikey met him halfway, impeding the policeman's vision inside the house. "Is India Kane in, Mikey?"

"Why would you think she's here?"

Stan cut him a cold look. "Everyone knows she's moved in. Gossip can't sit still without getting a scum on it in seconds, you know that."

Mikey shrugged. "She went out ages back."

The policeman glanced around and Mikey saw him ticking off the VW parked out front, the washing dripping from the Hills Hoist, the sound of water running inside.

"Ages?"

"Stan, just tell me why you're here, will you?"

The close set eyes narrowed. "I'd like to talk to her. That's all. Just a friendly chat."

"About a dead body? You reckon that's going to be friendly?"

"Not just any dead body," said Stan. "Elizabeth Ross's. Your housemate"—he loaded the word with sarcasm—"was seen leaving the Rosses' house with blood all over her at ten past twelve. That's exactly when the pathologist has estimated time of death."

Oh my God, thought Mikey. With a feeling of dread he watched Stan unholster his Glock.

"Your pretty little housemate's under arrest."

FIFTEEN

"WHERE'S YOUR WARRANT?" SAID MIKEY.

"You know we don't need one. Not when we know she's guilty."

Water was still running inside. He could hear it, and so could the senior sergeant. Stan turned and beckoned the dark-haired man to his side. "This here's Ben Thomas, from the federal police."

Mikey didn't offer to shake hands, nor did the fed.

"If you don't mind stepping aside, Mikey," Stan said, "we'd like to check the house. We've right of entry."

"Fine by me," he said, and stepped back to let them inside.

Stan immediately raised his pistol and headed for the kitchen, glanced at the taps, then skirted the living room and headed for the bathroom. For a man of his bulk he moved with surprising silence and agility. He held the Glock in readiness and seemed aware of everything around him. Mikey liked the way he worked. Cautious and in control.

The bathroom door was shut, and Stan stood there a moment as if contemplating his next move. He tried the doorknob. Locked. He turned and beckoned to Mikey. "Knock," he demanded in a low voice, "and get her to open it."

Mikey knocked on the door.

No response.

Again, he knocked, calling, "India! India, it's me, Mikey."

He found himself wondering how she came to be named. Had her parents travelled a lot? The continent of India was mysterious and exotic. She had been named well, he decided.

"India, open the door," he called.

Still no response.

"We'll have to break in," announced Stan.

"After you."

Stan raised his foot and smashed it just below the knob. The door shuddered, but didn't give.

He kicked again but the lock held. "This *never* happens in the bloody movies."

Mikey pulled him aside. Stepped back and charged at the door, right shoulder down.

With a snap, the lock popped. Mikey fell inside with Stan almost on top of him.

"Where the fuck is she!" Stan erupted back into the hall.

"Haven't a clue," Mikey said, and tried not to smile.

The fed brushed past him, shut off the shower and opened a window. He poked his head outside and withdrew. Mikey then peered through the window. Nothing, except for the faintest footprint on the warm wood, rapidly drying.

While Stan bolted around the house like a demented bullock, yelling his frustration, Mikey went into the kitchen and pulled out the stack of steaks. He contemplated them briefly. How many should he prepare?

Feeling optimistic, he pulled three free and set the rest back in the fridge. He crushed a handful of peppercorns with the blade of a knife and pressed them into the steaks. Next he mashed four cloves of garlic. He put two dried bay leaves on the board along with a sprig of thyme and poured some olive oil into a frying pan and set it on the stove. He brought out a tub of soured cream from the fridge, and some salad.

Stan entered the kitchen. His face was brick red and he was sweating profusely.

"Stan," said Mikey, "please don't have a heart attack or I'll get accused of murdering you, and since I really don't like prison food—"

"If you hadn't farted us about for so fucking long . . ."

"I'm sorry, Stan. What was I supposed to do, not ask any questions at all? I'm a citizen in your precinct and have every right—"

"Shut the fuck up!" Stan radioed for backup, torches, dogs and four-wheel-drive vehicles.

Mikey checked his ingredients. Something was missing. What was it? He couldn't remember. He crossed the kitchen for the pile of recipe books and paused.

India's backpack had gone.

He walked out of the kitchen and into the living room. The backpack was on the sofa and all of India's belongings lay in neat piles on either side of it. The fed had his back to him and Mikey watched as he picked up what looked to be a used shirt the color of terra-cotta and held it to his face.

"What the hell are you doing?"

The fed folded the shirt, put it to one side.

"Thomas, isn't it?"

The fed glanced at Mikey, and gave a little smile.

"You think she's left her forwarding address in there?"

The fed picked up a teddy bear the size of a pack of cigarettes with a tartan bow tie. He surveyed it for a few seconds before placing it on top of a frothy pile of lace and cotton. India's underwear.

Mikey strode across. "You can put that lot back where it came from. *Now.*"

Seemingly unperturbed, the fed meticulously repacked India's backpack. He folded each item of clothing around a book or shoe to avoid creasing and replaced the teddy bear on top with a little pat.

Mikey didn't look at the fed as he grabbed the backpack and lugged it back into the kitchen. He propped it against the divan where it belonged and reached for the cookery book.

———————

The manhunt gathered half an hour later. Mikey leaned against the screen door and watched lights fill the front drive as cars arrived. The sun had set and the night sky was clear. He saw a Nissan Patrol park with a leisurely spurt of gravel and Whitelaw hopped out, crossed to Stan and asked a question, then walked over to the fed. They shook hands, came inside. Mikey followed.

"We need all the firepower we can get," said Whitelaw to the fed. "Not for the woman, but for that trigger-happy lot outside. They'll start shooting one another out of sheer excitement if we're not careful."

Whitelaw unlocked his gun cabinet and withdrew two shot-guns. The fed expressed an interest in one of Whitelaw's pistols and handed the detective his own .45 to handle. Mikey left them discussing the merits of each and went to pour himself a bourbon, which he took outside.

He saw Donna, Cooinda PD's desk sergeant, climb out of what appeared to be a brand-new white Toyota four-wheel-drive Amazon. She gave him a little wave and came towards him.

"So, what's it been like, living with a killer?" she asked.

Mikey nodded at the Amazon. "What's it like winning the lottery? That must have cost you a fortune."

"It's Ed's." She turned her wedding ring around. "He bought it with his Christmas bonus. Mind you, it didn't cost as much as you think; he knows a bloke who knows a bloke, et cetera. Ed never pays full price for anything."

"Maybe I should become a rig driller," Mikey mused. "I like the idea of getting forty grand every Christmas."

"Yo, Mikey!" It was Reg Coffey, who'd donated half a side of beef after Mikey had chased a bunch of rustlers from his land two weeks ago. He held his broken shotgun over one arm and waved with the other. Mikey offered a half-hearted salute with his glass. Out of the corner of his eye he saw Donna wave her fingers at him before she returned to her husband's new car. "Not joining us then?" Reg asked.

"I'll leave you cowboys to it."

"Jimmy's with us," Reg said encouragingly. "He's brung his dogs."

Mikey laughed, earning himself a few frowns. Jimmy's dogs weren't trackers but hunting dogs; four Labradors, one spaniel and a raggedy Airedale. They had good noses but they spent most of their time running around enthusiastically chasing rabbits. Mikey recalled the Airedale, during a hunt for a psycho the year before, charging full speed after a dingo he'd flushed and not returning for twelve hours.

"I take it you're not planning on finding your quarry," Mikey said wryly, and took a slug of bourbon.

"What can we use to scent on?" asked Jimmy, a thickset man wearing a black cap emblazoned with the logo of the Melbourne Grand Prix. Six dogs were barking as they leaped excitedly around him.

Whitelaw handed over a plastic bag. "Shirt, socks."

"What, no skivvies?" Jimmy scowled into the bag.

"No skivvies," was all Whitelaw said, and Mikey thought: *He really likes her.*

"C'mon, how are my boys to find her without her undies?" Jimmy protested. "Everyone knows they give the best scent."

Another man, scrawny as a chicken, stepped forward. "Say, I heard mention of a five thousand reward. This right?"

"Five grand from the Crime Stoppers Division," Stan confirmed. "You collar her yourself, Ray, and you'll get your money. No one gets a fee for tracking, but there'll be hot coffee and sandwiches in the backup vehicles following."

"Is she dangerous?" Ray asked nervously.

Stan looked into the sky as if debating. Silence fell as they waited for his verdict. Even the dogs had quietened down. Finally Stan said, "Any cornered human being can be dangerous, so keep your eye out."

"She's not armed," added Whitelaw sharply, his voice carrying easily above the crowd. "Not even a kitchen knife. And she's only light, maybe one-twenty, one-thirty. So take it easy."

Growls and nods from the men and gradually they moved to the back of the house and headed for the low hills in the distance, Stan in front with Jimmy, the dogs straining at their leashes, the twenty-odd thrill-seekers spreading out in a fan. The fed, Mikey noticed, was in the center, positioned for maximum effect. He was looking at the sky as though thinking of nothing but what a nice night it was for a walk.

———

India stood, barefooted and sweating, on a square of smooth flat rock, trying to catch her breath. Her hands gripped her waist as she panted, and she stared in dismay at the sprinkle of lights bobbing before her. It hadn't taken them long to organize a posse; sixty minutes or so, quite impressive for such a hick town.

She had run all the way from Whitelaw's to the midst of these hills, following the trail she had walked the previous day in the hope she might be able to double back. Now that it was dark, she was stumbling and awkward and certain she had lost the right track. Her feet and ankles were sore and bleeding, and she wondered if she shouldn't give herself up.

Not yet, she thought. *When I'm tattered and torn and dead on my feet, maybe, but not before then.*

She rubbed her feet briefly, removed a thorn from her left heel, then turned away and set off at a brisk walk, not following a set course but heading away from the lights. After an hour, she reached the crest of some hills. Tussocks of spinifex hid jagged rocks, and she continually scraped her ankles as she clambered to the top. Cooinda squatted way behind her, shaped like a skittle. The moon was high in the sky and there were no clouds. The lights of the posse blinked and flashed below, but between them and her it was dark, just a smudge of black and gray that was the bush at night.

She kept moving. Dropping to the other side of the hills, she found a watercourse, powder dry, snaking through the thick scrub, and followed that at a smart jog for a while, but when the scrub ceased she was forced into the open. She made for a buttress of rock that was a deeper shadow on a dark landscape. On reaching it, she sank to her knees behind a tree. Her breath was rasping and she was conscious of her thirst. Where would she find water? Not out here. She'd have to sweep back now, making a big loop, and try to sneak back to Cooinda, hitch a ride away from the area.

Somewhere close by, a twig snapped.

Her heart jumped.

Crouching even lower, she fought to control her breathing, and a minute later heard a soft call.

"G'day."

She stayed quite still.

"You got no worries from me," the voice said, very close now.

India shut her eyes, as if she could will the man away by not seeing him.

"You in trouble, eh? It's a good place to get away from trouble. Middle of bloody nowhere."

Heart pounding, she opened her eyes to see a pair of dark eyes staring straight back, glistening in the half-light. The Aborigine was very old, and reed thin. He squatted with the ease of having squatted all his life, and surveyed her steadily. "No worries," he said, nodding, as if this would put her at her ease. He held a long, straight stick in his right hand and the hind legs of a freshly killed rabbit in the other.

A breeze picked up, flowing from the hills she'd just crossed. A voice, faint as a whisper, called out and India stood up, grunting with pain. Her feet were blazing and throbbing, but she started moving again, heading unsteadily away from the trees.

"You're going the wrong way," said the old man, and she stopped. She saw the outline of him against the sky; he had moved through the scrub and up the buttress without a sound. "C'mon. Follow me." And he beckoned with his stick.

She hesitated.

He jumped down, nimble as an eighteen-year-old. "Look, if you just go off like a frightened rabbit those blokes will get you. I know this place. I can find you somewhere to hide 'til they're gone."

He was close to her now, and she could smell a musty smell, like dried mushrooms, rising from his skin. "Your clothes'll have to come off. They're like wearing a bloody torch."

She shook her head.

"We could use them to divert the scent. Jimmy's dogs aren't great, but they can still sniff a sweaty shirt a mile off. Besides . . ." he gave a light chuckle ". . . travelling naked feels good. You should try it."

India paused, then muttered, "What the hell?" and hastily stripped.

"Everything," he insisted, and she looked into his eyes. They were enormous, but even in the darkness she could see they were smiling. "I'm an old feller. I couldn't even if I wanted."

He rolled up her clothes and put them under his arm. "I'll drop these off later . . ." He didn't finish, for a string of lights bobbed into view at the top of the ridge. The old man immediately turned and broke into a jog. India followed. They ran like that for several minutes, passing the buttress and heading for a region of steep undulations, covered by sand and mulga bushes. It felt peculiar running naked, her breasts and bottom bounced more than she'd thought they would, but the sensation of soft night air on her bare skin was a strange relief against the pain of her feet.

When they reached a rise, the old man stopped and turned to study the pursuers. Two vehicles had skirted the main ridge and were bounding towards them; they could hear the engines roaring. "Can't outrun 'em," he murmured, and loped away through the dark, effortlessly avoiding bushes and clusters of ankle-tearing rock with the ease of a dingo. Occasionally they stopped, to check on the pursuit, or to feel their way up a narrow gully. They were climbing, following a wild animal track up the side of a steep hill, when the old man paused and dived behind a dense clump of bush.

She kept moving, then stopped, peering around, but the old man had gone. A bubble of panic popped in her chest. "Where are you?" she hissed. A grunt sent her moving to the bushes where a hand was beckoning furiously. She forced some scrub aside to find he was squatting in a shallow cave, barely five foot high but quite deep. An aroma of woodsmoke and cooked meat drifted over her. India slipped inside on her haunches then sat up, brushing grit from her skin.

It was pitch dark, and the only thing she could see was the faint glimmer of the old man's eyes when they looked her way. She put her hand out to find the perimeter of the cave but it brushed something rough and prickly and she gave a muffled yelp.

"Put it on, why don't you? You'll be cold later."

India pulled the heavy woollen blanket towards her, draped it over her shoulders. Like the old man, it smelled of wild mushrooms; porcini and shiitake with a hint of dried sweat. He was busy with something, she couldn't tell what, but she could hear soft brushing and cracking noises, and smell ash and the scent of bloody meat.

"What are you doing?" she asked.

"I'll bugger Jimmy's dogs up real good. They'll find your clothes scattered over a mile square, but no trace of you, just me." He chuckled, a dry, hollow sound that she found comforting. "You stay here. I'll be back come dawn."

"What if they come to this cave?"

A thick silence settled all around.

"Hello?" she said, her voice small.

There was no reply. The old man had vanished without a sound.

———————

India peered out of the cave, parted the brush. The moon was high in the sky and only a few stars could be seen in the bright light. She could see a creek far below, sand shining like silver, and the glossy white trunks of ghost gum trees.

No sign of her pursuers, or the old man.

She lay there, watching and listening for another few minutes. The breeze had died, and she started to shiver. The old man had been right. It was still quite warm, but now that her sweat had cooled she felt cold. India wrapped the rough blanket closer and slithered back into the cave. Curled up like an animal on the sandy bed, she rested her head on her arm, and gazed into the darkness. She thought she could see the old man in the corner, his arms above his head, but it wasn't him, it was Lauren, rubbing her hands over her short-cropped hair, smiling.

So how do you like our good Australian bush?

I'd rather I wasn't here.

Sure you wouldn't, but you'll be glad later, I swear.

Lauren, I've never been so scared before.

Rubbish, 'course you have. This ain't no different, just a little more taxing on the physical side of things. Good thing you haven't run to fat or you'd be in big trouble.

I *am* in big trouble.

You'll come good as you always do, don't fuss so.

I'm cold, Lauren.

Tuck up tight in that blanket, hon. Think about that summer of eighty-two, the one we spent at Byron Bay. What a scorcher that was.

Lauren was laughing, her head flung back, joyous and carefree, and in her dream, India was sure she could feel the heat of that summer of eighty-two emanating from her smile.

———

When she awoke, dawn was close. The sky was flushed with lavender and the black shadows had melted into a deep blue. Nothing moved outside the cave, not even a bird. All was hushed as if in expectation of something magnificent.

India gazed from her aerie, wondering if this was how it felt to be an eagle. The air was clear, the sun a peeping yellow curve on the horizon, and if her feet hadn't been so sore, she would have revelled in the view. Her fingers traced the jagged lacerations around her ankles and down to the inner edges of her soles. She ached all over, from running half the night and having slept on sand and rocks. She was hungry and thirsty. She wriggled backwards into the cave and looked around her.

Light trickled through a shaft in the rock above the cold fire. Pale figures danced on the cave's walls, some throwing boomerangs after kangaroos, others catching fish. Several gourds were ranked neatly side-by-side in one corner, and India found fresh water in one, fresh rabbit meat—or was it kangaroo?—in the next, and dried leaves that smelled like thyme in the third. She took three small sips of water, wanting to drink the whole bowl, but wary of depriving the old man when he returned.

"G'day." The voice was soft.

The old man squatted by the entrance of the cave as if he'd never left, a long wooden stick by his broad dirty feet, a satchel at his side.

Did my thinking of him bring him here? she wondered, rather enchanted by the idea.

"No," the old man said. "I told you I'd be back at dawn."

She forgot all about her thirst, her throbbing feet, and stared at him. "Did I speak without realizing it, or did you just read my mind?"

"You white fellers," he said with a sigh, "too uptight for your own good." He gestured at the gourd, and told her to drink her fill.

"Are you sure?" she checked.

"I came by Easter Spring on my way here. Go for it."

India tipped the gourd back and drank until her thirst vanished. Wiping her mouth with the back of her hand, she sat on her haunches and watched him open the satchel. He carefully withdrew something she couldn't make out. "Betcha hungry, hey?"

India's stomach rumbled loudly in response. "No. Not particularly," she lied. She had no intention of eating raw rabbit meat or witchetty grubs—large white maggots extracted from trees—or any other traditional Aboriginal food he might offer.

He looked disappointed. "I went a long ways for this," he said.

I don't care how far you went, she thought. *I am not eating anything you offer me, and that's that.*

"Not even cross-ant?"

"Cross-ant?"

The old man shuffled forward, hand outstretched.

To her amazement, in his blackened, grimy palm, sat a large half-moon pastry: a croissant.

India thought of the dry landscape surrounding them, nothing but folded ribbons of brown and yellow stretching for miles and the odd white splash of a salt lake.

"Where on earth did you get this?" she asked disbelievingly.

"Eight 'til late," he said, his tone slightly waspish as if to say: Where else?

"Eight 'til late?" she repeated dumbly.

He rolled his eyes. "The BP shop. Open from eight 'til ten 'til they decided to stay open twenty-four hours."

"You've been to Cooinda?"

"Nowhere else around, but." Pushing the croissant towards her, he said with some anxiety, "Go on. I knew you wouldn't want bush tucker for brekka, no white fellers do."

Dutifully India ate, watched by the old man like a hawk would its young. "Delicious," she said, and licked her dirty fingers, one by one.

He leaned over and pinched her cheek, quite hard. "You're too skinny," he said disapprovingly. "But I've more grub if you want."

Expecting another croissant, she said, "Yes, please."

With a flourish, the old man whipped out two squares of yellow sponge topped with chocolate icing.

"Oh," India said, momentarily disconcerted. "Oh, Lamingtons, my favorite!" She took one and bit into it with a relish she could never have believed she'd muster.

The old man nodded approvingly as she ate. "Can't fight those buggers on an empty stomach," he said.

India felt like hugging him. Not only had he rescued her but he'd traipsed for miles to get her food he thought she might like, that she *did* like.

"I heard in town that your name is Indi," he said.

"India," she replied. "What's yours?"

"I am Milangga."

"Milangga, you're a good man," she said through a mouthful of sticky Lamington.

"And you're a good-lookin' woman," he replied, his huge black eyes on hers. "Why ain't there a bloke to help you out in this?"

At once she was aware of her nakedness. It was the words "good-looking" that had triggered it, and she was dropping the cake, scrabbling for the blanket, pulling it across her breasts and her groin.

Milangga shook his head in sorrow. "Why d'you hide? You liked your skin last night, why not now?"

India had wriggled into a defensive ball. Then, remembering her naked flight, she paused. He was right, she realized. While under pursuit, her lack of clothing had barely touched her consciousness. As she recalled the sensation of soft night air against her bare skin she smiled. She dropped the blanket, shrugged, and continued to eat. Milangga merely gave her a nod, casual, uncaring, and stirred the dead embers of the fire with the end of his long stick. "You should stay here a few days," he said. "After that, things'll settle down and you'll be able to move around."

India merely looked at him and thought: *I'm in your hands, old man. You're my guide out here and I'm in your hands.*

The look he returned was filled with pleasure. "You like witchetties?"

"No," she said, in her most definite tone.

"They're real good." He looked at the remaining Lamington with puzzlement. "Much nicer than that stuff. You might like 'em."

India didn't, as it happened, like witchetties. The flavor was okay, a bit like pureed chicken and sweetcorn, but it was the thought of eating a giant maggot—crunching through its outer coat into the soft juices below—that made her throat jam and her stomach rebel.

"Sorry," she said as Milangga carefully extracted yet another from the torn root of an acacia bush. "I'll stick to croissant, thanks."

He laughed at her, his teeth yellow and long as a horse's as they bit through the witchetty's skin. "Very good," he said, slurping noisily. "Protein, very good."

India ingested her protein through rabbit and kangaroo, both of which the old man seemed to catch without trouble. He told her he used a boomerang to hunt them, but on the second day she confronted him as a liar.

"I found a trap," she said indignantly.

"Anything in it?"

She looked away. "A rabbit."

Unabashed, he grinned at her. "I'm too bloody old to go chasing after them animals with nothing but a bloody boomerang. Didn'tcha think of that?"

That evening she asked him how old he was. His skin was like oiled leather in the firelight, his gray hair a woolly skullcap. To her he looked as ageless as the countryside around them. He shrugged. "My mother told me I was born on your fool's day, but I don't know what year. I could be sixty. Maybe seventy. What does it matter?"

She looked down at her own body, smooth and supple, and then at his creased skin. Out here all that mattered was your fitness, and your ability to hunt and gather food.

"It doesn't," she said.

Sixteen

MIKEY SAT ON THE HARD EARTH AND WAITED. THE MOON was behind a bank of clouds and the air was still. The Rosses' house had an abandoned look that gave him confidence, but still he waited, just in case. He wondered where India was, and whether she was awake too. He wondered at her courage. Her skill in avoiding Stan's manhunt. Anyone else would have stayed put rather than face the unknown dangers of the outback. But not India.

He checked his watch, and pressed through the greenery. A soft thudding told him he had startled a couple of kangaroos. They were obviously hanging around in the hope that the Rosses would return. He walked to the back door and broke the police tape, brought out a small leather pouch of tools he'd requisitioned from a burglar he'd caught five years ago and picked the lock easily. He slipped inside, took a penlight from his windbreaker and shone it around. The place was a mess. Cupboards and drawers were open, their contents strewn on the floor. He moved quickly from room to room. It had already been thoroughly searched, but what the hell. They might have missed something.

He started on the shelves, running his hand along the dusty wood. Then the cupboards, and the debris scattered in each room. It took him two hours to search the house, top to bottom, beneath carpets and rugs, behind skirting boards and window shutters, fridges and freezers. All the time his eyes were tuned for a slim square of plastic.

It was well after midnight when Mikey gave up. He left empty-handed, without a single computer disc.

———

Walking the same trail she had raced along the previous week, panicky and breathless, India found it hard to believe she hadn't been hiding for a month. An extraordinary calm flowed through her veins and, as she walked, she hummed a repetitive chant she'd picked up from the old man.

The sun bleached the sky hard white. She heard a repeated double whistle, *pee-yaa,* from a wedge-tailed eagle circling nearby. Its wing tips lazily stroked the rising thermals. She reached the top of the ridge that overlooked Cooinda and sat for a while to rest her bruised and heavily scabbed feet, enjoying the view. The town was a gray-brown smudge in the distance, barely distinguishable in daylight. At night it twinkled like a galaxy.

She pushed the sleeves of her shirt above her elbows. Milangga had presented her with the vast man's shirt the morning he'd decided she should leave. "White fellers don't respect a woman's bare skin," he'd said as he handed it to her.

"Where did you get it?"

"From someone that don't need it as much as you."

It was freshly laundered but unironed, and India had pictured an irate housewife going to her washing line to find it gone, and laughed. She chuckled to herself now as she slipped from the ridge and moved down the folded ribbons of the hills and across the dry landscape. The shirt felt constricting and heavy after walking naked for nearly a week, and India longed to throw it off; her chest and back were soaked with sweat.

The tail end of Biolella Road, as usual, was a ghost town late morning. Silently, she approached the rear of Whitelaw's house, watchful of his neighbor. She was hoping to grab her backpack, get properly dressed and hitch a lift out of town to Sydney to regroup with Scotto. Through the back screen door she could see that the kitchen was empty, and she paused, listening. Insects buzzed and clicked in the heat. All was still.

She slipped silently into the house. It was cool inside and smelled of toast and fried bacon. She froze when she heard water splash. *Someone was in the bathroom.* Softly, India crept into the kitchen, checking that her weight on the floorboards didn't make them creak. Fortunately the bathroom was on the way to the front door, and she could grab her backpack and leave without passing it.

She crossed the kitchen. Her backpack had been beside the divan, but it wasn't there now. Water splashed again, and she heard a man's grunt. Mikey, no doubt, trying to wash away another hangover. She searched the kitchen, checked beneath the sink, inside the broom cupboard . . . nothing. Laundry . . . second loo . . . amenity room . . . no. She padded into the living room, checked the cupboards next to the stereo. Piles of cassettes, LPs and CDs, but no backpack. Sod it! Quickly, she tiptoed into the front corridor. The bathroom door was slightly ajar. The water was no longer splashing; no sound to cover her movements.

Holding her breath, India quietly opened Mikey's bedroom door and peered inside. Sheets were tangled in the middle of the bed, a pile of laundry sat in one corner. No backpack. She was easing back into the corridor, skirting two tennis rackets and a tool kit, when the bathroom door flew open.

"India!"

She whirled around.

Whitelaw looked stunned. Freshly shaven and smelling of Armani, he wore red-and-blue tartan boxer shorts and red socks. There was a smudge of foam just below his right ear.

India exhaled. "Hey, cool shorts," she managed.

Whitelaw's expression remained stunned. "What are you doing here? I thought you'd be gone for good."

"I just came to get my backpack," she said. "Then I'll be off." It was only then she suddenly saw how tired he looked, how bruised and sleepless his face. "What's happened?"

He rubbed the back of his neck. "Do you want the bad or the good news first?"

"Doesn't matter."

"No. I don't suppose it does." He gave another sigh. "The good news is that the charges against you have been dropped."

For a moment she was too astonished to take it in. "I'm innocent?" she said. "It's been proved that I'm innocent?"

He nodded. "Frank Goodman came back on Wednesday and made a statement. You've an alibi set in stone."

India felt her face crack into a grin as broad as the Murray River. "That is great news! God, that's great!" She started to laugh, a slightly hysterical mixture of relief and elation, but another thought made her pause. "What about Elizabeth Ross's murder? Aren't I still up for that?"

"No. They've found someone else to take that particular rap, along with the others."

India punched the air with a fist, shouting, "YES!" and did a little dance of delight.

Whitelaw remained motionless, watching her. He didn't smile.

India stopped her dancing. "Sorry." She let her arms fall to her sides. "Okay, so what's the bad news?"

The muscles in his jaw were jumping and twitching. Now she saw how tense he was and regretted her outburst of glee. "God! What is it?"

"Someone's fitted me up." He blurted out the words. "The gun that killed Tiger and Lauren was found Monday. The day after you legged it. It's got my fingerprints all over it." He looked at the floor, speaking in a murmur. "I'm a suspect."

India felt a ripple of shock trickle unpleasantly down her spine. "What do you mean?"

He looked up. His burning stare was intense. "I mean, I've been framed. The hearing is tomorrow."

"Who'd frame you? I don't get it . . . How come your fingerprints . . ." She trailed off as the information finally permeated her brain. She took an unsteady step backwards. "I don't get it," she said. "Surely, you didn't . . ."

"No. I did not kill them."

"But you . . . just said . . . your fingerprints were on the gun . . ."

"That doesn't make me the killer."

"Then how did they get there? By magic?"

An angry flare lit at the back of his eyes and she muttered, "Sorry." She wanted to remain reasonable, but she'd been in too many courtrooms to accept his word just like that.

"It's the shock, I know." He rubbed the bridge of his nose. "I still can't quite believe it either."

"So where did your fingerprints come from?"

"I obviously handled the gun at some point. The question is, *whose* gun? It happened after Elizabeth Ross was killed because I'm up for that one as well."

"Elizabeth?" Her voice was faint.

"I did not kill Elizabeth either."

"But *who* do you think framed you? You must have *some* idea!"

"Could have been a cop, or maybe someone at the manhunt."

"Well, that narrows it down a lot."

She was finding it increasingly hard to believe him. She owed him that, after his kindness to her, but one thought blocked out all others: *Had he known from the start she wasn't the killer, because he was?*

"India, let's stay steady here and think a minute—"

"But why pin it on *you,* when I was already in the picture? It doesn't make any sense!"

He reached a hand towards her and she jerked away.

"Did you make me stay with you so you could keep an eye on me? Make sure I didn't find out too much about who killed my friend?"

"No!"

The next second Mikey appeared.

India and Whitelaw stood facing each other, breathing hard, faces flushed.

Mikey's eyes flicked from one of them to the other, as though measuring the tension in the atmosphere. "What's happening, Jed?" he said levelly. "She being rude about your shreddies?"

Whitelaw's furious brown eyes didn't move from hers.

"I wouldn't be surprised if she was," Mikey continued, "because tartan is for Scots and by no stretch of the imagination are you a Scot. Scots wear tartan and eat porridge. Abos wear paint and eat insects." He made a *tsk*ing sound and shook his head. "You really should know that by now."

"Suspicious cow," Whitelaw said.

Mikey's gaze travelled over her. "Bloody hell," he said. "What on earth have you been doing, woman?"

Vaguely she became aware of her grime, the countless scratches on her legs and arms. Her hair had tangled into a fierce mass and her skin was sunburnt. She must look like a madwoman.

He said, more gently, "Are you all right?"

"No, I'm not," she snapped. "I thought he was going to hit me—"

"Serve you right if I had," snarled Whitelaw. He turned to Mikey. "She thinks *I'm* the killer."

"Ah," said Mikey, and looked from one of them to the other. "Why is that?"

"Because she won't listen."

"Very good," India said acidly. "Award-winning, I'd say—"

"India! Go outside. Leave us for a minute."

Somehow India made it to the kitchen. She felt herself to be in a strange place between disbelief and horror. Disbelief because she liked Whitelaw, and horror because she knew it was all possible. Like a sleepwalker she filled the kettle. She spooned coffee into a mug, and poured water from the kettle onto it, not realizing she hadn't plugged it in. As she stared at the grains of coffee floating on the cold water she thought: surely not *Whitelaw.*

She'd started a headache when Mikey joined her five minutes later. "He's gone."

"Good," she said.

Mikey studied her grimy face, then her slashed ankles and calves. "Where have you been?"

"Walkabout." She sank onto a chair and massaged her aching temples. "Do you have any aspirin or some codeine? My head's killing me."

Mikey disappeared briefly, and returned with a packet of Disprin. "Take three," he advised. "Two's never enough."

India washed them down with water, leaned back in her chair. "Where's my backpack?"

"Under the house. I'll get it for you."

He returned a few minutes later, put it beside her. He peered into her mug, threw the contents out and turned on the kettle. "You can't blame him, you know. You're mates, or supposed to be. He thought you'd be on his side. He expected you to believe he's been set up. He expected you to believe in him, full stop."

Her agitation showed in the way her hands were clenching and unclenching.

"Come on, India. Surely you can't believe he killed Tiger and Lauren? And Elizabeth Ross?"

"People are capable of doing anything," she said, struggling to her feet. "Anything. I've faced the sweetest and kindest of men and women who've protested their innocence. One woman even killed her baby daughter for the insurance payout."

Mikey spoke evenly. "Jed's not one of your murderers."

"And you really believe that?"

"Yes."

"Even though his fingerprints are all over the gun that killed . . ." India took a deep breath. "Three people."

"Yes."

Her gaze levelled with his, then, on unsteady legs, she made her way out of the kitchen and headed for the shower.

————

"You can't leave," said Mikey. He plucked the backpack off her shoulder and dumped it on the verandah.

"Just try and stop me," she said icily. "I've had enough of this place."

He felt his gaze drawn to her. Her hair was still wet from her shower and her skin had darkened in the sun and gleamed as though it had been polished. She reminded him of a cheetah as she stood there, poised, all legs and grace. He had never seen a woman look more desirable. He looked away.

"Whitelaw did a run on the Beemer's plate," he said.

She glanced at him.

"It belongs to a company registered in Panama."

"Very helpful," she remarked, and made to pick up her backpack.

"It's Christmas Day tomorrow," he said, and saw her start of surprise. "You'll be lucky to get a lift over the next few days, and you can't fly abroad, not until you get your passport, clear things with Stan. How about you stay here over the holiday, free of charge of course, until you've sorted out what you're going to do next?"

She narrowed her eyes at him. "How come the change of heart? Last time I remember I was on your hate list."

He ran a finger around the neck of his T-shirt. "I guess it's because I had doubts about your alibi. The whole Frank Goodman thing." He forced himself to look her squarely in the eye. "I'm sorry. I'm a suspicious bastard. It just took a while because I couldn't . . ." He trailed off and scuffed the ground with his boot. He didn't know how to explain it. His initial dislike, his growing attraction.

To his surprise, she reached out and squeezed his upper arm. "Thank you," she said.

He didn't respond. He simply stood there, dumb as one of Reg Coffey's bullocks while she settled her backpack on her shoulder. "Well then," she said. "Since I have no intention of hanging around in this subnormal, retarded town any longer than I have to, I'll say goodbye." She held out her hand.

Mikey took it in both of his. His were hot and sweaty, hers cool and dry. He squeezed her hand gently and cocked his head to one side, projecting his most endearing expression.

"Do you do the little lost boy look often?"

"Sometimes," he admitted.

She glared at him. "Well, you can drop it with me."

Immediately he straightened up. "All right," he agreed. "How about this: I believe you're a woman of principle, and that if you don't give Jed a hand and he ends up with a life sentence in jail, your conscience will eat at you until the day you die."

"You're entitled to your beliefs," she said in a waspish tone, and walked down the steps, out of the verandah's shadow and into the sunlight. She turned and stared at him for a long moment, then walked away.

———

India regretted leaving almost as soon as her shoes touched the road. The sun thundered out of the bright-white glaring sky, making the pain behind her eyes almost unbearable, and when a car cruised into view she stuck her hand out without a second thought.

I hope he's got air-conditioning.

The silver Lexus pulled up beside her, its passenger window open. India peered inside. A gray-haired man, midforties or so, peered back.

"Miss Kane?" he said.

"I'm sorry, do I know you?"

"No." He gave her a charming smile. "I guessed it was you from the description the security guard gave me. I'm Robert Jones, I work for Karamyde Cosmetics. Glynnis Coggins, our PR manager sent me to see if I could find you. She wants you to meet our director for a quick briefing before his three-week break in the Far East. He leaves tonight."

India took a step backwards.

He gave another smile. "Where were you headed before I turned up?"

"Sydney."

His face lit up. "That's great," he said. "I'm planning on leaving for Sydney later today. How about you get your business over with and then I give you a lift? I could do with the company."

India looked up and down the road, undecided.

"You got relatives in Sydney?"

"Just friends."

"Come on, hop in."

"I really don't feel in the mood for interviewing," she protested feebly.

"He's flat out. Won't take more than half an hour, promise. We'll be in Sydney in time for breakfast tomorrow."

It was the thought of breakfast with Scotto that decided her. "Okay."

She glanced through the rear window as the Lexus purred down the road, tires sucking on loose stones. Mikey stood watching her go, and the sunlight through the dust in the air surrounded him like golden candy floss.

SEVENTEEN

ROLAND KNOX WAS IMMACULATELY GROOMED BUT HE WAS seven inches short of six feet and India towered over him. She shook the hand he offered, warily taking in his narrow mouth and pale, calculating eyes.

All her instincts were on red alert. There had been no Glynnis Coggins when she'd arrived. No PR director. Just Roland Knox, the owner.

Knox gave India a polite, professional smile before showing her into an impersonal room that smelled of lilies and bore the gray-and-chrome style of meeting rooms the world over. Beyond them an expanse of window looked out over what appeared to be a laboratory. Opposite hung a massive canvas, which took up most of the wall.

In oil and acrylic, a huge shark appeared suddenly and silently out of the green-blue gloom. Its eyes were matt black, its gaping maw hung with tatters of flesh and its razored teeth cut white against the aquatic darkness. Millions of tiny air bubbles formed a ragged halo of pearl-like droplets as it lunged. A mist of blood trailed after it. It was an image of sleek and ferocious power, of blind instinct and violent death.

India swallowed.

"Study of the Great White Shark, number seven," Knox said. "By Richard Hall."

"It's spectacular," India said truthfully.

"It should be, for twenty thousand dollars."

She nodded thoughtfully, as though impressed. In fact, she was thinking of Elizabeth's photograph. Was Knox the short young man standing aggressively with his friends around the dead shark?

She felt him studying her intently. "I wonder how you'd react if you faced such a creature in its own environment."

"I'd do my best to walk on water," India said.

"And when you discover you can't?"

"I'd poke its eyes out. Or try to."

"If it was the size of a bus, you might find that difficult."

India tried to contain her shudder but Knox seemed to see it because he gave a small, self-satisfied smile.

"What angle are you thinking of taking with your newspaper article?" he asked.

"Guinea pigs."

His eyes flared with a voracious light at odds with his urbane manner. "I'm sorry?" he said.

"You don't use animals to test products for safety. You use people."

"That is correct."

"Well, I thought a nice story would be to concentrate not so much on the scientific aspect of research but the testers. A sort of 'day in the life of a guinea pig' from when they first answer the ad to getting their check from Karamyde Cosmetics."

Knox waited for her to go on, his eyebrows raised a fraction.

She said, "In particular I'd like to interview those who earn up to a thousand dollars in an hour or so."

"Then you've come to the wrong place," he said. "The payment to our girls is pin money, no more. They can earn anything from thirty dollars for trying eyeliner or mascara to a hundred and twenty for a face treatment cream. None of them has earned over two hundred dollars for a single test."

India affected surprise. "Oh. I could have sworn I saw an ad that said you'd pay a thousand for . . ." she paused as if digging in her memory ". . . sleeping and taking drugs."

There was a perceptible pause. He's going to lie to me, she thought.

"I don't recall those exact words being used in any of our advertisements," he said. "One of our competitors must be running it."

"Any idea who they might be?"

"I'm afraid not." He turned towards the door. "Perhaps I can show you around the laboratory. You might find it interesting."

"Are any of your testers Aborigines?" asked India. "It'd be nice to get their view."

"No. We don't produce cosmetics for coloreds."

The way he said "coloreds" reminded her of her father. Curtly dismissive and condescending.

———

There was little to be seen on the tour of the Institute. Laboratories are very quiet places on Christmas Eve. In half an hour they were finished, and Knox ushered her outside. The Lexus was nowhere to be seen, but there was a taxi waiting. Her backpack was in the back.

No lift to Sydney, dammit.

Knox surveyed her with a cool half-smile as if he'd read her thoughts. "It was nice to have met you."

India concentrated on projecting back a warm smile. "Thank you for your time."

"And for yours. But despite your very exciting project, I don't think we'll be meeting again, Miss Kane. Do you?"

The smile was still there, the voice remained impeccably polite. The round face, the silver hair, the immaculate suit exuded nothing but friendliness and confidence, but she had caught the predatory glint in his eyes.

"No, I don't suppose we will," she lied.

As she climbed into the car he said, "Goodbye," and nodded, smiling a little to himself as though satisfied.

"Goodbye," India said politely as he turned away, and under her breath, "you smooth bastard."

————————

The taxi dropped her at the far end of Biolella Road and she saw a single branch of dry lightning tear through the sky in the distance. Someone yelled, "Happy Christmas, gorgeous!" from their front garden and she waved back without breaking her stride. Distractedly she ran a hand over her temples, wondering if her continued headache was due to an impending storm; she had always been sensitive to weather changes. Another white jag of lightning seared out of the blue-black sky, and seemed almost to touch the ground.

India approached the house with a fair amount of trepidation. She was unsure of her welcome having made it clear she wouldn't be returning. Mikey might throw her out. Then where would she stay?

She walked up the path and peered through the verandah rails at the slumped form in the cane chair. When she saw who it was, she glanced towards the front door, wondering whether Whitelaw had returned.

Only one way to find out.

All was silent, apart from the faint refrain of "Good King Wenceslas" from the street. She found some Disprin in the bathroom and downed three, then went into the kitchen to make herself a glass of iced chocolate. As the Disprin kicked in, she suddenly felt remarkably cheerful. Whitelaw wasn't home and that suited her fine. She would, she decided, slide onto the divan, get a good night's sleep, suffer whatever Christmas Day and Mikey had to offer her, then leg it to Sydney. She could almost feel the adrenaline surging through her body as she replayed her meeting with Knox. She didn't feel the least bit tired. She had a focus now: to team up with Scotto and nail Karamyde. She started to hum. Toasted Whitelaw's immobile tarantula with a flourish and raised the glass to her lips, closing her eyes as she gulped.

"So, Sly's returned," Mikey said.

India got the impression he was concentrating hard on his *S*s to appear sober. He was leaning against the wall, hands shoved casually in his pockets, but he was swaying slightly. She looked at him for a moment, then finished her chocolate milk, put the glass down.

He waved a hand at her face. "Moustache," he said.

She ran her tongue across her upper lip.

"Better."

"You're drunk." Her tone was purposely cold, making it sound like a dreadful thing, as if he had a disease that might be catching.

"Celebrating Christmas," he said, his tongue so slack the words came out in soft glugs.

"I'd say you've been celebrating all year."

He shifted his weight and lurched forward. India prudently stepped out of his way; he didn't seem to be in full control of his limbs and they looked as though they might collapse at any moment.

"You like turkey?" he said, hand on the fridge door.

"What, now?"

"No." He sighed as if dealing with an idiot. "Tomorrow. Christmas Day."

"Mightn't it be a bit hot for a traditional English lunch?"

His hand slipped off the door. "We can't not have it."

It seemed best to humor him. "Okay."

"Got to deliver it." He started nodding. She was reminded of a toy dog in the back of a sedan. "Or Jed'll hang himself. That's what Abos do, you know, when they're incarcerated. Hang themselves."

"You're going to take him Christmas lunch?"

"Jail foods' terrible. A hanging offense."

"Why can't his family?"

He blinked at her. "Come again?"

"It'd save you running around like meals on wheels if his family took it?"

"He doesn't have any."

She felt as though he'd punched her in the stomach. "Hell," she said. "I'd forgotten he was a stolen child."

"How's your head . . . still ache?" he said after a while.

"Better since I took some more Disprin. Thank you."

"So polite. So marvelously English. India, the jewel in the crown." He gave a deep chuckle. "I'm drunk, you know. Absolutely rat-arsed. That's what Christmas is for, isn't it? All good men and all that." He reached out and made to run a finger over her upper lip but she jerked her head and moved away, and he stumbled after her. "Stop moving about, woman," he slurred.

"I'm going to bed."

"Can I come too?"

She stopped and looked at him, her face impassive. "You can't be serious."

"Why not?"

"Do you really think I'd find a drunken slob like you attractive?"

"I'm not that drunk," he insisted. "And I'm not a slob."

She simply raised an eyebrow in return.

He caught her upper arms in his hands, pulled her towards him. "Don't."

"I bloody will," he murmured, and bent his head to hers.

His kiss was hard and demanding.

She could taste bourbon and woodsmoke, overlaid with anger, and a petal of rage unfurled inside her. She'd had enough of anger in her life. So she bit his lip.

Mikey reared backwards, a hand to his mouth.

"The difference between men and women never ceases to amaze

me," she said coolly. "Men don't have to love someone, or like them particularly . . . or even be sober. But you'll still sleep with them."

He blinked owlishly. "Either you're saying you don't like me, or that you're a cold fish. Which is it? I can't work it out."

"Men aren't as fussy as women."

"I'm extremely fussy," he protested.

"I am too. Goodnight, Mikey."

————

A clap of thunder woke Mikey in the middle of the night. He lay there with the consciousness—it felt worse than his hangover—of having made a terrible mistake. He got up. He felt shaky and slightly sick. He held out a hand, studied it. It shook a little, and he stared at it as if for the first time.

He couldn't remember going to bed. He probed cautiously at his memory as he watched the tremors in his hand, but couldn't get any further than the taste of India's lips. Then it all went blank. Had he passed out as he kissed her? *Had* he kissed her?

Absently he rubbed his mouth, felt his swollen and bruised lower lip. Yes. Yes, he had kissed her all right, and she'd bitten him. He'd deserved it.

He could feel a dark cloud of self-disgust gathering inside him. Mikey ran a hand over his face, groaning to himself.

A drink will take the edge off the way you feel.

But he didn't want one.

————

Mikey pulled on gym shorts, running shoes and a T-shirt, and ran seven Ks across the bush. He ran all the way to the base of the hills, startling a flock of cockatoos on the way, and looked back at Cooinda, twinkling through the darkness.

When he ran into the backyard his body was dripping with

sweat and his head was clear. He took a shower, dressed in the darkest clothes he could find, then headed for the kitchen to wake India.

———————

"Are you sure this is a good idea?" she asked for the third time. "It's barely two in the morning."

"It's Christmas Day. It's a perfect idea."

"What'll happen if you get caught?"

"I won't."

They were driving southeast through Cooinda. There was no traffic. The town was asleep.

Mikey cleared his throat noisily. "About last night—"

"You were drunk."

"Yes." He stared rigidly ahead, forced the words out. "I behaved badly."

"If I'm not embarrassed, you shouldn't be."

"But honestly—"

"Okay, okay, apology accepted if it makes you feel better." She sounded snappish.

God, she was hard, he thought.

———————

Mikey used headlights until they neared the clutch of houses in Jangala Vale. Then he doused them and did a U-turn before parking, so the car faced towards town. He left the keys in the ignition. The digital clock told them it was two-thirty in the morning.

They struck out across the bush together. A quarter moon supplied sufficient light. Mikey carried a big bolt cutter and a hunting knife. India had a heavy cosh of Whitelaw's. As they walked, he noticed how little noise India made. She seemed to avoid dry twigs and leaves with uncanny instinct, while no matter how hard he tried he crashed along beside her like a giant wombat.

It took them fifty minutes to get to his lookout on top of the ridge. They crouched low, staring down a rock-strewn slope towards the murky shape of Karamyde Cosmetics. Lights were off in every window, except the reception area. Spotlamps illuminated the car park and front of the building. Mikey scanned the area with his binoculars. No activity anywhere. Just two guards in the gatehouse, nursing white plastic cups and smoking.

He hunkered down, felt India do the same. He watched the guards. One of them started to laugh. The other reached for a bottle—it looked like Scotch—on the windowsill and topped up their cups. His movements were unsteady, and Mikey gave a little smile. They were celebrating Christmas. Maybe it wouldn't be as difficult as he'd thought.

He jerked his head at India and they started down the slope. Towards the bottom he slipped, sending an avalanche of loose rocks tumbling. He froze and flicked a look at India, who stayed motionless, waiting to see if the noise had attracted any attention. Silence.

Cautiously they crept towards the perimeter fence. When they neared it, Mikey squatted on the dirt again and raised his binoculars. The guards were still drinking and smoking. He scanned the fence carefully, checking for cameras. He couldn't see any, but that didn't mean they weren't there. He watched the guards for another two minutes. Not once did they show any interest in anything aside from their little party.

It was now or never.

Mikey rose and approached the fence. He picked up a handful of dust and threw it at the mesh. There was a sharp fizzing sound, then silence. He gave a low groan. An electrified fence. He flapped a hand at India, telling her to stay where she was, and skirted the perimeter, searching for a circuit box. When he eventually neared the car park he paused, concentrating his senses on every detail around him. He was conscious of a gentle breeze. The sweat trickling down his back. He couldn't see a circuit box anywhere. Shit. He'd bet his last dollar it was in the gatehouse.

He backtracked to India, whispered his plan.

"No way," she hissed at him.

"The only way," he whispered back.

———————

They had to wait thirty-five minutes for one of the guards to make a move. India watched as he stumbled out of the gatehouse, his hands already fumbling at his flies. She saw the big shadow that was Mikey slide around the gatehouse wall. The guard was oblivious.

Crouching low, India moved rapidly towards the gate. When she came to a low shrub opposite the gatehouse, she pressed herself against the ground, straining for the slightest sound. She thought she could hear the guard urinating, and held her breath.

There was a muffled thud and a groan, then the sound of scuffling.

India raised her head. Mikey was heaving the guard's inert form behind the gatehouse. The scuffing stopped. Silence. India lay still and waited. She shivered, not from cold but from fear.

Come on, she thought. *Come on.*

The minutes ticked past. Three. Five. Ten. When the second guard stepped outside, his footsteps seemed inordinately loud. "Curtis?" he called. "You all right?"

A long groan answered him.

The guard moved carefully around the gatehouse. "Curtis?" he called again.

Another groan.

"Piss artist," the guard grumbled, and as he rounded the gatehouse, his back turned towards her, India sprang to her feet and raced as quietly as she could for the open doorway.

———————

From the shadows Mikey watched the second guard try to rouse his mate. He was slapping the unconscious man's face. "Wake up, you sod, or you'll get us into trouble."

His friend didn't move.

"One-pot pisspot," the guard complained. "Not even half a bottle and you're bloody comatose." He hooked his arms beneath his friend's armpits and attempted to pull him around the gatehouse. He managed to jerk his friend about a meter, then gave up. "Sleep it off where you bloody are, then," he muttered, and turned back for his post.

Only then did Mikey launch himself at the man.

––––––––––

"Are you sure?" Mikey demanded for the second time.

"Yes! I'd like to walk through the gate too, but unless you've got the code to the key pad we're climbing the fence, okay?"

They were at the rear of the building, and he'd thrown dust and leaves and stones at the fence without a single warning fizz in response, but he still had his doubts. Big ones.

"What if the fence is on another circuit, like the gate?" he asked.

"Mikey, I did my best in there, but I didn't *know*."

"Christ!" he muttered, and hefted the bolt cutter.

India stood still as rock, watching him.

Mikey mustered his courage. Ignored the nausea in the pit of his stomach. He stretched out his hand, so the bolt cutter was a centimeter from the mesh. Do or die, he thought. And screwed his eyes tight shut as he jabbed the cutter against the fence.

Nothing happened.

He felt his knees weaken. "Christ," he said again as India murmured, "Thank God."

Mikey gripped the cutter with both hands and bit through the wire without difficulty. He made sure he cut a wide hole, about five feet square. He didn't want to get fried should the fence be reactivated.

They slipped through, heading straight for the fire door. India put a hand on his arm. They both stilled. She jerked her head, indicating she'd heard something. He motioned her to wait and crept to the corner of the building, peered around. Nothing, aside from a domestic tabby walking across the car park. India couldn't have heard *that*, surely?

He waited a few more minutes. Nothing. He returned to the fire door and took out his leather pouch of tools. During his stakeouts he hadn't seen any indication of a security system but they wouldn't know until they broke in. The scrape of metal made him sweat. It seemed painfully loud in the dense silence. He breathed shallowly as he worked, applying constant pressure to the cylinder. Suddenly the lock clicked back. The door cracked open. He held his breath. No sound. No alarm. India had told him she'd yanked every wire free from two circuit boxes in the gatehouse, but he still didn't like it. He wondered if there was a silent alarm, separate from the main system, perhaps more guards inside. No way to tell.

He slid inside and listened. A minute passed, then he gestured at India to wait by the fence.

"No," she hissed. "I'm coming with you."

"But I want you as my lookout."

"Don't fob me off—"

"I'm not sodding fobbing you off!" he retorted through clenched teeth. "I need a lookout and you'll be as much use as a flat battery if you come with me."

She gave him a hard look. "If I find out you're bullshitting—"

"Shut up, India, and go and keep an eye out."

He waited until she'd gone, and crept inside. He left the door open a crack behind him, felt his way along the corridor, listened, crept to the central stairwell, listened again. He slipped up the stairs to the first floor and approached the row of offices. He tried the first

door, marked with a little brass plate: IAN TURNER, HEAD OF RE-
SEARCH. Locked. The second too was locked, and Mikey prowled
quickly along the corridor, ticking off each plate as he went until he
came to the one marked GORDON T. A. WILLIS, DIRECTOR, opposite
the lift. Automatically, he glanced at the panel above the lift to
check it wasn't in use, and paused.

There were four floors.

He'd thought there were only three. Two above ground, and a
possible storage basement. But there was another floor below that:
B2.

He'd check it out later; first things first. He tried Willis's door, also
locked. He quickly freed the lock and entered, shutting the door behind him. Mikey crossed to the windows and pulled the blinds shut.
Then he switched on his penlight and scanned the room. His heart
gave a bump at the hammerhead shark jaws, and settled to a steady
pounding as he moved the beam around. Lots of chrome and black,
and trophies of fish and photographs of more fish on the walls. There
were four shelves filled with technical books and journals, a three-tier
filing cabinet and a computer on the desk. He crossed the room to the
desk and turned on the computer. Sweat pooled in the small of his
back; the hum of the machine seemed overly loud. He searched the
desk while the computer booted. Internal memos, a handful of checks
needing a countersignature. Nothing startling there. A book on big
game fishing. Another on sharks.

He shut the last drawer and leaned over and clicked the mouse.
The screen lit into blue and demanded a password. Mikey cursed
softly. He tried Willis's name, his initials and a handful of words including *Hammerhead* and *Great White*. Deciding not to waste any
more time he shut down the computer and went to the filing cabinet. Locked. He broke it open easily. Swiftly, he started his search.

It took him twenty minutes before he fell upon a register of
testers that told him when they had answered an advertisement,
what tests they'd undertaken and when, and what they'd been paid.

He saw Debs's name and Roxy's. He pulled out the next register and immediately his attention sharped because, while the previous register showed white testers, this register listed blacks—including the Mullett family.

He frowned. This register revealed the date when an Aborigine arrived at the Institute, but not what they were testing. None of them seemed to have been paid. Mikey folded both registers in half and pulled out his shirt. He stuffed the sheets in the back of his jeans and tucked his shirt over them.

A noise made him stiffen. He thought he could hear a low rumble coming from the corridor, like a distant engine. He hastened to the door, put his ear against it. Silence.

Cautiously, he opened it a crack. He peered up and down the corridor. Nothing. He stepped outside, shut the door and headed to the lift, pressed the button. The ping when it arrived made him flinch. He stepped inside, pressed B2. The lift doors closed. The lift dropped downwards, stopped at B1. Mikey pressed B2 again. The lift didn't move. He scanned the lift's panel. His pulse leapt. There was a tiny camera set above the panel. A camera with EYE TECH etched onto its bodywork. A camera that zoomed in to examine your iris for identification. He jerked his gaze away. His body streamed with sweat. He pressed G and the lift ascended. He decided to push his luck and try another route to B2.

The lift doors opened.

A low growl greeted him.

He looked down.

A pair of yellow eyes stared into his.

Oh, shit.

The dog was big, at least a hundred pounds, and jet black. Its ears and tail were cropped, and its teeth gleamed white in a dripping snarl. Its hackles were raised. Its massive chest emanated a deep continual growl.

Mikey started desperately stabbing the lift button. The dog's muscles bunched at his movements and the growl turned into a roar. Tortuously slowly, the lift doors started to close. To his surprise, the dog immediately stopped snarling, spun around and raced off.

Shit, shit, *shit!*

The lift rose silently, stopped.

Ping. 1.

The doors opened. Mikey craned his head into the corridor, listened hard, took one step, heard something moving. Put his finger on the lift button. The dog came charging around the corner, head low, ears flat against its skull.

Mikey stabbed G.

The doors were half closed when the dog appeared. It made no effort to spring inside, simply raced off again. Mikey's adrenaline was pumping. He slipped the hunting knife from its sheath, held it hard.

Ping. G.

He sprang outside and ran for the fire exit. He was two-thirds along the corridor when he heard something behind him. He ran harder. A rhythmic panting reached him. He pumped his legs faster, willing himself to reach the door before the dog reached him. The panting grew louder and louder, until it seemed to match his own frantic breaths.

Mikey hit the door with the full force of his left shoulder. He flew outside, spinning in midair, knife poised. The dog piled on top of him, snapping and snarling. Mikey tried to stab the dog but it was too close and trying to bite his face. He rolled onto his front, felt the jaws close on his shoulder. He tried to wrench free, but the dog had a good grip and was biting hard, shaking its head furiously. Mikey heaved himself off the ground in an attempt to pass the knife under his body and into the dog's stomach but there was no room so he jabbed the dog as hard as he could with his elbow. It simply bit harder, enraged.

Suddenly the animal went still, stopped snarling. Its body slumped, a dead weight on Mikey's back.

He pushed it off, scrambled to his feet. India stood there, Whitelaw's cosh in both hands. She was trembling.

"It wouldn't stop," she said. "I kept hitting it, but it wouldn't stop."

"It's okay, it's okay," was all he managed between gasps. His chest was heaving, his body shaking and sweat-soaked.

"It wouldn't stop," she repeated.

He grabbed her wrist and pulled her away. "Let's get out of here."

Something kicked up dust next to him. He heard the muffled *phut* from a gun with a silencer. "They're shooting!" he yelled to India. Another bullet whizzed between them. India veered away sharply. Mikey raced for the hole in the fence. He slowed abruptly, scrambled as carefully as he could through the hole, straightened up and sprinted dead ahead. A third bullet sang past his right shoulder and he started to zigzag, attempting to head for the rocky slope.

"Over here!" a man shouted behind him.

Mikey sprinted through the bush, dodging trees and shrubs. He risked a glance over his shoulder, expecting India to be hot on his heels. She was nowhere to be seen. Instead, three men were right behind him. Maybe more.

A bullet walloped into the tree ahead of him and Mikey dived left. More bullets slapped into the ground and snapped twigs. He ran in the opposite direction, trying to stoop, keeping his silhouette low.

The moon slid behind a bank of clouds. It was as though a light had been switched off. Mikey crashed into a rock, losing his balance and hitting the ground. He surged upward and kept running, straining to see obstacles ahead. He could hear men behind him, shouting urgently.

Mikey charged down a hill, bumping painfully against stumps

and rocks and overbalancing, sometimes falling to his knees, but he continued his charge, moving fast and hard as he could. He tried to figure out where he was. He had started out by heading for the rocky slope but in the darkness had lost his sense of direction. He had to find the slope, and then he could locate the car. Go and get help. Help India, wherever she was. He came to the bottom of the hill and pelted along the valley for several minutes before climbing the next hill. His legs were tiring when he reached the top, and his breath burned in his throat, but when a flashlight bobbed into view in the valley he accelerated downwards and then up for the next ridge, the thought of India keeping his body moving at a crippling rate.

He was going so fast he nearly fell when he got to the top of the ridge. He paused and looked back, panting. Flashlights bobbed below, hard on his trail. Men shouted. A dog barked.

A bloody dog! He could never outrun a dog. He hoped it wasn't the same black bastard. It was fucking *huge*.

"Over here!"

"This way!"

To his surprise, the flashlights changed direction. Moved directly away from him. He watched them for several minutes, his legs weary, his lungs aching. He couldn't see the Institute anywhere. Or anything, for that matter. Murky bush stretched endlessly in every direction. He saw the flashlights dwindle into tiny yellow dots, and eventually vanish. He sank to his knees and knelt there, gasping. When his breathing slowed and his heart rate steadied, he shuffled into a more comfortable position. He felt his sweat drying cold. His shoulder started to throb where the dog had gripped him. There was a deep ache at the back of his neck as well, and both his forearms and wrists, and his right knee. In the dark he couldn't tell how badly he had been bitten, just that his jeans and jacket were sticky with blood. He was aware that the sooner he treated the wounds the better. He looked around him again. Nothing but dark gray bush, as far as he could see.

And silence.

Dense bush silence. Nothing moved, not a bird or bat or a leaf on a tree. He looked into the sky. Nothing but thick clouds roiling in weighty slow motion across the moon.

He hunched there for quite a while, trying to ignore the increasing pain. Maybe an hour passed, but in the silence it felt like half the night. He decided to settle where he was, until dawn, and then move. If he set off not knowing where he was going, he might—

Something brushed his upper arm and he jerked wildly to one side.

"It's only me," said India. "Are you all right?"

He swallowed the yell that had formed in his throat.

"I . . . um, I guess." His voice was strangled.

"I've thrown them off your track for a bit."

"Ah," he managed.

"Are you okay to keep moving?"

"Sure."

She touched him again. "Come on, then. Follow me."

Mikey followed India through the thick dark gloom. She kept angling to the right, scooping around trees and bushes, heading downhill all the time until they reached the bottom of a valley, where she immediately increased her pace. They followed a wild animal track, bordered with saltbush and rocks and stones, for some time. He stumbled and lurched behind her, and found himself resenting his clumsiness. India hadn't tripped or faltered once.

They reached the end of the valley. Mikey looked upwards and at the steep cliff ahead, and groaned. He felt exhausted. In need of a hot bath, antiseptic, a stiff drink, a massage, cool sheets, a soft pillow . . .

The blanket of clouds parted for a brief moment, and the bush blazed silver. Mikey reeled in his tracks.

In front of him was a naked woman. Her head was held high, and her back and shoulders were straight, the dip above her buttocks pronounced. She had long muscular thighs and her calves curved to narrow ankles. She made no sound as she moved.

Cloud folded over the moon.

Mikey followed the gleaming shadow that was India until they reached the car.

EIGHTEEN

"DO YOU NORMALLY STRIP IN TIMES OF STRESS?" HE ASKED lightly as he drove.

India was curled on the passenger seat. She was wearing his shirt. It came down to her knees.

"Only when necessary." She sounded distant and distracted.

"Well, thank you. Without you I'd still be sitting frozen solid on that hilltop. Scared shitless I was lost forever."

She didn't respond.

"How in the hell did you divert them? And what about that bloody dog?"

"I picked up a few survival skills in the bush."

"Did you do a course or something?"

"Just last week's sojourn." Her face was turned to the window.

"You learned all that in a week?"

"I had a good teacher."

India was staring outside, as though she wished she were somewhere else. Mikey decided to leave her be.

———

When they got to Whitelaw's all he wanted to do was sleep.

"No," said India. She marched him into the bathroom, passed him a towel. "Get undressed." She started to run the bath, then opened the cabinet and pulled out a pack of cotton wool, sticking plaster, bandages and a bottle of Dettol, put them on the loo cistern. She poured half the bottle of Dettol into the bath, turning it cloudy.

"I'll be fine," he protested.

"We'll see about that after you've bathed." She glanced at her watch. "You've ten minutes. Then I'm coming in."

"Yes, commandant," he said wearily.

The water was hot and he had to grit his teeth as he slid down until he was immersed up to his chin. He couldn't see the damage on his shoulder or neck, but he could make out two punctures behind his knee, the way the skin was already turning dark purple from the pressure of those massive jaws. He exhaled and felt the heat penetrate his aching muscles. He leaned back and closed his eyes.

What seemed seconds later, India knocked on the door, demanded he sit on the loo seat. Towel intact, please. Feeling oddly vulnerable, he sat.

"Ready," he called, and gritted his teeth once more when she stepped inside, looking determined.

"When did you last have a tetanus shot?"

"Recently."

"How recently?"

"Recently enough, thank you."

He stared at the floor as she gently pushed his ponytail aside. Heard her hiss between her teeth. "This might hurt," she warned.

It did.

But he refused to make a sound.

With infinite care, India disinfected and bandaged each of his wounds, made him swallow two Panadol. When she'd finished, she said, "Look at me."

He raised his head. Slowly, she lowered her face to his, and pressed a kiss against his mouth.

"That's for being so brave," she said, and smiled.

He found himself grinning inanely as he headed for bed.

Mikey slept like the dead. Immobile. Comatose.

In the first instant when he awoke he wondered if he'd dreamed the past night, but then the pain in his shoulder and neck entered his consciousness. He struggled up and went to wash. In the bathroom he inspected India's first aid, downed some more Panadol and got dressed. He headed for the kitchen and coffee and toast.

India was struggling to open a jar of apricot jam. Her lips were compressed and her knuckles stood out white.

She thrust the jar at him.

"Having trouble opening it, India?"

She gave a curt nod.

"Not strong enough to open it by yourself?"

Another nod.

"Say: 'Please, Mikey, could you help me open my jar of apricot jam?'"

She sent him a look that could have stopped an elephant in its tracks. "Say: 'Please, Mikey, don't be a shithead,'" she said.

He couldn't help grinning. She may have resembled an untouchable wraith in the bush last night, kissed him like an angel, but deep down she was the same old India. Spiky and defensive.

He took the jar of apricot jam and with a single twist snapped it open. "Happy Christmas, India."

At eleven o'clock Mickey was basting the turkey.

"If Santa could bring you anything right now," he said to India, "what would you like?"

"A decent potato peeler."

"There's nothing wrong with it. You need more practice, that's all." He slid the turkey back into the oven.

"Please, Santa, make all potatoes skinless from tomorrow."

"I've never had a Chrissy pressie," said Polly wistfully. She was swinging her legs on the divan as she watched them.

"What's on the kitchen table, then?" Mikey said.

Polly shoved her hands beneath her thighs. "Pressies."

"Whose are they?" asked Mikey.

"Don't know."

"Hadn't you better look?"

Polly sidled up to the three gift-wrapped presents.

"Can you read out what's on their labels?" said India.

Hesitantly, Polly peered at the first. Her face split into a smile. "It says Polly!"

"And the others?"

"Another one for me! And one for Jed! Can I open them?"

"Only yours. Jed gets his when Mikey takes him his Christmas lunch."

"What's Jed's pressie?"

"A cake with a file in it."

———

The following evening, Mikey was sprawled on the grass with India and Polly at back of Whitelaw's house watching the sun set. It was ten past seven when his mobile rang.

"It's Sam."

Mikey stiffened. "So what's up?"

"I want to meet."

"Give me a time and a place, and I'll be there."

"Martin Place. Outside the post office. Eleven tomorrow."

Mikey's brain raced. "It's going to take me longer than that to get to Sydney. Can we make it Wednesday?"

"Not Wednesday."

"Thursday then."

"That's fine."

"Can you bring the—"

"No. I'm not bringing anything."

"That's okay." Mikey took a breath. "How will I know you?"

"Don't worry. I'll know you."

"Okay, I'll be—" he started to say, but Sam had gone.

———————

"I bet Sam's got Peter Ross's disc," said India. "My guess is Peter sent it to him."

"Sam never said anything about a disc. Just some files he found."

"I reckon they're computer files."

"I wish I recognized his voice," said Mikey. "He says he knows me but I don't know who the hell he is."

"Who's Sam?" asked Polly around a mouthful of turkey and honey-mustard marinade.

"A friend," said India.

Mikey had barbecued some leftover turkey and corn on the cob, and she'd eaten so much her stomach felt like a bowling ball. India found it hard to believe it was Boxing Day. Even harder was the sensation of peace and contentment. It may have been one of the most unorthodox Christmases she had ever experienced, but it was also unique. It was the first one she'd spent not being pressured to be someone she wasn't.

"You like India, don't you?" said Polly to Mikey after a while.

He raised his head to stare into the sky. India found herself holding her breath.

"Not always," he said finally.

"Me neither," agreed Polly.

India startled them by giving a bark of laughter. "Thanks, guys!"

———————

Scotto rang as they were washing up. He was so excited he could barely speak.

"I've found some notes of Lauren's," he said, "at her mother's. She was drafting an article. It's explosive stuff, Indi. Unbelievable. She hasn't anything to substantiate her story, but if it's true we've got to do something about it."

"God, that's great! Send it up!"

"No. No, I'm not trusting anyone with it . . ."

"What's it about?"

"Some pretty wild stuff about the Karamyde Cosmetic Research Institute. I think we should meet. Go over the stuff and form a game plan." He paused a second. "Can you come to Sydney?"

India didn't hesitate. "Yes. I can get a lift with Mikey." She looked across at him, eyebrows raised. He nodded.

"We'll be there Thursday. How about lunch?"

"Let's make it Friday," Scotto said. "We can celebrate New Year's Eve at the same time. And while you're here, you've got to see Geraldine Child. Remember I mentioned her before? The doctor Lauren saw before she left for Cooinda? It's important."

India took down Dr. Child's details again.

"Where shall we meet?" she asked.

"You still like oysters?"

"Absolutely."

"Broken your record yet?"

"No," she laughed. "It still stands at just two dozen."

"How about you go for broke and make it three? My shout. Sydney Cove Oyster Bar, one o'clock, Friday."

She hung up, and told Mikey about Lauren's article. "She was obviously close to breaking the story, but she needed evidence. Which is why she went to meet Peter Ross and Tiger."

Mikey was nodding. "She wanted that disc."

———

While India packed, Polly sat on the divan. She was wearing a new dress the color of saffron and had India's miniature teddy bear propped on her knees. She was gazing, downcast, at the backpack. "When will you be back?"

Not knowing how to respond, India pretended she hadn't heard. "I'll send you a postcard. Several in fact. Shall I mail them here?"

The smile she received made her feel even more guilty, and to compensate India knelt down to hug Polly. "I'll miss you," she said, and pressed a kiss on the girl's hair, which smelled of smoke and something that she couldn't identify. India took in some air over the back of her tongue, and breathed out, but she still couldn't identify it.

When they left for Rick Sullivan's airstrip the next morning Polly stood in the middle of the street, still in her saffron dress, watching them go. She clutched the little bear in both hands.

———

The pilot lit a cigarette and offered the pack around.

Ignoring Mikey's look of disapproval—which he tried to hide but she caught—India dragged deeply on the untipped Camel cigarette and exhaled, watching the thin stream of smoke being sucked through a hairline crack in the rubber lining by the window. Her head spiralled pleasantly with nicotine and she smiled as something clicked into place inside her head.

Nutmeg. Polly smelled of nutmeg.

———

The heat in Sydney was incredible. It was heavy as a wet woollen blanket, suffocating India. Hanging over the city was a haze of pollution the color of tobacco. The air-conditioning in their rental Ford was going full blast, but they were both sweating in spite of it.

If it hadn't been for Lauren's murder, she'd never have returned to Sydney. India stared at the city skyline, amazed at how much it had changed, how it was changing. Millennium fever, she supposed, as well as Sydney's hosting the 2000 Olympics later in the year. She could feel the fever of transformation in the cranes leaning against the sky, the foundations being built in massive holes, the glittering new office blocks and freshly planted parks and gardens. She found herself smiling, glad she was here—that Sydney still sparkled and danced like a professional performer never tiring of her audience.

"For goodness' sake, woman, concentrate," snapped Mikey. "We're meant to be heading north, not south. Don't you possess a sense of direction?"

"I'm sure Kent Street will get us on the Harbour Bridge," she insisted.

"It would if we were going the right way."

"Right, that's it." India leaned over and grabbed the steering wheel, and heaved the car to the side of the road. "I'm driving."

He sat there looking perplexed.

"If I haven't a sense of direction," she said reasonably, "then it's only sensible you map read."

They crossed the Harbour Bridge. India craned her neck briefly to glance through the windscreen and up at what was known as the coat hanger. In two days' time the bridge would be ablaze with lights and fireworks to celebrate the new millennium. The harbor would be filled with anything that floated: booze cruisers, dinghies and the smallest skiffs. It would be the biggest party Sydney had ever thrown, and India felt a trickle of excitement at joining in.

"What are you doing New Year's Eve?" she asked Mikey.

"Taking you and an Eski of champagne to the Cahill Expressway," he replied.

"We'll be run over!"

"Didn't you read the road sign back there?"

"What road sign?"

"The one that said they're closing it for New Year's Eve."

She took the Neutral Bay exit from the freeway and halted at a set of traffic lights.

"I'm going to stop at a bank," she said. "I need an injection of cash for DJ's food hall. We'll need some sort of sustenance with all that champagne."

She pulled over outside an ANZ on Military Road and Mikey slid across and drove around the block while she withdrew the maximum amount available. Five hundred and forty bucks. That should see her through the weekend and well beyond.

They headed east down the busy arterial Military Highway, thick with exhaust fumes and heavy three-lane traffic towards Mosman. Before their meetings with Sam and Scotto, they needed to follow up the photo that Elizabeth Ross had given India. Ten minutes later they dropped into a lush tree-bordered avenue lined with houses. The houses on either side were three or four storeys high and draped in hibiscus and bougainvillaea. Tall gum and palm trees stood in the gardens. Some houses had wrought-iron balconies and gates, others stained or painted wood, but they were all old, affluent-looking and splendid. Porsches and Mercedes were parked in broad open driveways and rosellas flashed from tree to tree, chattering madly. Little triangles of white sailed across the harbor, glittering silver in the distance.

"Wow," said India after a few minutes.

"No shit," said Mikey. "It's beautiful."

Erskin School blended into its surroundings perfectly. Sandstone walls gleamed like honey in the sun and a long lawn, perfectly mown, stretched to immaculate grass tennis courts and an Olympic-size pool. India drove up to the main steps, flanked by twin stone lions, and stopped the car. She pulled out Elizabeth's photograph and studied it. "I wonder if John Buchanan-Atkins is still here?"

"Only one way to find out," said Mikey.

She pocketed the photograph and climbed out of the car. She could smell fresh grass and hear the rhythmic tick of a sprinkler system.

"I wish the comprehensives in the UK were as nice," she remarked.

"Give them a few million each and they could be," Mikey retorted. "I'll pick you up in an hour and a half." He scrambled over to the driver's seat. "I'll wait until you're in, okay? Everyone might be on holiday."

———————

India walked up the steps to the school, which was deserted. She felt a longing to dive into the pool and wash away the sweat, lowering her body temperature by ten degrees.

As she put her hand to the door, a woman of about sixty with iron gray hair opened it. "May I help you?"

"I'd like to see John Buchanan-Atkins."

The woman continued to study India. "Why exactly would you like to see him?"

"I'm sorry. I can't really say. It's a personal matter."

"Are you a reporter?" She made it sound like child-abuser.

"No, I'm not," India lied. "I'm simply someone seeking an answer."

The woman arched an eyebrow. "To what?"

"I'm sorry," India apologized again, "but John Buchanan-Atkins is the only person who can help."

"Well, since he's dead," the woman said, "you'd best leave."

India could feel the shock register on her face. "Dead? When?"

The woman stared at her. "Why should 'when' matter?"

India was thinking of the body count. Of six people murdered. Or was it now seven?

"It's just that . . . several people have died recently." India wiped away the sweat from beneath her eyes with her fingers. "Including a very good friend of mine. I want to find out why she was murdered."

For a second the woman looked genuinely shaken, but she regained her composure fast. "You truly believe John might have been able to help you?"

"Yes."

The woman continued to stare fiercely at India, as though making up her mind about something.

"Please, come with me." She turned and walked into the building without waiting to see if India would follow. India turned and gave Mikey the thumbs-up before entering the hallway. Inside, the air smelled of toasted cheese and floor wax. There was a corridor to each side and a staircase straight ahead. Their footsteps echoed eerily in the silence as the woman turned left, past two open classrooms equipped with desks, chairs, blackboards and computers, and entered a third room.

Sunlight blazed across a thick royal blue carpet and lit up the pale silk Chinese rug in its center. India took in the large oak desk and the cabinets filled with silver trophies, but what really amazed her were the photographs.

Every square inch of one wall was taken up with photographs of varying sizes pinned to a massive board. They were all photographs of Aborigines. There were withered old men wearing battered hats, toddlers with enormous eyes and snot-caked noses, men with gray stubble, women with floppy breasts and cheap cotton dresses, children with impudent expressions . . .

Some were life-size glossy black-and-white portraits, beautifully lit, but the remainder were a jumble of Polaroids, color snapshots and passport photographs. Each picture had a sticker showing two names, one white name and one skin name, written in neat black ink.

For a moment India was so stunned she merely gaped at the photographs. "It should be in an art gallery. It's incredibly powerful."

The woman looked surprised. "How clever of you. The Australian National Gallery showed it last year. I hadn't meant it to be a work of art, but a visual document of my work." She looked casually at the wall. "All of these people are part of the stolen generation. Some still haven't met their real parents."

India stepped close to the massive montage and started scanning it. "I don't suppose there's a photo of Bertie Mullett here?"

The woman studied her for a few moments. "I can check for you, if you like."

"That would be great."

The woman moved to her desk and withdrew what looked like a ledger. She opened it and flipped through the pages. She ran a thin finger down a column and shook her head. "I don't have a Bertie Mullett, but there's a Louis Mullett. Apparently he's reunited with his family."

She crossed the room and scanned the bottom right corner of photographs. "Here." She plucked a Polaroid from the wall and passed it to India. A young man, early twenties, with his arm around a girl of about the same age, was grinning into the camera. He had a downy moustache, a scar the shape of a quarter moon at the corner of his mouth and happy eyes. LOUIS MEBULA MULLETT AND JINNY POLLARD.

India closely examined the picture. "I don't suppose you know where I can find him?"

The woman checked her large bound book. "No fixed address. But his girlfriend Jinny has one." She gave India an address in Redfern, Sydney. Then she held out her hand for the photograph and pinned it back on the wall.

"Now it's my turn," India said, and took out the photograph of the four men and the dead shark. "I take it the older man is John Buchanan-Atkins?"

When the woman looked at the photograph, she flinched as though she had been slapped and thrust it back at India.

"Who are you?" she demanded.

"Alice Gibbons," said India. She held out her hand.

The woman ignored it, saying, "That's not your real name."

India let her hand drop to her side. "India Kane," she admitted. "And I am a journalist. But I'm here for my friend Lauren."

"Well, India Kane, would you mind telling me what is going on?"

"My turn to ask a question." She fixed the woman with a hard gaze. "In what capacity was John Buchanan-Atkins involved with the Karamyde—"

"He wasn't." The woman's eyes flashed. "He never had anything to do with it."

Ah. A raw nerve.

"I'm sorry I suggested it."

The woman's features softened. "You weren't to know."

"Would you mind telling me your name?" India ventured.

The woman rearranged her scarf. "Catherine Buchanan-Atkins."

"He was your husband?"

She nodded.

"Would you mind telling me who the three young men in the photograph are?"

There was a long pause while the woman considered her.

"Roland Knox, Carl Roycroft and Gordon Willis," she finally said.

Knox was all too familiar to her while Gordon Willis, India recalled, was the ground-breaking scientist Mikey had spotted at the Institute, driving a Bentley.

"I know Knox and Willis, but who is Roycroft? What does he do?"

The other woman wouldn't meet her eye. "Roycroft's head of ASIO. Australia's secret intelligence organization."

India gulped.

"Where did your friend die?" asked Catherine Buchanan-Atkins.

"In a remote area of northwestern New South Wales. Fifteen kilometers east of a town called Cooinda and thirty-five Ks from the gates of the Karamyde Cosmetic Research Institute."

Catherine Buchanan-Atkins closed her eyes momentarily.

"What is it? What's wrong?"

The woman forced her eyes open. "Was your friend black?" she demanded.

"I'm sorry."

"Was she black?"

"No. She wasn't."

Catherine Buchanan-Atkins seemed to relax at that, so India decided to press the advantage. Keeping her tone soft, she said, "Your husband taught these three men, am I right?"

A nod.

"What did he teach them?" She knew from Mikey, but wanted the woman to tell her.

"History and political science, what else? He was a charismatic teacher, one of the best."

India nodded encouragingly.

"Amusing, quick-witted, able to encourage as well as discipline with a single word. The brightest of students adored him."

"Including Knox, Willis and Roycroft."

"Especially them."

India swallowed the urge to ask why and waited.

"This is all off the record," Catherine continued. "If you print any of it, I'll deny it."

"If that's the way you want it."

"I do. The three boys were exceptionally bright. Separately, they were very intelligent, each destined for a degree and a distinguished life in academia, but together they spelt brilliance. My husband used to say that if ever they got together as adults, working towards the same goal, they could rule the world."

She smiled wryly and went on. "The boys were mad keen on

fishing. John introduced them to the ultimate sport—hunting shark. Tiger, hammerhead or bronze whaler, they didn't care. They'd head out most weekends and come back sunburnt, backs red as brick, and John and I would light a barbecue and they'd feed on their catch." She paused. "He was the only teacher they respected. They worshipped John. Would probably have died for him."

"What went wrong?"

"In 1958 we officially adopted an Aboriginal boy, Robbie. Because of his fair skin, Robbie had been taken from his parents just after he was born. When we met we took an instant shine to him. He was intelligent and had a lovely nature." The woman pressed a hand to her forehead, her face drawn with emotion. "The three boys hated Robbie. Loathed him. They tormented the poor boy like a pack of hyenas. It was *racism*. Pure and simple. Because Robbie was black . . . I was at my wit's end. Even John, normally so calm, grew alarmed. He called them his little Hitlers, but despite his best efforts to guide them . . ."

Her blue eyes intense, the woman leaned forward. "Those boys murdered Robbie."

India stared.

"On a normal day . . . a fishing trip. They'd only dragged the burley a few miles when the boat was surrounded by sharks. John had never seen so many at once. He'd gone to fetch his camera from down below, when he heard a shout. He wasn't supposed to see what happened. The boys still don't know he actually saw them tip Robbie over the side. He lived for about a minute after he hit the water."

"Didn't your husband report the boys to the police?"

The woman rolled her eyes as though impatient at India's stupidity. "You obviously don't grasp the situation. These boys came from wealthy, well-connected families. Families who believed Aborigines were an inferior race, who taught their children the same, who wouldn't care if a dozen indigenous boys had been fed to the sharks that day. The police felt pretty much the same. John wouldn't have had a leg to stand on. They would have destroyed him and me."

India frowned. "Your husband was a man who was scared of the authorities. That was it?" She looked at Catherine Buchanan-Atkins. "Did something else stop him from reporting the boys?"

"What exactly do you mean?"

"There may have been something that made him vulnerable. Something the boys' fathers could have used against him."

"Why should you think that?"

"It's the only explanation I can think of for such a strong and moral man backing off like he did."

Suddenly the woman looked intensely weary. She gave a sigh and walked to the wall of photographs, staring at a picture of a young girl breastfeeding her baby. "Perhaps I should have done something about it years ago. But I didn't."

"About what?"

Catherine Buchanan-Atkins appeared to struggle with herself as she spoke. "John's life was this school. He built it. Made it what it was then, and is now. One of the best in Australia. It was his heart, his soul"—she paused briefly and took a breath—"but he made some mistakes. All to do with scholarship pupils. Children who were incredibly bright, but whose parents couldn't afford even the lowest fees. He ended up terribly frustrated. Thought how unfair it was that a child of low intelligence from a wealthy family could get the best education, where another child, extremely bright, couldn't. So John redressed the balance. Altered the accounts. Nobody knew, not even me for a while, that four scholarship pupils were paying less than fifty dollars a term."

"But the boys' fathers knew about this?"

Catherine pinched the bridge of her nose between her fingers. "Yes."

"So your husband never pressed charges?"

Catherine swung around. "John had no choice. It was either

that or lose the school. If it came out he'd been doctoring the accounts and favoring students, just about every parent would have taken their child away. Those men had him over a barrel. Eventually he came to the decision not to let three boys ruin the education of hundreds of others, present and future. Poor John," she said again. "He saw their picture in the newspaper last month. Said it was one of the most frightening days of his life, seeing them together as grown men. He had a heart attack two days later and now he's dead." She closed her eyes. "I blame those three for his death."

India was finding it difficult to stand still. The adrenaline rush of an explosive story was pulsing through every vein. "Are you sure you won't let me quote you?"

Catherine Buchanan-Atkins reacted violently. "Absolutely not. These men are not to be played with. They're dangerous. Cunning and dangerous. If you expose them in your search to find your friend's killer, all well and good. Otherwise I'll deny we ever met."

Nineteen

IKEY STOOD OPPOSITE THE POST OFFICE IN MARTIN place, waiting. Sam was five minutes late. He scanned the streams of office workers and tourists pouring down the broad pedestrian street, studied people sitting and eating out of takeaway cartons on the post office steps, searching for a man who might be nervous, perhaps checking over his shoulder.

Nobody. Mikey wiped his brow with the back of his hand, glad he was in the shade. If he had to stand in the sun with the humidity levels as they were, he'd melt. He touched the back of his neck, glad to feel the knobbly scabs that had formed. No infection, and no pain aside from when he knocked his bruises. India's first aid had done the trick.

A young couple were snogging on one of the post office's steps, and he watched the varying expressions of people as they passed; some amused, some disapproving. A fit-looking man with a buzz haircut, dressed in dark trousers and white shirt, stood a little distance away, seemingly oblivious to the snoggers. Mikey took in the man's alert stance and followed his gaze.

There. A balding man walking behind a fat woman laden with shopping. Mikey was sure he recognized him, tried to place him. When their eyes met the balding man looked away and slowed as though hesitating. Then he nodded once, and weaved through the crowd to come and stand beside Mikey. His shirt was wet with sweat.

"Nice to see you again," said Mikey. "Shall we take a walk?"

Sam fell into step beside him. Out of habit, Mikey checked the man with the buzz cut and breathed easier when he saw he'd gone.

"You don't remember me, do you?" Sam said.

"Yes, I do. I just can't recall your name."

"It's Stirling." The man's eyes were jumping over the crowd as he spoke. "Rodney Stirling."

"So, Rodney. What have you got for me?"

Rodney fiddled with his tie. "I want to show you something, but I don't want anyone to see us."

"The files, right?"

Rodney nodded.

"At the Australian Medical Association's offices?"

Rodney jerked his head around. His brown eyes were scared. "How did you know?"

"Come on, Rodney. They're just over the bridge in St. Leonard's. It's also where we met, albeit very briefly, during my investigation into your colleague's death. You do remember Alex Thread's murder, don't you?"

Rodney gave a jerky nod. "How could I not?"

They crossed over Pitt Street and to the left of a broad water feature. Mikey relished the brief sensation of damp cool as they passed.

"So, how do you like your promotion?" he asked.

"I wish I'd never got it. Jameson used to be our head of ethics. He died soon after he was transferred. Alex became head of ethics and then he was murdered. Now I'm head I'm utterly terrified."

"Where's the stuff you want to show me?"

"In the office."

"Tell me what it's about."

"I only found them by accident. I was changing a fluorescent strip, the maintenance man always takes so long, and the ceiling panel came loose."

Mikey glanced over his shoulder as Rodney turned left into Castlereagh Street. No buzz cut. Nobody seemed to be following them. Good.

"What's in the files?"

"Personal notes. Technical profiles. From a British defense establishment."

"Porton Down?"

Rodney halted outside a dry cleaner's and looked at Mikey. "I couldn't understand much of it. It's way out of my league. Apart from the DNA profiles and the notes Alex made. Some horrifying accusations. A list of names. Alex highlighted three though, which I suppose are important."

"Which three?"

"Sergeant Patterson, Lauren Kennedy and Peter Ross." He frowned for a second. "Oh, and a solicitor's name. Something Italian. I can't remember it offhand."

"Why don't we just go and get the files, then we'll know what his name is?"

"Christ," said Rodney, and ran a hand over his pate. He looked close to tears. "I've a wife. Two kids. I'm terrified for them, not just me."

"Come on, Rodney. You wouldn't be here if you didn't want to give them to me. Share the burden—"

"Okay, okay. I'll get them. Give me an hour and I'll meet you at Saint Leonard's station."

Mikey's mind flicked to India, who would be waiting for him at the same time. He said, "See you in an hour."

————

He looked across, saw the determination in her face. "You won't
up, will you?"

"Never." India braked smoothly for a red light. She turned her
and fixed him with her deep brown eyes. He felt something
in him as their eyes met, as though something dark inside him
being pulled into the light. He looked at her mouth, the full-
of her lips, the way they were curved in a slight smile, then back
eyes.

he Mack tapped its horn. India turned her head and pushed
ot on the accelerator. The car surged forward and within a few
ds they had caught up with the red Honda. They cruised
h Cremorne and Neutral Bay, with its palm trees dotting the
ents. India remained silent, but she kept flicking her eyes his

"ll right," he said. "If you really want to know I was convicted
ngling a man in custody, late at night, no witnesses."

wasn't sure what he expected, but he felt faintly surprised
he car didn't falter. She drove steadily on, glancing in the
mirror, concentrating on keeping her distance from the
in front. She said nothing. Simply waited for him to con-

e man, Harris, was an ex-employee of Karamyde Cosmetics,
hem for wrongful dismissal. One minute he's taking
le to court, and the next the poor sod's in jail for killing a
, his niece. He yelled his innocence, but we didn't listen.
me, but everyone in the station reckoned he'd been abus-
hild and was guilty of murder."

rned his head aside. The carriageway dipping to the Har-
lge slid across his eyes like a flattened worm.
n someone strangled him. Not me. But I took the rap. I
nded, which meant the investigation into Karamyde Cos-
s suspended too. They removed me without killing me to
entire police department landing on their doorstep. And

Mikey arrived at St. Leonard's and stood at the Pacific Highway entrance half reading his newspaper, half watching pedestrians and
streams of traffic pouring in both directions.

An ambulance, lights whirling and siren blaring, joined the
highway from opposite him and raced past. He watched it, not
thinking anything of it; the Royal North Shore Hospital was just
down the road. The ambulance roared to the next traffic lights and
swung left.

Then his stomach lurched.

The AMA's offices were just around the corner.

Mikey dropped his paper and belted after the ambulance.

————

He rounded the corner into Christie Street. A crowd stood around
the ambulance. Two paramedics were hunched beside a figure
sprawled on the pavement. Mikey pushed his way through the on-
lookers. Stared at the man the paramedics were trying to resuscitate.

His heart stopped for a second. He felt very unsteady.

Oh, God. Rodney.

Mikey swayed slightly. He heard a woman say, "Are you all
right?"

His poor wife, thought Mikey. *His two kids.*

"You know him?" the woman asked.

"What happened?" Mikey said.

"I think he got mugged. That man over there saw it. He's the
one who called the ambulance. He's got a mobile."

Mikey took in the man the woman had pointed out and went
over to him. "What happened?"

"Jesus," the man said, shaking his head. "I can't believe it. In
broad daylight—"

"What happened?" Mikey repeated.

"It happened so fast. I still can't believe it. I was behind him,
heading for the station. He was just walking along with his briefcase

when two blokes coming in the opposite direction jumped him. They snatched his case and he fell to the ground." The man paused. "I thought he'd get up, I really did, but he didn't. He just lay there. I got down to ask him if he was okay, but he didn't move. Then I saw he'd been shot. His shirt . . ." The man gulped. "All bloody. I called triple zero straight off."

"Where did the men go?"

"They were running for the highway. I'd have gone after them but he . . . he needed help."

"You did good."

"Thanks."

In the distance, Mikey heard the mournful wail of a siren and knew the police were on their way. He saw the paramedics rise to their feet. They were shaking their heads. Dully, Mikey walked away. His legs felt as though they'd been filled with wet sand.

———————

"Shit," said India when he told her how Rodney had died. "Shit, shit, shit." Her face had paled but she wasn't panicking. She had a lot of guts, this woman. She'd been waiting for him outside the school gates when he returned and didn't mention he was an hour late, just said, "You look awful. What's happened?"

Now he said, "It looks like it's down to your friend Scotto to deliver."

He watched her buckle her seat belt. They'd agreed that she should drive again while he map read. "That's not until tomorrow," she said. "I tried to ring him, to see if we couldn't make it tonight, but apparently the sod's gone sailing." She tossed the Gregory's Street Directory at him, and turned the ignition. "Where next?"

"North Sydney. I've some cop friends there. I want to see if any of them has an ear to the ground and might have heard something useful to us."

India pushed the stick into drive. They cruis[ed] gates and turned right up the hill, towards Mili[tary]

"I'll drop you off before I head for Cremo[rne] heaps of time. I'm not due to see Dr. Child un[til]

"Remind me," he said.

"Lauren saw her before she went to Cooi[important."

"What sort of doctor?"

"I don't know. But I think she's tied into[thing." He listened as she filled him in on[Atkins' story. "Lauren was searching for Ber[ine only had a record of a Louis Mullett, n[where his girlfriend is though. If we manag[down we might find some answers."

"According to that printout I nicked,[Research Institute."

India turned left onto Military Road[the second lane between a red Honda an[avoid a braking taxi in the bus lane. In t[the Mack flash its lights. India stuck her [waved with her thumb up. *Sensible girl,[to mess with those monsters. He smiled[short blast of its air horn and dropped [

The car thumped steadily on the [queue of cars outside a car wash an[nouncing food, videos and florists.

"Mikey?" India's tone was cautiou[lice anymore?"

"I didn't like the uniform."

"Seriously, what was it? A com[caught taking a bribe?"

He opted for silence.

"Too many unpaid parking tick[

they killed an innocent man and a little girl under the noses of Cooinda PD." He shook his head wearily.

"Bastards," was all she said, after a moment's silence.

"They'll pay," he said tightly.

When India dropped him off her face was troubled. "Take care, okay?"

"You too," he said. "Call me on my mobile later. I don't want to miss out on the oyster festival." He was glad when her expression brightened.

———

Dr. Geraldine Child was very old, amazingly tall—taller than India—wizened with age and appeared constantly alert. Her gaze was hard, blue and bright, her body lean, and she looked exactly how India wanted to look at her age. The room she ushered India into was small and immaculate, crammed to the ceiling with shelves packed with books and journals of various sizes. Each publication and book was, India saw, in alphabetical order by author.

Dr. Child sat on an upright chair behind her desk and smiled warmly at India. "I'm so pleased you came," she said. "Lauren told me all about you."

India found her nerves bristling, her insecurity rising at the woman's intimate tone.

Dr. Child gestured India to sit opposite her.

"How is Lauren? I haven't seen her or heard from her since she left for . . ." The woman paused, studied India's face. "She didn't tell you about me, did she?"

"No. Her husband suggested I come."

"Yes, I've met Scotto." Dr. Child didn't say any more. As she sat there, waiting for India to break the silence, she seemed less open, almost guarded. A truck rumbled past outside and India could hear a baby crying. The smell of freesias—there were a dozen, tall-stemmed, in a vase on the windowsill—fought with a deeper odor of furniture polish.

India took a deep breath. "Lauren's dead. She was murdered nearly three weeks ago. I'm trying to find out why."

"Murdered?" repeated Dr. Child faintly.

"Yes. She was shot."

Dr. Child closed her eyes. Her tall body seemed to shrink. She brought a hand to her eyes. Her lips trembled.

India rigidly suppressed her own urge to cry. "I'm sorry. I wish I could have told you more gently. I didn't know—"

"Of course you didn't." Dr. Child wiped her eyes. "We were quite close, Lauren and I."

"I'm sorry," said India again.

"Me too. I liked her enormously."

They sat in silence for a minute or so, then Dr. Child, more composed, studied India at length. She nodded to herself. "Lauren was a reporter," she said. "Do you think she was killed in the course of an investigation? For *Disclosure* perhaps?"

Surprised, India said, "Yes. I don't suppose you happen to know what she was working on?"

"I'm sorry," said Dr. Child. "She never mentioned her work, but I know how important it was to her."

"How did you know Lauren?"

"We met at a party in Rushcutter's Bay. I'm a genealogist, retired but bored. She wanted a family tree done. We did it together. I enjoyed it immensely. Lauren had an inquiring mind and a wicked sense of humor. She made it great fun. I shall miss her."

India was puzzled. "Why on earth did she want a family tree done?"

"It was a present. A Christmas present for you."

India's eyes widened. Her heart was thumping. "She said she'd found my grandfather but I didn't believe her. Not really. He's been dead for thirty years."

"That's what your mother told you, yes."

"Mum *lied?*"

"Yes. She had her reasons."

"Such as?"

"She didn't want anyone to know her true background."

India looked blank.

"Least of all your father."

"But why—"

"India . . . You don't mind if I call you India?"

She shook her head impatiently. "No. Not at all."

"India, over the past two months we have managed to trace several of your relatives."

India stared at Dr. Child. "*Several?* How many exactly?"

"At the last count, sixty-two."

"Sixty-two!"

"Your family includes a wide network of people, many of whom are only distantly related."

But India's brain was jammed on the number sixty-two and all she could say was, "Bloody hell." Then, after a minute or so, "Who are they? What are they like? Are they—"

"I'm afraid I can't say. Lauren went to meet them for the first time at the beginning of December." Dr. Child put a hand to her mouth. "You don't suppose they had anything to do with her murder, do you?"

"I don't know," said India, distracted. Sixty-two!

There was a lengthy silence, then Dr. Child cleared her throat.

"There's something else that I have to tell you. But I feel we should go into it another day. Give you some time to digest what we've learned so far."

India gave a shaky laugh. "It can't be anything like as dramatic as discovering I've so many relatives!"

"Yes, well, perhaps you're right."

India took in Dr. Child's tension, the way the lines had deepened on her face.

"It can't be that bad," India said.

Dr. Child looked away. "Will you be in Sydney for a while? Perhaps you could come back next week."

India thought of Mikey, then Scotto, and the unfolding story of Karamyde Cosmetics. "I'm not sure where I'll be tomorrow, let alone in a week."

"Oh dear. I rather hoped . . ."

"What's wrong?"

"Well, what I have to tell you could be somewhat emotionally devastating."

"It's that serious?"

Dr. Child shifted her fragile weight and gripped the edges of her desk as though steeling herself for a natural disaster. "Lauren was also searching for your brother."

"My *what?*"

Dr. Child said, "Toby was born on December the fifteenth—"

"And two days later he died in hospital." India was surprised at how belligerent she sounded.

"That's what your parents told you."

India felt as though her brain was staring to seize up. "Are you telling me Toby's *alive?*"

"As far as we know, yes. Unfortunately we're having trouble tracing him. Your mother gave him to your grandmother Rose, to look after, but . . ." She paused uncomfortably. "Sadly Rose lost him. He had a progression of foster homes, five in four years, I believe. His last caseworker reported that he misbehaved continually. Silly pranks . . . he seemed to like scaring people. For example, he'd catch spiders and let them loose at inappropriate times. Toby was ejected from his last home at the age of eight. We lost track of him then." Easing her frail body from the chair, Dr. Child walked around the desk and into the living room next door. She returned with a bottle of red wine, a corkscrew and two glasses. "Be a dear and open it for me."

India was only too glad. She'd never needed a drink so badly. She drank her glass of wine in three steady gulps.

"So," said Dr. Child. "You have a whole new family."

India poured herself another glass, downed it and topped it up, then sat there twirling her wineglass slowly between her thumb and forefinger. She was aware of the stem of crystal but she felt suspended and detached, as though she were aboard a space shuttle drifting in eternal weightlessness above the earth. "Where are they?" she asked quietly.

"They come from an outback town in northwest New South Wales. Cooinda."

"I've been in Cooinda for the past fortnight," she said faintly. "There was one family of Tremains in the phone book. They're from New Zealand. I couldn't find any more."

Dr. Child hesitated, but only for a second. "Your mother lied about her maiden name. It wasn't Tremain. It was Mullett."

India gazed motionless at Dr. Child, who continued, "In October, Lauren undertook some investigative work in Cooinda and discovered your mother had lied about her maiden name. Your mother, Mary, was the second daughter of Bertie Mullett and Rose Dundas. When she was in her teens, Mary turned her back on her family and moved to Sydney, where she married your father."

"I don't believe this," India said.

"Have you heard of the stolen generation?"

India managed a nod.

"I have a photograph of your grandfather, sent to us by Link-Up. Link-Up provides family tracing, reunion and support for forcibly removed children and their families." Dr. Child paused to let this sink in. "Would you like to see what your grandfather looks like?"

"He's black," said India faintly. "Bertie Mullett is black."

"Yes, he is Aboriginal."

"Lauren was searching for Bertie when she was murdered."

"She was also searching for Toby. Because he is, unfortunately, one of the stolen generation. Unlike you and Mary, he was born very dark, but his skin lightened after the first year . . ."

Suddenly the reason why her father had gone berserk that long-ago Christmas became clear to India; it wasn't a case of being overwhelmed by grief at Toby's death, it was because his son was *black*.

TWENTY

INDIA LAY IN THE DOUBLE BED IN DR. CHILD'S SPARE ROOM. She couldn't sleep. She couldn't keep her eyes closed for more than a few seconds at a time. The same thought bounced around her head like a superball and wouldn't let her rest.

I'm black.

Well, quarter-black. But it explained why she had skin the color of caramel, and hair that was thick and springy and black as jet. Little questions she'd had all her life were beginning to be answered: why she rarely burned in the sun, why her limbs were so straight and long.

She thought of the chart Dr. Child had showed her, and all those names—her relatives. Rose Dundas, daughter of a sheep farmer, married Bertie Mullett in 1955. They had six children, the second being India's mother, Mary, who left Cooinda and married a policeman. Mary eventually settled in Sydney's northern suburb of Dee Why. Bertie's eldest son, Jimmy, was born in 1957, married Nellie and had three children: Victor, Clive, and Rhona. Rhona married a man called Greg Cooper and they had five children: Albert, Bobby, Ray, Hannah, and Rosie. Clive was single but had a daughter called Polly. Victor married Lizzie and had two children: Louis and Clara.

Polly.

India slid out of bed and padded downstairs. Streetlights laid orange marks across the kitchen table, the cool blue floor tiles. The big station clock above the cooker gave the time as a quarter to three. She closed the door, turned on the light. Squinted as her eyes adjusted. She unrolled the chart Geraldine had shown her earlier, using salt and pepper shakers, a packet of muesli and a bag of flour to secure it. Wonderingly, she ran a palm over the paper. Dr. Child had told her Lauren had taken a copy to Cooinda. Planned to wrap it in red paper, with a gold-red blow. My relatives, sixty-two of them. My Christmas present from Lauren.

She gazed at the name Polly Cooper for a long time. Was this distant cousin the Polly she knew? She couldn't remember Polly's surname. Could it be Cooper?

You betcha.

Lauren?

Who the hell else would it be?

I'm half-black, you know. Isn't that weird?

Not half as weird as some folk here, believe you me. How're things going? Caught the guy who did it yet?

I'm working on it.

Well, get your bum in gear, babe, I want you to chew ass.

Lauren, is Polly a blood relative?

Who gives a monkey's? Either you like the girl or you don't.

I like her, Lauren. I like her a lot.

Then you're her relative. Blood doesn't mean shit. Remember that, hon, when the time comes.

India jerked upright, unsure if she had been dreaming.

Holy shit. The superball bounced back. *I'm black.*

————

The following morning she and Mikey were stuck in traffic at Bondi Junction. The road was being dug up and had caused a traffic jam half a kilometer long. Mikey had stayed the night with an old cop friend of his at the southern end of Bondi and she'd collected him, as agreed, at eight o'clock. They'd had croissants and coffee in the Lamrock cafe overlooking the beach, which India had thought was fabulous and said so.

"But it's crap," Mikey had said, expression bewildered. "It's full of fast-food outlets and money-scrimping backpackers and over-priced apartments—"

"It's so big!" she exclaimed. "Look at all that space and sky, right in the center of a major city. And look at the surf!"

Mikey had sent the breakers a disparaging look. "Small ba-nanas."

"Regular small bananas," she said. "Look at the hordes of surfers out there."

"The only good thing about this place is its shark attacks."

She sent him an alarmed look.

He tapped the cocktail list. "Shark Attack. Best Bloody Mary you'll find anywhere in the world."

Now India wished she were still in the cool of that cafe. The Ford's air-conditioning had packed up and she was uncomfortably sticky in the heat. *Surely,* she thought, *if I'm Aboriginal, I should like this heat. Shouldn't I?*

"India, what is it?"

"What's what?"

"You suddenly looked . . . I don't know, out of sorts. Like you don't feel well."

She squirmed in her seat. The temporary lights changed to amber, then green. The queue of cars and trucks began to move.

"Mikey," India began cautiously, "you know Jed's a lost child . . . Well, he joked about my skin. The color of it. How I could be an Aborigine."

Mikey looked blank for a second, then frowned. "I bet he didn't realize you'd be insulted. He'd have been teasing."

"I wasn't insulted," India said indignantly.

"So what's your problem then?"

"Listen," she said fretfully. "You know I saw Dr. Child yesterday. Well, she's a genealogist—"

"Ah, I see." Mikey engaged a gear, inched forward. "Does this mean that India Kane is Lady Kane of the Round Table, or the garter . . . which is it?"

"Neither." Something in her voice silenced him with that one word.

There was a long pause.

Her heart was beating a little faster, and she felt ridiculously nervous. "My name is Mullett," she finally said, and in a fit of insanity wanted to add: "India Mullett" in a James Bond tone.

For a second Mikey's foot came off the accelerator and the car slowed. The vehicle behind blasted its horn.

"Bertie Mullett is my grandfather."

Mikey went completely silent. He pressed on, past the traffic lights and down Oxford Street. Turned right into the heart of the chic suburb of Paddington and drove past its antique and homeware shops, boutiques, cafes, bars and pubs. They were in Hargrave Street when suddenly he took a deep breath and started laughing.

It was the last thing she expected. "Look, I'm sorry, but I honestly don't see the funny side of it."

"Oh . . . oh, God, I'm an idiot!" He clapped a hand to his forehead. "I mean, everyone knows Abos love hanging around the bush at night with no clothes on! I should have guessed then!" He gave her a look he'd give Polly; one of exasperated affection. She wasn't sure whether she welcomed it or not.

He leaned across and patted her knee. "Black and white or pink or purple, you're simply the person you are, and don't forget that."

Surprised, she said, "Thanks," and watched him calmly run a red light before diving left along New South Head Road and then right toward Darling Point. He pulled up outside a neat block of apartments overlooking the harbor. "I'll see you at one," he said, leaving the engine running as he got out. "If I don't turn up, report me missing, presumed garrotted."

She felt the horror show in her face. "I thought you were seeing Rodney's wife?"

Mikey grinned. "I am. But it sure got a reaction from you."

She stuck out her tongue at him before she drove away.

———————

India parked the car right outside the address Catherine Buchanan-Atkins had given her where she could keep an eye on it. From the looks of this neighborhood it wouldn't be wise to leave a vehicle unattended.

She rang the bell of a dilapidated semidetached house and stepped back. A dog started barking inside, then the door was flung open.

"What?" demanded an angry-looking woman of about India's age and height. She had bloodshot eyes and reeked of beer.

India's smile evaporated.

"I'm looking for Jinny. Louis Mullett's girlfriend."

"She scarpered ages back."

"What about Louis, he still around?"

"He buggered off months ago. She wouldn't stop her bloody crying. Went looking for him at Central, haven't seen her since. Glad she left, miserable cow."

"Are any of their relatives around? Any other Mulletts?"

The woman belched, scratched her belly. "Whole bunch scarpered together. Bought themselves a property out bush. Hadn't the money to pay for it, mind, but that didn't seem to bother them. Louis spoke about some weird job getting paid for taking drugs."

"Where's the property they bought?"

"Middle of bloody nowhere. Near Biloella." She suddenly looked suspicious. "Whatcha want to know for?"

"I'm a relative of theirs—"

The woman slammed the door in India's face.

India stood looking at the doorbell. The dog continued to bark. A truck roared past, belching blue smoke. India worked up her nerve and raised a finger, let it hover over the bell.

She jumped when the door was flung open and a handful of mail was thrust at her. "Jinny's. You're a relly of hers, you can have 'em." The door slammed shut again.

———

India read the letters as she walked. Three were from a school friend of Jinny's, the rest from Louis. They were love letters. Short, painstakingly written in capitals, and heartrending in their simplicity, they spanned a period of two years. The most recent was dated the seventh of July this year. It appeared to be the last.

Not gone long. Back quick. Wish words could tell what in my head. My body. Want you. Love you. Smell you.

None of them gave any indication Louis was disenchanted with his lover in any way. Pocketing the letters, India continued walking to Central Station.

———

It took her over an hour of scouting the station and the surrounding area, asking questions, before she hit on success. A taxi driver remembered seeing a dozen or so Aborigines hanging about on the steps of the station around July-August time, and being surprised when a new-looking white transit van had collected them. He'd expected them to be moved on by the police, not chauffeur-driven by a college-looking white bloke.

The taxi driver talked to his mates, who had by now gathered around India like bees to a honey pot, and she gleaned the information that small groups of Aborigines used to gather outside the station fairly regularly.

No, they hadn't seen any lately.

Yeah, mostly last year. Every two months or so, there'd be a bunch of them hanging about.

Yeah, a van usually picked 'em up. Yeah, reckon the last lot would've been November time. Early November, mind. Maybe even late October.

Nah, wouldn't know the rego of the van. It was white though, with a crumpled wing on the driver's side.

India thanked them, walked away. Her throat felt tight, her eyes scratchy as she consolidated what she'd learned. The Mulletts had answered a printed advertisement, gone to Central Station as arranged by the advertiser, climbed aboard a white transit van and vanished. Her family. Vanished.

India headed towards the Opera House. Circular Quay was crowded with tourists arriving off the ferries, and already people were staking their claim for the best vantage points to view the fireworks later on. Restlessly, she waited outside the Sydney Cove Oyster Bar, shaded by palms and white umbrellas. Tall purple and yellow flags fluttered in a slight breeze.

She scanned the street. A black Ford with tinted windows nudged its way through the crowds and around litter bins and benches. Must be a VIP, she thought, or an unmarked cop car. All traffic had been discouraged from entering the city since first thing that morning and the streets, although full of people, were virtually empty of vehicles.

India noticed a swatch of sun-bleached hair through the crowd and felt an immediate fizz of excitement, but it wasn't Scotto. Shifting from foot to foot, she tried to quell her agitation.

"You look like a kid." She heard Mikey's voice behind her. "Itchy with excitement."

"He's late," she said.

"I am too."

People were pouring past her. India was craning over the mob, looking for blond heads. Out of the corner of her eye she caught the black Ford sliding closer and was about to check it out when, striding into view, came Scotto.

He had lost weight and his jeans hung loosely on his hips. His face was longer than she remembered. He carried a briefcase in one hand and his expression was withdrawn. His eyes flicked across to the oyster bar, over India. Then they clicked back, and he looked straight at her. He smiled. A broad wide smile of delight that banished his earlier glum expression and filled his face with warmth.

India plunged into the crowd.

"Scotto!" she yelled.

He started for her. Panting with excitement, she dodged and skidded around the mass moving relentlessly towards the Opera House. Bouncing up, she could see Scotto being drawn to her, and she grinned. Then she saw a black shape pull up just behind him. She felt the first inkling of something wrong.

Two men piled out of the Ford, broke into a run. Straight for Scotto.

He started opening his arms to embrace her.

India saw, without quite believing it, both men lunge at Scotto and snatch him away.

For a second, she lost her momentum in shock. The two men were on either side of him, had grabbed his briefcase and pinned his hands high between his shoulders . . . They were hauling him away.

Instinct took over: India simply put her head down and charged for him. People were yelling in outrage, sprawling behind her, some on their knees. She ripped through the crowd, single-minded, unthinking. Someone lashed out at her and she found herself spinning around, her right arm in a grip like iron. A fist landed deep in her belly. She went down like a stone.

Immediately a crowd formed around her.

"Asthma, my wife suffers from asthma," a man was saying as he helped her to her feet, hands around her arms like steel cuffs.

She was bent double. She fought to breathe, to form a word.

"India!" Mikey shouted.

"Deal with him," the man snapped to his sidekick, who spun aside and vanished into the crowd.

"India!" Mikey yelled again.

"Does she need Ventalin?" a woman said helpfully. "I've some in my bag."

"No, no. She'll be right. My car's just here. Our friends will help. She's fine, thank you."

She was choking, gasping. Tears streamed down her face. The crowd parted as she was half-dragged, half-carried towards the black Ford. She tried to struggle but they simply hoisted her off the ground so her feet swung free. The Ford lurched alongside her, its rear door opening.

Her breathing suddenly eased. India filled her lungs.

Her scream split the air. "Mikey!"

People stopped to stare.

She was bucking and squirming furiously, her legs jerking as she took another breath, yelled, "Mikey!" but a hand clapped over her mouth, another on top of her head, and she found herself bundled into the back of the Ford and the door slammed shut behind her.

———————

Immediately the car moved forward. The interior was black leather and India could smell pine air freshener and stale cigarettes. Scotto lay slumped unconscious, half on the seat, half on the floor. There were two men in front, both about thirty, both in dark trousers and jackets. One held a gun in his hand, pointed at her.

"You try anything, I shoot you."

She was panting jerkily, her breath rasping in her throat.

The car did a slow three-point turn and eased through the

crowds, heading back to the city. For a second the man glanced away and looked forward.

India flipped off the door lock with her right hand, yanked back the door handle with her left and shoved with all her might.

Nothing happened.

She shoved again. The man snapped his head around.

She sat there, hands on the door, frozen.

They stared at each other, immobile, and all she could think was that he had missed a patch of stubble, the size of a five-pence piece, shaving that morning.

"Didn't you hear what I said?"

She didn't think he'd shoot her, but she couldn't be certain. So she sat there, quite still, willing him to be lenient.

The seconds ticked by. When the journey had been going on for some time, the man moved the pistol away from her. India brought her hands onto her lap. Began breathing normally again.

———

Mikey had seen the man come for him and immediately spun away for Phillip Street. He saw the black Ford start its three-point turn and pelted for the Intercontinental Hotel and the taxi stand outside, praying there'd be one, that they weren't all taken . . .

He ran up the hill. Two taxis, thank God.

He raced to the first, a blue Holden, and yanked open the driver's door.

"What the—"

"Sorry, mate," Mikey said, dragging the man out and shoving him into the street. He jumped into the cab, locked the door, turned the ignition key.

The cab driver was yelling at him, banging on the door.

Mikey slammed the car into gear and roared off with a squeal of rubber.

The car was cruising south. They'd passed Haymarket and were on South Dowling Street, heading towards the airport.

India tried to work out why she was there, why they'd grabbed Scotto too . . . and a sinking feeling of dread settled in her stomach. There had been no blindfolds. No concern about hiding the kidnappers' faces, or their route. This was bad news. Very bad news.

When they reached Mascot, the car pulled off the expressway and turned right. After a set of traffic lights it swung suddenly to the left and bumped onto an ill-kempt road lined with warehouses. After a while it slowed, and turned into a huge courtyard that spread over several acres. The whole place was empty. A single dusty gum tree stood like a sentinel beside a rusting gate hanging from one hinge. The building ahead was white, with great cracks running down its walls. The car drew to a stop outside a metal door. The driver switched off the ignition. Everything was silent, aside from the faint hum of traffic speeding down South Cross Drive.

There was a rattle from the warehouse and the metal door opened. Two more men appeared, walked to the car. One had a buzz haircut, the other short curly brown hair.

"India." Scotto drew the word out slowly, as though he were drunk.

Instantly the gun trained around. "Shut up," the man said tightly.

Scotto acted as if he hadn't heard. "Indi, darling, I've missed you. Terribly."

Holding the gunman's eyes, she reached across and gripped Scotto's hand. It was surprisingly warm, and when his fingers clenched around hers with a remarkable strength, she had to concentrate on keeping her expression bland. The gunman didn't notice, however; he was watching the two men approaching. But the gun never wavered.

"Who are these apes?" Scotto said, then as the gunman swung around, "Shit, my head hurts."

There was the all-around click of car doors unlocking, the clunk as they opened, and then the instant heat as the humidity rushed in and blanketed the air-conditioning.

"He's awake," said the gunman, jerking his pistol at Scotto.

"Good," said one of the men outside, and yanked a protesting Scotto through the door by his hair and an elbow. "I didn't fancy carrying the bastard."

India found herself being hauled out of the car and marched into the warehouse behind Scotto, who was still protesting about his head, how it hurt and wouldn't they give him a break?

Inside, the warehouse was enormous. There was a stack of packing crates to her left, and on the right, just yards away, a silver Mercedes four-wheel-drive. Scotto's briefcase was put next to the Merc, then he was handcuffed with what looked like police-issue cuffs and led towards the crates, where they tethered his feet together. India was guided to stand in front of the four-wheel-drive car. Two men took up position behind her. She felt something small and hard pressed into the small of her back. She had no doubt it was the barrel of a pistol.

"Come on, guys," Scotto said, loudly aggrieved. "Let us in on the secret, will you? What's going on here, huh?"

There was the sound of a car door being opened and shut. "Very good, Mr. Kennedy. Acting as if you haven't a clue. If I didn't know better I could even fall for it myself."

India recognized the voice. Felt sick.

Roland Knox.

He was dressed as he'd been when she met him at the Research Institute, in a city suit. Dark gray, snowy white shirt, and a vivid blue tie that paled his eyes to water.

Scotto looked bewildered. "What the hell is going on here?"

"I'm fed up with him playing the whingeing innocent," said Knox. "Break a finger."

"Which one, sir?"

"I don't give a damn," Knox snapped. "Just do it."

He stepped forward, quite close to India. He was watching her with a strange intensity.

She felt a moment of complete disbelief as two men approached Scotto. He jerked wildly as one man pinned him against the wall, another gripping his handcuffed wrists.

Her eyes opened wide in shock, wider than they'd ever been, as the man holding Scotto's wrists gripped the little finger of his right hand, bent it back. The snap of bone when it came had a slightly succulent popping sound, like a chicken drumstick being pulled from the raw flesh of torso. Scotto paused in his fight and turned pale.

A wave of dizzy nausea washed over her. The other two men were behind her, one on each side. She could hear their breathing they were so close, too close for her to make a run for it.

"Christ," said Scotto weakly. "Christ. Oh, Christ." He cradled his hands to his chest. He was deathly white.

Knox clicked his fingers at one of the men behind her. "The briefcase," he said. "Open it and bring it here."

The man in question did as commanded and held Scotto's brief-case open in front of Knox, as though he were offering him a giant box of cigars. Knox glanced inside. His voice was full of satisfaction as he held up a tattered green folder stuffed with papers and waved it at Scotto, then dropped it back inside. "Just as I thought," he said, and waved the man away. Knox gave Scotto a nasty smile. "You took it sailing with you, didn't you, Mr. Kennedy? I respect your caution. Wary of sharing its contents with the average Australian family, no doubt."

Scotto jerked his head up as though electrified, and when he spoke his voice was steady and strong. In ringing tones he said,

"Indi, if you don't remember anything else, remember it's the *water.* It's the WATER—"

"Shut up!" snapped Knox. He made a sharp gesture to the men holding Scotto. "Keep him quiet. Yank that finger of his, break another bone, I don't care."

Knox came to India, looked at her. She knew he hated his lack of height, loathed looking up at her, and she made sure her chin was well tucked in as she peered down, so that from his position her nose would seem elongated and her attitude haughty.

"I want to know everything," he said. "I want to know how you set up that Abo cop to take the fall. I want to know about Rodney Stirling. I want to know who you've talked to, who you've seen . . . I want to know about every minute of every day since we last met."

Distantly she registered the fact: *Whitelaw was innocent.*

"Start talking, Miss Kane."

India didn't say anything. Where would it get her? Especially with Scotto guarded by two men, and her with a gun in her back. So she stood there without moving, and thought about life and Scotto and sunshine and how Mikey had looked when he was laughing about her being an Aborigine.

"You think you're so tough, don't you?" said Knox. "Tough as nails. Not scared at all."

She held his gaze, didn't reply.

"How about Mr. Kennedy here? You're scared for him, aren't you?"

Involuntarily, India's head jerked.

Knox came close to her, so close she could smell his aftershave: a hint of citrus, sharp, but not unpleasant.

"I want to know why the AMA started investigating my business," he said.

India stared at him. A feeling of dread started in her lower belly, moved to her heart.

"Answer me," he said.

She didn't move, not a centimeter.

Knox clicked his fingers at the man who had brought him the briefcase. He came forward and gave him a small handgun. Knox quickly pulled back the slide and a bullet slipped into the chamber. Then he gave a nod to the two men holding Scotto, and said, "Hold him down."

India made to go to Scotto but the man behind her grabbed her hair and twisted it around his hand and pulled from behind in a grip that made her eyes water.

Like an animal who senses its doom, Scotto struggled the instant he felt their hands on him. The man who'd given Knox the pistol went across and helped. It took three men to subdue Scotto and even then he was bucking and squirming furiously as Knox approached, gun held at the ground.

"No!" Scotto shouted. His limbs were flailing, and spittle flew from his mouth. "Don't! Please, don't!"

India made a lunge towards Scotto but her head was jerked backwards so hard she thought her hair would come out at the roots.

Roland Knox stepped towards Scotto and swung his arm so that the black barrel was pressed against Scotto's left kneecap. Scotto was shouting, but India was deathly quiet. A wave of horror drenched her from head to toe.

Knox turned to her, and smiled. He said, "You're not enjoying this, are you, Miss Kane?"

Then he pulled the trigger.

———————

Scotto screamed incoherently for twenty-five seconds before he lost consciousness. India knew she would hear those screams in her cold dawn dreams until the day she died. She could see blood soaking his jeans like red ink spilled onto blotting paper. She could smell burnt powder and the acrid stench of her own fear. Her ears were ringing from the gunshot and her head was beginning to throb; the grip on her hair had tightened unbearably.

Roland Knox came and stood in front of her and lowered the pistol until it was pointed at her stomach.

India jerked against the man behind her, tried to twist away from Knox, then lashed out with her feet in panic, a strangled whimper bubbling in her throat.

"Hold her still."

Frantically she kicked out at the men as they neared, but they were too strong and she ended up with two of them restraining her legs and arms.

"Pull up her shirt," he said, "and undo her jeans."

The man holding her hair started to relax his grip but Knox said, "Not you, you idiot. Aikin."

The fourth man jumped to do his bidding. Knox slowly brought the barrel to the tender skin of her lower belly and stroked it. She could feel her muscles leap and contract against the metallic caress and tried to drop to her knees, twist away, but the man behind held her head relentlessly. Knox watched her closely, his face intent.

He raised the pistol.

Fear liquidized her insides. It swept through every vein, every nerve, made her whimper in every cell of her body. She tried not to let her fear show, holding Knox's gaze with her own without blinking, but she couldn't stop the trickle of urine that escaped and wet her pants, seeped down her jeans.

His voice was calm, serene, almost as though he were reassuring or comforting her. "As you can see, I can demolish your intestines if I choose. Turn your stomach, your bladder and your bowel into juice. I doubt if you'll ever be able to have children." He stroked the hard gunmetal in a circle around her belly button. "What would you do to prevent that happening?"

India opened her mouth. Worked her tongue drily. Choked out, "Anything."

"How very accommodating of you. Does this mean you will tell me who tipped off the AMA and set you on my trail?"

She closed her eyes and immediately felt the gun barrel jab hard into her belly.

"Open your eyes and answer me."

Her voice was hoarse. "Yes."

He put his head on one side and studied her, the sweat trickling down her forehead, her cheeks. "So start, Miss Kane. Go ahead. Start talking."

There was a long silence while he contemplated India and India hung from the trap of her hair, shaking and trembling and thinking: *Please, God, let me live, don't let him pull the trigger, don't, please don't.* Finally, he took the pistol away from her stomach and pushed it against her right kneecap.

"This is going to hurt, Miss Kane."

TWENTY-ONE

NDIA MADE A FINAL, WILD STRUGGLE, URGENTLY TRYING TO free herself.

"Keep her still!" snapped Knox.

Every muscle, every nerve was flooded with adrenaline as she fought, and she was kicking and bucking and yelling when somebody screamed: *"Police!"*

Knox immediately trained his pistol towards the sound.

The same voice yelled: *"Drop your weapons or I'll shoot!"*

Nobody moved.

A single gunshot split the air. Spat cement chips to India's left.

Knox fired twice and ran.

The three men dropped India and scattered behind the Mercedes.

She sagged there for a second, bewildered.

A bullet whacked into the Mercedes. Another whizzed past her. A surge of adrenaline reenergized her. She twisted sideways and ran in the opposite direction, for the door, for freedom. She heard the blast of guns. Men were shouting behind her. A bullet struck a shipping crate just ahead. India stretched her legs. More bullets struck the crates, splintering wood. She swung left.

"India!" a man yelled ahead of her. "I'm here!" Mikey's voice was hoarse.

A bullet nicked her shirt. Another zinged past her ear.

Gunshots roared in the warehouse.

"Mikey!" India screamed.

"Stay down!" he yelled.

India dropped to her hands and knees, scurried for him.

"Are you okay?"

"Yes." She hastily did up her jeans.

"Let's go." He grabbed her wrist. "I'll come back for Scotto. Hurry!" He pulled her after him. She strained to keep up. Her ears, deafened by the gunshots, were ringing and, in confusion, it took her a moment to realize they were outside.

Bullets struck the ground. The shots continued from behind them.

Without warning Mikey stumbled. Dropped her wrist. Sprawled facedown. A bullet parted the air by her head. She barely paused. Kept sprinting across the forecourt. *Have to reach the road. Have to get out of here. Have to run. Run, run, run.*

The next thing she realized, she was running along Botany Road, traffic was lumbering along, and then she was slowing, putting her hand out, walking, gasping.

The truck that stopped was headed for Newcastle but she didn't care.

————

Mikey scrambled to his feet. He saw India race through the court-yard gates and disappear. He ran for the Holden taxi, jumped in and locked the doors. He started the engine. He became aware that the gunshots hadn't stopped.

Who was shooting who?

Mikey drove onto the street, took the next left and tucked the taxi behind a truck. Heart thumping, he watched the street through his wing mirror.

Three minutes later a silver Mercedes M-Class shot past, followed by the black Ford.

A minute later, a black BMW cruised by. OED 128. India's Beemer. He cursed. He still hadn't found out who owned the sodding thing. The Panama connection had led nowhere.

He waited another couple of minutes then started the car and sped back to the warehouse. Before he went to Scotto, he quickly checked the surrounding area. Nobody. Inside the warehouse it was empty, aside from Scotto's still form.

He was glad Scotto was still unconscious. As carefully as he could, Mikey untied the ropes around Scotto's feet. There wasn't much he could do about the handcuffs. He had to get Scotto to a hospital pronto. His heart was still banging away. He picked up Scotto. Adrenaline helped. Scotto wasn't exactly a featherweight. Mikey eased him onto the backseat of the cab and headed for the Prince of Wales Hospital.

———

The truck dropped India at North Sydney, where she took a taxi to Manly, the easiest place she could think to hide. She tried five B&Bs and three hotels without luck. The fourth hotel was on North Steyne and had a double room with ocean view at an exorbitant price. She didn't care about the expense, she was lucky to take a last-minute cancellation; every room was fully booked for the New Year celebrations. India paid cash, glad she'd barely spent any since her last withdrawal. She didn't want Knox to track down her credit card.

She was so numbed, so traumatized, that she wouldn't have believed she could feel any emotion, but when she let herself inside the room, she began to shake from head to foot.

She closed the door and locked it. She fumbled her way into the bathroom and vomited. She bent over the loo and retched over and over again as if she could rid herself of her experience in the warehouse. She could hear Scotto's screams, smell the cordite, see his blood. Every detail was imprinted on her senses whether her eyes were open or closed.

She dashed water over her face and neck, cupping some and rinsing her mouth to ease the acid burning in her throat. She grabbed a towel off the floor and wiped her face, let the towel fall in the sink. At that point she glanced in the mirror.

The years drained away.

She was kneeling on the kitchen floor, trying to help Lauren.

She was walking out of *The Courier*'s office without a backward glance. She was stubbornly refusing to go to Sydney to see Lauren. She was watching her own sanctimonious face as she condemned Whitelaw's guilt before stalking into the street and turning her back on Cooinda. She was running away from Mikey sprawled outside the warehouse, and was deep in the heart of her worst memories. She saw herself clearly, stripped of self-regard, vanity and ego. The very foundations of her being were crumbling and toppling around her. She had thought she had outrun the person she used to be. She'd believed she had outrun the past, but she was wrong. It had followed her all the way here.

————

She was six years old. She was at the rude little house in Dee Why with her mother. Her mother had returned from the hospital and was crying for Toby, who had died that morning. Her father came home and when he saw her weeping he started pushing her around the kitchen, slapping her hard, and India knew he was going to hurt her really badly this time, that he was stoking his rage, and her mother was sobbing and all the time India was shivering, huddled in the corner.

"You bitch!" he kept yelling. "My God, I'll kill you, you lying bitch!" And his hands clenched and he was punching her and she was bleeding from her nose and mouth and India just huddled there, so frightened, so tiny against his huge bulk and his burning rage she couldn't move, couldn't help her mother, and suddenly Lauren was there and she was shouting, yelling at him to stop or she'd get her parents, fetch the police, anyone, if he didn't stop.

He stopped. He came to Lauren and grabbed her, and she was trying to fight him but she was so skinny and small that he simply shrugged her off and handcuffed her to the radiator, and India was crawling to Lauren, desperate to reach her, when he suddenly turned and looked at her.

His face was red and his mouth caked with spittle and he had blood on his fists and on his shirt. Holding her eyes, he reached for the baseball bat beneath the table and took a step towards her and she screamed.

He came for her.

India ran. She catapulted out of the house, running as fast as she could, blindly, without any plan. She ran on bitumen, on grass, sand, gravel, her bare feet pounding, and she couldn't stop, couldn't stop running. When at last her legs gave way, she was on a beach and she was crawling on her hands and knees, her feet raw and bleeding, her lungs and heart like razor blades, but she couldn't stem the urge to keep running . . .

It wasn't until dawn the next day that she returned to the house, quaking and weeping with terror, to find her father gone, her mother unconscious, and Lauren still handcuffed to the radiator, but with both arms broken.

She had left her friend like that all night.

She was so ashamed.

———

The phone was ringing and she was in Sydney, had never left Sydney. She began to cry, not as she had before, quietly and in control, but great racking shouts that tore her throat and convulsed her shoulders and lungs. Helplessly she fumbled for the towel, tried to muffle her roars. She found herself stumbling backwards and clutching at something, and she grabbed at it but there was nothing there and she began to fall, and saw Lauren as clear as day.

Hon, you'd better get a grip, or you'll be in serious trouble.

Scorching pain licked at her. Her closest friend was dead. Dead, dead, *dead.* And by abandoning Scotto and Mikey she felt as though she had abandoned Lauren all over again.

———————

An hour later she still couldn't get herself under control. Clumsily, unable to see properly, she folded the towel and hung it neatly as she could on the rail, and because she didn't know what else to do she went out onto the balcony overlooking Manly Beach, and leaned her head on her arms and wept. After a while, she sank onto one of the chairs, exhausted, her eyes puffed almost shut and her mouth was so distorted and swollen it felt like a pig's snout.

She felt hollow and drained. She sat there and stared unseeingly at the surfers rising and falling on the deep blue of the Pacific Ocean. Everything looked exactly the same as it had all those years ago. Same pine trees, same angled parking, same blue ocean rimmed with booming surf. Nothing had changed, not even herself. She was the coward she always had been.

India sat there for two hours, watching the surfers, and only went inside to use the bathroom, or drink some water. She couldn't think about Jeremy Whitelaw sitting in jail for something he hadn't done. She couldn't think about anything connected with Cooinda; Polly or Albert or Mikey.

At five-thirty that afternoon, she felt no better. She didn't know what to do. She didn't want to leave the hotel. She wanted only to stay here in retreat, hiding. She watched a 747 crossing the sky and thought about flying to London, China or Brazil. She pictured herself in Rio de Janeiro, then Beijing, and came to the miserable realization that wherever she went, inside she would still be the same person.

She watched the surfers in the late gold haze of afternoon then went inside and made some coffee, but didn't drink it. She took the plastic wrapper off a biscuit, then threw it in the bin. She needed something to occupy her, something to take her mind outside itself and give it a rest from this continual torture.

She left her room and went in search of a swimsuit.

————

The sea was cold, colder than she'd expected, and the waves quite big, about six feet. India ducked through each as they reared above her, plumes spraying in the breeze, and snorted salt water from her nose when she broke through on the other side. It didn't take long to get past the breakers, and after half an hour or so she trod water and looked back.

The beach was littered with glistening bodies sprawled on multi-colored towels, some beneath umbrellas, some not. There was a volleyball game going on, and a crowd of people carrying Eskis and picnic hampers poured down the central steps.

India turned seawards and struck out once more in a strong, steady breaststroke. Her mind was calm, absorbed with nothing but the motion of swimming, the chop of the water, the sting of salt on her mouth and in her eyes. After an hour she began to tire, so she floated on her back for a while, staring up at the hazy overcast sky and the seagulls with their sharp-cut wings shaped like boomerangs. Then the emotional agony returned, so she swam some more, until she tried again. She floated awkwardly this time, her legs seeming to drag her down, and she wasn't sure if she wanted to keep swimming right now, but it felt so good being out there that she rolled over and continued.

She was tiring again and thinking about flipping onto her back and floating some more when she heard a voice behind her.

"G'day."

Treading water, she saw a very brown, very lean man in his midtwenties sitting astride his surfboard.

"Hi," she said.

"You sure are a long way from shore."

India looked back. Her hotel was a sugar lump on the horizon and she could only see the thin yellow strip of beach when a wave came and lifted her. "Yeah, I guess I am."

"Going anywhere in particular?"

"Just felt like a swim."

"Mighty long swim."

She squinted at him. "What are you doing out here, then?"

"I'm a lifesaver."

India was surprised into laughter. "I don't need saving."

He gave her a smile. "Are you tired yet?"

She didn't reply.

"If you want to tag onto my board while I paddle back, you're welcome. It's no extra effort for me."

"Thanks, but no thanks." India turned away from the kind young face that reminded her of Tiger's and continued swimming. It wasn't until fifteen minutes later, when she paused for breath, that she saw him out of the corner of her eye, just over her shoulder, lying flat on his board, paddling easily with his sinewy arms.

"Don't mind if I come along, do you?" he asked.

"It's a free ocean."

India floated for a bit while the lifesaver sat on his board, humming an operatic tune she recognized from *Carmen*. When she tilted onto her front again, facing east towards the northernmost tip of New Zealand, he said nothing, merely paddled after her silently, just out of her vision.

She didn't really think about what she was doing, register how far she was from shore and how close she was to exhaustion. All she knew was that her conscience had eased, her guilt had abated, and that her psyche wasn't in perpetual pain.

A wave, larger than the rest, slapped her in the face and she swallowed half of it the wrong way. She was choking, coughing, trying to grab a breath of air when the next wave hit her. She felt she'd taken in half the ocean and was sinking with the weight of water in her lungs when the lifesaver came into view.

"Need some help?"

She continued to choke, but she didn't take his outstretched hand.

He raised his head, looked into the distance before glancing back at her, his expression serious. "Looks like a ship the size of the *Titanic* cruised past a while back. We've got some real big waves coming."

India gave one final cough, hauled air into her lungs.

"Why don't you hang on to my board 'til they've gone, then we'll get back to what we were doing before."

For a minute she thought he was making up a story about big waves to get her onto his board, but then she saw it. It wasn't that high, but it was travelling hard and fast for them.

I can dive through that, no problem, she thought.

"There's about eight of them back to back," he said, quite calmly, as if he'd read her mind. "And you won't get a breath between the last five."

The wave came closer, a greeny-blue opaque curve with no white cap, no spume. She thought she saw a shadow move inside it. It was shaped like a torpedo and could have been a porpoise, but her mind yelled: *Shark!*

"Shit," said India, and grabbed the board.

It was as if the lifesaver had been waiting for that exact moment. In one swift and powerful movement, he grabbed her wrists and hauled her up in front of him, straddling her legs around his board and hugging her from behind, her fingers clamped beneath his. His chest was pressed against her back, his chin on her shoulder.

The wave sped towards them.

"Sit tight," the lifesaver said into her ear, "and let me do the steering."

Then they were rising to meet the wave. The board's nose tilted sharply and she thought she might slide backwards, but he was there behind her, solid and impregnable . . . Suddenly they reached the top of the wave. The surfboard levelled out, and for a single, breath-taking second, paused.

She could see the other waves—no time to count them—ranked ahead in varying shades of blue, cobalt blue and black, and then they were sliding downwards. Barely had they reached the bottom of the trough than they were climbing again. Another swift climb up another wave to the crest, a second's pause to marvel at the view, and then the exhilarating swoop down the wave's back before the next climb.

All the time the lifesaver held her tightly, cheek against hers, their hands like limpets around the edge of the board.

They were climbing a wave, she had no idea whether it was the fifth, sixth, or seventh, when he said, laughingly, delighted, "You're enjoying this, aren't you?"

A flash, a thunderbolt from nowhere: *You're not enjoying this, Miss Kane, are you?*

She gave a single cry, an inhuman sound like a seagull's shrill scream, full of anger and rage and grief. The lifesaver's grip tightened but she made nothing of it; she thought her cry was lost in the spray of sea, the sound of water churning.

Finally, the ocean returned to its habitual chop and occasionally unpredictable waves. India sat limply on the board, motionless. Her skin was cold, her mind smooth. Eventually she felt the lifesaver lift his head from where it rested against her shoulder blade.

"Will you come quietly now?" he asked, his voice amused. "Or will I have to tranquillize you?"

She gazed at the seemingly endless silver-blue ocean. "I'm al-ready tranquillized."

"Okay then. It's best if we lie flat, you on the back. Is that okay?"

"It's fine."

She did as he said and lay with her chest and belly on the board, her legs in the water, while his wiry shoulders and arms paddled them both.

The beach was busy when they returned. Groups of people had started celebrating New Year's Eve early and she could hear laughter, the sound of music blasting from boom boxes. She saw another group of people standing by the twin flags at the far south end, and lots of surfers, in the water and out, about twenty of them.

India found her legs wouldn't work properly when she clambered off the surfboard and tried to walk. She stumbled and fell to her knees, the surf churning around her waist, beating her and remorselessly keeping her off balance.

"Here," said the lifesaver, and took her hand and slid it across his back to hook her fingers with his over one shoulder. His other arm went around her waist and like lovers they walked through the kicking, churning, white-bearded surf and up the beach. Each time she stumbled, it was only his strength that kept her upright. She concentrated on nothing but putting one foot in front of the other, leaning against him, battling with the soft sand underfoot and her exhaustion.

He deposited her gently on the bank of warm sand outside her hotel and sank down next to her. He sat up, looking alertly out to sea while India sagged, empty and drained.

"Did you leave a note?" the lifesaver suddenly asked. "Write up your obituary?"

"Don't be ridiculous." God, it was an effort to speak.

He was matter-of-fact when he said, "Suicides rarely do. Sad for their relatives. They seem to like an explanation. It exonerates them from guilt, I suppose. Helps them understand what's going on."

India didn't know what to say to that, but she faintly registered the fact that she didn't particularly like being categorized as suicidal.

"Leave me alone." She was surprised at the strength of her voice.

He gave a shrug. She felt his right hand sweep up her spine, encircle the nape of her neck and squeeze it briefly, affectionately, as a fellow footballer might to another, and then he got up and walked away without another word. She realized she hadn't even thanked him.

TWENTY-TWO

INDIA SAT IN HER ROOM, SIPPING CHAMPAGNE WHILE SHE watched the millennium celebrations on television. Millions of people thronged the foreshores; specks of flag-waving and face-painted humanity in good-humored mayhem. She saw the Cahill Expressway was packed and wondered if Mikey was there. She thought about Whitelaw in jail, Scotto with his smashed knee.

Through her open balcony door she heard claxons and happy shouts and the occasional *bang* of a flare being let off.

She watched the Harbour Bridge light into a giant smiley face, above which hung the word *Eternity* in gold.

She finished her champagne and went to bed. She slept deeply.

———

The next morning, she went in search of her lifesaver. It was breezy on the beach and the surf was booming in, making the air hazy with salt spray. The safety flags were at the far southern end of the beach, indicating a dangerous rip farther north, and two lifeguards stood ten yards back from the twin red markers, muscular arms crossed, chatting to a sun-oiled girl with cropped blonde hair and short legs.

India introduced herself, allowed them to do the same—Lance and Trevor—then she quickly explained the events of the previous evening and asked where her lifesaver was.

Both of them looked blank. "We were the only ones here," said Lance, the taller of the two.

"What was his name?" asked Trevor.

"He didn't give one," she said. "And I didn't ask."

"Was he wearing our uniform?" Trevor pointed to the rear of his black swimmers and white shirt, which had NORTHSLEYNE emblazoned in gold.

India frowned. "No. His shorts were plain black."

Not one of us, Lance and Trevor agreed, nodding together.

"Why say you're a lifesaver if you're not?" she asked, puzzled.

"Probably didn't want to panic you. Everyone loves a lifeguard but not everyone likes being rescued by a stranger."

———————

From the beach, India walked down The Corso, amazed at how quickly Sydney returned to normal after an all-night party. The pedestrian street was immaculate. Not a bottle or paper cup could be seen. When she neared the Esplanade, there seemed to be more people cleaning up than there was rubbish. She estimated that within two hours nobody would believe the city had even held a party, let alone such a momentous one, the previous night.

She turned right and crossed over Whistler and into Belgrave Street, heading for the Manly police station. Part of the council buildings, it was two-storey and built from purple-hued brick. She paused on the bottom step and looked at the blue and white plastic sign on the door: WELCOME. Two female police officers brushed past her and clattered up the steps. Both gave her a smile.

She followed them through the glass and wood door, and felt the sweat break out on her body. She might be determined to fight Knox, and to win, but it didn't lessen her terror.

The atmosphere inside was busy. Behind the counter she could see two desks, both manned by policemen who were on the phone.

A woman in a pink dress walked briskly past. India could hear music playing and the sound of people speaking into radios.

There was a uniformed policeman at reception, typing on a computer keyboard to the left of a wood counter. He gave her a friendly smile. Her knees were weak, but she managed to smile back.

"Can I help?"

"Yes," India said. "I want to report two possible murders."

The policeman looked startled.

"Yesterday I was kidnapped with a friend of mine by a man called Roland Knox. He shot my friend in the knee and was going to shoot me when another friend, an ex-policeman called Mike Johnson, rescued me."

"Yesterday?" He was frowning.

"It took me a while to get my courage up to come here."

"Can you hang on for just a second?" He cleared his screen and tapped some keys. "Could you give me your name?"

"India Kane."

He tapped some more. The computer beeped. He stared at the screen. Then back at her.

Her heart began to pound.

"Is something wrong?"

He looked at the screen. "No," he said, "nothing's wrong." He swallowed.

She tried to control her breathing, but adrenaline was coursing through her veins.

He cleared the screen, looked up at her. "I'll get someone more senior to take your statement."

Someone more senior was about fifty with iron-gray hair and a wary look in his eyes. "Hello," he said. "I'm Senior Sergeant Llewellyn. You say you are India Kane."

"Yes."

"And you'd like to make a statement."

"That's right."

He was inching closer.

"How about I get Lee here to get us some coffee, and we go to my office and talk?"

Lee was edging towards the door. *If he looks like blocking my exit,* she thought, *I will run.*

"That sounds fine," said India, but she didn't move.

Llewellyn was really close now, and Lee halfway to the door.

The iron-gray cop reached for her elbow and she slapped his hand away. "Don't touch me."

Lee was nearly at the door. He was definitely going to block her exit.

Llewellyn moved quickly, gripped her arm hard. Instead of jerking away, she plunged straight for him. Broke his grip. Broke into a run, crashing past Lee and into the bright light outside.

They were shouting as they chased her. She raced down the street, trying to dodge the council cleaners and their black plastic bin liners, crashing against people and sending bags flying. India's legs pounded, her mind fixed on nothing but putting distance between herself and her pursuers.

She swung left past the council chambers and raced over the road. A horn blared. She dived right down a narrow alley flanked by tall buildings. It looked like a dead end.

Please, God, don't do this to me.

She pelted along the alley. The right wall gave way to a small cafe. She burst inside, knocking over a chair. A man stood there with a broom, his mouth open. India raced past him and into a car park. She could hear a row behind her, men shouting, something crashing.

She tore along another alley and onto the street, swung right and hared towards the harbour and Manly Wharf and its ferries and buses and taxis.

She ran across East Esplanade. She saw a bus by the bus stop. Its doors were closing.

"Wait!" she screamed.

She didn't think she'd ever run so hard. She heard the doors hiss, spring open. India sprang inside. The bus driver was shaking his head and smiling.

"Jesus, when's the baby due?" he said. The doors hissed shut.

"Soon," she panted, digging in her jeans for some change. She paid her fare. The bus moved off. She stumbled to the rear of the bus. Gulping convulsively, she peered outside. Nothing but a smattering of people. The bus turned the corner. Her lungs continued to bellow in and out. India collapsed onto the nearest seat, buried her face in her hands.

She was on her own.

———

Scotto Kennedy's guard was awake and alert when Mikey padded down the corridor. Ahead of him, a doctor marched out of a room on the right and spoke to a nurse. The air smelled acrid and pungent, of things Mikey couldn't identity, didn't want to identify.

As he neared Scotto's room the guard looked at him. He frowned. Mikey kept walking. He turned the corner and saw the guard was still watching him. He was speaking into a radio.

Mikey left the hospital. No point in hanging around and getting banged up, he told himself. Yesterday he'd gone to North Sydney PD and seen his cop friend, who had warned him to get the hell out. India was wanted by the police. And anyone who had anything to do with India Kane was up for grabs as well. Keep your head down, his cop friend said, so low you can see your ass, okay?

Mikey ran a hand over his face and exhaled noisily. At least they hadn't found her yet. He thanked God for that, if nothing else.

May as well face the next hurdle. Break into the Karamyde Cosmetic Research Institute again, but this time with a gun for the dog and a handful of Semtex for the lift door. Mikey knew the answers lay in floor B2 of the Institute.

———

Two hours after being chased by the Manly police, India was in the public toilets of the Queen Victoria Building. She rummaged in a carrier bag on the floor and pulled out the items she'd bought from the only shop open, a chemist near Town Hall station. The scissors were sharp and it didn't take long to hack her hair reasonably short. She swept it up and flushed it down the loo then picked up a packet of hair colorant and read the instructions. They seemed relatively simple, but she wished it wasn't New Year's Day, and that she could go to a hairdresser.

"Maroon tint," the packet read.

Just do it, she told herself, and pulled on a pair of rubber gloves. She stuck her head beneath the tap then drenched her scalp with treatment cream.

She didn't think Knox's men could possibly track her to the public toilet, but when the door opened she spun around, adrenaline surging.

An Asian girl came inside. "Looks like you lost the bet," she remarked, and went and locked herself in a cubicle.

India looked in the mirror. Her hair had definitely changed color. She waited until the Asian girl had left then quickly rinsed and blow-dried it beneath the hand-dryer in the corner.

She blinked several times when she checked her appearance. She looked as though she was wearing a shaggy woollen cap. It made her face longer, more haunted.

Her hair was purple.

So much for trying not to draw attention to herself.

———

India spent the night in a small, dirty hotel near Central Station. The train didn't run until the next day and although she wanted to leave Sydney immediately, it would take her less time to take a direct route a day later than leave today.

At midday she left her room and walked to Central and bought her ticket, coach class, for a hundred and eight dollars.

She had some time to kill until the train left, so she went to the Grand Central bar and bistro. India sat on a stool beside a man in a cheap suit at the bar and ordered a coffee. She craned her neck to cheap suit's newspaper who obligingly turned it so they could both read.

"Thanks," she said.

"No worries."

The headline read: "Flu epidemic hits Darwin—23 dead."

"Lousy news," said her neighbor after a while.

Not good, India agreed. The only people suffering from this new virulent strain of flu—that scientific and health experts seemed to think came from Indonesia—were Aborigines; whites appeared to be completely unaffected.

"Reminiscent of when us whites first came here with our new diseases," he remarked. "The Abos got wiped out by the common cold, measles, chicken pox. You name it, they died of it. I remember an Abo called Billy Muran dying of flu back in the eighties. My dad said he remembered a whole bunch of them getting wiped out in the fifties. Looks like it's happening all over again, poor buggers."

Absentmindedly, India finished her coffee, less concerned at the flu epidemic five thousand kilometers away than whether Knox's men would be waiting for her in Cooinda. Over the loudspeaker, a man with a nasal voice made a crackling announcement about the departure of an Indian Pacific train to Broken Hill. She set off through the echoing hanger-shaped terminal, stopping at the newsstand to buy a copy of *The Fatal Shore*. It might help her understand

Australia, she thought. And it would certainly last the seventeen-and-a-half-hour train ride.

She didn't want to hire a car, leave a trail for Knox, so she hitched out of Broken Hill from the Silver City Highway. Her lift was a Toyota Amazon, a huge four-wheel-drive with leather interior and icy air-conditioning and tinted windows. Her driver, a bulky man called Larry Thomas, owned two sheep stations outside Tibooburra. He sang along lustily to his collection of Neil Diamond CDs as they flew northwards. In the blinding sun it wasn't possible to tell where the desert or the sky began; the heat haze made it seem as though there was a shimmering lake between the two. They overtook trucks, several pickups, passed a couple of road trains packed with cattle travelling in the opposite direction, and gradually the sandy terrain turned to a vast rock-strewn plain.

Soon there were some homesteads, a clutch of wooden houses, and in fifteen minutes they reached the center of Tibooburra. Larry parked outside the Caltex garage and trotted inside, gesturing for her to remain in the air-conditioned car. He had insisted on finding her another lift from his hometown to Cooinda.

"Jerry's always going up there," he said, "to see his women friends. He'll be glad of the excuse."

Jerry was, indeed, glad of the excuse, and after filling his pickup's tank and two big jerricans with four-star, he checked the tires and the oil then cheerfully popped India in the passenger seat and drove out of town singing Robert Palmer's "Addicted to Love." The sun continued to beat down. Occasional red sand dunes rose through the rocky plains and there was no habitation, no sign of life other than the odd crow hopping across the road.

Two hours later they came to the low rise of hills overlooking Cooinda. It felt like a year had passed since Tiger had driven her here, India thought.

Jerry asked her where she'd liked to be dropped, and she said down the Biloella road would be nice. No problem, said Jerry, and deposited her outside Whitelaw's with a grin. The road was deserted. No black BMWs, no silver Lexus or white transit van with a crumpled right fender.

She pushed open the fly-screen door and stepped inside.

"India?" Mikey said, his voice astonished.

She stopped dead. Their eyes met. He was scanning her while she was trying to decide whether he loathed her for abandoning him outside the warehouse. They stood in tense silence.

"Nice haircut," he said eventually.

She continued to stare at him. Something about him was different. His jaw seemed bigger, his nose larger, his green eyes more vivid.

"You too," she said finally.

He gave a faint smile and ran a hand over his short-cropped hair. He said, "What are you doing here?"

"I want to nail Knox."

He gave his head a little shake. "Last time I saw you, you were legging it at a hundred miles an hour."

She looked away. "I'm sorry."

He came to her. Put his arms around her. Gave her a strong hug. Thigh to thigh, belly to belly. She felt her feet leave the floor as he tightened his grip and lifted her into his embrace. "I'm bloody glad you did. That you're all right." He pulled back, looked down into her face. "I've been worried sick."

She felt her muscles relax. Thank God. Thank God he didn't hate her. He pulled her close to him again. Kissed her hair. She hugged him back with surprising strength. They stood in the corridor like that for some time before Mikey told her about Scotto.

"He's doing okay. I rang the hospital this morning and although they wouldn't let me talk to him, I gather he'll be up and hobbling about soon."

"Were you hit during the gunfight?" she asked. "I mean, you fell . . ."

"Tripped over my big feet as usual."

"Thank heavens you turned up when you did. You saved my life."

"No, I didn't. I came in after the shooting had started."

She frowned. "So who yelled 'police'?"

"Not me."

India was shaking her head. "I don't get it."

"Me neither." He grinned. "Perhaps you've a guardian angel."

"Who screams 'drop your weapons or I'll shoot'? Somehow I don't think so."

"Well, if it hadn't been for whoever it was, I'd be dead. They covered me until I'd gotten the heck out of there, and I saw Knox and his blokes leave, then the black Beemer. When I went to get Scotto I couldn't see anybody." He scratched the side of his jaw with a finger. "Maybe there's another party involved here. Secret Services or something."

India remembered Arthur Knight, the man who'd paid her bail. Whitelaw had said he was a fed. Was it Arthur who had covered them? If so, *why?* She wished she'd written that letter now. The one she'd meant to before Stan rocked up and wanted to arrest her, but she'd been too busy surviving to think about it since.

They went into the sitting room. India pulled out a tattered map of Australia from the bookshelf and studied it. Biloella was northwest of Cooinda, a pindot in a spot surrounded with symbols for desert. It didn't look far, about fifty kilometers, but she knew distances were deceptive and driving time depended on how good the roads were.

"How long will it take me to get to Biloella?" she asked Mikey.

"An hour. In Whitelaw's rust-bucket, four."

She glanced at the VW outside, tried to ignore the continual heated inner voice demanding she forget it, that she leave town, climb on to a plane and flee to England.

"I don't suppose I could borrow yours for the day, could I?"

India found herself sweating, unsure whether she'd be relieved or disappointed if he said no.

"All yours." He dug in his front jeans pocket and tossed her his keys. "What are you going to do up there?"

"Try and track down the Mulletts. See what they got paid, if anything. Get more information."

"A family reunion!" Mikey grinned again and India rolled her eyes at him. "Okay. While you do that, I'm going to get supplies. I want to find out what's in the basement of the Institute."

"What, break in again?"

"Absolutely. But this time I'll be better prepared."

"You'll need a lookout."

"You betcha."

She glanced at her watch. "When were you planning your assault?"

"We can prep this evening, go in tonight." His eyes lit up. "It'll be dark. Does this mean you'll strip?"

She took a swipe at his head, which he ducked.

He was still chuckling when she climbed into his ute.

India cruised into the baking wilderness, anxiously checking the rearview mirror, her knuckles pale as white chocolate buttons around the steering wheel.

She drove on the speed limit all the way to Biloella. Later, she couldn't remember anything about the journey; it was one of those times when she didn't care to think about what she was doing.

The main street of Biloella was deserted, dusty, and about four hundred yards long. India parked nose-in next to an ancient gray Land Rover with blistered paintwork and crazed windows. She climbed out of Mikey's ute and walked along the street of aluminum and weatherboard dwellings. They were not well kept and many of the houses had crudely built lean-tos attached for additional living space. An aura of dirt and poverty hung over the settlement and the air was thin and hot, and pulsed with the sound of insects.

She passed a hotel and an all-purpose general store, then a milk bar. India entered the milk bar. An angular woman in cut-off dungarees was serving banana splits to an old couple at a table in the corner. She walked behind the counter, asked what India would like. India ordered a glass of water and a banana milkshake.

The glass of water was from the tap, the milkshake freshly blended with ice cream and soft fruit.

"Hot enough for you?" the woman said.

"Sure is."

"You're from the city, am I right?"

India hesitated. "I suppose so."

"Sydney, right?"

"Er . . ."

"Wouldn't pick you for a Melbourne girl. I'm from Melbourne myself."

"London."

The woman's eyes rounded into saucers. "Strike me pink, I don't believe it. We've a tourist in town."

India smiled.

"Passing through or stopping for a while?"

"Depends if I find what I'm looking for or not."

The woman's face lit with curiosity. The old couple looked up.

"And what's that, darl?"

India lit a cigarette, dragged the smoke into her lungs and exhaled. "Three families."

The woman leaned her skinny arms on the counter and shook her head in a parody of wonderment. "Don't keep us in suspense, then. Which families can someone like you be after out the back of Bourke?"

India took a long drink of water, set the glass down, then picked up her milkshake. "The Mulletts. Do you know them?"

The woman shook her head. "Can't say that I do."

The milkshake was thick and sweet, and as she sucked hard on the straw India decided to try the all-purpose store, then the hotel. And then she'd start knocking on people's doors. Across the street, she noticed a sand-colored dog cock its leg on a cardboard box and trot off, the white tip of its tail waving like a freshly laundered handkerchief.

India jumped when a hand touched her elbow. The old man withdrew his gnarled and liver-spotted hand, his face anxious. "Sorry," he quavered. "Didn't mean to give you a turn."

"That's okay," she said. "Us city folk take a while to relax."

The old man's lips trembled into a smile. India smiled encouragingly back.

"We couldn't help but overhear." He turned to look at the old woman in the corner, who nodded obligingly. "We were wondering if you were talking about Victor and Lizzie Mullett?"

Her voice was an octave higher than usual when she said, "I'm looking for Greg and Clive too, and Greg's wife."

"And seven kids."

"Are they here?"

The old man shuffled his feet, looked sideways. "Well, as it happens, no. I'm just the solicitor, but Dorry—that's the owner selling up to them—heard from Victor when they were in Sydney. Victor told Dorry he'd be moving up here after they'd completed some contract out bush somewhere. That was the last we heard. They just never turned up."

India was frowning, trying to work it out. "So where did they go?" she thought out loud.

"I don't know," he said, sounding as puzzled as she. "It was all sorted, that September sixth they would take on Ringers Soak . . . it's a beaut property. Tough to manage, but we met them and reckoned they'd make it work. They're all from the outback. The back of beyond. This kind of country is their type of country and they would have made a good go of it. They had a waterhole for their stock and nature would have provided the food." He turned a bewildered gaze on her. "Why the devil didn't they take it?"

India shrugged helplessly.

"I know they needed more water, in different locations, Dorry was always up front about that. And they'd been thinking long and hard about underground reservoirs. Clive was a rig driller. He was convinced one existed beneath the property. He planned to drill holes. He'd have sorted their water out in seconds."

Twelve of my family missing, she thought. If what she'd learned so far was true, they had climbed into that white transit van at Central, and vanished.

"Damn shame," the old man was saying, shaking his head. "I still have their deposit. Invested it for them in case they turned up. Had to sell Ringers Soak though, couldn't wait for the Mulletts forever."

"How much did they give you?"

"Three grand. There's two hundred or so on top of that now."

India wondered whether Polly could inherit the deposit, should her relatives have perished, or if Bertie was first in line. Which reminded her. "I don't suppose you've heard anything of Bertie Mullett?" she asked. "The grandfather."

The old man looked surprised. "Sure. He's staying with the Dungarins just down the road. Got in last week after going bush for three months." His face fell. "He doesn't know where his kids are either. Right cut up, he is."

"How do I find him?"

TWENTY-THREE

NDIA STOOD OUTSIDE A SMALL TIN SHACK WITH AN IDEN-
tical neighbor on one side and a vacant lot overgrown with
spinifex and weeds on the other. The shack was streaked with rust.
An old woman sat unmovingly on a tattered beige armchair beneath
a small lean-to that offered some shade. Gaunt and twisted with age,
she stared at India through rheumy, purple-rimmed eyes.

India had brushed her hair, put on some mascara and lipstick,
but now felt out of place wearing makeup.

The old woman called out something to her that could have
been a greeting, but it was drowned in a coughing wheeze. India
walked across a sandy patch of ground prickly with tough grasses to
join the elderly Aborigine.

"I was wondering if Bertie—"

The old woman made a loud choking sound, which turned into
a series of racking coughs.

India surveyed her anxiously. "Can I get you some water?"

"Too late for that," the woman rasped and turned slowly to spit
into a bowl sitting on the seat next to her. Then she leaned back and
closed her eyes, exhausted.

"Have you seen a doctor?"

The woman nodded. "Flu. Whole town's down with it. We'll be
right as rain next week, but."

India remembered the twenty-three Aborigines dead in Darwin.

"Johnnie's out," the old woman said. "So's Elsa."

"I was hoping to catch up with Bertie Mullett," India said. "I was told he was here."

"You missed him. He's gone back to Cooinda."

India cursed and the woman chuckled.

"Doesn't he ever stay in one place for more than a day?" asked India. "I've been trying to get hold of him for over two weeks now."

"You'd catch him at home this minute," said the woman, her smile showing purple gums. "He caught a lift with Liz Jollie. Promised he'd stay put for a bit 'til he heard from his family."

"I gather no one's seen them for months."

The old woman nodded, managed to say, "Not since July back," then started to cough again. Finally she stopped, wheezing heavily.

"Isn't there anything I can get you?"

She shook her gray woolly head and India watched helplessly while the old woman withstood another attack of uncontrollable coughing.

India left her staring out at the hot street, at the dust devils spinning in powdery cones. Deep in shadow, she looked like a fragile branch of mottled, rough-grained wood that had been torn from a tree.

———

Mikey was in the hardware store when Jerome Trumler came in. He bought some twine, a hammer and two tubs of Polyfilla. Mikey watched him. There was something pushing at the corner of his mind. Something about Jerome. Something that Rodney Stirling had said.

Mikey followed the solicitor outside. Fell into step with him. "How's it going?" he asked.

Jerome sucked on his elongated lips. "The wife wants me to do some DIY. I'm not terribly good at it."

"I'm sure she'll be glad of your efforts." They walked a bit farther. "I don't suppose Peter or Elizabeth Ross left a will?"

Jerome paused, looked Mikey in the face. "I wouldn't know. Coscarelli represents the Rosses."

Mikey waited until Jerome had climbed into his Mitsubishi Shogun, then headed along Main Street, past the post office and the Royal, past the little courthouse to a squat, blue-painted building next door with peeling white shutters. The window was thick with grime, but Mikey could see Giancarlo Coscarelli at his desk, an ashtray and a whisky glass in front of him, reading the midsection of *The Australian.*

"Hey, Mikey," he said, shoving aside his paper, grinning widely when Mikey came through the door. His face was broad and red, with purple veins across the nose and cheeks. "What's happening?" He knocked back the whiskey in a single swallow, then exhaled loudly.

"Rough day?" Mikey said.

"No more than usual." Coscarelli mopped his forehead with his shirt sleeve.

"I need a small favor."

Coscarelli put his head on one side. "Which is?"

"Did the Rosses make a will?"

Coscarelli considered Mikey through watery bloodshot eyes. "Yeah. They did that all right. Left their bloody 'roos to the National Parks. It's proving hell to sort since all the bloody 'roos have run off."

"Did Peter Ross give you anything to look after? Anything to be opened after his death?"

"Like what?"

"A package of some sort. A book or something smaller, like a CD."

Coscarelli was scowling. "Not that I recall. Bert Roach did, I remember that. Sent me some bloody stuff about a rustler. Convinced he was going to get done by the bugger."

"It could have been a while back. Maybe early- or mid-December."

Coscarelli was still scowling. "My memory's not so good."

"Can you check for me? It's quite important."

"You working in an official capacity or what?"

"Which would you prefer?"

"Bollocks to both." With a loud grunt Coscarelli got to his feet and shuffled into the next room. Boxes bulging with beige files lay everywhere. There were carrier bags stuffed full of papers, padded envelopes propped against the walls, and on the two chairs were more files stacked in piles two feet high.

"Great filing system," remarked Mikey.

Coscarelli flapped a hand. "You find it, I've other more important things to be getting on with."

Mikey decided to work from one end of the room to the other. He peered inside each envelope, every carrier bag. Scoured the shelves and cupboards. Upended boxes, piled their contents back inside. He was a third of the away across the room when he found it, buried in the middle of one of the cardboard boxes. A small yellow padded envelope. TO BE OPENED IN THE EVENT OF MY DEATH: PETER ROSS.

Mikey hastily slid a finger beneath the seal and peeked inside. His heartbeat quickened. One computer disc. He resealed the envelope, pulled out his shirt and forced it inside the rear of his waistband. He ducked his head into Coscarelli's office. "No luck," he said.

"Told you so."

"Thanks anyway." Mikey left.

———

Back in Cooinda, India went into the chemist and bought some aspirin. She felt slightly shivery and her head was aching, a tight band that pulsated just behind her eyes.

I hope I haven't caught the flu.

She bought a half pint of Moove chocolate milk at Albert's, to wash down the pills, then headed across the street. A horn blasted and she leaped into the air. It was Mikey, face alight. He drew up beside her.

"Get inside!"

She yanked open the door, and jumped in.

"I got it," he said. "I got the bloody thing!"

"Got what?"

He glanced in the mirror. "The disc! Peter Ross gave it to Coscarelli for safekeeping."

"Where?" She was looking around urgently. "Where is it?"

Mikey reached across, snapped open the glove box.

India held the little padded envelope gingerly, reading the slanting script. "You are the most amazing, wonderful, fantastic person," she said.

"Aren't I just?" He was grinning fit to burst.

"Shall I open it?"

"Go for it."

Carefully she opened the envelope. A floppy disc lay in her hands with a pale blue Post-it note stuck on its underside. The sticker had some Chinese character printed on it, and the initials CTW.

Mikey was craning to read the note. "What's CTW?" he said. Suddenly he put his foot hard on the brakes, narrowly missing a Holden turning right.

He roared down the Biolella road and turned left into Whitelaw's driveway. They both ran for the sitting room. Mikey switched on his laptop while India slotted the disc inside. Mikey started tapping on the keyboard.

The screen went blue. Demanded a six-digit access code.

Mikey tapped CTW anyway, and the screen responded with: ACCESS DENIED, PLEASE TRY AGAIN.

Mikey tried combinations of Knox's name and initials, Gordon Willis's and Carl Roycroft's, to no effect.

"Hell," he said. "This could take hours, if not weeks."

India's teeth were clenched. "I can't believe Peter Ross didn't leave some sort of clue. Why lodge it with a lawyer if it can't be used?"

Mikey pointed at the Chinese characters on the Post-it note.

"Great," she said. "So which one of us can read Chinese?"

Mikey continued to tap. India picked up the envelope and turned it over and over in her hands.

"It may only need six digits," he said after a while, "but considering they could be numbers or letters, or a combination of both, it may take some time."

Something nudged at the back of her mind. Six digits.

In the kitchen she put on some coffee to perk. Six digits. She stared unseeingly at Whitelaw's Mexican red-knee tarantula and let her mind run loosely over phone numbers, street numbers and people's initials. She poured them both coffee, brought the mugs into the sitting room.

"Thanks," said Mikey.

She sank onto the sofa, mug cupped in both hands. Six digits.

Time ticked as Mikey tapped.

ACCESS DENIED . . . ACCESS DENIED . . .

"We'll have to get an expert to crack it," he said after a while. "Take it to a computer whizz." He opened the envelope wide and peered inside.

"I've already done that," she snapped.

"Okay, okay. Just making sure we didn't miss a vital piece of paper or something."

You can lose a piece of paper, darl, but you can't lose your arm.

"CTWGN1," India blurted.

"What the—" Mikey said, but tapped anyway.

The screen cleared. It showed a logo. An image of the world spun leisurely inside a red band imprinted with: CHANGING THE WORLD.

Mikey gave a whoop. "You clever, clever girl!" He turned around, eyes shining. "How the hell did you do that?"

She was grinning at him. "Lauren had written it on her wrist. I guess Peter Ross gave it to her." She moved to stand beside him, put a hand on his shoulder as she leaned closer to the small screen.

The world faded to be replaced by a multimedia presentation program. "Holy moly," said Mikey. "It's a video."

He clicked on "maximize" and the image of the slowly spinning world returned. Then faded to be replaced by a violent scene. Men and women in some sort of square, throwing rocks at a building. The women wore striped smocks, the men dark trousers and thick jackets. The building was alight with flames.

"Quick, the sound, the sound," India demanded, and Mikey turned up the speakers.

The people were shouting. The camera panned back. The square was dominated by a monastery in the distance. On its roof was a gold wheel flanked by two gold deer.

"What the hell . . ." Mikey was scowling.

"It's the Jokhang," said India, astonished. "The Jokhang monastery. They're bombing the police station in Lhasa."

"You mean Lhasa, Tibet? What's Tibet got to do with . . ."

The image faded to be replaced by the same square, but this time there was no violence, no rock-throwing. Blue-uniformed Chinese men, women and children walked serenely across the square and in and out of the monastery. There was not a single Tibetan to be seen.

The picture faded again. Showed a Chinese man in a white coat sitting in front of the camera. He had thick lips and glasses and looked comfortable and relaxed. He started to speak, in Chinese.

"What on earth—" India began as Mikey said, "Shit," then they both went silent.

After a minute, no more, the Chinese man rose and walked to a broad expanse of window and looked out. The camera zoomed in on two Aboriginal men weeding a patch of grass. One wore a blue shirt, the other red. A man with a white coat approached them, gave them each a glass of water, which they drank straight down.

"Oh my God," said India, staring at the Aborigine in the red shirt. "Stop it, stop it!"

Mikey paused the screen presentation.

"Go back. Go back to the man in the red shirt."

"I'm not sure if I can . . . we'll have to start it again."

"Okay, do it."

He re-ran the program and paused it exactly as the Aborigine in the red shirt raised his head to drink the water. He had a wispy moustache and a scar like a quarter moon at the corner of his mouth.

"It's Louis," said India faintly. "Louis Mullett. Bertie Mullett's eldest grandson. My cousin."

Mikey took her hand in his and held it tight as the Chinese narration continued. The screen faded once more, than back. The two Aborigines were lying on single beds side by side in some sort of cell. They still wore the same shirts. They were both coughing. Great racking coughs that shook their bodies. Yellow sputum rimmed their lips and their eyes were sunken and watery.

The Chinese man came and stood between them and spoke briefly, with a smile.

The picture faded again. Bloomed to the same two single beds, the two Aboriginal men. Their skins were tinged with gray, their eyes rheumy, and their breathing was thick with mucus. The Chinese man stood between them, looking serene as he spoke. The camera zoomed in to show chapped lips and eyes hollowed in be-wilderment and fear. Their hands were clenched into claws when they coughed.

Fade. Bloom.

Two bunk beds. Two rigid corpses. Eyes open and opaque. Their hands were still clawed.

The same Chinese man in between. Composed, placid.

The picture of the corpses returned to the two Aboriginal men weeding a patch of grass. One in a blue shirt, the other in red.

The Chinese man's face split into a smile as he held up a single glass of water.

At once Scotto's voice was thundering in her ears.

Indi, if you don't remember anything else, remember it's the water. It's the WATER . . .

TWENTY-FOUR

I NDIA THOUGHT, *OH MY GOD, MY RELATIVES WERE GUINEA pigs for a genetic weapon.*

The next thought punched beneath her diaphragm and left her breathless with disbelief. *I drank a glass of water in Biloella.*

"India?"

Bound by this horrifying new thought, she made a strangled sound.

"Did that make any sense to you?"

She stared at the image of the world spinning on the screen. CTW. Changing The World.

"They've contaminated the water," she managed, "with a virus or something that has, I assume from this video, been genetically modified to target Aborigines. They're all going down with the flu. Darwin's last count was twenty-three dead."

Mikey's expression was appalled. "Christ!"

They stared at each other.

"That's why Knox went to China," Mikey said. "He's selling the technology to the Chinese. So they can have Tibet without the Tibetans." He jumped to his feet. "We've got to get this to someone," he said urgently. "Now."

India leaned weakly against the wall and closed her eyes. She was trembling.

CAROLINE CARVER

"Who do you know?" he demanded. "Who's trustworthy? Someone with clout. Who do you know in the government? State, national, I don't care. The papers. Who's at the *Sydney Morning Herald, The Australian* . . ."

A short pause. India swallowed. She tried not to think of that glass of water. She tried to fix her thoughts on Peter Ross, brave Peter Ross, smuggling the disc out of the Karamyde Cosmetic Research Institute. Courageous Peter Ross, meeting Tiger and Lauren. And his stalwart wife, Elizabeth, giving her an old photograph to expose the three young boys who had killed Robbie, now grown men in positions of power.

"India?" demanded Mikey. "Are you all right?"

"Yes," said India. She felt peculiarly detached, as though she were encased in glass.

"This is serious shit we're in," said Mikey.

"Pulitzer Prize-winning shit. Do you have a fax modem?"

He shook his head.

"E-mail?"

He looked away.

"But your games, surely—"

"Who would I E-mail? My thousands of friends around the world?"

"Christ, Mikey—"

"Now is not the time, India. I don't have E-mail, so we'll have to communicate the old-fashioned way, okay?"

"Okay."

Suddenly an enormous sense of urgency descended on her. "I'll write it up but I've something to do first," she said swiftly. "Before it's too late."

Mikey didn't ask why or where. He simply nodded. "I'll see if I can copy the disc," he said. "And then we'll deliver it . . . Scattergun effect. Police. Government. Media." He glanced at his watch.

"Let's meet in town, it'll save time. Say five, outside the court-house."

————————

Images flashed before her as she drove, like stills from a film. *Mi-langga grinning, holding a rabbit. Five men playing cards and smoking beneath a eucalyptus with silver peeling bark. Polly flying towards her, skin streaked with dust, skinny legs pounding.*

Fine sand ballooned around the tires as she drove into the center of the settlement, narrowly missing the sow who decided at that moment to trot briskly across the track in front of her. The car was still rocking from the force of her fierce halt when she opened the door and looked into Polly's grinning face. India's throat tightened and her eyes were suddenly wet with relief.

"How are you doing, sprat?"

Polly wrapped her arms around India's thighs and continued to grin up at her. "Doing good, thanks."

India sank to her knees and hugged the girl, breathing in her smell of dust, butter and nutmeg. Polly unhesitatingly returned the embrace, giggling and squirming with pleasure. Eyes closed, India took a long breath and let it out.

She could feel Polly looking at her curiously. "What's wrong, Indi?"

"Nothing. Nothing's wrong."

"Why you in such a hurry?"

"Listen, I'm going back to Cooinda in a minute and I want you to come with me and stay with Mikey and me until we've sorted something out."

"What's going on? Are you in trouble again?"

"A little bit, I guess. And I need you to promise me something, okay?"

Polly nodded solemnly, her eyes wide and unblinking.

"I don't want you to drink any water. Not today or tomorrow or the next day. Not until I tell you it's okay. We'll go and stock up on bottled drinks and when you're thirsty, you won't go to the tap, you'll have mineral water instead."

"Has an animal died in our tank?"

"I don't know for sure, but it could be something like that. Whatever it is, it's poisoned all the water, everywhere."

"Can I have Coca-Cola?"

"Anything," promised India, "so long as it's not water."

Polly leaned back in India's arms and beamed. "I like Coca-Cola."

"I know," said India. Then, "Let's go and warn everyone else."

———

The aspirin she had taken hadn't yet kicked in. The pain behind her eyes was increasing and a hot current of nausea was overtaking her. Involuntarily, India gave a dry cough, then another.

Dust, she told herself. *That's all it is. Just dust.*

She poured Polly an apple juice from Whitelaw's fridge, then put the television on for her. Clearing her mind of everything else, India sat at the kitchen table with a pot of coffee and a large pad of paper, and jotted some notes, trying to get her story in chronological order.

Only when she had it planned out did she start writing. She wrote for a full straight hour and when she finished her nerves were jangling and her headache had worsened. She wasn't too concerned; having drunk all the coffee and chain-smoked full-strength Marlboro she ought to have a headache. India swallowed another two aspirin and microwaved two Hawaiian pizzas for herself and Polly. At four o'clock she telephoned the *Sydney Morning Herald.*

"Tom? It's India. I've something explosive for you." Quickly she filled him in on what they'd discovered.

"What it comes down to," she said, "is that these guys want to wipe out the entire Aboriginal race. Already people are blaming it on a flu epidemic. Unless we do something extremely fast, they're going to succeed."

"Flu?" he said disbelievingly.

"Yes. The Karamyde Cosmetic Research Institute has invented a selective genetic weapon that targets Aborigines. They've put it in the water."

"Why the hell—"

"The three men behind it are pathological racists."

He sounded doubtful. "I didn't think viruses could survive in water."

"Perhaps they've found something in the water it can cling to for longevity. I don't honestly know, but what it comes down to is they've poisoned the water and hundreds of Aborigines are dying as we speak."

"It's a bit circumstantial, isn't it?"

"Get a scientist, someone who knows what he's looking for, to test the water in Darwin. Alex Thread, from the Australian Medical Association, was investigating Karamyde Cosmetics when he was murdered. His boss, Dr. Nathaniel Jameson, head of ethics, was gagged by being transferred to the UK. Where he was killed in a mugging just a week after his arrival."

"How did the AMA get wind of what was going on?"

"One of the scientists working at Karamyde had a conscience."

"Name?"

"Peter Ross. After Thread's death, he made another attempt to divulge what was going on to the press and the authorities, via Scotto's wife, Lauren, and a policeman called Terence Dunn, but they were all murdered."

"Let's hope your phone is secure."

She went ice cold all over.

"What did you say?"

"Well, if what you say is true, and your phone is tapped, I'm a dead man and you're a dead woman."

She sat there, staring at a packet of Special K on the sideboard, her mind frozen.

"Can you get copy to me today?" he asked. He went on to say that if the water checked out as contaminated he would print her story, and if the story was as good as he thought, she should write a book that he could serialize and perhaps do something for TV.

"Tom." India was barely listening. "I've got to go. I'll fax it . . . Soon. As soon as I can."

After she had hung up she folded the papers in two and grabbed the car keys and bundled Polly into the ute. She felt dizzy and light-headed and blamed it on too many aspirin. After she had been driving a while, the seed Tom had planted grew and she considered Whitelaw's phone, whether the house could have been bugged.

If it wasn't, how else could Knox have known she was meeting Scotto in Sydney and that he had Lauren's notes?

A feeling of pure dread descended on her now. As she thought of her missing family climbing into the white transit van her foot pressed harder on the accelerator and her heartbeat increased.

I am a dead woman.

"Indi?"

She saw Polly watching her, her eyes squinting as though she were thinking hard.

"What is it?"

"You're driving awful fast."

"Awfully fast." India braked heavily as she came to a T-junction, spewing gravel beneath her tires, then swung the pickup hard for the center of town. "Yeah, I know. I'm in a hurry."

"Where we going?"

"To fax a letter."

There was a one-person queue at the post office, formed by a very old, very slow man whose counter order was being placed with an air of great importance and complexity.

"One package for England." He pushed a small brown parcel beneath the glass plate to the tall, thin-lipped postmistress.

"Small packet rate? Or normal delivery?"

"I wouldn't know," the old man said. "You tell me."

"Look, I'm sorry," India interjected, "but I just need to send a fax, it's terribly urgent—"

"You can wait your turn," the postmistress snapped. "Exercise a little patience, will you?"

Polly giggled nervously as India jerked aside with a flush of anger and stood there tapping her foot until the old man had finished his transaction. India handed the woman her seven sheets of closely written paper and asked for it to be faxed to Sydney.

"I'm sorry," the postmistress said, not sounding sorry at all, "but we don't have a fax machine. Just a copier."

"Telex?"

"Sorry, nope." She looked faintly smug.

"Computer? With a fax modem?" India felt desperation wash over her.

The woman shook her head.

"Which couriers are there in town?"

"Have you thought of using the mail?" the postmistress said acidly. "The courier companies operate out of Broken Hill and take the same amount of time."

India bit back a sharp retort and politely asked if the copier was working. Of course, said the postmistress just as politely, how many copies would you like? Five, please, said India. The woman stuck her long nose in the air and asked if twenty-two cents a copy was all right.

Fine, India said, and picked out five strong envelopes and addressed them. Polly was sitting on the steps outside with a look of bright curiosity, as if she'd never seen the town before. She looked over her shoulder at India and smiled happily. Behind her, a truck growled past, flashing silver from its tall metal flanks and making India crease her eyes.

"That's twelve dollars exactly," said the woman. "Eight seventy-five for the copies and three dollars twenty-five for the envelopes."

"Do you have a stapler I can use?"

The postmistress gave India a cold look. "Sorry, no."

Thanks a bunch, India thought, and put the loose pages into the envelopes, asked for stamps for four of them, and went to mail them outside. Although the temperature was in the early forties, when the first two dropped into the box she gave a violent shiver.

I can turn your stomach, your bladder and your bowel into juice.

India thought of the postmistress, her thin lips, and instinct kicked in. She mailed the other two a few blocks away. With the last envelope in one hand, Polly's sticky palm in the other, India headed up the main street. Once she and Polly had handed the last envelope to Jerome she would meet up with Mikey and drive to Sydney and the *Sydney Morning Herald*'s offices. Then they'd get lost in the city until they could be guaranteed some protection.

She felt a surge of electricity go through her as she headed for Jerome's office; a mixture of elation and fear. She had mailed the biggest story of her life and she was in the greatest danger of her life. She'd never known how intense the sensation of feeling alive could be until faced with the possibility of death maybe hours or minutes away.

India had just passed the Royal when the door banged and someone came out, fell into step behind her and Polly. Nerves prickling, India pulled Polly against one of the verandah posts and waited until they'd passed. She stood there, heart hammering, studying the street. Farther up, Jerome was walking into the police station. Three women in brightly patterned dresses stood on the opposite corner in animated conversation. Pulling up between a Falcon ute and a Toyota Hiace was a white transit van.

Her heart gave a single giant leap.

It had a dent in its nearside wing as though it had hit a large rock.

Trying to appear calm, India hunched down, looked gravely into Polly's face.

"I've something very important for you to do for me."

Polly's face lit up.

"I want you to take this envelope to Jerome. He's just gone into the police station."

Polly's eyes were round and unblinking. "Why can't you?"

"I'd like you to deliver it for me. Only to Jerome. Not to Stan, okay? Or Donna or Constable Crawshaw. Just Jerome. It's got to get to him, Polly. It's really, really important. I'll be counting on you, okay?"

The girl gave two uncertain nods.

"Now, can I tuck it beneath your dress? It's so important that I don't want anyone to see it. Only Jerome."

Polly let her lift the dress and slide the envelope into the rear of her knickers. India pulled down her dress and smiled in what she hoped was an encouraging manner, but she knew it was strained. "Okay, Polly. Who are you going to give the envelope to?"

"Jerome," she said in a small voice. "Not Stan. Not nobody."

"That's right."

India pulled her against her shoulder and kissed the top of her head. She could smell the sun-warmed nutmeg of her hair.

"You'll do good, I know," she murmured as she rose. Her legs felt weak, like putty, but she made herself appear confident. "You go now, Polly. Take the envelope to Jerome for me."

Polly walked away uncertainly, looking back over her shoulder.

India turned her back on the girl and walked in the opposite direction. The white transit van had parked, but nobody was near it. They could have climbed out while she was talking to Polly. They could be anywhere. She walked down the street, her legs unsteady, her breathing shallow.

Where could she go that might afford some protection? She'd get fifty kilometers out of town before Knox's henchmen caught up with her. There was no train station in Cooinda. No planes, helicopters or hot-air balloons for hire. She could almost feel Knox's breath against the back of her neck as he scented her trail and tracked her down.

Involuntarily, India's throat convulsed in a groaning whimper of fear that she would always remember. Because at that moment, as she turned to cross the road and head for Jerome's office, she found herself facing two men with guns in their hands. One wore a buzz haircut, the other had short brown hair. Two guns, black, with long barrels: silencers.

TWENTY-FIVE

"Don't move," Buzz-cut said.

India's eyes were flicking behind them, to left and right. She was in an outback town, a lonely street that held nothing but three middle-aged women and a skinny cat slinking beneath a Falcon ute. Dust and sun and the smell of heat in her nostrils.

"Not a muscle," he added.

"Or what? You're going to shoot me?"

"You think you've got a choice here?"

"I'll scream," she said. "I'll scream so loudly your eardrums will burst. They'll explode with such pain you'll remain blind for a week."

"Oooh," Brown-haired drawled in a mock falsetto. "I *am* scared." He turned aside contemptuously and made a gesture with his left hand that brought the white transit van to their side.

India was watching it out of the corner of her eye. The driver jumped out, opened the rear door expectantly.

The three of them stood there silently. The two men held their guns pointed at India's gut. She felt they'd all been fixed in this position for an age, but she knew that it hadn't been more than a few seconds or so.

As if in slow motion, Brown-hair reached up to India's neck and grabbed her collar. He bunched it in his hand and twisted, pulling her towards the van. She started to fight, her legs scrabbling in grit and gravel, but the other man grabbed her hair, then her right arm.

Her head was jammed against a muscular armpit. Her nostrils were full of a stranger's acrid scent. Struggling, she managed to turn her head. She opened her mouth, brought the soft skin inside the man's upper arm between her lips and clamped her teeth down.

Hard. Hard. *Hard.*

Her jaws bulged with the effort, her eyes watered.

The man screamed so loudly a flock of galahs exploded from the gum tree opposite in a burst of pink and gray.

———

Mikey heard the man's scream from inside the general store. He had just picked up six padded envelopes for the discs in his back pockets and was standing in the queue to pay.

He dropped the envelopes and spun around, raced down the aisle and erupted into the street.

He saw Polly racing up the path for the police station's door, chest out, matchstick legs pumping; two brick-shaped women staring at the Royal, shocked, and three men having a fight . . . no, two men struggling with someone at the back of a transit van.

Mikey's eyes clicked to Polly, but she vanished inside the police station.

He sprinted for the van.

———

India was bucking and kicking against two men. Mikey saw her knee come up. She jabbed it hard into the first man's groin. She brought it back and spun and tried to jab the second man but he swung away.

The first man was bent double, his hands between his legs, groaning. India was thrashing at the air with her hands and feet.

Mikey gave a bellow of rage and charged. He seized the second man by the arm and spun him around, smashed a fist into his nose. The man staggered and fell to his knees and Mikey kicked him in the face. The man flew backwards, clearing the ground and smacking onto the road, blood spurting from his shattered nose. Mikey lunged for the other man, and distantly heard India scream his name.

He was bringing back his bunched fist to smash the man's face when he felt a thud in his right shoulder blade. He jerked sideways, stumbling and losing his balance. For a second he thought someone had punched him from behind, and he tried to turn to fight his attacker, but his knees began to tremble.

Dear God, no, he thought.

The driver of the van came into view, nodded once as though satisfied. He holstered his long-barrelled pistol and helped the second man to his feet. Blood was clotting around the man's nose and mouth and when he said something, his front teeth moved like loose planks in a fence.

India was suddenly in front of Mikey, holding his face in her hands. She was shouting something but he couldn't hear her. He seemed to have gone completely deaf.

Slowly, he felt himself topple sideways. There was a numb area in his lungs, his whole chest. He tried to raise his head from the road, but it wouldn't budge. He attempted to lift himself with his arms, but they lay uselessly at his sides.

"India," he whispered.

"Mikey," she said.

"Run."

"Never."

———

Mikey regained consciousness as they flew over Broken Hill. Rivulets of sweat ran down his face and neck. A nauseous pain filled his veins, his whole body.

He was lying sprawled across the rear seat, his legs jammed behind the pilot's seat. He couldn't feel his legs. He wondered if they
were numb from the position they were in, or whether his injury
was worse than he thought. Irrationally he decided: *I don't care, because my head is in India's lap.* He could feel one of her hands cupping the side of his face, the other brushing the hair rhythmically
above his right ear and down to his nape. It felt good. It felt so
good . . .

A little later when he opened his eyes again it was to see India's
chalk-white face close to his, set with anxiety. He saw his name on
her lips. He turned his head to indicate he couldn't hear above the
clattering of the engine. She put her face close to his. "God, Mikey."
Tears spilled. Angrily she wiped them away.

It took an immense effort to speak. "Sorry."

"You idiot." Her voice faltered. "You bloody idiot."

"Missed the third."

She was crying.

"Sorry," he said again.

"Don't," she choked. "Don't apologize, for God's sake."

"Wanted to help."

She tried to smile. "And got yourself into a whole lot of trouble.
As usual."

"As usual." A dark shadow nudged the corner of his mind and
he closed his eyes again. Succumbed to blackness. When he awoke,
fresh cool air was on his face and he could smell dew on grass. It was
night. He heard the pilot shutting down the engines. He was lying
in a field, India by his side.

"Where . . . discs?" he asked her.

"I'm afraid they've got them. I mailed four pieces to newspapers
though. One's with Jerome . . ."

As she talked he found it hard to concentrate. He closed his
eyes. Drifted again. When he came around, he was rocking on the
floor of a covered ute. In the gloom he saw two benches fitted

lengthways, two wheel wells and a spider's web beneath the nearest bench. Long legs were stretched on either side of him. Long and clean and brown. Once again, his head was in India's lap. He listened to the engine's constant drone. Took in the steady juddering motion, the regular clicking of small stones and rocks against the bodywork. They were on a well-maintained dirt road.

"How you doing, soldier?"

He felt her hands supporting his head while she brought her legs up beneath her, then it was resting on something solid and soft. She knelt beside him, swaying with the motion of the ute, and quickly stripped off her T-shirt. Her breasts swelled against her brassiere. His kind of brassiere. Cotton with lacy edges. A soft apricot color. Very feminine.

Distantly, he realized his head must be resting on her balled up shorts, because he could see she wore matching knickers. High-cut, with a lace band, they barely covered her sex. Almost a G-string, he thought, but not quite. Her skin was the color of caramel, the texture of silk.

"Nice," he managed, but she didn't seem to hear him.

She dabbed his face and neck with her T-shirt. His lids started to droop. He felt her press a kiss to his forehead. Then her palm resting gently against his cheek. A shaft of perfume pierced his pain; cinnamon and allspice. He was going to say something banal, about the scent of an Aborigine, but a shudder went through him as the sickening pain spread, and he began panting hard. His clothes were now soaked.

"You hang in there, okay?" India demanded.

He found he couldn't even manage a nod. He simply lay there, staring at her.

"Jerome will be on our case. We'll have you in hospital before you know it."

Mikey gazed at India, the way she knelt in her underwear, glaring fiercely at him through her tears, willing him to live. He'd never wanted anyone or anything so much before. He loved her for her spirit. He guessed he always had, and always would.

As if she'd heard his thoughts she bent her head and very gently, very tenderly, kissed his lips. Then she moved back a little. Her expression was solemn and intense.

The ute started to slow, taking a long smooth curve upwards and to the right, as though breasting the crest of a hill.

"Want . . ." he said, with great difficulty.

Her hand came to stroke the scar on his eyebrow, then the hair above his ear, smoothing it between her fingers as she caressed his cheek with her thumb.

"You," he managed.

Tears sprang in her eyes.

"Me too."

The ute hit a pothole and he heard himself moan.

"Take it easy, my love," she whispered, leaning close. "I'm here, okay? I swear no one's going to fuck with you while I'm around, you get it?"

"Got . . . it."

They went quiet. The engine note started to slacken as the ute dipped downhill. The driver took up the brakes, and as it lurched around the first corner, India slid to his head, his shoulders, to steady him.

In second gear now, the ute howled downwards.

There was a bump when they reached the bottom, and the tires slipped on loose gravel as the ute veered to the right.

"India."

She bent over him, expression taut and anxious.

"Kiss . . ."

Her gaze became unsteady.

"Me," he added weakly.

As he lay there, her soft lips on his, it suddenly struck him she had felt the same way all this time.

The dirt road seemed to last forever. India was working to free a two-inch nail from the bench. She knew it wasn't much of a weapon, but if David could topple Goliath . . . With her thumb and forefinger, she rocked the nail back and forth, loosening it little by little. Her head was pounding and she felt faintly sick, but she was so absorbed in working the nail, in arming herself with something, that she didn't think about the flu.

The ute lurched off the dirt road, slowed to a snail's pace and bumped over some large potholes. It picked up speed again, but not as fast. The tires started scrunching as though they were driving up a finely gravelled drive. Their destination, she assumed. India hastily pulled on her T-shirt and shorts, apologizing to Mikey's unconscious form, and went back to urgently tugging and twisting at the nail. She felt the ute ease to a halt. The engine note rose for a second, then died. Silence.

She heard doors opening, the men talking as they came down either side of the ute, but India didn't stop; the nail had started to move.

She took a deep breath, tightening her hold on the nail's head, squeezing her left hand over her right thumb and forefinger. She yanked with all her strength, felt the flesh of her forefinger tear. With the edge of her palm she knocked the nail hard one way, then the other.

One last yank, and the nail tore free.

"On your feet, bitch," said the driver.

She slipped the nail into her shorts pocket and bent to squeeze Mikey's shoulder. To her surprise his eyes were open, their expression urgent. "Run," he whispered.

Her heart was jumping, adrenaline pumping through every vein at what she imagined was coming, but she managed a smile.

"No."

He tried to rise, but she pushed him back gently.

"Come out!" the man yelled.

She brushed her lips against Mikey's, then crabbed around his inert form and out of the ute.

They were outside a large beach house. India could smell the salty tang of the sea, the more pungent odor of seaweed. A boatshed stood to the right, and a jetty stretched over green-blue water dead ahead. The sky had turned purple and black to the east and rain clouds were building out to sea. A big Bertram motorboat, maybe thirty-four feet long, was surging against its ropes at the end of the jetty, causing the wood planks to shudder and creak.

She watched the man whose face Mikey had shattered stumble up a set of curved wooden steps and into the house. The driver stood behind her, his pistol aimed at her back, while the other man stood by the open doors of the van, smoking. Then she heard a faint thumping sound. The sound of a helicopter. Sweat ran through her hair, down her neck as she gazed around, looking for weapons, escape routes. Jetty. Boat. Van. Car. Sea. Bush all around.

Her eyes snapped back to the car parked beside a broad flat patch of mown grass. A black BMW with tinted windows. OED 128. She blinked.

She stood there, breathing in the smell of sea-spray, pretending her fingers weren't throbbing from the nail, trying to work out the significance of the black BMW.

Gradually the rhythmic pounding of rotor blades grew louder. The helicopter swooped low from behind and thundered past them, banking sharply over the water before settling like a giant metallic fly on the flat patch of grass. India squinted against the fine stinging sand raised by the machine, to see the pilot shutting down the engines and unclipping his belt. The passenger's door was opening. She knew who it was before the stubby legs came into view.

Roland Knox.

The pilot climbed out and stood there, stretching, arms to the sky. He dropped them and turned around. He was still flexing his hands when he looked directly at her. She couldn't make out his features, he was too far away, but she felt the intensity of his gaze and, without knowing why, she shuddered.

Knox was coming down the drive, expression hard.

The pilot turned and loped away, along the jetty. She swallowed. An odd, hollow feeling settled in her chest as she watched him vault effortlessly onto the Bertram. There was something familiar about the way he carried himself and she felt more frightened, even more vulnerable than she had before she'd seen him.

"Miss Kane," said Knox. "You really have excelled yourself."

India made no reply.

He held up four sturdy brown envelopes. Each had been slit open. "You failed," he said abruptly.

Irrationally, she felt an intense urge to burst into tears. Not because he was going to kill her, but because he was right: she had failed to get the biggest story of her life into the world's media.

"Sir," said the driver hesitantly, and Knox moved past her, peered inside the ute.

"What the hell's he doing here?"

"He attacked us. Smashed Forbes's face to pieces, then went for Curran. I had to shoot him."

So, Brown-hair was called Curran, and Buzz-cut Forbes. Buzz-cut suited Forbes much better, she thought dimly.

Knox made a strangled, angry sound.

"He was going to kill us," the driver protested.

"I wish he had," snapped Knox.

"We used silencers." The driver's tone betrayed a slight desperation. "No one heard a thing."

"Carl told me you were the best," said Knox, "but he knows nothing. You're shit."

The driver remained silent.

Ten seconds ticked past. Knox gave a grunt. "I want you on the boat. Her too. And him."

Tension ebbed as Knox continued giving orders.

"Shepard, when you're done, drive the ute behind the house beneath the trees, where it will be hidden from the air. Lock it. Stay with Forbes in the house until we get back. Curran, bring the woman. I want to leave in ten minutes."

He turned around sharply, made for the boat.

The driver, Shepard, swapped positions with Curran, who jabbed his pistol into the small of India's back.

"Move."

She started to walk slowly for the jetty, listening to the ute start up, the sound of a gear being engaged and the whine as the vehicle reversed. Then the engine faded. She was trembling inside, but she held her back straight and her head high. Waves slopped against the jetty, making it rock slightly. Anvil-shaped thunderheads slid across the sun and a solitary raindrop splashed on her cheek.

The helicopter pilot was on the bridge of the Bertram, his head turned towards the horizon as though studying the coming storm. Knox clambered up the narrow chrome ladder and gestured sharply at the helm. The pilot responded by pointing first at the sky then directly at India, saying something to Knox that he didn't like because he started stabbing the air violently with his hands.

Then she heard another helicopter. The faint but distinct sound cut through the increasing noise of the wind. She felt the gun ease fractionally from the small of her back as Curran looked around.

Sensing that everyone was distracted, India pretended to stumble and went down on one knee.

"Get up," said Curran.

"I can't," she said. "I've hurt my ankle."

The sound grew louder. It was a small helicopter, with coast guard markings, not police. Moving fast, it was following the coast in a westerly direction. India had no idea where it was headed, and didn't care, because it had given her the moment she needed.

She waited until she felt the brush of Curran's hand on her shoulder, and the air was filled with the beat of the rotors. She whirled around and lashed her foot upwards, hard between his legs, and then threw herself onto his body sideways to spill him into the ocean.

He shouted and rolled towards the edge. She swarmed over him, pushing him for the water with all her strength, hitting him in the face, trying to hook her fingers into his eyes, anything to disable him, give her a chance. He raised his arms around his head and she bit a wrist, her rage out of control, something she'd never expected to feel. He scrabbled backwards on the jetty, trying to get away from her.

The first crash on her head made everything go dim. A boot thudded into her ribs, another her kidneys. India found herself groaning involuntarily, lying on her side, felt a thin trail of saliva dribbling down her chin. Shepard stepped back and kicked her again, and then again.

She heard Curran say, "Hey, go easy."

India ignored the pain thumping and howling through her, and concentrated on keeping her anger white-hot. She thought, *If you think I'm going to give up easily you've made a big mistake,* and with a monumental effort she lunged for Shepard, gripping his left leg, pulling herself onto her knees and hanging on tight.

She dived a hand into her pocket, drew out the nail and slammed it into his thigh.

For a second there was silence.

Then he screamed.

The second crash landed on her head, laid her flat on her front, jerking for a moment and finally lying motionless on the hard wooden jetty. *I did my best,* she thought dimly. *Shame it wasn't good enough.*

TWENTY-SIX

INDIA CAME AROUND WITH HER FACE ON WHITE DECKING, to hear Knox bark an order.

"Start the engines. Head for Sinker Reef. Now!"

"I advise against it," shouted a man's voice.

India blinked slowly several times.

"I don't care what you advise, Bishop," called Knox. "Just do it."

"Sir, the southerly is coming in extremely fast. It's going to make things very difficult. Not just because it'll be uncomfortable in the swell, but visibility will be down to a few yards within the next half hour. I don't know if I'll find the jetty again."

"We have sat-nav," insisted Knox. "Radar, radio. A whole array of dials on the dashboard. We're going. We can't risk not going. Not since that chopper flew over. Start the engines."

India took in the way the boat writhed against the jetty, the sporadic spatter of raindrops the size of dollar coins, the sound of wind moaning around the hull. She empathized with the cool-headed Bishop. She knew the pilot was right: the southerly was whipping into a ferocious storm.

"Perhaps I could remain ashore, sir."

"No," said Knox. There was a distinctive wet metal click that India recognized as the hammer of a pistol being drawn back. "Start the engines or I'll blow your head off."

"If you insist, sir." To her confusion, India thought she heard a thread of humor in Bishop's voice, as though he found Knox amusing.

She moved her head fractionally but she couldn't see where Bishop was. She could, however, see a sprawled leg about eighteen inches from her nose. Blue jeans. Battered leather boots.

"Mikey," she said, but all she heard was a coughing wheeze that was drowned in the rich roar of twin diesels starting up.

Her cheek vibrated against the deck and she closed her eyes as she listened to Bishop issuing commands about casting off, pulling buoys in, and—surprisingly—asking who wanted a life jacket. She told herself she would rest a little before raising a hand to request two life jackets, but in all honesty she knew she wouldn't be able to move any of her limbs.

She felt bad. Sick. Throbbing. Quite unable to think clearly, wanting to lose consciousness just to stop the awfulness of it all.

She wanted to stretch out a hand to grasp Mikey's ankle, feel the comforting warmth of his skin against hers, but she couldn't move.

Everything hurt. And Mikey, she saw, didn't move a centimeter either.

The throb of powerful engines picked up, going from a gentle burble to a smooth howl as Bishop swung the boat hard southeast to meet the weather. Almost immediately India heard the wind's moan turn to a shriek, and felt that moment of weightlessness before the prow of the Bertram met the first wave.

Her whole body juddered as the boat slammed into a wall of water in an explosion of spray. She found her face pressed against the denim of Mikey's thigh. The Bertram faltered a second, then her motion steadied as she settled herself squarely to meet the oncoming waves.

I have to move, thought India. *I must.*

Rain began to fall in earnest. At first it was bearable, but when her clothes grew sodden and she started shivering, she put every ounce of effort into rolling onto her side. Rain streamed from her hair across her face. She saw Knox standing under the hard canopy, hands gripping the near side of the boat, sturdy legs spread well apart to retain his balance. The boat started to corkscrew as she wound her way between the swells. India found herself swallowing salt-laden air over a tongue that felt like cotton. She was shuffling her palms up the side of the boat, dragging her torso after them.

Knox was facing determinedly into the heavy swell and didn't seem to notice.

Inch by inch, India hauled herself upright. The movement of the deck became shuddery. Knees bent to absorb the pressure as the boat hit each wave, she looked around her.

The waves were black below a darkening purple sky, looming like curved and silent scythes out of nowhere. India watched them curl above the boat, then lift the hull high into the air and ease it downward. Heavy spray rattled on the deck and streamed back to the sea.

Mikey was watching her, eyes fogged, and she gave him a nod, which he returned with a sluggish blink.

The engine note eased a little and the Bertram swung in a broad arc. Through the spume India saw a hem of cream to the right, indicating rocks, or a reef. Five minutes later the diesels slowed even further as they began to swing for the frothy fringe.

Knox was leaning out of the boat, scanning the water.

The boat was creeping now, feeling her way closer to the seething aquamarine foam to leeward of the reef. It was calmer here, and the boat didn't lurch so high or so violently.

Knox suddenly jerked up, leaned out farther. "There's one! What a beauty!"

India craned her neck to see a long mottled-brown shape sliding through the waves like a slow-motion torpedo. About eight feet long, with a broad rounded head, the tiger shark didn't seem to notice the storm above and came to cruise steadily alongside the boat, dorsal fin barely cutting the surface of the water.

They were within twenty yards of the reef when Bishop turned the Bertram into the wind, letting her shoulder the surf while keeping the engines running to avoid being swept aground.

"Aren't they beautiful?" Knox said.

India was staring at the sea, riveted with a mixture of fascination and dread. A heavy, no-nonsense shark with a tawny hide and pectorals tipped with gleaming white moved in a concentric circle around the boat. Another three sharks, thinner, with pointed snouts and small black eyes, nosed the rear of the boat before darting away. In the slop of the sea the big shapes became so numerous she couldn't count them. They glided effortlessly, crisscrossing in a seething stack as far down as she could see, like the well-oiled parts of an engine.

India started to sidle warily across the deck, heading for the hatch, but Knox turned almost instantly, pistol in hand. "Stop right there," he barked.

She realized he had been aware of her all along.

"Curran!" Knox shouted.

Curran ducked warily through the hatch.

"Give Miss Kane a hand over the side, will you?"

"I'm sorry?"

"Throw her overboard."

Curran glanced at the sea, where several long backswept pectorals moved in slow circles, then back to India.

Christ, she thought. *No, no, NO.* Her eyes were drawn back to the churning sea.

God, no. NO.

"But she's not an Abo," Curran said.

"We need to get rid of her, and her policeman friend. Can you think of a better way?"

Curran ran a hand over his head, staring at his shiny city shoes.

India found herself swallowing convulsively, with no saliva. She couldn't bear to look at Mikey. She felt a desperate urge to urinate.

There was nowhere to run. Weaponless, outnumbered and with a seriously injured partner, she stood on legs ready to crumple, waiting for a miracle to save them both. Never had she felt so powerless. Neither trickery nor cunning would work against a passionless shark.

"If I said I was Aboriginal," said India, her voice surprisingly steady, "would that make it easier for you, Mr. Curran?"

He didn't answer.

"I take your response for a yes," she said. "I also take it you've tossed a few Aborigines to the sharks recently."

"Only when they're dead," protested Curran.

Two beats of her heart, and she knew what fate had befallen her family.

"Jesus," she said, and closed her eyes briefly.

"That's enough," snapped Knox. "Just do it."

Curran hesitated.

"For Christ's sake," said Knox. "You want me to shoot her first?"

He aimed his pistol at India's stomach.

Oh, God, she thought. *No. Not yet. I'm not ready.*

She turned her head, wanting to see Mikey, feel his eyes on hers, but he'd gone. Moved. Was crawling for Knox with infinite, painful stealth. Nostrils pinched, lips stretched over his teeth, he was stalking Knox on his belly. A thick smear of blood lay on the deck behind him, the rain thinning it as he went.

Knox was smiling at her, his eyes hooded. She saw his finger tighten on the trigger.

Ridiculously, she braced herself for the blow, as if by tensing her muscles she might deflect the bullet.

A cloud of spray hissed between them.

"NO!"

The word was a shout, but only because it wanted to be heard.

The voice wasn't panicky or stricken with rage. It was calm and hard.

Knox glanced up, Curran too. India could not think, couldn't reason as she stared at Bishop, looking down at them. He held a submachine gun in his hands, and his face was oddly bland, devoid of emotion.

India continued to stare.

The lifesaver who had paddled his board after her off Manly Beach.

"India," he said, "I want you to move away from Mr. Knox and go below deck."

Knox had swung his pistol on to Bishop. Bishop had his submachine gun on Knox.

"What is this?" demanded Knox.

"Go on, India," Bishop urged her. "You'll be safe inside. I'll take him out if he so much as blinks your way, I promise."

India slowly backed around Knox, but veered away from the hatch and headed for Mikey, knelt by his side. She picked up his hand, interlaced her fingers with his. Feebly, his fingers twitched in response.

"Okay," said Bishop. "We can do this. But Mr. Knox will have to drop his gun before we go any further."

"What the hell's got into you?" Knox said. "Is this a strike or something? You want more money?"

"It's much simpler than that." Bishop gave a short bark of laughter. "I just changed sides."

Curran stood, knees bent as he rolled with the motion of the Bertram, looking baffled.

"Steve," said Bishop, "I want you up here and keeping the boat steady."

The two men locked gazes.

Bishop moved the submachine gun a fraction. "Your choice," he said.

Steve Curran sidled up the ladder.

Bishop looked down at Knox.

"Drop it."

"No," said Knox.

"You've got five seconds," said Bishop.

"And you've—" said Knox.

"Five," said Bishop, and a burst of gunfire exploded from his hands, shattering the air with flashes of white fire and spurts of red. India ducked her head into Mikey's chest, felt his hand grip the back of her neck. She could taste salt and the metallic tang of blood from his shirt.

The wind whipped sheets of water across the deck. Mikey's hand dropped from her neck and gripped her hand, hard. He said, "Get up, India. Get up."

She raised her head to see Knox lying spread on the deck, holes the size of ten-cent pieces in his dark blue sports shirt.

Water streamed down her face and neck as she stared at Knox's corpse, her body rocking in time with the swell beneath the boat. Knox, the man who had terrorized her, was dead. She felt no elation, no euphoria, just a faint throb of relief.

"India." Mikey's voice was urgent.

She turned, looked into his face.

"Don't trust him." Mikey jerked his chin at Bishop, who was climbing down the chrome ladder. "He was at Whitelaw's. Searched your things. Said he was a fed but something's not right." She saw his leg extend as he tried to hook Knox's gun with his foot.

"India, for God's sake *get up*."

"But he saved us."

"Why?"

"He's on our side—"

"Why?" he repeated.

"I don't know. But he's okay. I swear, he's—"

"Get it," Mikey urged, eyebrows arched at the pistol a handful of inches from his foot.

India obediently grabbed it, surprised at its weight.

Bishop gave them both a nod as he passed, as though he were a fellow soldier, a pal, before he vanished beneath deck.

"Is it loaded?"

India felt a surge of frustration, at odds with the situation. "How the hell should I know?" she said, and shoved it at Mikey.

He spun the cylinder, clicked it into place. "Loaded," he confirmed.

India leaned close. "He's okay," she said again, her tone fierce. "Believe me. I swear he's okay."

"Okay," said Mikey, but she heard the doubt in his voice.

As if on cue, Bishop slipped out of the hatch and came over to Mikey. He had a first-aid kit under one arm. "I'm going to move you beneath the awning," he said. "Give you a bit of cover. Keep you dry while I do some home surgery. But first I've got to knock you out."

Mikey looked alarmed. "No," he said, "I want to remain awake."

Bishop popped an ampoule and filled a syringe with colorless liquid.

"India, don't let him."

"He doesn't trust me," said Bishop to India, unruffled. "Sensible fellow really, except I'm on his side."

"Perhaps . . ." India started to stay, but before she or Mikey could protest further, Bishop flicked the needle into Mikey's thigh and squeezed the plunger.

"Christ," said Mikey, then desperately to India, "be careful, for God's sake, darling . . ." His words faded as the drug took effect and the tension went out of his muscles.

India found herself trembling.

A gust hit the boat, sweeping a sheet of water over them.

Bishop didn't look at her as he rolled Mikey onto his side, took a look at his wound. "He wouldn't have let me treat him, you do realize that, don't you?" he said. "Knocking him out like this may well save his life. I'll take his shoulders if you grab his feet."

With difficulty they maneuvered Mikey out of the worst of the weather.

"Unwrap these, would you?" Bishop passed her packets of surgical swabs, bandages and tape, and a packet of stitches.

Another gust shook them. The Bertram took it with a heavy roll. Bishop looked up, yelled at Curran, "Use the throttle!" and bent back to his task.

Quickly and expertly he cut away Mikey's sodden shirt and trousers, fetched some blankets from down below, and wrapped him in them. He started to clean the wound.

"Not too bad," he remarked. "I wouldn't have thought it's done him much damage, but he's lost a lot of blood. That's our main concern—getting him hooked up to a blood bag."

India watched Bishop and his spare long fingers, fast and nimble in their delicate work.

"Are you a doctor?"

"Today I seem to be."

Again, India heard that edge of humor.

A little later he said, "That should prevent him from losing any more blood." He glanced up and grinned at India, his dark eyes twinkling. For no reason she found herself smiling back. "Bush medicine," he said, still grinning. "The best there is." He snapped the first-aid box together, got to his feet.

India smoothed a lock of wet hair from Mikey's forehead and bent to press a kiss on his lips. *You see?* she told him. *You've got to have a little faith in the unexpected, is all.*

She thought she heard him say, "*Watch him . . .*" so she did.

Bishop stood over Knox's dead body. "I'm very respectful of sharks," he said. She wasn't certain if he was talking to her, or the corpse. "I've always respected sharks and I always will."

He bent down, grabbed Knox's hands, started to drag him to the stern of the boat. "They're at the top of the ocean's food chain, and you can't not respect that."

Bishop hooked his elbows beneath Knox's armpits and hauled him upwards and across the stern.

India's breath hissed between her teeth. God, he's strong, she thought, slightly awestruck. This was followed by a weird sense of pride as she watched the lifesaver heave around 155 pounds of dead weight to the edge of the stern. For a few seconds the body hung there, unmoving. Then Bishop gave it a final shove, and it slipped into the water without a sound.

"Bye-bye, Mr. Knox."

India scrambled to her feet, peered over the side. Knox wallowed heavily in the oily sea, a slab of gray stuff, like a floating rock.

The first shark appeared within six seconds. In fifteen there were eight in sight, then eleven. Their first attack was tentative, until a tiger bit hard and churned, rubber body twisting like a corkscrew, to pull a gobbet of flesh away.

A slick of red surrounded the bobbing corpse.

It was as if someone had sounded a dinner bell, India thought numbly, staring down from the deck. *What a grisly graveyard my family had.*

A long blue shark forced its way between the heavier white-tips and latched on to the torso, filled its jaws, then rolled over onto its back to twist a chunk free. Another bit and rolled, then another.

"They're coring," said Bishop quietly. "As in coring an apple."

India was surprised she didn't feel sick. If anything, she felt a sense of justification. Roland Knox had worshipped the shark, therefore it was fitting he should be disposed of between their gnashing, chomping jaws.

Afterwards, India estimated it took just two minutes for Knox's corpse to be devoured, but at the time it felt more like an hour.

Bishop came to where she stood and paused, studied her face. "So you toughed it out."

She smiled twistedly. "Yes."

He nodded, squinted out to sea. "Thought you might. I never took you for a pushover, not since I first saw you."

She ran a dry tongue over her lips. "When was that?"

"On the road to Cooinda. With your busted car." He looked down at Mikey, then back at the bridge. "Better get going. Your friend needs a hospital, sharpish."

Twenty-seven

They didn't get back to shore until late evening owing to the worsening weather. Rain and wind howled up from the Southern ocean. The boat bucked steeply all the way and heavy spray poured across the deck and cockpit.

India had started to shiver again, from shock as well as cold. By the time Bishop drew the Bertram up to the jetty, her teeth were chattering like power drills, her fingers numb. They had to shout to make themselves heard above the gale, but with Curran's help they managed to secure the boat.

Bishop pushed his head close to India's so she could hear him above the din. "Let's get Shepard," shouted Bishop. "He can help us bring Johnson out."

Together they clambered from the boat, Bishop gripping her right arm until he was sure she had her balance on the jetty, then he took hold of her wrist and they ran for the house, ducking past palm trees whipped against a sky almost the color of night.

The silence inside made India feel unsteady.

Bishop charged from room to room; she could hear his footsteps pounding up a set of stairs, then walking above. He returned fast. "Forbes took Shepard to the Royal Adelaide. You hit his femoral artery."

"God," said India. "He might die."

"I'm more concerned about the shit hitting the fan when they get there. It'll be crawling with cops."

India turned, made for the front door and Mikey.

"Wait."

She halted, head turned over her shoulder.

"You've got to get changed. You're soaking wet and in shock. In the master bedroom at the top of the stairs you'll find everything you need. Strip off everything, I mean everything, underwear included, and wrap up warm. It'll help. And bring another blanket for Johnson."

India hesitated, realized it made sense, and went up the stairs.

The bedroom was huge, with wall-to-wall windows overlooking the wild churning sea. She pulled open the built-in wardrobes and yanked out handfuls of clothes. She shed her sodden T-shirt and shorts, then her underwear, and dumped them on the thick silver-gray carpet. She was buttoning up a checked men's shirt that hung just below her groin when she caught a movement out of the corner of her eye.

Bishop stood in the doorway, one ankle hooked around the other, arms crossed, watching her.

"You're very beautiful," he said.

India felt a shiver run over her skin at his tone. Soft. With undertones of wonderment and surprise. She forced her hand to do up another button. There were seven on the shirt, and she'd only buttoned two. She had started from the bottom, had five more to go. Her hand slid to the next button. Bishop stood upright, came and stood in front of her. She took a step back. He said, "Don't!" so intensely that she stopped.

He raised his right hand and, with his forefinger, traced the line of her jaw. His touch was both sensuous and frightening, and she could feel her breathing falter.

Her hand slid up to the third button, fastened it. Bishop stroked her fiercely arched brows, then her lips, his expression absorbed, intent. She fastened the fourth button, her fingers fumbling.

Mikey was right. Oh, God, he was right.

Bishop dropped his hand and captured hers before it could slide to the fifth. Slowly, he brought her hand up and turned it over, so her wrist was exposed. He stared at her beating pulse for several seconds, then raised his hand and looked at his own.

India didn't dare move.

Gently, he pressed two fingers to the side of her neck, feeling the pulse there, then with his other hand did the same to himself. She stood utterly still while he felt the blood pulsating through their veins.

He sighed. A long, slow sigh that could have been regret but could have been deep pleasure, she never knew.

Bishop withdrew his hands, let them hang by his sides as he gazed at her. Then he gave himself a shake and bent over to pick out a pair of jeans. "These should fit. Size ten." He passed them to her.

Unsteadily, India took the jeans and slid into them while Bishop rummaged in the bottom of the cupboard. He pushed a pair of Timberlands towards her. "Size thirty-eight, right?"

"Right," she echoed.

He handed her a vast fisherman's sweater, waited until she'd pulled it over her head. "Cute," he said, and with a grin, boyish as a ten-year-old's, ruffled her hair with one hand.

India stared at him.

"What are you waiting for?" he said. "Let's go."

———

With Mikey on the metal floor, Curran on the rear seat and India in the co-pilot's, Bishop eased the helicopter's engines out of idle. The thumping increased to a shuddering buzz and India pushed her headset closer to her skull, trying to block out the noise.

"Okay?" she heard Bishop say. His voice was surprisingly clear through the headset. She nodded and immediately felt the aircraft rise off the grass.

The helicopter lifted straight up, well above the trees, then eased away from the house until it was facing north. The nose dipped forward and it accelerated hard. The engine settled to a steady roar. Although the storm had lessened it was still raining and water streamed over the Plexiglas, making it difficult to see the coastline flashing past below.

India twisted her mouthpiece and spoke into it. "Where are we headed?"

"The Royal Adelaide Hospital."

"How long?" she said.

"About forty minutes. All going well. It's not the best weather for flying."

She took in the black clouds and spray. "No. I guess not."

He fiddled with a dial and called up Adelaide Radar and explained the situation, where they were headed, that they had wounded on board and could they please have every assistance?

Of course, said the tower controller. We'll be with you every inch of the way.

Five minutes on, a small clump of houses came into view, then what appeared to be an average-size town. Bishop swung the helicopter around to follow a road snaking through the bush. India craned forward, staring down.

"Next marker, Meningie," said Bishop.

The helicopter was hurtling above the road, nose down, flying fast. There was little traffic. Everybody had taken shelter from the storm. Then they were above the Princess Highway and following the coastline.

India stared at the ocean. "Why are you doing this?"

"Because." Bishop shrugged.

"Why did you change sides?"

"I didn't," he said. "I was always on the same side."

She looked over at him.

"Your side," he said.

She kept looking at him.

"Why?"

He was quiet for a long moment, then turned to meet her eyes.

"Families should always stick together."

Her stomach gave a little lurch. "I'm sorry?"

"Families," he said again, "should stick together. Don't you think?"

She was staring at him, her skin crawling.

"I mean, I know we're at opposite ends here, me with my mercenary work and you trying to blow the lid on our little operation, but I still couldn't throw you to the wolves." His head tilted slightly to the side and his eyes narrowed as though puzzled. "I don't know why that is. It's not as though I know you. Or that we're at all alike. I'd never have swum out so far from Manly, for instance. Or trusted that Aboriginal copper."

India felt as though all the air had been sucked from her lungs.

"Mind you, you're quite tough for a woman. A lot of stamina. I was really proud of you, the way you survived in the bush for so long. Dodged the dogs and the trackers."

She sat there, wondering if this was real, if any of it were real, or whether she would wake up in a minute and marvel at herself for imagining the clear calm voice coming through her headset.

"Toby?"

"David Bishop's a much better name, don't you think? Toby reminds me of a little round clockwork toy, or a tubby bank clerk. You grow into a name, I reckon, and I didn't want to grow into my real name so I chose another when I turned seventeen and stuck with it."

No wonder they had lost him, she thought.

"But they said you were *black.*"

He chuckled. "I was. Black as pitch. When I was born anyway.

But by the time I was four I was pale as a ginger biscuit." He angled his elbow to lie against her wrist. "Almost the same color."

A trail of misty vapor whipped past and suddenly they were in cloud and had lost sight of the ground. Bishop immediately dropped the helicopter, searching for the cloud base. The aircraft was hit by turbulence and tossed sideways. Bishop slewed it back and swung around, still dropping the nose.

India was gripping the sides of her seat, palms clammy.

Then they were below the cloud, buzzing a thousand feet above Coorong National Park, rain spattering on the screen.

"You're saying you're my brother," she said weakly.

He shot her a grin. "One hundred percent."

"Are you sure?"

"I'm sure all right."

"But you can't be."

"Okay. So who paid your bail?" he said. "Who set up the Abo cop to take the murder raps?"

Pause. Beat. "You paid my bail?"

"Sure did. But you don't owe me anything. That's what brothers are for."

"So who's Arthur Knight?"

He chuckled. "King Arthur's a guy I've always admired. I chose Knight because I've always fancied myself in shining armor." He peered at a dial in front of him and slanted the craft eastwards a fraction. "Cops. They bleat they don't want dirty money but when there's two hundred and fifty grand in cash in front of them . . . well, when they start to ask questions, all you've got to do is show them a badge."

"Are you a fed?"

"Not really."

When she remained silent he continued. "I've been watching out for you, you know. It's been a bit difficult to manage it without compromising myself, but I did my best. Like trying to warn you off with that kangaroo. Arriving in the nick of time to stop Knox from shooting you in the warehouse."

"How did you know"—she paused, marshalling her strength—"we were related?"

"Your friend Lauren wrote to me." He raised his hips, withdrew a crumpled envelope from his back pocket and passed it to her.

India extracted a single sheet of paper.

She felt her throat constrict when she saw the familiar handwriting.

Dear Mr. Bishop,

I have drafted this letter many times and cannot find a way to soften what I want to say, so I will be blunt.

I have a very close friend, my best of friends, India Kane. She has no family that she is aware of, but over the past few months I have managed to trace over sixty of her relatives, including yourself.

India Kane is your sister. She doesn't know you are alive. I think it would be great for you guys to be reunited . . .

She let the letter fall to her lap. "How on earth did she find you?"

"She'd managed to trace the ad I placed in the *Sydney Morning Herald,* announcing my change of name. She found it via their archive. Talk about tenacious." He stared through the windscreen. "I'm sorry about Lauren. I really am."

"What do you know about her murder?"

He made a noise somewhere between a groan and a growl.

"What is it?"

"It was a mistake."

"In what way, a mistake?"

"My mistake."

A sensation of dread curled around India's heart. She took a deep breath.

"You killed her?"

He nodded slowly. "Yeah."

Disbelief and horror flooded her. Time rolled past. Five minutes. Ten. Homesteads became more numerous. Roads converged below. They had reached the outskirts of Adelaide.

"How . . . why . . ." She couldn't think what to say.

"She met Peter Ross and that young copper, Terence Dunn. They all knew about the Institute. Lauren had to go. As a potential threat, that is, not as your friend."

"Jesus," she whispered.

"I know. It's a bugger. I wish I'd got Ross first, then Lauren would still be around. But as it is . . ."

India was staring at him. She felt lightheaded and faintly sick.

"Don't you feel any regret?"

"Regret?" He sounded surprised. "Well, I guess so. I mean, I've looked out for you as best I could. You could say I doubled my attentions over you because of my previous cock-up. Not that it was my fault. I didn't even know you or Lauren existed when I went out that night. I hadn't got the letter then. At the time I was just doing my job: terminate whoever Dunn was meeting, and they happened to be Peter Ross and Lauren Kennedy."

"Jesus," she said again.

"But life does go on and all," he finished.

He's a psychopath. He has to be, not to feel any remorse.

"Nearly there." He started to ease the helicopter downwards.

India sat back, chilled with horror. She stared at the windscreen, utterly silent. Tears rolled down her cheeks, but she was barely aware of them and made no move to brush them away.

Bishop drifted the helicopter over the helipad and hovered briefly, then set it gently down on the asphalt. One of the hospital doors burst open and a crowd of people spilled out and ran over.

Four in white uniforms; doctors and nurses. Several policemen. And Stan.

"Oh, no," she said.

"What's wrong?"

"Stanley Bacon . . . Isn't he on your payroll?"

He flung back his head and laughed. "God, no! Old Stan's straight as a die, a perpetual thorn in our side." He started to slide off his headset, but she stopped him with a touch on his arm.

"Who, then?"

He looked at Stan and said, "Donna. My guess is she's spilled the beans or he'd never be within cooee of here, even with that coast guard helicopter buzzing past when it did."

"Thanks," said India. She clicked her belt free, pulled off the headset, and swung open the door.

Stan reached them first. He pulled out India, covering her head with his hand as though to protect her from the rotors spinning above. The downdraft tore at their clothes. Curran clambered out behind her, helped two doctors ease Mikey onto a stretcher. India pulled herself away from Stan and leaned inside the cockpit, shouting at Bishop, "Aren't you coming in?"

"No."

"How can I reach you?"

"You can't."

"But I want to—"

"I'm out of here," he yelled. "Gone for good."

He released his harness and leaned across to hook his hand around her neck. Gave it an affectionate shake like he had on the beach. She put her hand over his briefly. Then he withdrew his hand, belted up and gestured for her to close the door. He snapped it shut from inside. Then the helicopter's engine note rose. She watched his movements at the instruments, economic and precise. Bishop waved everyone away from the machine. Stan was tugging her back from the aircraft.

"India," Bishop mouthed at her.

She mouthed, "Toby."

He shook his head, made a slashing movement across his throat.

"David," she mouthed.

He gave her the thumbs-up. Then the helicopter was rising, soaring into the air. The last India saw of her brother was as he banked the aircraft sharply around, to go back the way they'd come. His face was absorbed, glancing at his instruments, then looking ahead. Concentrating on the job in hand.

TWENTY-EIGHT

SUNDAY MORNING, INDIA WAS DOZING IN MIKEY'S BED. HE had an arm hooked over her hip and she could feel the warmth of his breath on her neck.

So whatcha think of my Chrissy present?

You certainly outdid yourself.

Yeah, didn't I just. Found out your skin name yet?

No. But Polly's started calling me Damala, as in the ancestral eagle hawk, because she says I'm so brave.

Sounds good to me. The bad guys behind bars yet?

Pretty much. One scientist, a Chinese man, hasn't been found yet, but Willis and Roycroft are under lock and key. Neither made bail.

Good on you, girl.

India could hear a phone ringing. She opened her eyes. The ringing stopped. There was a tap on the door. "It's for you, India," called Whitelaw.

She scrambled out of bed and pulled on Mikey's bathrobe. Mikey made a snuffling sound and rolled onto his front. She padded out of the bedroom and into the kitchen. She went and gave Whitelaw a good-morning kiss on his cheek before picking up the phone.

"I'm out, Indi. They discharged me yesterday." He sounded dull and dispirited.

Short silence.

"I gather I've your brother to thank for my life. Shooting up the warehouse when he did." India felt her breathing catch. "The man who took Lauren's life saves mine. Christ. I'm having some trouble with this as you can imagine."

"I'm sorry," was all she could think to say.

"Not your fault." She heard his sigh gust into the receiver. "Any news of him?"

"Gone for good, I'd say. He flew the helicopter back to Knox's beach house and took the boat. At least that's what we think, since his Beemer was still there. A fishing trawler found the Bertram drifting off Port MacDonnell. Nobody was aboard, but he wouldn't have drowned or anything. He'd have planned it like that."

"Hope he stays away."

"He will, I'm sure of it."

They talked a while longer, about Scotto's physiotherapy and when he'd be able to go sailing again, then he said, "Could you call Lauren's mum? She's terribly upset she froze you out, but you understand, don't you?"

"I'll call her today."

"Oh, and Tom's been at me to put you on our team. We're totally impressed with your articles. What do you say to working with us reprobates?"

"I'd love it! Mikey's starting work with the North Sydney Police next month, so that would be brilliant."

They sent love and said goodbye. Whitelaw poured her a coffee and put an ashtray next to a pile of newspapers. She lit a cigarette and looked at the headlines a hundredth time.

SEVEN HUNDRED KILLED BY THREE MEN . . .
DEATH BY STEALTH . . . NOT THE FLU BUT

MURDER . . . HUMAN GUINEA PIGS
SACRIFICED . . .

She pulled Saturday's *Sydney Morning Herald* free and took it to the divan with her coffee and cigarette.

SCIENTISTS BAFFLED OVER DEADLY CODE

By India Kane

SCIENTISTS are still trying to discover how the virus that killed over seven hundred Aborigines works. The virus, introduced into mains water, is the first of its kind. In the past, biological weapons have been airborne.

It is thought the virus infects an engineered bacteria and as the bacteria multiplies, so does the code for the virus. At some point, after drinking the water, the bacterial infection releases the viral code inside the victim's cells, triggering a massive and lethal infection.

"We will have the answers very soon," said Paul Barnett, a spokesman for the CSIRO. He described the technology as "groundbreaking and extraordinary."

Dr. Ruth Reid, head of science and ethics at the Australian Medical Association, said this development heralded a new era of germ warfare. "Such technology could be applied to destroying armies, or for blackmailing governments into cooperation." She went on to say there is an urgent need to develop biological tests to detect dangerous new pathogens in seemingly innocent civilian research establishments.

All water supplies in the Northern Territory, Queensland and New South Wales were sealed off when a national alert was given on fourth January, by the Cooinda Police Department. The authorities confirm that Tasmania, Victoria and Western Australia have not been polluted with the deadly virus. All stocks of mineral water were sold out within twenty-four hours. Army units have been supplying water by truck to cities and outback towns from these states.

Whitelaw pushed a copy of *Newsweek* onto her lap. A shot of Polly, India and himself, taken outside Cooinda Police Station, was on the front cover.

"Don't you look beautiful!" she said. "Personally, I think it's the haggard expression that makes it, along with the pouches under your eyes."

"Nobody'll be looking at me. They'll be fixated by your purple hair."

"Don't you like it?"

"It won't matter if you're moving to Sydney."

"I'll make sure it's back to normal by the time you come and visit, okay?"

He smiled. "Okay."

———————

Come eleven-thirty, India was in the kitchen, burning onions. Mikey was rolling his eyes at her and asking why God had sent him someone who couldn't cook. She was rolling her eyes back and asking God to give her the strength to deal with the world's worst patient. He responded by telling her she'd won that particular prize; all she'd had was a head cold and she'd thought she was going to die of the flu. Whitelaw walked out of the kitchen for somewhere more peaceful. Twenty minutes later, a loud knock on the front door sent India into a panic.

"How do I look?" she asked Mikey for the third time.

"Like an Abo."

She sent him a look of desperation.

"Gorgeous," he amended.

Half a minute later, Bertie Mullett walked into the kitchen. He wore jeans and a work shirt and stood tall and straight, his right hand holding Polly's. His hair was gray and woolly, his skin dark, so dark it seemed to glow with a bluish tint. For an age he stood there staring at India, and then he smiled. It was as though the sun had exploded from behind the blackest, darkest thundercloud.

"Hello, granddaughter."

India was gripping the side of the kitchen table with both hands. When she spoke, her voice was faint. "Hello, Milangga."

Her grandfather came over, pinched her cheek. "You're still too skinny. How about I bring you some witchetties to help fatten you up?" He cocked his head to one side. "Or do you still prefer croissant?"

ACKNOWLEDGMENTS

I would like to thank my agent, Elizabeth Wright, who for five years encouraged me to keep writing. My thanks too to Kerith Biggs for representing me so well overseas, and Darley Anderson for sharing his wisdom with me. All your advice and support has proved invaluable.

I am grateful to Jane Wood, my editor, who has been a joy to work with, and to Orion.

In particular I would like to thank for their support the Romantic Novelists' Association, the Crime Writers' Association, the First Paragraph writers' group in Bristol and my mentor, Terence Strong.

I have imposed on a number of friends to help me as critical readers and technical advisors, my thanks to them: Dr. Michael Seed, Tania Harper, Iain Cassie, George Kimball and Peter Lamb. Any errors of fact are purely mine.

Lastly, my thanks to Sarah Cunich, for her belief in me.

WITHDRAWN